THE FACE OF THE ENEMY

THE FACE OF THE ENEMY

WALKER BUCKALEW

Providence House Publishers
PROVIDENCE PUBLISHING CORPORATION
FRANKLIN, TENNESSEE

Copyright 2003 by Walker Buckalew

Printed in the United States of America

07   06   05   04   03   1   2   3   4   5

Library of Congress Catalog Card Number: 2003107909

ISBN: 1-57736-306-X

Cover illustration by Jeff Whitlock, Whitlock Graphics

Cover design by John Tracy

This book is a work of fiction. Names, characters, places, and incidents are products of the author's imagination or are used fictitiously.

PROVIDENCE HOUSE PUBLISHERS
an imprint of
Providence Publishing Corporation
238 Seaboard Lane • Franklin, Tennessee 37067
www.providencepubcorp.com
800-321-5692

This story is offered to readers

in honor and in memory of:

C. S. Lewis (1898–1963)

Thomas Merton (1915–1968)

M. W. Buckalew Sr. (1911–2000)

"The word of the Lord was

rare in those days; visions

were not widespread."

—*1 Samuel 3:1*

Prologue

COULD THERE EVER BEFORE HAVE BEEN A NIGHTMARE like this? Of course, the thing could hardly have been a true "nightmare," I suppose, since it happened in broad daylight—warm, comfortable, sunny, early fall daylight—and came just as I was strolling across Clare Bridge.

After all, I was wide awake.

Wide awake, yes, but no less terrified than if asleep.

And—humiliating thought—I find that I am still terrified.

Dear God in Heaven . . . What does it mean simply to be walking to prayer service in King's College Chapel, thinking of nothing in particular, and then to see such things as I saw this day?

What could it mean? What must I do? How should I be?

Oh, You'll insist that I know quite well.

Right, then. Martha Clark, ordinary Christian person, shall proceed to set down, here on paper, just what I saw, leaving out nothing, and then I shall read my story to Paul when he comes home, and then to Elisabeth and Jason. And then we four, together, can think, and pray, and, perhaps, do . . . if doing is somehow called for.

Yes. That's the thing.

And so here I will begin, in this little book. Here is everything that I saw this morning, just as I remember it. And if these words make me appear (to my husband and friends) a crazed woman, well, that's just how it will need to be.

I came across the little bridge, intending to walk into town through Clare College, and just as I reached midpoint and turned to look downriver—the Cam is so tranquil at that time of day—my view of the water was, first, interrupted, and then, by degrees, completely obscured by what I can only call a vision. I began to see a picture before me, one with bright outlines and clear contrasts. It formed itself right in front of my gaze, blocking out the Cam, and then it began to grow and grow until it occupied my whole field of sight. I remember that I held on to the railing as tightly as I could, because I was afraid I might actually fall prostrate on the bridge.

And then the nightmare proper began. I was not at first so much frightened as I was confused. After all, it was, when it started, just a "perplexing optical phenomenon"—as my psychologist husband might call it—that scared me in one way (*What could be happening?* I thought to myself.) yet not in any other way.

At least I don't think it scared me, at first, in any other way.

But following a perfectly innocuous beginning—with, in the center of the dreamed landscape, perhaps a dozen men stacking little books, hundreds or thousands of little books, in a small clearing in a woodsy place—the thing changed. It all became somehow bigger than that. Everything became quite large: the men, the individual books themselves, the number of books . . . all perfectly huge . . . and all somehow perfectly horrid. (I can't quite say how.)

And then suddenly there was fire. The books were burning. And the men seemed to cheer and clap their hands. And I tried—we all know how frustrating dreams are—to cry out to them that they should stop, and when I did, they stopped cheering and looked right at me. One pointed toward me, and several of them began to advance in my direction. Quite menacing, really. I tried to cry out, but, of course, it was just a dream and nothing happened when I tried.

And then the thing began to go away, and yet, before it was quite completely gone, I saw that the fire was spreading from the books to some buildings that I had not noticed before. I don't know if they had been there at the start of the vision, or if they were made present while my attention was drawn to the men. But the buildings were, I'm quite certain, churches. Big ones, tiny ones, ancient ones, young ones, stone ones, frame ones . . . all shapes and sizes and types . . . but quite definitely churches, every one of them. And I saw the fire beginning to run toward them.

And that was the end.

The vision just vanished, and I was left there on Clare Bridge, holding on to the railing for dear life. There were people around me all the while, mostly students, I believe, crossing the bridge and, as I think, paying me no mind.

And when it was all over, I felt so weak I could hardly stand. And so I didn't try to walk for some time. I remained and looked over the Cam, and tried not to be so frightened. I suppose I appeared to others altogether normal the whole time. No one stopped to inquire. People just continued to pass behind me.

I stayed a long time, just standing, looking, thinking. And, of course, praying. And praying desperately, I'm ashamed to admit even to this page of my own writing. After all, when something like that happens to a Christian person, one can't just say, "Father in Heaven, I'm terrified by something that just visited my mind and I am awfully keen on never seeing such a thing again."

So, my desperate praying was quite silly, I now think. Whatever the thing—the vision or nightmare—actually was, reason suggests to me that it should be regarded as holy, in some fashion, and that my prayers should take the line that I require assistance in understanding what it all meant. It's not as if God is to be regarded as unaware of the event, after all.

And I can't believe that it was all just the result of my failure to have a proper breakfast this morning. This wasn't about bad digestion or no digestion or running a fever or slipping into an elaborate daydream at an inconvenient moment. No, this was something done to me, or with me, or for me, with clear purpose and exquisite timing. There is holiness here somewhere, and I must come to understand it.

There. I'll have done with this now. It is all set down here on paper. I only wish I could know what will be next.

Then, after nearly three decades,

a new generation has come,

and a new story—

the new generation's own story

has begun. . . .

Chapter One

THE DAY THAT CHANGES OUR LIVES FOREVER DOES NOT introduce itself by that name. It just comes.

We awake. We arise. We move about. We may pray. If we do, we may ask God for His protection. From what, we do not yet know.

United States Navy Lieutenant Matthew Clark, age twenty-seven years and one day, stretched to his full six-foot four-inch length on the upper bunk of his diminutive stateroom. He smiled as the aircraft carrier's steam catapult, anchored within the flight deck's superstructure just above his head, slammed an F-4 Phantom into a summer morning. This was the flyoff of the air group to Oceana Naval Air Base after a seven-month patrol in the Mediterranean, and it meant that in twenty-four hours the ship would be berthed at Norfolk and he would begin processing out, his active duty at an end, and on his way to Charlottesville to begin graduate school.

Matt was genuinely excited. He had enjoyed his military experience even though it had meant enduring Naval ROTC in the years of an unpopular war, especially so on university campuses. And it had meant serving on active duty at a time of low morale throughout much of the United States military. But his country's involvement in an Asian morass had finally come to an embarrassed, miserable end, while the resignation of a United States president had seemed to place an exclamation mark on an interminable paragraph in the nation's history. The chance to return to his alma mater as a graduate student was delicious to him.

He was proud of his military service and happy with his prospects. He felt that his British parents, Martha and Paul Clark, were, too, at

1

least to the extent of endorsing graduate studies as a worthwhile post-Navy step. His father had loved his academic career in psychology, first at Cambridge, then, after their immigration to New York City shortly before Matt's birth, at Columbia. Matt, as an only child steeped in his parents' love of ideas and, especially with regard to his mother, of books themselves, understood academic life. His intention was to complete graduate studies, then immerse himself in the business world just long enough to achieve a "financial platform." He told himself that at that point he would, having proven himself in that fast-paced, competitive world, move into academia for a second career of teaching and research in economics, marketing, or international finance. Matt had thought it through with his usual intense care. He relished this future, played it out in his mind often, and at times could scarcely contain his impatience to begin after five years in the military. His father shared his excitement. His mother did not, but only because, he felt, she did not really value either business or money. She would come around soon enough once he began to find his way.

Another F-4 cranked its twin jet engines to a fury directly over his head, engines capable of driving the huge fighter plane into a completely vertical ascent when necessary. Matt had not been counting the launches that morning, but he knew the flyoff had been underway since 0600. It was now 0745 on this June Thursday, and, even at the relatively leisurely launch pace of an end-of-cruise flyoff to Oceana, he knew that by now few of the carrier's eighty-five warplanes would still be on board. He swung his long-muscled frame out of the upper bunk and dropped to the polished deck. He would go topside as soon as the "secure from flight operations" announcement came. He intended to walk the flight deck one last time while still at sea. He wanted to stroll aft, to the fantail, and watch the seventy-five-thousand-ton vessel's enormous wake churning toward the bow of the dutiful rescue destroyer, a mile to stern.

As he laced on his scuffed brown shoes, the telephone at his elbow emitted its jangling alarm, a unique sound he despised, even though, in comparison with the roar of steam catapults and Navy jet engines, it ranked far lower on a decibel scale. He lifted the receiver.

"Mr. Clark speaking, sir," Matt responded with practiced military elocution.

"Matt? This is the XO. Can you come down right away?"

"Yes, sir, Commander." He replaced the receiver, making sure the heavy weather clamp was in place. The clamp, designed to prevent the telephone receiver from being dislodged from its cradle in turbulent seas, served no purpose on a ship the size of a Forrestal-class aircraft carrier, a ship almost completely impervious to the sea's violence. But it was a useful reminder that this was indeed a warship, one that could be as susceptible to other kinds of threats as the smallest minesweeper in the fleet.

Matt finished with his laces and straightened his uniform, careful to align his shirt buttons' vertical seam with his slightly tarnished gold belt buckle. When he had the alignment perfect, thereby calling the eye's attention away, he hoped, from the wrinkles his khaki shirt had developed during his fully clothed, two-hour post-mid-watch attempt at sleep, he snatched the clipboard from his desk and stepped gingerly into the brightly lit passageway. The last time he had been in the ship's executive officer's cabin had been two years previous, when he had first reported aboard after having served nearly three years on a new frigate. Matt assumed that the XO had summoned him for the same sort of procedural conversation with which he had been greeted twenty-four months ago.

Yet there was something in the XO's voice that did not suggest routine. An edge. A slight discomfort, undefined. Matt pushed the disquiet from his mind with practiced dispatch. He stepped purposefully through two of the regularly spaced watertight hatches that interrupted the carrier's longitudinal corridor, wheeled left into the starboard escalator shaft, and waited for three of his junior officer colleagues to reach the top. As they cleared the ascending escalator with nods of morning recognition, he twice slapped the rubber-coated directional switches to reverse the gears, descended the now rapidly downward-moving stairway at full gallop, switched off the escalator mechanism with a deft open-hand punch, and, fifteen seconds later, stood at the executive officer's closed door. Matt squared his shoulders, breathed deeply one time, knocked twice, and heard the *basso* response: "Come in."

As he entered the spacious living and working area of the XO, three senior officers rose to meet him. The XO was one. Matt's immediate superior, the operations division officer, was another. The third was the ship's Protestant chaplain, a Methodist minister with the rank of commander. None was smiling. The sight of the chaplain sent an alarm to Matt's brain. Why would the chaplain be present for a routine exit interview? He tensed, eyes narrowing. He turned slightly to face the executive officer.

But it was the chaplain, whom Matt scarcely knew, who spoke, without preliminaries and with all four men still standing at a sort of informal attention. "Matt," he said with set jaw and what he may have thought was a don't-be-alarmed voice, "something may have happened at home. It may be nothing, but we wanted to relay the information to you immediately. Your parents' whereabouts . . . That is, it appears that your parents have been missing for several days now. Police just now reached us."

Matt, unmoving, stared, first at the chaplain, then at his division officer, the only one of the men whom he knew more than superficially. But they simply turned their own eyes back to the executive officer. When Matt's eyes followed theirs, the XO spoke.

"The flyoff is finished, Matt. We're holding the mail plane for you on the flight deck. Grab your shaving kit out of your stateroom and go. We'll take care of your gear and of your processing out in Norfolk. Here's the name and phone number of the New York detective who spoke with me by radiotelephone half an hour ago." He paused. He stepped forward. "Good luck, Matt. You did a fine job for us. Let us know if we can help."

With that, the XO thrust a folded piece of ship's notepaper into Matt's hand, then attempted to shake that same hand with his own. Matt did not reciprocate. He stared down at the paper in his right hand, still unmoving.

Then he felt his division officer's hand on his arm. "I'll fly with you to Oceana, Matt. Let's go."

Seven minutes later, at 0802, only two minutes behind scheduled departure, the ship's twin-propeller mail plane lumbered down the flight deck, assisted not by catapult, but only by the thirty-five knots of wind streaming over the deck as the ship's massive engines drove her through the green swells of the Atlantic. Near the bow, the stubby craft rose and, reluctantly airborne, lifted into the June sky. Matt Clark, near-civilian, was going home.

At 0945, standing at a telephone placed on the edge of an otherwise bare metal desk by the teen-age yeoman serving as receptionist in the lobby of the Oceana Naval Air Station BOQ, Matt fought the infuriating rotary dial with an adrenaline-driven index finger. Plowing through a formidable long-distance bureaucratic barricade comprising abrupt New York City questions and surly transfers, he heard finally the guttural, two-syllable response, spoken as a well-rehearsed challenge.

"Belton!"

"Detective Sid Belton?"

"Belton!"

"This is Lieutenant Matthew Clark," said Matt, dropping the pitch of his voice and placing emphasis on his Navy rank. "My executive officer gave me your name. I've flown to Norfolk from the ship. What's happened to my parents?"

Despite his effort to match the detective's brusqueness with his own, the words began to tumble from his lips, faster as he spoke each one, words competing nervously with each other and progressively weakening themselves in contrast to the detective's finely honed bark. There was a pause at the other end of the line. Matt could hear drawers opening and closing, papers shuffling, and finally the leather-and-rusting-spring complaints of an ancient swivel chair. When Sidney Belton spoke again, his vocal demeanor had changed. He was no longer speaking, it would seem, to an inconsequential distraction to his mid-morning paperwork. His voice maintained its guttural tone, but the pace of his words now traced a measured trajectory, one filled, it seemed to his listener, with omen.

"Twenty-four hours ago, we got a call from Columbia. Your father's department chairman told us that Dr. Clark had not come to work on the day before, that he had also missed an eight o'clock meeting that morning, and that there had been no response to repeated phone calls. Asked us to check on him. We did. Found nobody at home. Interviewed several people in your parents' apartment building, and three of Dr. Clark's colleagues at the university. No one could say they had seen either your father or your mother since Monday morning, almost seventy-two hours ago now. We wanted to go in the apartment yesterday, but your father's colleagues wanted us to wait until we talked to you. It took us a few hours overnight to track you down through the Navy. I finally got your boss on the line about 7:30 this morning. You want us to go in the apartment, Lieutenant? We can be in there fifteen minutes from right now, and I can call you back from inside the apartment."

When Matt did not respond immediately, the detective resumed his original tone. "Hey! Are you there? We got missing persons here!"

Matt, accustomed for five years to being spoken to with some deference by all those not clearly of higher rank than he, was instantly livid. "Why don't you go to the devil! Why, you . . ."

"Hey! Take it easy, kid! We're on the same side here. Just gimme a 'yes' or 'no.' We go in the apartment now, then give you a call? Or not? What do you say, kid? Just gimme an answer."

Matt was easily chastened. The word "kid" had done it instantly. He felt like a child and responded in kind. "Well, I suppose it's the best thing. Sure. What? Oh, here's the yeoman. He'll give you this number."

Just over an hour later, the same yeoman handed the phone to Matt, and Matt's ear was assaulted by the same rough New York City rasp: "Lieutenant Clark? Belton here. No luck in the apartment. No sign of a struggle. Nothing out of place." The detective paused, then modulated his voice to a caricature of persuasive intimacy. "Understand from your boss that you're practically out of the Navy now? Yes? Come on up to New York, Lieutenant. Go through everything here in the apartment and see if you can come up with anything. We'll notify police and highway patrol personnel across the country. We'll find 'em. . . . I *always* find 'em."

Ten minutes later, Matt replaced the receiver with a certainty that he must not stop and think about anything at all. Experience told him that when things seemed most confused to him, he needed to delineate a course of action and move on it immediately. This New York detective's suggested course would do just fine. If he stopped to think . . . to try to sort everything out . . . to imagine the possibilities of foul play that his parents might somehow have encountered on the streets of Manhattan . . . to weigh the consequences of this unforeseen emergency for his life, for his entry into graduate school, for his imagined sequence of careers . . . above all, to decide how he actually *felt* about any of this . . . he would become frozen, mentally and physically inert. So, thinking about little other than the next five minutes' demands, he moved efficiently from one step to the next: meeting with the base transportation officer, securing passage on a Navy cargo flight that evening to Dover Air Force Base in Delaware, arranging for lodging that night on the air base, and reserving a civilian rental car for early next morning. It would have been possible to drive from Norfolk to New York immediately, but he had served the midwatch the previous night, with less than two hours' sleep just before the XO had summoned him, and now, in late afternoon, he knew he could not start an eight-hour-plus drive that would bring him to New York City well after midnight. He would accept the military cargo flight, sleep for several hours at the Air Force Base in Delaware, and then start the three-hour drive from Dover to Manhattan. He did not want to think. He only wanted to rest, to gain his parents' apartment by noon tomorrow, and then, in that familiar sanctuary, begin to make sense of this catastrophic intrusion.

For that was still Matthew Clark's first response to nearly every unexpected, uninvited interruption, small or large: resentment that "his time" had been encroached upon. It was not that he did not love his parents. It was not that he was not desperately worried about them. It was that his habitual response to unplanned events was irritation borne of a sense that, once something was planned, the time thus allocated for it had become, quite simply, his own.

And so it was an angry, irritable Matt Clark who began his journey north to New York, a Matt preoccupied more with this newly unsettled quality in his own life than with the ominous uncertainty surrounding his parents'.

Still clad in the clothes he had been wearing on board ship when the executive officer's summons had come the previous morning, Matt Clark entered the borough of Manhattan via the Holland Tunnel, extricated himself from the snarl of tunnel traffic, and raced north surrounded and buffeted by a flight of New York City Yellow Cabs toward his parents' West Side apartment. As agreed, Sid Belton and several uniformed city police officers awaited his arrival. Two police cars held a place for his rental car in front of the apartment building. Matt stepped from the car, self-conscious in his now thoroughly disheveled at-sea working uniform, and shook hands with a stooped, rumpled mid-fortyish man nearly a foot shorter than he. "I'm Belton, Lieutenant. Glad you made it. You tired? Hungry?"

Detective Belton's physical presence was a revelation to Matt. Heretofore the disembodied voice of arrogant, authoritarian rudeness, he seemed in person almost cuddly, with a crooked smile that by itself softened the harshness of the voice, and with deep-set, almost black eyes peering with something like naïve inquisitiveness at the world at large. Matt's long-distance anger and frustration dissolved in a surge of wholly unexpected gratitude at the detective's demeanor and at the extraordinary preparations he had engineered in anticipation of Matt's arrival. Not only had he been waiting as promised, and personally solicitous, he had assigned one police officer to turn in Matt's rental car, another to pick up a ham sandwich for his lunch, and still another, after having estimated Matt's height and girth with the critical eye of the *gendarme*, to go to one of the neighborhood haberdasheries to buy a few "civies" with taxpayer money, on the correct assumption that Matt's clothes—military and civilian—were still on his ship or in storage. When Belton explained all of this, Matt found himself staring at the detective, stunned by such generosity and thoughtfulness. Belton smiled his crooked smile again: "Hey, kid, we're rude, but we're not bad people. We do try to help, y'know?"

Together, the two of them went up in the elevator to the ninth-floor apartment. They were silent as they entered, using Matt's own key. Matt shivered involuntarily as he stepped into the familiar living room. He had a sense of somehow entering his parents' tomb. An uncanny feeling of abandonment enfolded him in the silence. The door closed behind them.

Belton spoke: "We've dusted for fingerprints, and tried to find out if valuables have been taken. I don't think we have anything, but that's why we need you to go through their things and see if anything looks wrong. And another thing, son. Everything we can find out about your parents leaves me confused as to why anybody would kidnap them or do anything to them at all. There is such a thing as randomly targeted crime and violence, of course, but your parents . . . they're boring, son. Know what I mean? They're not rich; they're not controversial; they don't hang out with anybody except their university and church friends; they don't gamble; they don't have anything to do with drugs. I don't know what they left behind in England, but in more than twenty-five years in the U.S., they haven't done a thing that makes them targets for anybody . . . for anything. And, of course, if they were actually kidnapped for any reason, we'd expect the kidnappers to contact somebody long before now. So, I don't get it. But I want you to look carefully at this apartment, and then I want you to just sit down and *think*. Think about their lives. Think about anything they may have written to you recently that meant nothing to you at the time, but might fit into this puzzle somehow.

"I'll leave you to it. Your lunch and a few clothes will be here in a couple of minutes, and we'll station one officer just outside your door and his partner out front in their squad car. You come up with anything at all, you tell the guy at the door, okay? You need anything at all, you ask for it, okay?"

Matt nodded. "All right, Detective. I might as well get started." He thought for a moment and spoke again. "Detective? Why all this trouble? I don't mean the sandwich and the clothes, which, believe me, I do appreciate. I mean . . . why are you . . . why are the police so . . .

interested in this? Is there something that you suspect that you haven't told me? I need to know. Really. I want to know."

Belton shook his head. "Nope. Don't know anything that you don't know. But it's not every day that a Columbia professor and his wife go missing for a week, son. I don't know if anything bad has happened to them or not, but I don't like it. When someone does something to good New York citizens, I take it personally, son. Understand?"

As soon as Matt was alone, he quickly walked through the apartment, scanning every surface for something amiss. Then he dropped to his hands in front of each piece of furniture, peering under each. He did not know why. He did not know what he was looking for. But he had immediately trusted the detective, once he was face to face with him, and he wanted to comply with Belton's directives as best he could.

After nearly two hours, he sank into his father's living room chair, and allowed his mind to run free in his parents' past. He tried to do what Belton had asked, tried to think of anything his mother and father had said in their letters during his seven months' cruise in the Mediterranean. He tried to imagine sinister meanings behind their stories of university politics and church pettiness. Campus intrigue. Parish scandals. He laughed aloud, softly. His parents were so . . . upright. What had the detective said? "They're boring, son."

His gaze, unfocused until now, absently scanning the rooftops and balconies visible just across the street, moved idly to the left of the window. Without conscious effort, his eyes brought into focus a framed print. The print was a striking, snowy depiction of King's College Chapel, Cambridge University.

Matt sat straight up in his father's chair. His eyes narrowed again as they had in the XO's cabin thirty hours previous. King's College. Cambridge University. It was long ago, but . . . if there did happen to be any "intrigue" in his parents' past, perhaps it lay there, in England, not here in New York. What had Belton said? "I don't know what they left behind in England. . . ."

What *had* they left behind in England? He searched his memory. They had left Elisabeth and Jason Manguson, their best friends. They had left Dr. and Mrs. Ashford, their "campus parents." They had left that strange story of a "war," something to which they alluded from time to time, usually somewhat cryptically, his father, lightly and jokingly, his mother, always with deadly seriousness. Waged just after the real Second World War, this apparently clandestine conflict had somehow been conducted above and below and behind the public's consciousness. Yet it had been fought, if one could accept his parents' characterizations of it, in deadly earnestness and would have become real enough, and public enough, had it turned another way. And Matt knew even as he thought it through that he actually knew almost nothing about it. He had listened to his parents' accounts of the conflict with the polite interest with which he listened to his history professors' accounts of Persians fighting Greeks. His war interests had always been kindled by aircraft carriers and aerial torpedoes and dive bombers . . . modern Naval warfare. *Real* warfare. But this other thing, the "Cambridge War," as his parents had termed it, or the "Prayer Book War," as Matt himself had once jokingly called it, seemed to Matt to have been fought over some ludicrously obscure threat to the Christian church in England, something about corrupting or replacing the Anglican prayer book. He had never even tried to understand any part of the story. Religion had never "taken" with Matt. He had no idea what all these religious conflict tales had been about. And none of it had ever mattered to him in the least. Until now. He frowned. Detective Belton hadn't known "what they left behind in England." Well. Neither did he.

Matt rose quickly from his chair, crossed the room, and stopped at the doorway of his mother's study. He stood for seconds, looking around the compact room with new eyes. He knew his mother wrote here, always at the small desk tucked just inside the doorway. He knew she prayed here daily, a fact that made him uncomfortable at this reminder of her unabashed piety, the image of her here in this room suddenly highlighting by way of contrast his own breezy and cynical materialism in a fashion that made him flush with an unexpected and unfamiliar sense of shame. He brushed the feeling away with a characteristic, nearly imperceptible wave of his right hand. It was a skill borne of long practice.

He let his eyes fall to the floor while he processed the prior thought. He knew nothing about this room, precisely because he knew his mother prayed here, read Scripture here, wrote in her diary here. And he wanted nothing to do with any of that. He shook his head slowly.

Then he looked up sharply. Her diary. Where was it? He knew she wrote in her diary each day, but he could not recall ever having actually seen it. He turned to face the desk. It was orderly, of course. His mother's Bible was placed carefully just to the right of the lamp, itself on the left corner. To the right of the Bible was her red leather-covered Episcopal *Book of Common Prayer*, with its slender, graceful, gold cross on the cover, and with three red-ribbon page markers trailing from it onto the desk surface.

He turned his head away, looking back into the living room without moving from his position in front of the desk, and thought. There had been no signs anywhere in the apartment of his parents packing for a trip, and all their luggage seemed to be in its expected place. But this, his mother's desk, was the most telling sign that, wherever his parents might be, their departure was not planned . . . and not voluntary. His mother never went anywhere overnight without her prayer book. It was unthinkable.

He reached for the prayer book, cradled it in his huge left palm, and fingered the first of the ribbon markers, sliding the ribbon upward while the pages separated obediently. A small heading announced the start of the Nicene Creed. He read to himself: "I believe in one God, the Father Almighty, maker of heaven and earth, and of all things visible and invisible; And in one Lord Jesus Christ, the only-begotten Son of God. . . ." His only son, our Lord..."

The words further heightened his discomfort, his sense of alienation from the room itself. Replacing the first marker, he quickly turned to his mother's second ribbon-marked passage. The italicized phrase at the bottom of the page announced, *"Ministration to the Sick."* The prayer just above that phrase began, "This is another day, O Lord. I know not what it will bring forth, but make me ready, Lord, for whatever it may be. If I am to stand up, help me to stand bravely. If I am to sit still, help me to sit quietly. . . ." He shivered. The words dripped with piety and resignation. Why was this page marked? Was his mother ill? Or did she simply pray daily for the sick as part of a regimen?

His discomfort nearly overwhelming him now, he turned to the third of the marked pages. His eyes fell on the heading at the top of the right-hand page: *For those in the Armed Forces of our Country.* Under that heading, he read, "Almighty God, we commend to your gracious care and keeping all the men and women of our armed forces at home and abroad. Defend them day by day with your heavenly grace. . . ."

He smiled as he read the words to himself. He knew exactly why this page was marked. He read the words a second time. The words of the prayer seemed to go deep down into his mind, and beyond. He read them still again. And he realized that he was actually beginning to relax. He pictured his mother reading and praying that prayer, and he knew that she would have had Matt's image before her, in her mind, as she prayed. He smiled again. As the seconds and minutes passed, his discomfort subsided, at length leaving him in the midst of a rising sense of his mother's presence, her maternal protectiveness and love for him enveloping him as of old. Eventually, for perhaps the first time since his shipboard meeting in the executive officer's cabin, he sensed outrage mounting in his chest, radiating outward to the muscles of his forearms and hands. He closed the prayer book, replaced it on the desk, and saw both hands tighten into fists. Although he could not have put it this way, the fact was that he was just now beginning to think about someone other than himself, for the first time since his parents' disappearance had been announced to him. The thought that actually formed itself was this one: "How is it possible that anyone could do something to this woman? And if God were *here* for her prayers, how, exactly, might He permit something to happen to someone this . . . this . . . *good?*"

Now genuinely angry, he forced his mind back to the diary. He saw that nothing else graced his mother's desk except for her pens and two photographs of his father and himself together, one taken on his last leave, just before the Mediterranean cruise, with his mother standing between them in the picture, and one taken by her five years before, when he had reported aboard his first ship. He then noticed for the first time that the desk had no drawers; it was just a writing table. His eyes moved to the bookcase just to the right of the desk, and fastened quickly on a rectangular lock box on the lowest shelf, probably dark green once, now presenting a near-colorless, metallic image, almost military in its studied dullness. He stepped to the bookcase, stooped, and lifted the box with both hands, placing it in the center of the desk. He moved the clasp and raised the hinged handle, testing the lid; it yielded. He saw that the box contained a small stack of near-identical booklets. He was certain even before opening them that the tattered, spiral-bound, untitled volumes were his mother's diaries.

Matt pulled the chair away from the desk, took a deep breath, and seated himself. He removed the topmost booklet from the box, turned to the back, and paged forward until he encountered the most recent entry. His mother's familiar script—as familiar to him as his own—met his eyes. As he turned back two more pages to the start of her final entry, his eyes were attracted to a grouping of words that were set off from the rest. He leaned forward in the chair and stared at them uncomprehendingly. Martha Clark's careful formation of letters left no doubt that he was reading what she had intended to write:

Unig-genedledig Fab Duw,
cenedledig gan y Tad
cyn yr holl oesoedd,
Duw o Dduw,
Llewyrch o Lewyrch,
Gwir Dduw o Wir Dduw . . .

Chapter Two

AT NOON ON A HAZY ENGLISH FRIDAY—THAT SAME FRIDAY on which Matt Clark was driving his rental car from Delaware to New York City—Dr. Jonathan Foster, director of the University of Bradford's Institute for the Study of Society, closed the door behind him as he stepped into his college rooms. He placed his briefcase on the floor beside his antique roll top desk, crossed into his sitting room, and snapped on the television. He hoped he was in time to catch the BBC interview with Cambridge theologian and historian Meredith Lancaster.

Foster hated meetings in which he was not the chair; they could run late and often did, placing him in the position of asserting his authority to end a meeting at which he was merely *ex officio*, or enduring the wasted minutes to the bitter end. Having just endured, he was in ill temper. He would be doubly so if he had missed the Lancaster interview. Turning the volume high enough to be audible from the scullery, he quickly put on a pot of tea, then returned and stood in front of the screen.

He was rewarded a moment later when Lancaster's introduction began. As the host provided background on the timing for the interview, a second camera framed Lancaster's face. His pale blue eyes focused, steely and unblinking, on his host. He seemed unaware of the cameras, though Foster was certain that Lancaster, veteran of many years of television interviews, was fully aware that the live camera was his. Lancaster's mouth traced the relaxed, poised smile of the famous and handsome, of the public figure confident that he was not merely famous and handsome, but compellingly telegenic under all circumstances. As the introduction drew to a close, Lancaster provided his viewers with

15

his familiar lift of the chin, signaling his preparedness to illuminate, to enlighten, and to reassure.

Lancaster had begun to speak, his baritone voice resonant, completely in charge of his audience: both the interviewer himself and those countless fellow countrymen viewing from TV sets throughout Great Britain. "Yes . . . yes, I do think that, when we make our full disclosure in the appropriate venue, Christians and non-Christians alike will be led to a somewhat altered view of who our Lord actually was, and of how we should come to understand Him. Most certainly we will experience a shift in our understanding of early Christian history, particularly as it developed here on this great island. I've no doubt that this will be, to some, unsettling at first, but I ask simply that our viewers at home and in the workplace . . ."—here Lancaster leaned toward the camera, smiling gently, looking earnestly into the lens, expressing with great effect his sympathy for the fragility of his audience's belief system—". . . *trust me.* Each one of you understand how loathe I would be to introduce anything whatsoever that . . . that . . ."—here he appeared to search for precisely the right phrase—". . . that might somehow be construed so as to seem to . . . to *diminish* our Lord, and our sacred history and traditions."

Lancaster sat back in his chair while his interviewer probed further. Again came the characteristic lift of the chin, the confident smile, the steady gaze, and the power of the blue eyes to make contact with the television viewers. "No . . . no, I'm afraid I cannot yet go further in disclosing the full nature of the discovery. I can only say that soon . . . quite soon, in fact . . . we will be ready to announce the date, time, and location of the full *revelation,* if I may use that word. You may *all* rest in assurance that it will have been worth the wait."

With that, Meredith Lancaster crossed his legs and relaxed in his chair, rewarding the viewers with his most ingratiating smile, satisfied that he had again piqued the curiosity of the faithful, the unfaithful, the anti-faithful, and the religiously uninterested alike. It was, as always, *exactly* what he had wanted from the interview. He had controlled his host and his message from the first moment, and had closed the session when it pleased him to do so.

Foster switched off the television, smiled to himself, and shook his head in wonder. The man was a master. An absolute master. Still standing motionless just in front of the darkened TV screen, Foster's smile faded as he pictured Lancaster's televised gaze—unblinking, steady, intimate—and the televised smile—warm, welcoming, self-assured—in contrast to those very features as Foster himself had so often experienced them from close range. From very, very close range.

He turned away from the quiescent television, and crossed the room to his desk. Seating himself, then leaning down to open his upright briefcase, Foster reached inside and removed a sheaf of papers, spreading the papers before him on the desk's massive writing surface. Most of the material related in one way or another to his upcoming retirement ceremony. He half-absentmindedly looked over the material, noting the most recent changes, his eyes moving rapidly from one announcement, agenda, or text to another, nodding his head occasionally in satisfaction. Some of the festivities and encomiums seemed, he had to acknowledge, a trifle overdone, but one could certainly appreciate the eagerness of the College Visitor to celebrate the career of one universally regarded as the institute's modern-day savior.

It had seemed clearly the result of divine intervention nearly three decades earlier that he—then the institute's deputy director—had been spared death in the Great Disaster, as he and his colleagues from that era had christened it. Divine intervention, certainly, though in retrospect Foster had to acknowledge that his response in the immediate aftermath had been too sanguine.

He brought easily to his memory, for perhaps the several hundredth time, that long-ago day when he had stood in the morning silence of Magdalene College Chapel at Cambridge and, still a young man, had listened to an equally young Meredith Lancaster recount for him in hushed tones the story of the previous night's events. Both Lancaster and Foster himself had been scheduled to ride the late train from Yorkshire to Cambridge with their allies in their secret battle to replace the Church of England's *Book of Common Prayer* with something radically new, *The Anglican Book of Community Service*.

The new book had represented an exciting change. Its text would have subtly, yet forthrightly, updated the language and the emphasis of the worship services and prayers so that the faithful would have been led to a clear recognition of the full range of charitable obligation falling upon those who wished to honor the Christian traditions. And it would have sought discreetly to ignore out of all existence such primitive concepts as heaven, hell, resurrection, sin, salvation, eternal life, and the like, except as imaginative and, certainly, enriching metaphorical constructs.

Attempting such changes through regular ecclesiastical channels would, in all likelihood, have proven fruitless, and, in any case, would have been altogether unnecessary. Arrangements were quite in order to accomplish the thing in Parliament, thanks to the established nature of the Church of England. Lancaster, Foster, and ten other prominent scholars, politicians, and churchmen had operated for several years in complete secrecy, or so they had thought. And so they had been surprised to find themselves opposed, within days of their first public statements, not by any sort of officialdom, but by an even smaller band of unstable and unbalanced individuals who deemed it their business to confront the movement by methods that were, in some ways, just as forceful, secretive, and unconventional as their own. The Parliamentary outcome had become suddenly less certain.

In any case, on the very eve of the day that might conceivably have marked their final triumph, the train had been somehow derailed and all ten of their colleagues had gone to their deaths. At least, that was how it appeared to the authorities. As Lancaster had explained to Foster that morning in Magdalene Chapel, the bodies of their colleagues had not actually been found. Their rail car, having been reserved just for their group, had been the last on the train and, unlike the cars ahead, had actually plunged all the way down the embankment and into the swollen river that ran alongside the tracks just at that point. They had apparently managed to escape the rail car, but had been swept downstream in the flood waters so rapidly that their bodies were never found. An incomprehensible thing. But there it was. And, without the ten, which included all the senior members of the group, the chances of moving forward successfully with the coup shrank to nothing.

It had clearly been through divine intervention, then, that Lancaster and Foster, both by far the youngest members of the group, had been spared. They had been sufficiently detained at a meeting at the institute that they missed the death train's departure. Since the dead included the director and one other key fellow in the Institute for the Study of Society, Jonathan Foster had been asked to rebuild the institute from the ground up. And he had done so with the sort of deft purpose and political dexterity that had made him, he knew, the envy of all those who perhaps had stronger ideas but less of the craft that could bring those ideas to complete organizational fulfillment. Yes, the modern-day savior. That was how he was thought of. And with good reason.

Foster had known then that this would be the turning point of his life. From the first moment he had received the staggering news from Meredith Lancaster on that morning after they had been driven to Cambridge by automobile, he had sensed divine intervention in the whole conflict and, even then, in its outcome, disappointing though that outcome seemed both to Lancaster and to himself at first. The more he had thought about it, the more fully Foster had realized that the whole shaping of the institute would now rest with him. There would be no new prayer book—no *Anglican Book of Community Service*—but, at least, he would have on his resume the rebuilding of a quite visible academic community. It was a less dramatic call to service, but also less controversial. And it certainly had its own kind of importance.

And so it had in fact happened. No statue in his honor had yet been proposed, admittedly, but plenty of time for that, once he assumed his role as Director Emeritus, presiding sagely and with more effect than most would be aware, from a position both behind and above the new director. The new appointee to the post was, after all, an amiable enough chap, but one in rather obvious need of direction from the esteemed savior of the institute.

His thoughts lingered . . . and then he sighed . . . knowing that his mind would not be allowed to close the story there, even in imagination. Foster shut fast his eyes and awaited the inevitable. And it arrived. The fairy tale began to deteriorate. He took a deep breath. Knowing what would come now, he pushed his chair away from his desk, and slowly leaned forward until he held his face in his hands, elbows propped on knees. For the ten thousandth time—for no day had passed for almost thirty years without a visitation regarding this portion of the tragedy—he saw in his mind Meredith Lancaster's then-young face, appearing at his hotel door in Cambridge within days of the Great Disaster, the final action of the Cambridge War. He saw as if it were yesterday the rapid transformation before his eyes of that handsome countenance, as it had confronted him in his private hotel suite: the pale, steely eyes beginning to shift continuously as if directed by automata; the warm and welcoming features dissolving into repeated grimaces in satanic imitation of a human smile; the then-dark goatee, its irregular contours exaggerating the strange fluctuations in Lancaster's freshly sinister visage; the lift of the chin coupling arrogance with furtiveness in a complex and confusing manner. And then the threats had come, spoken by Lancaster's lips but in a voice strangely unlike Lancaster's own voice, *ordering* Foster to continue his plans to rebuild the institute with himself at the center. Then, again, *commanding* Foster to accept the fact that henceforth his chief authorities would be "spiritual" authorities.

"I find your manner of speaking rather . . . ah . . . overbearing, Meredith," Foster had replied. "But I will say, regarding your allusion to *spiritual* authorities, that, in the light of these astounding developments, I have indeed come to appreciate the providential aspects of all this, and am quite willing to entertain the likelihood of divine influence. . . ."

"Silence! Fool!" Lancaster's alien voice had shouted. "You have been *saved* from the Disaster by *my* Masters for *their* purposes. *They,* partly through me, will develop your agenda for the institute. *They,* with my assistance, will arrange for you to become a wealthy man as the years pass. *They,* served and aided by me, will provide you with your *vision* for the rebuilding of the organization. Simply know that your orders, whether penned by my hand or not, will come from those who fully intend to establish their domination over this planet once and for all, and who will kill you . . . or worse . . . at a moment's notice, should you hesitate to carry out the program with which you will be provided."

Lancaster's *faux* voice had by then risen to an inhuman screech. "Do you understand this, *you miserable wretch . . . you moronic cipher . . . you insipid ass?*"

Foster recalled for the ten thousandth time the terror that had overcome him in that interview as he saw the young academician transformed before his eyes into an agent of . . . he could only call it Evil, despite his previous disbelief in anything that could be imagined as an "anti-Divine force." He remembered afresh the sense of overwhelming heaviness that had come upon him as that "conversation" had continued on into the night, feeling again in memory the crushing weight upon his head and shoulders that had forced him literally to his knees, and then to the floor, prostrate. His disbelief had, he knew, been fractured beyond repair in those minutes, there having been absolutely no recourse available to him . . . not logic, not reason, not previous experience of any kind.

He recalled—again for the ten thousandth time—how, after Lancaster's departure that night, he had searched for escape. He remembered his tortured admission to himself, well after midnight, that up until that evening he had in fact believed in nothing except, as a result of his survival of the Disaster, some vaguely formulated idea of destiny, and even that only because it flattered and suited him. And now he called once more to his mind, knowing that he had no choice but to do so, his desperate collapse as morning had approached, his falling again to the floor in the hotel suite in submission to . . . nothing that he could conjure in his imagination. And he remembered still again how, as dawn had broken on that decisive morning, he had admitted to himself with an inconsolable finality that, with belief in an actual, tangible, irrefutable Evil having been forced upon him, and, having no protection of the sort afforded his believing colleagues from a creative, redeeming goodness that, even if "real," he could not believe in, he would have no defense—none—against this threat to his very existence. His life, he sensed, was over, just at the moment that it would seem to the English public to be at its true beginning. He had *seen*—no, more than that by far—had *felt* Evil itself. He had been given certainty that this reality existed and had been physically present with him . . . and he knew that he could not believe in any antidote . . . any cure . . . any personal, active, countervailing force.

And now, at his desk, once again, as had been the case each and every day for nearly three decades, Jonathan Foster felt the nausea rising. He rose swiftly, left the room, and, for the ten thousandth consecutive day, was sick.

His hatred for himself was infinite.

On an uncomfortably warm, threatening Monday morning in Cambridge, three days after Meredith Lancaster's television interview, and the same three days after Matt Clark, sitting in his parents' living room an ocean away, had fixed his eyes on a print of King's College Chapel, Jonathan Foster stepped from the train and paused to assess the overcast skies above him. Shortly before daybreak Meredith Lancaster had summoned him, as he had, when it pleased him, for nearly thirty years. Foster had perforce responded, as he had, when thus summoned, for the same interminable span of time. He had swiftly instructed his assistants at the institute to cancel his day's agenda, had packed an overnight bag with accustomed dispatch, and rather easily had found a seat on the 8:12 to Cambridge.

Foster loved Cambridge, and since, even with his train's tardy arrival there, he had well over an hour until his meeting with Lancaster, he resolved to enjoy the time as much as he could. Excising the approaching appointment from his mind with modest success, he walked north from the station toward city center, turned left onto Downing Street, then right onto King's Parade. As he walked, he distracted himself from thoughts of Meredith Lancaster by encouraging history to play through his mind, solemnly imagining the old "presences"—Wren, Milton, Newton, Wordsworth, Byron, Tennyson, Inigo Jones—and stopping to gape, *like some ordinary tourist*, he thought to himself, at the late-Gothic magnificence of the university's signature, King's College Chapel. He stopped briefly in two bookshops, then, feeling the first tentative raindrops of what might become a downpour at any moment, purchased an umbrella with a distinctive dark-grain handle from the men's store on the corner. Then, with a start, seeing his appointment time almost past, he walked purposefully, anxiety building in his stomach, past Trinity and St. John's Colleges, doing his best not to interfere with, or be struck by, the bicycles swarming around him from all directions. He hastened miserably across the bridge over the Cam and turned right into the arched entrance to Magdalene College. When he reached courtyard center, he turned briskly left, aware that perspiration was already beginning to work itself through his patterned shirt. Foster pulled open the courtyard door to the college chapel, strode to its interior entrance, and glanced at his watch. He was nearly five minutes late for his rendezvous with Lancaster.

Foster folded his new umbrella loosely, not using its self-binding strap in deference to the scattered raindrops that it had collected, then stepped through the interior doorway to the chapel. He looked to the right immediately, despite an earlier resolve not to do so, and observed the discreet plaque to the memory of the late C. S. Lewis, whose last years had been spent in this very college. Foster remembered Lancaster's grudging compliment, issued privately, upon Lewis's death: "That damnable Lewis did more damage to our cause in this century than all the Archbishops of Canterbury stacked on top of each other." Foster, sensing in himself some odd difficulty in moving his eyes away from the Lewis plaque, at length succeeded in looking toward the front of the chapel. There he saw his nemesis standing near the altar, talking with two students. Lancaster saw Foster in the same instant, and looked at his watch with a dramatic flourish.

He shouted from the altar: "You're late, Jonathan. Trying to assert your independence?" Before Foster could issue a disclaimer, Lancaster turned his back to him, spoke earnestly to the two students who responded with obedient nods of their heads, and, smiling broadly, turned again and walked up the aisle to shake Foster's hand. "Just joking. Thank you for coming. I've just finished here. Let's go up to my rooms for a few minutes."

As they walked, Foster found Lancaster ebullient, talking expansively about the "mounting international excitement," the "gratifying political enthusiasm," the "surprising ecclesiastical anticipation," and the "humbling corporate support" for his upcoming announcement. How had Foster liked Friday's television interview?

"Oh, I felt you were absolutely masterful, Meredith, in your . . ."

"There are a number of individuals I will want you to contact next week," said Lancaster, ignoring the obsequious response he had elicited from Foster and clearly relishing his right of interruption. He opened the door to his rooms, stepped inside while Foster followed, and continued, reaching for a packet on the entryway table. "Here is your file, containing instructions and brief biographies on each man. We'll have Ms. Thompson and Ms. Levy get in touch with the women, while Samuels and Ms. Waidlaugh telephone the Americans and others out-of-country.

"Why don't you have a seat here, Jonathan, and have a look at your lists, while I put on a pot of tea. You've had lunch?"

Not waiting for an answer, which, they both knew, was going to be a lie, Lancaster, who himself never seemed to eat except at banquets at which he was the speaker, left the room. In the silence, Foster tried to concentrate on the data in front of him and, when Lancaster returned, the two men conversed for several minutes, clarifying details and points of emphasis, person by person.

Without warning, Lancaster abruptly stood and announced that it was time to go.

"I have just a few more questions, Meredith . . ."

"Give me a call on those when you get back to the institute. I want to show you something now. We'll need to drive."

"I thought I was to remain overnight. I have brought . . ."

"You may indeed stay overnight. But not here. Let's be going."

With that, Lancaster left the room again, turned off the tea that he had not served, and reappeared, carrying an unusually long, thick umbrella with a massive, curiously formed handle that gave it more the appearance of a saber than a rain shield. Lancaster clearly intended to leave that very moment, and Foster swiftly collected his scattered materials, fumbling them in his haste, sighed to himself, and followed Lancaster out the door.

The rain shower had passed for the moment, though the cloud color and texture looked more ominous than before. They departed the college by the same archway Foster had used an hour previous, turned left, crossed Magdalene Bridge, then turned left again to follow the footpath beside the placid river's graceful curve around city center. The two men did not speak to each other. Meredith Lancaster spoke, however, to every person they met, occasionally by name. He was the picture of relaxed cheerfulness; his companion, the embodiment of anxious misery. At the footbridge that would take them back over the river to Chesterton Road, they were slowed by the bridge's switchback approach to its span, and by clusters of students, some of them walking bicycles in obedience to the bridge's large-lettered instructions to that effect. Finally joining the slow-moving procession across the narrow span, they encountered a bespectacled student, pedaling his way across the bridge in oblivious defiance of signage and custom, squeezing past those crossing in his direction and dodging those who, like Lancaster and Foster, were walking against him.

As the young man guided his teetering two-wheeler past the two men, Lancaster, in the blink of an eye, thrust the point of his heavy-shafted umbrella through the bicycle's rear wheel, moving with the fluidity and force of the accomplished fencer that he had once been. Spokes burst instantly from their moorings in the wheel, the cyclist was launched over his handlebars, and the resulting crash scattered students in every direction. Suddenly the heavily trafficked bridge appeared as a still life. No one moved. Students, stunned, looked from the fallen cyclist to Lancaster and back. Seconds passed. Then, as if on signal, Lancaster whirled and marched away, the weapon pointing straight skyward as if it were a knight's lance, while transfixed students swung into action again, some attending to their fallen comrade, others continuing in their original directions. Lancaster completed his bridge crossing as if nothing had happened, speaking to several more students whom he met, ignoring the carnage and confusion behind him, and looking for all the world like a man on holiday.

Upon reaching the roadway itself, Lancaster swung to the right, Foster continuing at his heels. Suddenly, treating oncoming auto-mobiles as unworthy of acknowledgment, Lancaster strode straight across the traffic-swollen Chesterton Road while drivers did their best to avoid him and his terrified companion, continued in the same direction on the opposite sidewalk, and, some fifty paces later, stopped and faced the left rear door of a black Mercedes sedan. A muscular, impeccably attired young man bolted from the left front seat, opened the rear door, and stood at near-attention as Lancaster gestured for Foster to enter. Foster found himself gaping in astonishment and in some fear at Lancaster and at the open door. It seemed to him that the car's interior was a kind of pit from which he might never emerge.

He hesitated.

At that moment, he felt himself struck sharply on the back by Lancaster's astonishingly heavy umbrella. Shocked into action, Foster virtually leapt into the vehicle's rear seat, moving without pause to the right-hand side while Lancaster followed him. The door was slammed shut. The apparent bodyguard swiftly and almost soundlessly returned to the left front seat. Only then did Foster realize that there was a driver already in the car, that the engine had been idling, and that they were already in motion. The bodyguard then turned all the way around in his seat and made eye contact with Lancaster, who nodded. With that, the young man reached under the car's dashboard, lifted something out, then turned in his seat to face Foster. He gestured for Foster to lean forward and to the left, toward him, and Foster realized that the man was holding a blindfold.

Foster's verbal paralysis left him. "No," he shouted. "I say! Stop this car this instant! I say! Stop it now!"

There was no discernable response from any of his three captors. There was a longish pause before, without visible signal from Lancaster, the driver pulled to the curb and stopped, still on Chesterton. Finally, no longer shouting, Foster turned to face Lancaster. "I demand an explanation. I demand to be released from this car. What do you have to say for yourself? Answer me!"

Lancaster, who had not so much as turned his eyes in Foster's direction until now, slowly turned his face to Foster's, a slight smile playing across his lips, the gray-streaked goatee providing punctuation for the distinctiveness of the chiseled features. Still he did not speak. Ten full seconds went by. He simply stared straight into Foster's eyes, impassive.

It was Foster who broke. He dropped his eyes, then raised them in the direction of the blindfold. The young man had not moved the blindfold even an inch throughout Foster's diatribe and the ensuing silence. Foster dropped his head to his chest in an agony of humiliation at his own cowardice and submissiveness. Then he leaned forward and accepted the placement of the blindfold. Darkness covered him. The Mercedes moved forward again.

For several minutes Foster knew where they were. He sensed that the car had turned right onto Elizabeth Way, then, at the roundabout, left onto Newmarket Road. That, he knew, would take them immediately out of the city.

But as the drive continued, the car's occupants completely silent, Foster soon gave up his guesswork regarding direction and location. At every roundabout he found himself uncertain whether they had gone 90 degrees round, 180, or more. He only knew that eventually they were no longer on a highway. The Mercedes had slowed, its turns had become continuous, and the roadway was no longer smooth. Finally, after what seemed to be a long, steep, switchback climb, the car stopped.

Lancaster spoke. "Remove your blindfold, Jonathan. We have arrived."

The bodyguard opened Lancaster's door, while the driver opened Foster's. Foster stepped out and, following Lancaster's prompt, moved around the rear of the vehicle toward the entrance of a rather unkempt country home, much of it covered in some sort of wildly aggressive vine, and looking uninhabited to Foster's quick glance. The four men entered and, without pausing, Lancaster gestured for Foster to follow him up a staircase that rose just from the left of the front door. They reached a landing and Lancaster turned to Foster, indicated one of several closed doors in the passageway before them, and said, unsmiling, "I have a surprise for you, Jonathan. Old friends."

With that, he stepped to the door indicated, rapped once, turned the handle without waiting for a response, and followed the door as it swung open in response to his pressure. They entered a large and nearly dark room that appeared vaguely to be a parlor. Foster entered dully. His eyes, having begun to adjust to light after the blindfold, attempted a reverse adjustment to the room's shuttered, single-bulb illumination.

Next he heard Lancaster's voice announcing with feigned formality, "Jonathan Foster, please renew your acquaintance with . . ." and here he motioned sweepingly to his right while Foster's eyes struggled to focus on two seated figures, ". . . my house guests, Martha and Paul Clark, recently of New York City and Columbia University."

Chapter Three

CATCHING THE METROPOLIS BY SURPRISE, THE SATURDAY sunrise reached toward the east-facing windows of a small flat in one of London's less distinguished neighborhoods. It was the morning following Matt Clark's Friday arrival in New York, and two days prior to Jonathan Foster's encounter, in Cambridge, with Matt's mother and father.

Inside the flat, a woman struggled to extricate herself from sleep by the sheer force of her considerable will. Violently, her long, muscular legs thrashed and scissored under the light summer bed coverings.

And suddenly she awakened as a sleep-wounded animal, struggling in consuming desperation, nightclothes drenched. The dream that had broken her slumber still held her, forcing from her a twisting, pawing lurch from the bed to her feet. Pushing away the clinging suffocation with immense effort, she dragged her unresponsive body from the nightmare's embrace. Groggy, moaning involuntarily, she gained the bedroom door, staggered into her closet library, and faced the near wall, chest heaving. Her fingers gripped the sides of her tall, narrow bookcase. Raising her eyes, she focused on a reality inches from her elegant face: as the early morning light followed her path through her bedroom and into this passageway *cum* bookroom, she fixed her gaze on the relaxed features of her parents, smiling from the picture frame on the top shelf. And her mind began slowly to clear.

Rebecca Manguson, twenty-six years of age, six feet tall, strong, erect, and handsome, was anything but a coward. Gasps subsiding, her thoughts beginning to organize themselves, she forced her mind back to the terror with the outraged intention of confronting it immediately, now alert, no longer awash in an unfathomable medium.

Still gripping the bookcase, her breathing now measured, Rebecca's gray eyes dropped one shelf from her parents' photograph to the small, dark blue Church of England prayer book. *Of course*, she thought. The dream was extraordinary, horrifying, and disgusting all at once, but her start of day need not be. First, begin the morning as she had done for more than a decade. There would be prayer. Then, in the clarity of that regimen, she would confront whatever terror the nightmare might still hold. And after that, to act. Rebecca was designed for action. She would not, could not, simply "be done to" by these preposterous dreams.

For this was not the first such nocturnal violation. It was, in fact, the third in the last fortnight. Each had been more or less the same. The starting point was a face. The face itself was unremarkable. It was a face that drew one's attention to itself simply because of the unpleasantness of its movements and the strangeness of its contours: the eyes, shifting almost continuously; the mouth, grimacing repeatedly in imitation of a smile; the small goatee, narrowing and tapering the features oddly; the lift of the chin juxtaposing arrogance with the furtiveness of shifting eyes and a nervous mouth. From this beginning, each dream had broadened to include two other faces: the first, a stoic, elderly, enigmatic face adorned with an Anglican cleric's collar and bishopric regalia; the second, a rugged, weathered, full bearded, vibrant countenance of indeterminate age, radiating enormous force of will, consummate intelligence, and uncompromising and explicitly Christian charity.

As the dreams had continued, progressing each time in the same pattern, she had perceived background features: a parchment or scroll, a small vial, and, stretching darkly behind and beyond every foreground component, a massive, medieval ruin, strangely purplish in color. None of this frightened Rebecca who, in waking life, was an extremely difficult person to frighten.

Soon after these faces and ancillary features had materialized, that disquieting first face began to spawn undulating shapes that added confusion and clarity at once. Emerging from a point behind the face itself, the shapes began to inject fear, then outright horror, into Rebecca's sleeping mind. This they accomplished more through their inexorably expanding aspect than in their plain appearance. For in appearance, they seemed nothing more than a sort of multiplication of the face itself: if anything, they were enhancements, less devious, even ingratiating. But unlike their primary manifestation, these emanations communicated clear intent, and that intent was unambiguously lethal. Thus, the clarity. As each dream moved into full nightmare, the emanations, soon too numerous to count, grew steadily to fill nearly the whole field of dreamed vision. And worse, they began to approach both the third face, with its commanding and radiant countenance, and Rebecca herself, threatening each of them with . . . not death, but something worse.

And it was that which induced both confusion and the full horror, the frantic half-dreamed need to intervene and yet to flee, which eventually woke her each time in an agony of imagined flight and rear-guard combat with the spectral beings. It was something beyond mere death that was being forced on the two of them—the rugged, full bearded third face and Rebecca herself. Or, perhaps, *offered* the two of them. She could not say what, even to herself. She simply knew.

Rebecca broke through her reverie, relaxed her grip on the bookcase, and lifted the prayer book from the second shelf. She turned toward the sunlight just beginning its full cascade into her bedroom, strode back through the scene of her struggle, and knelt at her desk. She composed herself, opened the book, and read the General Thanksgiving, whispering the sentences aloud to herself, savoring the seventeenth-century prose.

> Almighty God, Father of all mercies . . . We bless thee for our creation, preservation, and all the blessings of this life; but above all for thine inestimable love in the redemption of the world by our Lord Jesus Christ, for the means of grace, and for the hope of glory. And we beseech thee, give us that due sense of all thy mercies, that our hearts may be unfeignedly thankful, and that we shew forth thy praise, not only with our lips, but in our lives. . . .

She closed her eyes and continued her prayer, focusing with practiced concentration upon praise, upon thanksgiving, and upon the daily miracle that for her comprised prayer itself. She asked for guidance in the face of an intrusion of a sort unknown to this point in her life.

Perhaps the repeated nightmare meant nothing. Perhaps it was simply to be endured. She prayed for understanding, for direction, and for courage to act upon that direction.

Finally, a clean peace centered in her consciousness, muscles finally relaxed, she looked up, placed the prayer book on the edge of her desk, and rose from her knees. Moving with her mother's unselfconscious, straight-backed grace, she prepared herself for this newly dawned Saturday and its long-promised rendezvous with her parents in Oxford, then strode rapidly down the short hallway of the flat to her brother's bedroom. She knocked twice. "Luke . . . Luke . . . it's time."

Rebecca and Luke Manguson were twins. They had decided some months previous to reduce expenses by rooming together in the compact flat while they pursued separately their low paying starter posts with neighborhood junior schools, hers, a girls', and his, a boys'. They were poor by the standards of London's other university graduates in mid-to-late twenties, but they were happy, very happy, with the lives they were building there.

Inseparable as children, Rebecca and Luke had drifted apart during years in boarding schools, and even more while at university. But they had begun to grow close once more while still geographically far apart, Rebecca immersed in volunteer service in Birmingham's underside, Luke at sea with the Royal Navy as a radar control officer (surface warfare) during the last eighteen months of his military service.

Rebecca's center-city work placed her face-to-face with her persistent fear that her lofty academic studies of economic history and the development of metropolitan cultures, coupled with her pristine but untested determination to serve those whom Christ had called "the poor," would be no match for the flesh-and-blood-and-soul human beings whom she would engage hourly in that setting. Meanwhile, Lieutenant Luke Manguson, RNVR, found that his daily contact with the British military's variegated mix of humanity, from the sons of privilege to the rough and tumble products of the same environs in which his sister now labored, pushed him similarly to a reassessment of previously abstract notions and career goals. Their intermittent correspondence, heretofore undertaken more as a sop to their mother's wishes than in genuine desire to communicate with each other, became more frequent and gained depth by the letter. The eventual result had been mutually supportive decisions to teach junior school youngsters in the city.

The twins, with their maturing vocational understandings and newly discovered respect for each other, liked one another in the same ways that fast friends do: they were comrades and confidants. They enjoyed each other's company now more than that of anyone else they knew, male or female. They had each "fallen in love" more than once, but each such incident seemed, in retrospect, little more than a diversion from a developing sense of vocation. Neither of them seemed to need to be in love any more, if indeed they ever had, and so neither displayed the debilitating habit of searching incessantly for it.

And both honored their parents. Elisabeth and Jason Manguson had been attentive to their offspring, but had never "lived for" their children. And as Rebecca and Luke had grown, their parents had progressively shared as much as they felt they, in conscience, could possibly reveal concerning the obscure, life-changing series of events in their own young adulthood that they referred to within the family as the Cambridge War, and occasionally by its other name, the Prayer Book War. The second name, the twins knew, had been coined as a joke when they were teens by the one-year-older son of their parents' best friends. Those friends had remained close to the Manguson family despite having moved from England to the United States at the conclusion of the "war."

Partly as a result of these parent-child disclosures, the twins' already close relationship with their parents had gradually strengthened. A great deal of plain mystery about the Cambridge War remained unrevealed to the two young people and, they understood, with reason. They experienced no resentment, since, the more they were told, the more strongly they felt a sense of trespass.

Rebecca knocked again on her brother's door. "Luke . . . it's time."

She waited until she heard a sleepy acknowledgment, then turned into the cramped kitchen to prepare sandwiches for this excursion to Oxford where their parents, driving from Birmingham, would meet them for a day of Oxford-browsing and a meal. Rebecca forced herself to keep the nightmare away for the present moment and, partly as a diversion, she encouraged her mind to play swiftly across their family's history.

Their father had developed in his youth a promising career in academia, but at the conclusion of the "war," Jason Manguson had had no further interest in his university career at Cambridge. He and Elisabeth had moved to a spot near their current home in Birmingham, had borrowed enough capital to purchase and then renovate a decaying Victorian mansion, and had begun a life together as boarding house proprietors.

But that was not "who they were." As Rebecca moved with a two-fisted tennis player's strong, dexterous hands to complete the steps of sandwich preparation for Luke and herself, she smiled as she recalled the many times she had tried to "explain her parents" to her friends as she grew up. It was not easy. To say to a new friend that her parents were best described as full-time Christians seemed both the truest thing and the most impossible to say. Usually, she could craft a circumlocution that hinted with more or less success that the Mangusons' real vocation had little directly to do with the boarding house, but rather with their engagement with the people of Birmingham's center city, frequently, but not always, through their parish's outreach ministry. Rebecca and Luke had themselves often been included as children in this ministry, and eventually learned not to fear it. They also learned that their parents' forthright, unpretentious, unsanctimonious approach to conversing with others about their Christian engagement was in the long run the only sensible way to do the thing.

Rebecca wrapped their food, actually a breakfast of sorts, placed it in the small picnic basket, tidied the kitchen, and went to Luke's door once more. She listened, then prepared to knock again. The door swung open to display her brother, fully dressed, shaved, and ready. They laughed. "It's the Navy," he said. "Get ready quick. Get ready quiet."

Luke was an inch shorter than his twin, and looked not at all like her, except perhaps in his ramrod posture. While she displayed her mother's upright, willowy strength and grace, he marked his father's triangularity. His shoulders and chest were of great breadth, with supple, rippling muscles prominent through almost any clothing he chose to wear. They were both strong and athletic, but in Luke those were the dominant physical impressions left upon any observer, whereas in Rebecca those characteristics were mostly obscured by her height, bearing, and eyes that were striking both in their grayness and in their fixed penetration of any object on which they fastened.

Together they started for their dilapidated motorcar, and began the drive around London's perimeter and on to Oxford. They consumed their breakfast sandwiches while negotiating the London orbital, whereupon Rebecca moved into the first action step of her morning resolve, reinforced in prayer, not to allow the nightmare to strike her at will without counterattack. She placed her hand on her brother's shoulder to make certain that he understood that the small talk of the holiday's onset was over, and punctuated that warning with the request that he pull off the motorway so that he could give her his full attention. He complied immediately, turned off the motor, and faced her.

As she began to describe the thrice-recurring dream, Luke's eyes widened with what seemed to be recollection. He appeared so struck by her description that, well before she had reached midpoint, she paused. "What are you thinking, Luke?" she asked.

"Sorry . . . didn't intend to stop you . . . please, go ahead."

"No, really, tell me."

He paused and looked away for a moment. Then, still looking away from her, he asked, "Rebecca, do you remember Mrs. Clark's dreams? The ones that presaged the Cambridge War?"

"Martha Clark? Mum's friend?"

He nodded.

"Oh!" she exclaimed, her hand going to her mouth. "Oh, no!"

They stared at each other, wordless . . . their minds racing . . . racing first into the thirty-year past . . . then back into the glare of the present.

Their silence continued for minutes, while their eyes eventually moved off into the distance, each one fighting against the obvious, searching for an escape from the conclusion that, irresistible, returned again and again.

At length, Luke spoke. "But you weren't finished, were you, Rebecca? I'm sorry to have interrupted, but there was just something in the character of the dream . . . something in its complexity and in your feeling that it was *imposed* on you somehow . . . that brought Mrs. Clark's experiences to mind. Go on. Please."

She nodded and, now with some effort, brought herself back to her description. The idea that this could in fact be some kind of recurrence of the Martha Clark dream sequence, and that she and Luke could actually be on the edge of some corresponding drama or crisis, distracted her, clamored for her attention. She fought her way back to concentration on the nightmare itself, trying to include every detail for her brother. Finally, as she concluded, she exclaimed, "Luke! I'm remembering something in the telling that I'd not remembered at all until now. During my third dream . . . the last one . . . that scroll . . . there were *words* written on it, and I was beginning to see the words just before the . . . the growths . . . the emanations . . . the spectres . . . began to obscure everything." She paused again, shaking her head slowly. "I didn't recognize the language, but I can still actually picture one or two phrases."

She stopped, covered her eyes with her hand, and tried to see still more clearly the unfamiliar words—if they indeed were words at all— as they had appeared in the final vision. Still covering her eyes, she spoke, softly, haltingly, sounding out the unfamiliar syllables as best she could:

> *Unig-genedledig . . . Fab Duw . . .*
> *Cenedledig . . . gan y Tad . . .*
> *Cyn yr holl . . . oesoedd . . .*
> *Duw o Dduw. . . .*

Chapter Four

REBECCA READ HER MOTHER'S NOTE ONCE MORE, SITTING in the car with her brother in front of the Eagle and Child Pub in Oxford. They had been met there at the rendezvous point not by their parents but by a Birmingham friend of the family, who had issued apologies and delivered the note. "My dears," it read, "we shan't be able to see you today or, possibly, for some time. When we got news and instructions this morning, you had already left home, so we couldn't telephone to keep you from driving all this way to Oxford. I'm so sorry. Will get in touch when we can. Try not to worry. Must run now. Love, Mum and Dad."

She looked at her brother, who was staring straight ahead. "Luke? Luke? Say something!"

He turned to her and smiled affectionately. "I'm sorry," he said, "I was doing it again, wasn't I?" Luke's lifelong habit was to concentrate silently on a problem regardless of whether or not he was in anyone's company at the moment. Rebecca had been trying good-naturedly for some time to pry him out of the habit when he was with her.

Luke turned his head and looked up and down St. Giles, searching for something. "There's a telephone just down the street. I'm going to try to call them, Rebecca. Wait for me?"

In five minutes he opened the driver's side door and slipped behind the wheel. Rebecca looked at him.

"A recording: 'This number has been temporarily removed from service.'"

The twins were silent for several moments.

36

Rebecca spoke softly, her face now turned away from her brother's. "Luke, what should we think? This note from Mum is . . . well . . . strange . . . even mysterious. *Look* at her words: they may not see us 'for some time' . . . and they have got 'news and instructions' . . . and they'll 'get in touch' when they can. And now you tell me their telephone is 'temporarily removed from service,' which means they have taken it out of service within the last hour or so. . . .

"Luke, I'm frightened."

He reached for her hand. Looking hard into her gray eyes, he replied to her, his voice tense, "They're cutting themselves off, Rebecca, . . . establishing, for some reason, a defensive perimeter . . . and they're trying to avoid involving us in whatever this may turn out to be."

He looked away. "Something is happening to them. They expect something to try to get to them . . . to try to get *at* them . . . and they're making preparations for siege."

They were silent again, their hands still joined.

"Luke?"

He faced her again.

"My dreams . . ."

He nodded.

She continued. "Martha Clark's dreams . . . thirty years ago . . . the Cambridge War . . . and now this . . . whatever *this* might be. . . ."

He nodded again. "Yes."

"And this time it's I, rather than Martha Clark, who has been given the secret *intelligence*."

After a pause, he nodded again. "Maybe," he said simply.

After another moment, Rebecca spoke again. "Luke," she began, "we have to go to them. We . . . at least, I . . . must tell them about these dreams. The dreams may be nothing. But they may be everything. We can't just go back to London and go about our business. We can't . . ."

Suddenly Luke covered his sister's hands with both his own.

"Rebecca! Yes!" her brother responded with his first real sign of animation. "Of course! If we didn't at least make a report . . ."

Not finishing the sentence, he added, "You and I have no idea what your dreams mean, but Mrs. Clark, you'll remember, didn't either, at first."

Releasing his sister's hands, he sat back, breathed deeply, and, now looking away from her, continued. "What would you think of going back home right now," he said slowly, deliberately, "just long enough to speak with our headmistress and headmaster, giving them time to arrange substitutions for us at school on Monday, and then starting for Birmingham this afternoon? It's Saturday. The administrators would have time to work on this. And neither of us is scheduled to read tomorrow morning in church."

Rebecca nodded her head slowly. "Yes. Yes, I think we simply must."

She sighed. "We may be fools to do this. After all, Mum's note certainly does not invite us to go to them. And, of course, there is the possibility that my dreams are ordinary nightmares having nothing to do with anything. And there is also the chance that there is some perfectly benign explanation for their change of plans this morning. I may turn out to be the biggest fool . . ."

Once more Luke's left hand covered his sister's hands as she began to clench and unclench them in her lap. "You know in your heart," he said to her softly, "that those dreams are not ordinary, my dear. And you know in your heart that our parents do not send us cryptic messages canceling plans and saying that they may not be able to see us 'for some time,' while at the same time they, in haste, move to have their telephone service suspended. And we both know where our duty lies. We've no choice, Rebecca."

No further discussion was needed. Luke put the old car on the motorway back toward London and, as the twins retraced their morning's path, they began to focus upon their pupils and the next few weeks' lessons. They remembered enough about their parents' stories of the old Cambridge War to know that the fight had consumed their parents and their parents' allies for at least several weeks' time, though they were as uncertain of that as they were about most details associated with that mysterious conflict. But they assumed that, once they plunged in, their involvement would not end in a matter of just hours. In fact, though neither actually said so, they both knew that, when one chose to engage this type of enemy, the battle might well be joined for a lifetime. And they also knew that lifetimes under such circumstances could become very short indeed.

As Luke drove, Rebecca made notes for them both, addressing one set of instructions to her headmistress, and the other set to Luke's headmaster. Throwing themselves into the task, they completed their work shortly before arriving home, finding in the end considerable confidence that their junior school youngsters would be well served, even if they should be away until end of term.

Once in the flat, the twins helped each other put things away in the kitchen, then went to their own rooms to pack. Luke had rung up his headmaster soon after they had arrived and, once they were both ready for departure, Rebecca spoke for a half hour with her headmistress. When she finished the call, she turned to find Luke standing in the doorway, looking at her oddly.

She raised her eyebrows in question. "Someone has been in the house, Rebecca," said her brother with the military edge to his voice that meant he was on guard, ready to "repel boarders," as he liked to say jokingly.

He was not joking now.

She stared, incredulously.

"When we first came in, we were both in the kitchen and, since you were the last one in that room, I couldn't very well notice if anything had been moved. But as soon as I went into my room, I saw that the extra house key and the extra car key were not in the positions in which I had left them. I noticed, but I just thought I must have brushed one of them when I put on my wristwatch and ring this morning. But later, after I spoke with Mr. James about my classes, I began to see other things: two of the drawers were not closed fully; the note pad on my desk was askew, and so were the three books just next to the pad; and my Bible was *face down*, Rebecca."

Rebecca knew her brother better than anyone else knew him. She immediately shared his complete certainty that someone had broken into their flat; she knew that he *always* left his personal things in precise geometrical relationship to each other, and that the idea that he would ever leave his Bible face down was preposterous. It was not that Luke thought there was something actually wrong with not closing drawers fully, or leaving his own materials at angles other than 90 degrees or in parallel, or leaving a Bible face down. It was simply that Luke, even before his years in the Royal Navy, organized his own things with such care that this series of, by Luke's standards, unthinkably careless placements could mean nothing else. No, she was as certain as he. Their home had been violated. She shuddered. But it was anger that rose within her, not fear. Her powerful hands tightened.

"Rebecca," he continued after a pause, "I've taken a while to think about this while you were still on the telephone with the headmistress. I fear the same thing that you fear . . . that somehow all of this connects both with your dreams and with mother and father's message to us. Somehow *they* have located us, and have some special interest in what you and I are doing. We are almost certainly going to be watched as we load the car, and then we will be followed out of the city . . . perhaps even prevented from leaving the city, though I think it is more likely that whoever was in our flat may be more interested in learning our destination than preventing our leaving town. Did you tell your headmistress?"

"No, I simply told her what you and I agreed would be appropriate: that it had become extremely important that we assist our parents with a family matter over the next several days or even weeks. That we couldn't guess for exactly how long. That we had prepared detailed packets for our substitutes in class.

"She didn't need to hear more than that about our reasons for leaving. Our conversation was all about the pupils."

"Good. I've a preliminary scheme of action, Rebecca. Tell me what you think. . . ."

Several hours later, having unpacked everything and restored the flat to its everyday appearance, the twins were ready for a different kind of departure than their original, heavily laden one would have been. They each surveyed the other's work, rendering judgments. Finally, satisfied that indeed the apartment appeared no different than it might at any time, and that there seemed no hint that the occupants were away at all, they then marked the time until nightfall by reading and doing their evening devotions. Then, without the need for further signals to each other, they passed through the flat, turning off all lights but two, as they did every night.

They stood in the darkened kitchen and, with his small, hooded, Navy flashlight, Luke read aloud their final checklist: credit cards; cash;

passports; driving licenses; detailed map of the city; detailed map of the region; keys to the flat; small bath kits; the instruction packets they had prepared for their heads of school, now ready for the post; and Luke's multi-purpose, sheltered knife blades, a set of clip-on blades of varying size and contour, fitting a universal handle, and thus useable as utensil, tool, or weapon. They each wore dark clothes and caps. Rebecca's attire included her midnight blue, full-length, tennis warm-up trousers. Her long, thick, black hair was pulled into a tight ponytail, which protruded through the slit in the back of her cap.

Luke pulled aside the curtain covering the small window in the kitchen's outside door to the alleyway behind the apartment. He was thankful now that no one had repaired the street lamp that had once illuminated a portion of the alley. He nodded to his sister, pulled open the door just enough for each of them to pass through, slipped onto the back stoop, waited for Rebecca to pass, and closed the door behind her. In seconds the night had swallowed them.

Earlier on the same Saturday morning on which Rebecca and Luke Manguson had started for Oxford for holiday with their parents, and two days before Matthew Clark's own parents were to be reintroduced to their old enemy, Jonathan Foster, near Cambridge, Matt opened his mother's lock box in a New York City police precinct office. He removed her current diary, turned to a page near the back of the small book, and began to explain the passages he had marked, during a long Friday night of reading, for Detective Sid Belton. "See, Mr. Belton," Matt said carefully, "just over two weeks ago, starting right here, Mom records the first dream. I mean, the first *special* dream . . . the first *special* dream in almost thirty years. She describes it in detail. It appears to be centered on a man's face . . . a face that does weird things in the dream . . . a face that seems to generate other, similar versions of itself. These multiplied faces then start to spread out with what Mom calls 'lethal intent' and they begin to approach . . . what is it, Mr. Belton?"

The detective had stopped following Matt's finger as it traced his mother's passages in the diary, and had begun to stare at Matt. The crooked, mischievous smile was already beginning to crease his elfin features. "Whad'ya mean, 'What is it, Mr. Belton?' You're gonna waste my time telling me that your mother has had some dreams? Go back to the apartment and get some sleep, kid. I got stuff to do here, even if it is Saturday morning."

"No, wait . . . you have to understand something, sir . . ."

"Don't call me 'sir,' kid. And don't call me 'Mr. Belton,' either. Makes me feel one hundred years old. I'm just *Detective*. It's who I am. It's what I am, too. Call me that. And now get outta here so I can do my job."

Matt closed the book and faced the detective. "Please . . . listen to me. I *have* stayed up most of the night, again—I admit that—but I'm still thinking straight, Detective, and we don't have any time to spare. We've got to go . . . I've got to go . . . to England . . . and right away. I just need for you to understand something about why I've got to go. Please . . ."

"England?" The detective seemed to reflect for a moment. "All right, all right. Let's hear what you got, kid."

Matt, pulling his thoughts into ordered form with some difficulty, given his fatigue, began to explain. He outlined for the detective the salient features, as best he could, of the Cambridge War, drawing both from his memory of his parents' sketchy allusions and, to a somewhat greater extent, from some of the passages in his mother's oldest diaries. The "war," he explained, had formed the final chapter in a still little-known series of events in England, just after the Second World War, in which his mother's special dreams had provided a small group of . . . well . . . "Christians" . . . he supposed might be the most appropriate term for them . . . with critically needed assistance in thwarting a plot. And, he continued, it had been a plot that, had it worked, would have made *by political fiat* a number of dramatic changes in the Church of England, with longer-term results that might well have done significant damage to the faith and to the faithful and, if fully successful, to Christianity itself. And, even if one didn't take Christianity with much seriousness, one had to admit that these unscrupulous people, who were . . . well . . . he supposed . . . actually "evil" . . . had been prepared to do a lot of damage to something that was of fundamental importance to a lot of human beings and, just as bad, they had planned to do it in ways that were irregular, heavy-handed, and, possibly, even criminal.

Matt stopped again. Belton's crooked smile had returned and he had begun to shake his head at Matt in apparent wonderment and disgust at the naïveté—or perhaps delirium—of the young man in his office.

"Look, Detective," began Matt with renewed impatience, "even if you don't take seriously a thing I have just said, think about this: something huge happened to my mother—and, by the way, to my father, too—back then. It may make no sense to you, or to me, for that matter, but Mom's diaries do make one thing clear. After nearly thirty years, the dreams that precipitated her involvement with those Christian people started again just over two weeks ago. And in some of her final diary entries she even refers to several of those very people by name, and is actually in communication with them when the diary stops. It's all right here, Detective. And now she and Dad are gone, and without so much as a trace. So . . . I'm going to England. I just wanted you to know. If you don't have any interest in this, that's fine. But I'm going." Matt had begun placing his mother's diaries back into the lock box, when Belton's hand gripped Matt's wrist gently, stopping him in mid-motion.

"*She refers to several of those very people by name?* Y'know, that might have been a pretty good starting point for this conversation, kid. Then you might not have had to come across as nuts, either."

Matt looked sharply at the detective, ready to snap at him, but, as before, found himself disarmed simply by the look of this strange man. How could a person's words fit his demeanor so poorly? Belton's deep-set black eyes communicated a child's simple ingenuousness and inquisitiveness more fully than those of any adult with whom he had ever conversed. And the crooked little smile softened everything the detective said, melting his confrontational words into some kind of appealing, liquid mush. It was magical. Now Belton was speaking again, and Matt, whose gaze had drifted, looked at him once more, hope returning that the detective would help him to think through his next steps. For Matt could not, in his exhaustion, think further than the need to purchase a plane ticket to London, and there to start looking for the individuals named in his mother's diaries, starting, he thought, with their old friends Elisabeth and Jason Manguson. He could not form the first thought as to how.

"Son, you said this was a Christians-versus-evil story thirty years ago? What does that mean? Who were these *Christian* people?"

Matt sighed. "Detective, I know you think all of that stuff is nonsense. I can see it in your reaction to everything I've told you. The part that interested you was my mother's having named some people, and her having speculated in her diary about getting in touch with them. Let's just stay with that part, since it is the only part you can take seriously."

"Look, kid, what you don't know about me is a lot. It was you, not me, who looked like you wanted to crawl under the table when you had to use the word *Christian*, or when you had to say the word *evil*. You wanted to be sure I knew that *you* wouldn't be fool enough to take those words seriously. You don't believe in anything, kid, but your mother does, and so you're embarrassed for yourself, that you *don't* believe in anything, and you're embarrassed for your Mom, that she *does* believe. Isn't that about it, kid?"

Matt's face flushed bright red and he looked away, astonished and further embarrassed. Who *was* this little man, who couldn't speak grade-school English decently, yet who seemed to see right through him? Matt's only visible response beyond uncontrolled blushing was the nearly imperceptible wave of his right hand that signaled his dismissive wish to move on to something else.

"Son, am I right? Gimme a 'yes' or 'no.' I need to know stuff like this. Helps me do my job. You *want* me to do my job, y'know."

Matt sighed again, this time audibly. "I suppose so . . . Yes!"

"Okay. So don't make decisions for me, son. I want the names of those people, I want to know what you meant by *Christians* and *evil*, and I want to read those entries where your mother is talking about contacting people. Tell me. Show me."

The two men spent the next ninety minutes immersed in Martha Clark's diaries, old and new. Detective Belton made notes to himself as they moved through the pages. Near the end, Belton placed a gnarled index finger on a page and asked, "What's this stuff?"

"I don't know what it says, Detective, but Mom writes, just before and just after that entry, that these words appeared repeatedly in each of her recent dreams. She doesn't know what language this is, or even if it is a language. She just reports that these words appeared . . . and they appeared every time she dreamed. And she notes somewhere that, when she had these dreams years ago, she dreamed in a long series of dreams that led from one to another. This time, it's the same dream, over and over. I don't know what that means, either."

"Hmm . . . I'm no shrink, but I have to say . . . that's interesting to me. She can reproduce the words without knowing what they mean . . . without knowing even what they are? I'd sure like to know whether or not this actually says anything in some language or another. Let's run these lines over to our language experts . . . see what they can make of it."

"You've got language experts in the police department?"

"Not *in* the police department, but, sure, *available* to the police department. Kid, this is New York City. Every third person is speaking something other than English."

Matt, having slept for several hours that Saturday afternoon at his parents' apartment, and having tossed his police-issue civilian clothes into one of his father's small pieces of luggage, had gratefully accepted the standby seat, left aisle, center section, on British Airways' 10:15 P.M. flight from JFK. He had hoped for a few more hours' sleep en route, but his mind, thus far, was racing as fast as the Boeing 747's engines, as the huge aircraft climbed out over Long Island and set a northeasterly course toward the Newfoundland coast.

He had been dismayed at Sid Belton's response to his queries about how to find any of the individuals who, because his mother had mentioned them in her current diary, in her older diaries, or both, might be of assistance to him in locating his parents. Belton had simply asked a series of questions, none of which Matt could answer.

"These people your mom writes about . . . why aren't any of these people in her address book? You've said you looked for each name in her address ledger, and not one of them is there. Why is that, son?

"And if she knows where they are, and had wanted to talk to them in person, why wouldn't she have just packed a bag and bought a plane ticket? We've checked every international manifest for the past ten days and found nothing. And you've told us that your Mom's bedroom and study show no evidence of her preparing to leave. And you made special note that her prayer book and Bible are still in her study. And so, obviously, were her diaries.

"And if *bad guys* have kidnapped your parents—or, I have to say this—worse than that, what is the point in looking for people who, whatever else they might be, are *not* themselves the bad guys?"

Matt had tried to stop the detective at this point, having felt sufficiently beaten down so as to wish fervently not to hear any more, but Belton had continued.

"If foul play is involved, son, how are you gonna do anything other than create more headaches for us by setting out on your own? Did you think about that? *Would* you think about that?

"And what are you gonna do in England that Scotland Yard couldn't do a thousand times better and faster? You're gonna find these people in the telephone books of England? What for? You're one guy in a foreign country with a pathetic little list of names out of a diary. You're crazy, kid. Let us do our job."

At the end of this barrage, Matt had held his head in his hands in dejection. And immediately he had felt the detective's hand on his shoulder. "Son, you're exhausted and you're nuts, but do whatever you think you gotta do. If you gotta go to England, okay. Go to England. If you need something once you get over there, gimme a call. If I can do something to help, I will. Meantime, I'm gonna look for your parents, son. And I'm gonna do a better job than you will. Now get going. No sense sitting here."

Despite the withering list of unanswerable questions, Matt had, in the end, found unendurable the prospect of sitting in the apartment for hours, days, weeks, or longer, doing nothing about his parents' disappearance. By the time he had reached the door to the apartment, having walked the eight blocks from the precinct office, he had decided he would rather launch a search of his own for the people his mother wrote about, checking in by phone as often as he could with the detective, than any alternative he could imagine.

Now, as the British Airways flight attendants began their evening cabin service, Matt, declining food and drink, reached under the seat in front of him and pulled his mother's lock box towards him, placing it between his feet. He opened the lid, pulled out his mother's current diary, then reached to the bottom of the stack, and removed the oldest. He closed the lid, pushed the box back under the seat, switched on his overhead reading light, and began again, at the beginning.

Feeling momentarily refreshed after two hours of airborne sleep to go with a four-hour afternoon nap in his parents' apartment, and still energized by a second review of his mother's diaries, Matt cleared customs on a warm Sunday morning at Heathrow, and waited for his single piece of luggage to find its way to the conveyor. He smiled, despite his impatience at the wait, as he thought again about the diaries and the conclusions he had drawn from his study of them. And he knew that he felt a certain relief that Detective Sidney Belton was not there to quiz him on his findings and, no doubt, to turn his too-eagerly seized conclusions into jelly.

Those admittedly amateurish conclusions were twofold: first, that his parents were facing some conflict that was larger than their kidnapping itself; and second, that he should go to Birmingham, to the renovated Victorian mansion that Elisabeth and Jason Manguson had converted years ago into a boarding house. The first conclusion he had reached by systematically comparing his mother's recorded descriptions of the circumstances leading up to the original conflict with those leading to what he had decided to regard as a second one. And while he had decided this in part, he knew, for emotional reasons—he felt less anxious with a working hypothesis than without one—it was not just that, and it was not just the dreams. It was her increasing frequency of contact with the small cluster of individuals who had formed the opposition to, in his mother's recorded words, ". . . the forcible corruption of our church's central beliefs." The same build-up of communication with this group that had gone hand in glove with the first threat seemed to have been repeating itself over the last few weeks.

And it was obvious from the tone of Martha Clark's recent entries that she was worried about all of them. His mother was frightened, and every indicator pointed across the Atlantic toward the source both of her comfort and her fear.

Matt's second conclusion, that he "should" find the Mangusons' boarding house, was one that simultaneously embarrassed, dismayed, confused, and delighted him, the first three because he had spent an entire adolescence and young adulthood forming a view of anything religious as, quite simply, beneath him intellectually. To find himself suddenly and unaccountably being pulled, however nonspecifically, in a religious direction had stirred a deeply felt humiliation within him that he could not fail to acknowledge. And yet he could recognize that he also felt delight. The detective, after all, had been right about him: He *was* embarrassed for his mother that she was a Christian, and yet just as embarrassed for himself that he believed in nothing. Thus, despite the humiliation of sensing a fresh spring of belief welling up within him, he felt an odd sort of happiness, too.

It must, when one thought about it a certain way, be a very exciting thing honestly to believe in God, especially the Christian one, insofar as Matt understood what that might mean. To believe—*really* to believe— that the Almighty was active on this planet, "cared" in some unimaginable way about its individual inhabitants, could actually be prayed to . . . could be thanked for some things, could offer one forgiveness for other things, could actually intervene in still other things. What a colossal idea! What if it turned out to be a fact? If it were, *everything* would be different.

And when he tried to determine analytically why he suddenly had developed this sense of being pulled and tugged by something, he had no trouble knowing the answer. It was his mother's oldest diary, the one she wrote as the Cambridge War made its approach, reached its maturity, and moved to its sudden end. For during those several months long ago, she had written quite clearly a description of her having found God. Well, no . . . of her having been found *by* God. Her description was detailed, compelling, and, he knew, as factual as any such account could be. That was who she was, his mother, this Martha Clark: factual. And while Matt had read, airborne over the Atlantic as he crossed the time zones and while his New York Saturday became his London Sunday, he became more confident by the hour that he had grasped both the intellectual underpinnings of his mother's faith and at least some flavor of the interplay between, as she had written, "the Holy Spirit and my very soul."

Just then Matt saw his luggage emerge onto the conveyor belt, but he did not move toward it. In fact, he turned away because he wanted to finish his thought. He smiled to himself again. The most fascinating part of the story of last night's flight had been this: at the same time that he felt himself gaining a grasp on the intellectual structure of his mother's recorded transition, and a sense of what she meant by that interplay between Spirit and soul, he actually experienced something that seemed at least analogous to that interplay. In his case it took the form of what he could only call a message, though the word itself, he knew, illustrated the poor power of language to represent things supernatural. And the message was straightforward: *Go to the mansion.* He knew exactly what mansion. It was, of course, the only one that played through this story. And the received message was not one that suggested his parents would be there. But *someone* would be there. And that was enough.

And then, standing there in the Heathrow baggage claim area, Matt Clark laughed aloud, and with such joyous gusto that several fellow passengers turned their heads to look at him. He had just pictured in his mind once more what had happened hours ago, high over the darkened ocean. He had been carefully returning the diaries to the lock box and, just as he had lifted his mother's current diary to place it on top of the others, a small slip of paper had fallen from it, directly into his lap. He had held it under his reading light and there, in his mother's familiar script, was an address:

Liz and Jay Manguson
4 St. Martin's
Birmingham, England

Chapter Five

UNDER THE NATURAL COVER PROVIDED BY A MOONLESS Saturday night, two dark-clad figures ran steadily through the back streets and alleyways of London. Having by now covered more than two miles, Rebecca and Luke Manguson came to a halt at the end of another narrow, trash-filled, concrete corridor. Though both were perspiring, neither was breathing hard.

Rebecca trained almost daily at three to six miles distance, usually at a pace much faster than this cautious, gliding run through London's bleak streets and alleys. And she played tennis on most Saturdays with other women and men of her own considerable ability. Now, on this evening of danger uncertain, she would be capable, if necessary, of running at this restrained pace for at least ten miles without difficulty.

Her brother knew her capabilities just as well as he knew his own, and had formed their escape plan with their substantial physical stamina in mind. Stronger than his sister—indeed, stronger than almost anyone, male or female, of comparable height and weight—and faster in a sprint, Luke played soccer with regularity sufficient to fuel his legs and lungs for the two-mile run to this point. But he knew that eventually he would not be able to keep pace with his sister.

"Give me a moment to rest my legs, Rebecca," he said softly. Still breathing easily, he removed the London city map from his zipper case and unsnapped his belt-clipped, hooded flashlight. "I want to make sure we can get all the way to Roger's without using any main streets."

Having satisfied himself regarding the route and remaining distance, Luke pointed to a bright red upright enclosure a half block from where they stood. "I'll just ring up Roger from there. I won't be a moment."

Rebecca waited while Luke ran easily to the booth, dialed, and conversed. She thought about the evening's surprise developments to this point, and discovered that she was filled with excitement and even a sense of pleasure. She felt joyously certain that this mission of theirs was the right thing. She had, as the afternoon had passed, become settled in her conviction that her dreams could be of importance not just to their parents, but perhaps in the resolution of a larger conflict or threat about which she had been somehow selected to provide insight and information. And she had complete confidence in her own and her brother's ability to escape their apartment and London itself, and to reach Birmingham without endangering those who unknowingly awaited them. She found herself smiling broadly as Luke returned at a run.

Luke stared at her, incredulously. "You're looking happy, Rebecca. Do you know something I don't? I was under the impression that we might be courting at least a modicum of danger this evening."

"Oh, I suppose we are. But isn't it *lovely* to be out running in this warm night? And doesn't it feel . . . well . . . gloriously *right* to be a courier under such circumstances?"

Luke laughed quietly. "Actually, I must admit that I've been mostly angry from the moment I realized that the flat had had uninvited visitors. Enjoyment of the evening had definitely not crossed my mind. I've seen a potential enemy in every rubbish can, every telephone booth, and around every corner. When that dog emerged from behind the fence a few yards back I nearly went for its throat."

Rebecca gripped her brother's arm. "I'm sorry, Luke. It's really quite unfair. I've placed myself in your care and given no thought to what you would have had to prepare yourself to do . . . and at any moment, too. I just feel safe when you are like this . . . as if nothing could actually happen to either of us."

"I hope your confidence is well placed, dear." He holstered his map and clipped his flashlight to his belt. "Are you ready?"

They resumed their guarded run through the city, stopping only once more to verify their position. In twenty more minutes, they turned into another alley and slowed to a walk. They saw at once their friend's "for sale" vehicle, a small, swift-looking, six-year-old Alfa Romeo, parked just behind Roger's new automobile. As they reached the Alfa,

Roger himself emerged soundlessly from his darkened back door, obviously having been alert to their approach. Luke accepted the keys wordlessly, placed his hand on his friend's shoulder in gratitude, and watched him slip back immediately into his apartment. Luke unlocked the car for himself and Rebecca, and they slipped from opposite sides into its bucket seats, Rebecca behind the wheel. He handed the keys to her. Only then did they speak, and softly.

"Will Roger need the car soon?" Rebecca inquired.

"He said on the phone that he would simply resume his efforts to sell whenever we were finished with it."

"He had no questions?"

"I told him that I would not be able to answer any, that you and I needed his extra auto in twenty minutes, and that we were moving fast and quiet. He didn't need more than that." Roger and Luke had served together in the Royal Navy during their last eighteen months of service. They saw each other rarely as civilians, but their level of trust remained high and well developed. Luke had known that his request would occupy his friend's mind for no more time than it took to find his spare keys and watch for the twins' arrival out his back window. It was the trust of comrades-in-arms, common even among those whose military service has included no enemy fire, and it would remain available on demand for as long as each might live.

While Rebecca studied the Alfa's controls, Luke, using his hooded flashlight, resumed his review of the maps. Suddenly her powerful left hand covered the light and pushed it to the floor. Luke, without taking time even to look up, hit the "off" switch. Their eyes then focused on the distant shape of a slowly moving, darkened sedan moving past the end of the alley in the direction from which they had come. They watched as the car came to a stop, reversed, and crept back several feet to provide its occupants a fuller view of the alley's length. Before the twins could react, a spotlight beam from the sedan penetrated the darkness, illuminating their surprised faces and then disappearing again as they ducked below the dashboard. After several seconds, seeing no beam above them, they slowly raised their heads in time to observe the sedan backing further, switching on its headlamps, then stopping, and now creeping forward and beginning to turn into the alley.

Wordlessly, Rebecca turned the ignition key, heard the nicely tuned Alfa engine spring to life, and felt the gears grinding together as she fumbled, at first uncertain, to find reverse with the unfamiliar shift lever. Then, headlamps still off, Rebecca turned her head over her left shoulder to face the rear, placed her left hand on Luke's seat back, gripped the steering wheel with her right hand, and sprung the clutch in perfect coordination with the fuel pedal, now pressed hard to the floorboard. The rear wheels spun, screamed briefly in protest, then bit into the gravel and asphalt. The Alfa leaped backward toward the alley's opposite end. Accelerating, the car did not waver under Rebecca's hand. It arrowed straight down the center of the narrow alley.

Luke, looking only at the other vehicle, saw its headlamps jump as its driver observed their movement and began to race forward from the opposite end of the alleyway. Rebecca exited backward at full throttle and braked, simultaneously spinning the steering wheel first to her right, then, still skidding backward, to the left. She slammed the shift lever from reverse into first, worked the pedals in a blur of foot movement, and pulled away from the alleyway exit, now already into second gear and preparing for an accelerating, no-brakes right turn onto the thoroughfare in front of Roger's home. As the Alfa had sprung forward, Luke had glimpsed a shadowy movement as the pursuit vehicle raced past Roger's apartment. In a microsecond's glance, Luke had seen two barrels rolling into the speeding vehicle's path, its headlamps dipping and swinging to the driver's left in a last-instant avoidance maneuver. Faintly, over the roar of the Alfa Romeo's engine, he then heard a metallic, crunching noise from the alley, coupled with the sound of glass breaking. As Rebecca swung the car into the hard right turn, Luke held on and realized he was smiling. Roger, it would seem, had not been content merely to hand over his keys.

Halfway through the turn, Rebecca saw another large sedan approaching the corner on a collision course, fast, no headlamps. Reflexively, she corrected her turn to the left to swing wider, then snapped the wheel back to the right as it became clear that the onrushing driver intended to broadside the small Alfa. The steering was precise and quick, and Rebecca's skillful fishtail to the left took the Alfa's rear out of the new attacker's path by a foot, even as its driver bore to his right in a desperate effort to make contact. As Rebecca deftly halted the fishtail with a flick of her wrist and steered into her lane, building speed and shifting through her gears rapidly, she saw in her rearview mirror a flash of metal against metal, and she knew in a moment's recognition that the opposing driver, having missed his target by inches, had been unable to gain control of his vehicle and had careened, skidding sideways, into the opposite corner's lamppost, sliding through and under the post, which began a slow collapse over the sedan's roof. Rebecca had no time to take note of further developments, already gauging speed and selecting gears for a still-accelerating left at the next corner.

As she came out of this second turn, she saw automobile lights in her mirror at the same time that Luke, now facing the rear, said quietly to her, "Two more, Rebecca." She immediately geared down and swung the Alfa right, into the next alleyway, pursued by two more dark sedans, both much larger and more powerful than Roger's small, quick Alfa runabout. At first glance in the poorly lit alley, and with her headlamps still off, Rebecca thought the alley was blocked entirely by its residents' haphazard parking. Then, seeing a narrow opening halfway through the block that, she estimated, would accept the diminutive Alfa, she downshifted briefly, slowed for a moment, then accelerated hard into the tiny gap. She cleared the parked vehicles with no more than an inch to spare on each side beyond her side view mirrors, then heard, two seconds following, the metallic detonation of the first pursuit vehicle as it smashed into both parked cars, followed almost instantly by the second pursuer, which, in a screaming, prolonged skid, spun into all three. She whipped the Alfa left out of the alley, flicked on her headlamps, powered right into the next turn, then left into the next, until, five minutes later, she slowed at a corner long enough for Luke to read the street signs. She then wheeled into the next alley, moved the car into a position hidden from either alleyway entrance, turned off the lights and the ignition, rolled down her window, and listened, her fingertips on the ignition key.

After a silence that reached nearly fifteen minutes, Luke, moving his map to the floorboard, examined their position with his flashlight. After he had extinguished the light and folded the map into its case, he leaned toward his sister and said, a quiet smile on his lips, "Rebecca, I believe you were explaining to me how . . . ah . . . *lovely* it was to be out in the warm night?"

Returning his smile, she placed her hand over his face and shoved him playfully back to his seat. "Leave me alone," she said, still smiling. "That wasn't much fun."

"Well, you'd never know it from watching the performance. You looked like the *grand prix* driver you probably should be."

"Luke," she said, suddenly serious. "How did they do that? How did they find us?"

"I underestimated their determination and their resources. These people are not *casually* interested in us. They want us very, very badly. I'm sure they simply staked out the four corners of a perimeter, two or three blocks beyond our own block, positioning themselves so that they could see each other, and could thereby cover any exit we would attempt. I'd guess they saw us cross Maple Street a couple of minutes after we slipped into our own alley.

"Then they simply shadowed us on parallel streets as we moved through the city. With four vehicles at their disposal, it wouldn't be difficult."

"But . . . who are they, Luke? Why do they want us this badly?"

"As for *who* they are, I would imagine that they are simply hired guns . . . thugs . . . but capable thugs. As for *why* . . . well, we won't know until we get to Birmingham, if, indeed, we are allowed to know even then. I simply assume that someone is carrying on the legacy of the Cambridge War, and knows the players from decades ago. And, I assume that without too much research, that same someone would also know that those players, at least in the case of our own parents, have adult children. It wouldn't be hard to find out any of that, if you really wanted to know. And it certainly would not be hard to find us, Rebecca. We're in the London phone book!"

They fell silent again for several minutes, still listening. Then Rebecca asked quietly, "Will Roger be in danger, Luke? He gave us his car, and you said he blocked the first sedan with barrels. What will happen to him?"

"Roger is of no interest to these people. Oh, they'd treat him pretty roughly if they got the chance. But that's nothing to the purpose for them. They'll have no personal stake in any of this. Unless Roger is fool enough to walk up to them and start a fight, they'll be away from there just as quickly as they can be. Roger will be fine. And so far, his car is still in one piece."

"Yes, and I'd like to keep it that way. Do you think we should move on now?"

"Yes. I think we can get to Birmingham by midnight. Provided, that is, we have no more adventures tonight."

Without need of word or signal, each then reached to the floor to retrieve the small kit bags of sundries they carried, and each removed a copy of the Anglican prayer book. Propping the flashlight against the shift lever at an angle that afforded enough light for reading, the two leaned down close to each other and to the light.

After several minutes, Rebecca said, "Luke, do you want to say the Deliverance Prayer together?"

He nodded.

"Good."

They read in unison in quiet, strong voices:

O Almighty God, who art a strong tower of defence unto thy servants against the face of their enemies: We yield thee praise and thanksgiving for our deliverance from those great and apparent dangers wherewith we were compassed: We acknowledge it thy goodness that we were not delivered over as a prey unto them; beseeching thee still to continue such thy mercies towards us, that all the world may know that thou art our Saviour and mighty Deliverer; through Jesus Christ our Lord. *Amen.*

Then, after closing the prayer books, they silently continued for several more minutes their individual prayers of gratitude. As Rebecca, eyes closed, neared completion of her prayers, she heard from her brother the rustling sounds that marked the completion of his. And then she brought her silent prayer to a pause as she heard an unexpected sound, that of a steel blade—a very long steel blade—sliding slowly into its case.

During the chase, she now realized, Luke had prepared to defend her with steel, and with his life, if it had come to that. And she thanked her God for her brother, his great courage, his great strength, and his great love.

Rebecca ended her prayers, squeezed her brother's hand tightly, and started the engine. The night accepted them as once more their journey began. And this time, no one followed.

Now in the same city from which the twins had managed to escape just twelve hours earlier, Matt Clark, son of the first dreamer, stood alone in Paddington Station and studied the train departure schedules. Like the twins, his destination was Birmingham. If he understood the rather difficult schedule postings, they seemed to tell him that the Sunday afternoon trains to Birmingham's Moor Street Station could be expected to depart on the odd half-hours, starting at 1:30, with the final departure at 7:30.

Matt was tired. The random waking-sleeping pattern he had followed since the Wednesday night mid-watch on the ship was overtaking him, and he knew that. Still, he was determined to remain awake for the scheduled 1:30 departure. He would catch a short nap on the train.

And so, afraid to sit down in the station for fear he would fall instantly asleep, he checked his suitcase and his mother's lock box at the station, keeping with him only Martha Clark's current diary, and began to walk the streets of Bayswater and Notting Hill. Despite his fatigue, or perhaps because of it, he was ebullient. In fact, the embarrassment of what he had begun to imagine a religious awakening of sorts—an embarrassment that had dogged him during the hours spent that morning processing through customs, arranging ground transport to Paddington Station, and, finally, riding the jitney into the city—had seemed somehow to vanish. It was a strange business, he thought to himself, as he walked in bright sunshine along Craven Hill. Here he was, Matthew Clark, well-educated twentieth century skeptic . . . a man of the world who, like most, believed that he accepted only what was "proven," without delving too deeply into what that might actually mean . . . and yet a man who, incomprehensibly, seemed somehow to have developed, in a matter of hours, a *belief*. If he could have said what he felt he "knew" about himself at that moment, he would have said that he had a freshly developed belief in a God . . . no, that was too strong . . . a freshly developed belief that there might be a God, and that he, Matt, might believe in Him. But he would have drawn back from the notion that that made him a "believer," much less that it made him a "Christian."

Whatever this was, and whatever it meant, and whatever might have happened to him while studying his mother's diaries in New York and, especially, on that airplane last night at thirty-nine thousand feet over the Atlantic Ocean, he was certain of these things: first, that he was happy; second, that he felt, beyond mere happiness, joy; and thirdly, that he felt . . . yes, he could make himself say it, at least to himself, "sent" to a place . . . sent to the Mangusons' mansion in Birmingham. And the more he thought about it all, the less he wanted to think about it all. He just wanted to be joyous. And so he began increasingly to relax in his joy, and soon found himself sauntering, not merely walking, along the sidewalks in the vicinity of Kensington Gardens, and actually smiling at people for no reason he could articulate. He was interested to notice that some people smiled back at him. Were *they* joyous? Were they "catching" it from him?

One couldn't be quite sure how to think about any of this.

That was his mood when, having strolled idly into a bookshop, and having leafed through a half-dozen volumes without much thought as to whether or not he might really want to read any of them, his eyes fell on a title that sent a thrill through him. It was a rather fat little paperback with a cream cover and black lettering on its spine: *The Seven Storey Mountain*. Thomas Merton. He was startled to see it, because he had never heard of the book or of its author until his study of his mother's diaries. In several of the middle and late diary entries, it became obvious to him that his mother had found this book compelling, so compelling that she apparently reread the book, and more than once, as she moved into her thirties, forties, and early fifties. He found the idea of rereading something to be, in itself, extraordinary, accustomed as he was to reading "for credit" and, in that mode, accustomed to reading the minimum amount of anything that might allow him to perform satisfactorily on examinations. Further, it intrigued him that his mother would choose to reread *this*, apparently the "spiritual autobiography" of a man who, a mere forty years ago, had been a thoroughgoing atheist and an enthusiastic and reckless *debauchee*, a student at Cambridge and then at Columbia, and, following a slow conversion to Christianity, eventually a Trappist monk—whatever that might be—and a prolific author. All this mixed itself into Matt's newfound state of joy and led him unhesitatingly to pull the book from its shelf and to leave the shop with his first British purchase under his arm.

He walked several blocks, idly thumbing through the book and reading odd paragraphs while he walked. Once when he looked up, he realized that Kensington Gardens was but one block away. He stopped and checked his watch. Half an hour until the 1:30 departure to Birmingham. He could walk back to the station in time if he started back right now. Or he could stroll through the park, sit in the sun, and read a chapter or two in his new book. The choice seemed to be made for him. He would take the 3:30 train.

Merton's writing captured him immediately, and he read, randomly selecting a mid-book starting point, for almost twenty minutes without so much as looking up from the book. When finally he did, it was for the purpose of pausing to give some extended thought to something Merton has just taught him. Matt raised his eyes, focusing on nothing. A quick movement from a fellow reader seated on the bench directly across the pathway from him captured his attention in a flash, and Matt knew instantly that he was being watched. The man's eyes dropped to his paper, which he jerked upward to cover his face.

Matt, three days out of the military and long accustomed to the outwardly imperceptible process of moving from utter relaxation at one moment to full-bore mental and emotional tautness the next, felt himself aroused to a condition of maximum alertness in the length of time—perhaps one second—needed to recognize what had just happened. He dropped his eyes to his Merton, but he did not read. Instead he thought: if his mother and father were in danger, and if they in fact had been kidnapped and brought to this country, what would lead him to think that he himself might not be similarly in danger for no other reason than his being their son? It was a completely new thought, and as soon as the thought occurred, he was amazed that it had not occurred until now. For all he knew, he now realized, he might have been followed continually from the moment he arrived at his parents' West Side apartment in Manhattan until the moment he had taken his seat on the park bench twenty minutes previous.

His nostrils flared and his biceps and forearms tensed with real anger. Was this man sitting no more than twenty-five feet from him party to violence against his parents? Against his will, but not *much* against his will, rage began to infuse his body with a tingling, deep-set fury. Determinedly, he kept his eyes on his book while he began to breathe deeply and slowly, calming himself gradually and purposefully. He was not yet sure what he wanted to do next. To his mild surprise, he felt no fear whatever. He felt instead a sense of aggressive protectiveness. These people, whoever they were, had his *mother.* Never mind about his father for the moment. He loved them both, but anyone cowardly enough to do something to his petite, never-harm-an-insect *mother. . . .* Matt allowed his eyes to rise from his book. He looked across at the figure on the bench opposite, its face still covered fully by the newspaper. Matt studied the man's clothing, such as was visible, satisfying himself that he could recognize his adversary if he saw him again in a few minutes, as he intended.

Matt slammed the Merton book closed, picked up his mother's current diary from the bench beside him, stood, and walked briskly south toward the interior of Kensington Gardens. He had nothing in his hands other than the two small books, and was simultaneously thankful that he had checked his suitcase and the lock box at the station and mildly worried that he might have been observed there, and his belongings taken. He shoved this new thought aside; nothing could be done about that now.

He had not come to a rational decision as to what his best course of action might be; he simply felt unable to sit for another second. He continued to walk in his erect, rapid, military stride toward the Round Pond. Matt had been walking for almost two minutes when, as he neared the water, he suddenly pivoted, wheeled in a flash, and began walking still faster, almost running, in the direction from which he had just come. Instantly he focused his eyes on the same man, following him at a distance of forty yards, newspaper under his arm. In the split second it took the man to realize that Matt had reversed course and fixed him with a glare unmistakable in its hostility even from that distance, Matt saw that the man was not alone. Two others were with him, one on each side.

The men were professionals. He would give them their due. There was no sign of alarm, nothing to indicate their dismay at having been made. Reaching a crosswalk after several strides, two of them turned right and the other left. Matt was still twenty-five yards from them. He continued to the same crosswalk and stopped. Alternately he watched the twosome, then the singleton, as they moved steadily into the distance, never turning to look back.

The telephone beside Matt's bed rang harshly in his room at The Commodore. It was five o'clock Monday morning. This was the day on which, in mid-afternoon, Jonathan Foster would be taken by Meredith Lancaster to Matt's parents, sequestered in the isolated, ramshackle farmhouse near Cambridge.

Matt's intention was to be out of the hotel before sunup. Following his encounter in the gardens on Sunday afternoon, he had wasted no time, taking a fast but circuitous route to this fine hotel, one he had noted appreciatively on his walk from Paddington Station. He had decided quickly, while still standing at the crosswalk in Kensington Gardens, that he needed time: both time to sleep and time to think. Accordingly, he had checked into the hotel mid-Sunday afternoon, requesting a wake-up call at 9:00 P.M. He had arisen then, ordered a late meal, and, finally well-rested, well-fed, and alert, had considered his next steps.

It had not taken him long. Matt was no less committed on Sunday night in his hotel than he had been Saturday night on the plane, or

Sunday morning at the airport, to the idea that his "charge" was to go to Birmingham. That was a given. The new awareness, that he was being watched and followed, changed two things: first, his luggage and his mother's diaries, other than the current one that he had kept with him, would have to remain indefinitely in the locker at the train station because he was unwilling to risk returning there; second, he would proceed to Birmingham by cab, rather than by train or bus, leaving before dawn and proceeding straight to the Mangusons' mansion. The cost of such a lengthy cab ride would be exorbitant, but he had plenty of cash, and nothing better to do with it than complete what he had come to view as his mission by any means that he deemed safe, quick, and direct.

Upon entering the Navy five years previous, Matt had found it impossible to spend his salary while at sea, living and eating on the warships on which he served. Thus, he had accumulated a considerable amount of money, money that he had expected to use for graduate school tuition, but now had without hesitation begun to use for his transoceanic flight, the unanticipated night at The Commodore, and, now, the more than two-hour cab ride from London to Birmingham. And so, at midnight, he had placed a request with the front desk for a shaving kit, a 5:30 cab to Birmingham, and a second wake-up call, this one at 5:00 A.M., and had returned to his bed, confident in the course of action he had chosen. He slept soundly.

Matt stepped into the waiting automobile at 5:30 exactly, clean shaven but wearing the same "police civies" that he had donned Saturday afternoon for the flight from JFK to London. He carried only the shaving kit, his Merton, and his mother's current diary.

As his driver gradually extricated them from the darkened, still sleeping city, Matt found himself repeatedly checking behind them for evidence that they were being followed. Finally, satisfied that they were not, he relaxed and began to consider what he might find at the mansion. He quickly found that line of thought fruitless. He had not the slightest idea what he might find. At length he decided simply to acknowledge this, and turned again to his book as daylight began to make reading possible. But that failed as well. He could not focus on it, and so he lay down as best he could on the cramped back seat and tried to sleep. Dozing off and on, he found that just seconds seemed to have passed before the car stopped and he became sleepily aware that the driver was speaking to him.

They were in Birmingham's suburbs in Monday morning's rush-hour traffic. The driver had pulled into an unfilled parking lot to examine his map of the city. Matt sat up, leaned over the front seat, and together they began to develop a workable route from their intersection to the address—that of "Liz and Jay"—shown on the slip of paper that had fallen with such obvious serendipity onto his lap on the plane. Traffic was heavy, but shortly before 9:00 they found the street, and the cab turned onto St. Martin's.

Immediately they found themselves waved over to the side of the road by two uniformed security officers. One checked the driver's identification, while the other examined Matt's.

"The lodge is closed, sir," said one, looking at Matt. "You have business with the Mangusons?"

"Yes, sir," he responded. "I do."

"Step out of the car, please. We'll need to do a pat down on the both of you. This street is a private drive, you'll understand. All the property of the Mangusons."

The roadway seemed to be a country lane that in a matter of yards moved them so far visually from the main thoroughfare that only an act of imagination could create the metropolitan area surrounding this miniature forest. The cab struggled steeply upward through densely wooded, suddenly rugged terrain that reminded Matt of the lush hills and ravines of Charlottesville, that Jeffersonian environment which he had grown to appreciate so fully during his undergraduate days. After a mere three-quarters of a climbing mile, St. Martin's came to an end. They had driven the entire length of the roadway in about two minutes. They now saw before them, running perpendicular to the road, an old, but not ancient, eight-foot high wall that disappeared into the woods on each side. The road tapered narrowly to conform to the strictures of the massive wooden gate, just wide enough to accommodate European autos, but doubtless built with horses and carriages in mind. The gate was actually higher than the wall itself, set into an arched entryway perhaps twelve feet in height. Ten feet to its left was a low, narrow, pedestrian doorway. Its oaken door, though much smaller, appeared hardly less formidable than the first. The entire arrangement was foreboding.

Matt completed his financial transaction with the driver and stepped from the car, waiting for the cab to manage its stop-and-start turnaround and begin its descent. Then he turned to face the wall and its dual gates. Matt realized he was nervous. It wasn't that he had suddenly developed new doubts about his charge and his mission. It was just that, now, after flying across an ocean and then passing across miles of English countryside, he was actually here. In just minutes, he would find . . . what? Would he be turned away at the gate? Would he be invited in and then treated as the utterly confused foreigner that he would appear to be? Would he find himself retreating on foot down this very hill in just minutes, embarrassed again and without a clue as to how to proceed?

He made a conscious effort to push these clamoring thoughts away and, as if to help himself with the effort, he brought his mother's face to his mind. He felt sure, somehow, that she was not here, but he was as certain as a person could be, just prior to unveiling the portrait or hearing the verdict, that this step was the only one he could possibly make in her direction. The mansion awaited; it would not disappoint him.

He approached the pedestrian gate. As he had done on board ship, standing outside his executive officer's cabin just four days before, he faced the door, squared his shoulders, and took a deep breath. There was beside the door a small black switch set in a copper plate. Below it were the words, "Guests of the lodge: Please operate the switch. Expect a five minute wait. Thank you for joining us."

Matt operated the switch, then stepped back and examined his surroundings more carefully. Although the forested hillside obscured his view to either side of the roadway, he could see by looking back down the lane to the south that he was at considerable elevation in contrast to the countryside that lay in that direction. The city center, he knew from his review of his driver's maps, lay to his west, and was not visible at all. He then turned and peered at the wall as it disappeared into the woods in each direction. As far as his eyes could follow it into the undergrowth, it remained at least eight feet above the ground that it fronted, and it appeared already to begin to curve away from him and, thus, to fold back on the grounds within, by way of providing, he assumed, both privacy and protection.

He waited a very long time.

Finally he heard footsteps faintly clicking on a hard surface walkway far away, somewhere on the other side of the wall. As the sound grew nearer, he became sure that this was a woman's approach, and he realized that he had prepared no introductory words. Would this be Mrs. Manguson—"Liz," according to his mother's address slip—or someone else?

Now the latch was being worked from the inside, apparently a cumbersome maneuver. And now the heavy door was being pulled inward, swinging heavily, complaining on rusting hinges. A woman in somewhat drab, matronly garb stood before him. His eyes rose to meet hers, and then he saw . . . the grayest, deepest, most penetrating eyes he had looked upon in his lifetime. They were set in an elegant face with high cheekbones framed by jet black hair that disappeared in a silky cascade behind the woman's shoulders. She was very tall, and appeared to be his age, and yet, of no age. Seconds passed. He became conscious of the fact that his mouth had been open to speak, but that he had said nothing. She returned his gaze, noncommittal. Finally she spoke, and the voice sounded to Matt like that of an angel, as he imagined an angel's voice might sound: low, for a woman, musical, authoritative even in speaking a simple interrogative. "May I help you with something?"

Matt cleared his throat and blushed bright red. He looked away from the gray eyes in hopes of regaining a measure of composure. He failed. Yet he knew he must speak, and so he tried. "I . . . ah . . . am looking for my parents . . . ah . . . I don't think they are here, but . . . I . . . ah . . . thought someone might help me. . . ."

He stopped, miserable.

The woman smiled, and he was in that instant completely undone. It was easily the most beautiful smile he had ever seen. No, that was wrong. It was her face that was the most beautiful he had ever seen, and the smile accentuated the beauty to such an extent that he could no longer think at all. He could only blush, still redder, still deeper.

She had perhaps thought to put him at ease. The smile accomplished the reverse. Matt raised a hand to his forehead and looked straight down at his feet. Weirdly, the thought flashed through his desperate brain that he was glad no one from the United States Navy could see this humiliation. He was supposed to be poised under fire. But this was not mere gunfire; this was the most devastating onslaught. . . . He heard a noise, looked up, and realized that, though still smiling gently in his direction, the woman was beginning to close the door. "I'm sorry," she was saying.

Matt was stricken. With all his strength, he called his voice to action. "No! Wait! Please! I . . . I'm Martha and Paul Clark's son! Please!"

The door stopped inches short of closure. It remained in that position.

Slowly, the door began to open again. The woman's eyes bore into his once more, and he was once more undone. He thought he might actually faint. Now she was speaking to him. He tried to listen. "Do you mean . . . ," she asked, "do you mean that you are Matthew Clark?"

He nodded helplessly, unable to trust himself with speech. Then, struck by the improbability of her question, he blurted his own: "You know my name?"

The angel extended her hand. "I'm Rebecca Manguson," she said.

Matt fought off a powerful impulse to raise the hand to his lips and bow deeply, or even kneel, if only he knew how, to the vision before him. But he managed to extend his own, and felt the strength in her right hand. Mere contact with that hand, however, communicated something like electricity that ran through Matt's body, hand to head to toe. He actually shivered, then hoped the shiver had not been visible to her. He knew his mouth had again fallen open, but fortunately she had taken the initiative to add, "Our parents have been great friends through the years."

Then her brow clouded, and he felt immediately crushed, as if the sun had been extinguished at just the moment that it had been shining on him alone, and for him alone. "What did you mean when you said that you are looking for your parents? Are they not in New York? Has something happened?"

"No . . . Yes . . . They've been reported missing, and I thought . . . I thought that someone here . . ." He stopped. "Please," he said, "just give me a moment."

Matt looked down again. Despite the clumsiest introduction and deepest embarrassment he had experienced since early adolescence, he sensed that here, in this context, with this person, the plain, undisguised truth should be spoken. He had come partway around the globe to be *here*. It was incumbent upon him to behave accordingly. If the fact of his arrival meant nothing, changed nothing, invited nothing, then he would go away. But at least he would have spoken the truth. He steeled himself to confront Rebecca Manguson's countenance again, and now forced himself to engage the gray eyes and, for the first time, to speak as an adult: "Please forgive me. I have certainly behaved like a child. I actually *can* string words and even complete sentences together."

She smiled again, but he forced his way through the fog that she continuously generated in his brain.

"I have felt that, somehow, I *should* come here. I have not felt that my parents *are* here, but that this is where I should be. I don't know why, but I think that this *place* is where I am to be right now. I know that doesn't make much sense, but it's the truth."

The smile faded then, honoring the seriousness and obvious difficulty of Matt's disclosure. "I think you may find that this is exactly where you should be. And I think that you *will* find that I and my brother and my parents will view your being at the mansion with us as something that makes a great deal of plain and good sense." Here she stepped aside, motioning for him to join her on the inside of the wall. He passed through the doorway, coming within inches of her arm and feeling his heart race at the thought.

Only then, with a start, did he see the faces of two men, standing thirty yards from him, and approximately that distance from each other. The woman had not been sent alone to open the gate for a stranger. He nodded at them and turned to face Rebecca Manguson.

He waited while she wrestled the locking mechanism into place, his eyes averted, afraid that looking upon her would again strike him dumb.

Then she turned earnestly, and said, he thought, with a hint of something he could only associate with threat, not directed toward him, but toward . . . whom? "Now, tell me about your parents . . . No, don't. I want to introduce you to the others. Then we will want to hear. We will want to hear everything."

She stepped past him, again almost touching him on the narrow walkway. "You'll have to forgive me if I walk in front of you. The walk is not wide enough for us both. And I hope you'll forgive my clothes. I have been wearing my mother's dresses for two days now."

Matt looked steadily at the ground in front of his feet and followed.

Chapter Six

HOURS AFTER MATT CLARK HAD FOLLOWED REBECCA Manguson into the perimeter of the Birmingham mansion, far to their east, near Cambridge, Jonathan Foster stared, open-mouthed, at his "old friends," as Meredith Lancaster had referred to them, seated side by side in the artificial dusk of the upstairs parlor. "Why . . . Paul . . . Martha . . . I don't understand. . . ."

"Of course you don't understand, Jonathan," observed Lancaster dryly. "But try not to be rude to my guests. Ask after their health . . . their son's health . . . Paul's post with Columbia . . . all the usual things. I'll rejoin you in just a moment. You would all like a cup of tea, surely?"

Lancaster left the room, noisily closing the door behind him. Foster turned again to face the Clarks. "What's happened? I don't understand."

"Hullo, Foster," said Paul Clark, rising and extending his hand. "Nice to see you. I understand things have gone well at the institute under your hands. Congratulations. It must be gratifying for you."

Foster was nonplussed. Clark seemed to be ignoring the obvious just as thoroughly as Lancaster himself. With his brow furrowed in honest bewilderment, Foster managed to stammer out the pertinent question. "Why . . . *why* are you here? What is *happening?* Really . . . I just don't understand."

"*We* are here against our will, Dr. Foster," Martha Clark replied icily, unsmiling and unmoving in her chair, sitting so erect that her shoulder blades no longer made contact with the chair back. "What is *your* excuse?"

Martha was as physically trim at fifty-two as she had been in her twenties, when she and her husband had known the young Jonathan

69

Foster in a distant, formal way. But her diminutive stature and soft appearance masked a formidable presence, still easily aroused when confronting injustice, especially involving her family. She had never had the slightest use for Foster, and the sight of him after so many years, under these circumstances, had brought to her a surge of the distaste, even disgust, that she had developed for him in her youth when the Cambridge War had first intruded upon their lives.

"Now, Martha," said Paul, still standing. "There's no need to assume that Jonathan knows much more about this than you and I do." Paul looked from his wife's eyes back to Foster's, but continued to address her with a trace of amusement in his voice. "He really doesn't appear to be the one in charge here, wouldn't you agree?"

Martha found Paul's light tone utterly false, but said nothing, looking away and, in an internal gesture misunderstood by both men, turning her attention inward to consider the complete absence of charity she now felt toward both Jonathan Foster and her husband. Her eyes and face still averted, she made a conscious effort to relax her tight shoulders, and to respond to her conscience by shifting mentally from an attitude of accusation to one of compassion. Foster might deserve the words she had just spoken to him, but not the malice behind them. And he was, in her eyes, merely a dupe, just as he had always been. His misfortune was to be the unwitting accomplice of some of the worst people in the world, then and now.

Both to Jonathan Foster and to Paul Clark, she appeared simply furious, leading neither of them to want to risk speaking again, either to her or to each other. The awkward, lingering silence thus imposed was finally broken by the doorknob's metal-and-glass clatter. The parlor door swung open once more, and a young man entered with a pot of tea and three cups, noiselessly placing the tray on a table near Martha, then swiftly leaving the room. As he disappeared, Lancaster reentered, leaving one hand on the open door and addressing Foster. "Pour yourself a cup, Jonathan, then come to my office down the hall . . . at the front of the house. I'll need to see you for a few moments before you resume your conversation with the Clarks."

Lancaster left the room. Foster stepped toward the tea, then stopped, realizing that he had no interest. He looked up at the still rigidly silent Martha, mumbled an apology, and followed Lancaster out the door and down the hallway to an office at the end. Entering the open door with a perfunctory rap on the doorframe, Foster saw that the room's windows overlooked the front of the property, and noticed the black Mercedes, still parked where it had stopped moments before, the driver now standing at the front of the car. He looked to Lancaster, then, having caught a glimpse of something unexpected as his eyes had moved away from the driver, Foster turned his head back toward the front windows, and found himself staring in astonishment, confounded. The driver held in both hands, at port arms, what appeared to Foster's inexpert eyes to be a lightweight machine gun.

Lancaster saw Foster's frozen stare, followed Foster's eyes with his own, and laughed aloud. "Don't be concerned, Jonathan. He doesn't seem to be pointing the thing in our direction."

"Meredith, what are you *doing?*" said Foster in a question stripped of all the political sensitivity and genteel courtesy within which he habitually wrapped every utterance.

"Well, Jonathan, as regards the automatic weapon out front, I'll just observe that one cannot be too careful. The unveiling will be, after all, just days from now, and my announcement of the date and location of the unveiling is less than twenty-four hours from this moment. As you'll remember, I will be making the announcement personally, in the House of Commons, and will follow that with a series of televised interviews."

"Of course. But . . ."

"You seem still somehow to maintain the fiction that our enemies will not resort to force to stop us, Jonathan. I should have thought that the events of thirty years ago might permanently have rid you of that view. Not to be armed and ready at this point would be tantamount to issuing an invitation to them to raid this place and divest us of every- thing we have prepared."

"Well . . . yes . . . yes . . . I suppose that line might be taken with some justification, Meredith. Still, a machine gun just in front of the door . . . I would have thought that a location so apparently secluded would have been sufficient precaution." He stopped, then turned his back to the window. "But why do you have the Clarks here, Meredith, under circumstances that look very much like kidnapping? And why was it necessary to blindfold me, treating *me* as your enemy, in order to bring me here?" Foster was trying not to bluster, but his natural bent in that direction carried him further than he perhaps intended.

There was a fresh tautness in Lancaster's voice, which in itself should have provided Foster with ample warning of danger, as Lancaster made his reply. "As regards the latter, you were blindfolded so that, when you return to the institute, you will be literally unable to report the location of this place to anyone."

"But can I not be trusted to keep secret . . ."

"You can*not* be trusted, Mr. Foster, with anything whatsoever. Pressure of almost any sort, from almost any quarter, would lead you in short order to reveal anything and everything that you might actually know. This is safer. You cannot reveal what you do not know.

"As to the former, the Clarks are here because I have laid plans, as you at least dimly know, for a second Cambridge War, this one waged with, if I may say it, a considerably more sophisticated strategic objective and plan of battle than the original. Implied by the objective itself is the foreclosure of our enemies' opportunities to interfere. We have the Clarks here simply because, if they are here, they are not *there*. They are not with their mischief-making colleagues. They cannot plot and scheme and organize their pitiful threats against us.

"Unhappily, we have not been able to bag the rest of them, and it begins to appear that we shan't succeed with the majority of the scum. That vile Manguson couple, of course, have for years been sequestered in what has, since the first war, become enemy headquarters, and, thus, protected from both our natural and supernatural forces by their own special resources. They have, it would seem, beaten us to both Dr. Sutton and Dr. Ashford. We cannot be certain that both have managed to slip through to the Birmingham fortress, but they may indeed have done so. Our real hopes, then, for reducing the number of combatants on their side, are concentrated upon the adult children of the Mangusons and Clarks. The former have twins, a woman and a man; the latter, a man raised in the U.S.

"Both of the young men have been Naval officers, something of a nuisance by way of their preparation and competence to execute this war. But the real problem among the three is, embarrassing to admit, the young woman, whose name you may have seen in connection with her tennis prowess. Not only is she infernally blessed with a wealth of talents—Oh! The unfairness—but our Spirit Masters have strong reason to believe that she may, like Mrs. Clark, have been *gifted* with those damnable dreams which so plagued us in the first war.

"We have tightened the net on the twins, who live and work in London itself. It may be that they are in our custody even at this moment. I expect an in-person report—I have prohibited telephone usage on this effort—from the eight-man team assigned them, later today.

"And the Clark youngster is slated to process out of the U.S. Navy this very day. If all goes well, we may have him by nightfall in Virginia. All said and done, we expect to have not only the senior Clarks, but their son and the Manguson twins, right here in our hands by this time tomorrow. If so, we will have crippled our enemy before the thing even gets off the ground. Their prospects will lie in rubble before the first shot is fired."

"I see," Foster responded carefully. His mind was racing. One voice in the background of his thinking was busily berating him for his own obtuseness in not foreseeing any of this. After all, he had been at least somewhat party to this new thrust against the Church of England, and, beyond that, Christianity itself, from the first, or so he assumed. Why had he not also foreseen that this sort of skullduggery, which he detested, would not be part and parcel of the whole endeavor?

The second voice was just as busily reminding him that this was surely a great opportunity to become truly indispensable to Meredith Lancaster, a man already near the pinnacle and transparently poised to claim the summit. If he could possibly impress Lancaster now with his willingness to serve and assist, he knew he absolutely must.

And so, after a thoughtful pause, Foster inquired, "Is there something I might do to further the cause at this stage, Meredith? I certainly stand ready to do everything in my power . . ."

"I have you here this afternoon," interrupted Lancaster with typical relish, "because I would like you, as a former adversary of the Clarks' who was, however, never in the forefront of the *contretemps,* and who, as I am sure became obvious to them five minutes ago, has not been complicit in their . . . ah . . . forced removal from their home, to draw them into your confidence."

"Do you mean you want me to . . ."

"I want you to speak with them now, Jonathan. Have a chat. Explain to them that Mrs. Clark will need to describe for *me* the details of the dreams that our Spirit Masters report she has recently begun to experience. Make clear that I will need to be apprised of every detail, no matter how minute or seemingly insignificant to her. Make clear that she must do it now, this very evening. Not tomorrow. Not the day after. Tonight."

"But why should she do that, Meredith? What leverage do we have to induce her to cooperate in that way? She was clearly not, shall I say, delighted to see me, nor, in fairness, can I imagine why she should have been."

"Did you not attend to my words, Mr. Foster?" Lancaster thrust his face toward Foster's menacingly. "We know that Martha Clark's *son* is processing out of the United States Navy today, in Virginia. He will then be completely unprotected. How can you possibly think that we are without *leverage*, as you so quaintly say, when we are within hours of securing this woman's only child?"

Several minutes passed while Meredith Lancaster prepared a fresh cup of tea for himself. Studiously, he ignored Jonathan Foster during this ritual, taking considerably more time than necessary, prolonging and heightening with practiced skill whatever discomfort his guest might be feeling.

"What I shall need from you, Jonathan, is for you to extract from Mrs. Clark, in my presence, the details of her new dreams, partly as a matter of routine intelligence gathering, and partly for a more urgent reason. And that's this: when we secure the new dreamer and bring her here, I want to be already in full possession of the content and import of these insidious dreams. I want the dreamed intelligence in hand long before I begin to interrogate the young Manguson woman. Now do you follow me, Jonathan, or must I try to make this somehow more explicit for you?"

Foster nodded gravely, feigning a degree of understanding that was somewhat beyond that which he actually felt. "I take it, Meredith, that our Masters expect the two dreamers' visions to mirror each others'?"

Lancaster smiled, almost, though not quite, in a kind way. "That's good, Jonathan, that's quite good." Lancaster paused to sip cautiously at his tea. "It is difficult to imagine a scenario in which the enemy would place one set of dreams in one mind, while instilling another, wholly different set, within some other mind, particularly when the two dreamers are, at least in terms of their spiritual genetics, within the same enemy circle.

"The mere fact that the senior Mangusons and the senior Clarks were side by side in the first war means, I'm afraid, that any number of interactions of that sort may well have occurred. When Christians gather together into tight-knit groups of this sort, they are as likely as are we to be spiritually *infected* with one another's *divine gifts*, as some of them might put it.

"In any case, your job is simple, Jonathan. Go back into the parlor, serve the Clarks an ample portion of your most refined political skill, and endeavor to persuade Mrs. Clark to provide you with details. And go as far as you can before you play your trump card.

"When and if that becomes necessary, just make clear to the two of them that we know where their son is . . . and that he is altogether unlikely to . . . ah . . . survive the week unless we are provided this information in full."

Foster grimaced. His hand went to his mouth. "Meredith, I really do not think that I am cut out for this kind of job. I really think that . . ."

Lancaster closed the distance between himself and Foster in two swift strides: "Shut up!" Lancaster hissed into Foster's face from very, very close range. Lancaster's usually impassive, haughtily handsome face had changed like a lightning bolt, even during the first few syllables of Foster's protestation: the eyes instantaneously beginning their macabre dance, shifting continuously, animated and empowered by Lancaster's Dark Masters; the mouth distorted by rippling flashes of his demonic caricature of a smile; the gray-streaked goatee accentuating every movement of hatred's face; the lift of the chin at such close range giving the impression to Foster of diabolical height, despite the fact that Lancaster and Foster were within a fraction of an inch of each other's actual height. Foster felt himself looked down upon from a great distance by Evil itself, though Lancaster's face nearly made contact with his own. And then Jonathan Foster felt the weight of dark eternity beginning to press down on his head, his shoulders, his back . . . and he was driven slowly to his knees, and, under crushing weight, inch by excruciating inch, all the way to the floor at Lancaster's feet. His chest and his face were forced by the unseen pressure into the dark carpet. As he gasped for breath in the grip of the unyielding force, Foster heard Lancaster's otherworldly rasp inches above his head, and felt Lancaster's scalding spittle spraying and burning onto the back of his neck: *"You will do as you have been told. You will do it now. You will* . . ." And here the words dissolved into something not English. It was, no doubt, language. But it was not human.

This made little difference to Foster. Time after time, through the years, he had found that once the dark weight had begun to press upon him, he was never able actually to hear the words, English or other, that sometimes accompanied the physical humiliation. In fact, it was the sound of prolonged, multi-car automobile collisions, replete with metallic concussions, glass splinterings, and rubber shriekings, all punctuated by the agonies and horrors of animal or even human groanings, that had always comprised the dominant auditory sensations.

Minutes passed. Foster slowly began to recover a semblance of consciousness. He heard eventually Lancaster's normal voice speaking from what seemed a great distance. "Get up. Go across the hall and be sick. Get it over with. Be quick."

Foster struggled to his feet in obedience. Holding to, first, the nearest chair, and then, successively, windowsills, bookcase, and doorknob, he crept unsteadily from the room. And this time he actually welcomed the familiar sickness. At least, vomiting, he was alone.

When he returned, pale and weak, after an interval of several more minutes, Foster experienced the same unsettling sensation that he had sensed earlier that day upon entering Magdalene College Chapel.

There he had recognized in himself a discomfiting inability to move his eyes away from the Lewis plaque, despite his brain's own "orders" to his eyes to look in the direction of Lancaster, who had stood waiting for him at the altar.

Now, similar sensations, similarly insistent, seemed eerily to prompt him to ask a question that he had no wish to ask, and the answer to which, he was certain, he already knew. "Meredith," he began with a sense of not quite having control over his own decision to speak, "what will you do with the Clarks and with the young people after they tell us, or after they do not tell us, what we need to know? How will you deal with them, whether they cooperate or not?"

"We will kill them, of course," Lancaster replied without hesitation. He looked at Foster with contempt. "There'll be no need to emphasize *that* when you speak with them, Jonathan. A threat to Mrs. Clark's own life, and even to her husband's, will be of little interest to her, once you have made clear the threat to their son's. He will become her only issue. From that moment, she will be yours. You'll have no trouble at all, my *dear* friend.

"Oh . . . and you'll want to use the young man's name often in your presentation, Jonathan. He is Matthew Clark. Refer to him— affectionately, of course—as *Matt*."

Chapter Seven

REBECCA ENTERED THE SMALL UPSTAIRS BEDROOM THAT had been hers for most of her life. She closed the door softly and pulled the upright chair away from her corner desk, placing it in front of the window. The room still maintained many of the trappings of her youth: framed school photos on walls, school yearbooks and memorabilia on shelves, old tennis rackets and trophies scattered throughout the room, even a few of her stuffed animals from early childhood. But she was not now in a mood to reminisce. She sat and looked out her window. The mid-afternoon view from the mansion's second floor was magnificent at any time of year. Now, in early summer, the pastel shades stretching before her to the east seemed to fill her soul with their warmth.

She let her mind play over the hours since her arrival with Luke at midnight after their Saturday evening escape from London. The twins had used the secret entrance to the property, a barely visible, completely unmarked, woodsy opening off of a minor, unpopulated suburban roadway to the north of the mansion. The pathway accessed by this gate, just large enough for an automobile, followed a serpentine route to the mansion's hilltop position from the direction opposite the public's southerly approach by way of St. Martin's Lane. Near the top of the hill the twins had used their own set of keys to open the gate and squeeze the Alfa Romeo through the "family entrance," a small opening cut into the old wall by their father as part of his reconstruction work in the early years of the Mangusons' occupancy. The twins' set of keys, used at this secluded northern perimeter entry, automatically disabled the alarm system that was designed to alert the family to any unauthorized penetration—whether through the wall or over it—of the wall itself.

78

Rebecca and Luke had left the auto just inside the gate and had approached the mansion on foot so as not to awaken their parents. They had not entered the house itself, but had simply turned the north screened porch into a makeshift bedroom.

Their initial welcome had been mixed. Elisabeth Manguson had been genuinely angry that they had come; their father had seemed more incredulous than angry, but the twins knew that his anger, though slow to build, could easily exceed their mother's if he were unsatisfied with the rationale underlying their actions. As soon as Rebecca had reported the fact of her dreams, as distinct from their content, which she did not immediately attempt, Jason Manguson had nodded his acceptance of their decision. But their mother, if anything, had become more distraught, and it was obvious to the three of them that her emotions were driven by fear for her children. She knew there was to be great danger. She accepted it for herself. Not for her children.

Over Sunday lunch, they had learned that others were expected. Dr. Lawrence Ashford, emeritus professor of language studies at the University of Bradford and a widower since Arianna's death two years previous, was expected that evening. And Dr. Thomas Sutton, a lifelong bachelor and surgeon, would be arriving from Oxford next morning. The twins had seen immediately that their parents, taken by surprise by their arrival, were going to tell them nothing about the situation until they had time to converse in private and, possibly, to meet with Drs. Ashford and Sutton. They understood this, and so the conversation had remained rather easily focused on their lives and work in London, much as it would have had the Saturday rendezvous in Oxford actually occurred.

Sunday afternoon events had forced their parents' hand, however. Thomas Sutton had arrived a day early, using his own set of keys to the family entrance, and had explained to the senior Mangusons that he had received a phone call from Lawrence Ashford. Dr. Ashford had reported to Sutton that he was being watched and followed, and would need assistance getting out of Yorkshire, to say nothing of reaching the Birmingham mansion. And Sutton had reported that he, too, having decided to leave Oxford for Birmingham as soon as the call from Ashford had come, found himself followed, eventually being forced to abandon his own vehicle in Oxford and maneuver through the campus by a variety of interior passageways through the colleges, finally to travel by cab to the exterior northern gate of the Mangusons' Birmingham property. He had then walked the mile from the hidden gate to the family entrance in the perimeter wall, and finally to the mansion itself.

At that point, Jason Manguson and Tom Sutton had been able to persuade Elisabeth that Rebecca and Luke simply must be brought into the impending conflict as full members of the group. There seemed no choice. The first consequence of that decision was Luke's being directed to retrieve Dr. Ashford next morning.

Using his medical connections judiciously, Tom Sutton had then arranged for a private ambulance to pick up the frail, frequently ill Lawrence Ashford at his home, and to drive him to the hospital. From there, one of Sutton's lifelong associates had driven Ashford quietly to his home and gave him a guest room for the night. Luke departed the mansion at daybreak Monday in the Mangusons' sedan, was to collect Dr. Ashford from his Yorkshire hideaway, and was to bring him back to the mansion, probably by mid-afternoon.

Rebecca, still sitting in the chair in her room and gazing across the countryside to the east, reflected to herself that she had been disappointed to realize that she would be required to wait perhaps twenty-four hours or longer to report the specific content of her dreams to her parents and the others. But she understood, certainly, her parents' desire to have the complete group assembled before her report, and perhaps other reports, were to be made.

Now, the day following their arrival, her suppressed impatience had been multiplied by the fact that, in this very bedroom, a new dream had come to her on Sunday night. It had been the same as the others in its essential development, and yet it had brought new and disturbing aspects along with it. Rebecca wanted desperately to understand the implications of this and the original dreams. And she wanted to move into action. She felt certain that something would be required of her. She wanted to know what it might be, and she wanted to prepare for it now. And the astonishing disclosure of the Clarks' disappearance from their home in New York, learned only in conjunction with Matthew Clark's arrival, had simply added to Rebecca's impatience and eagerness.

Rising from her chair and pacing slowly through her bedroom, she began to consider, too, the intriguing fact that, in the midst of the *crescendo* in the new dream last night, she had awakened, as with each of the others. But here, at the mansion, in her own room, she had awakened undisturbed, even relaxed. The contrast with her other awakenings was so striking that she had sat up in bed, turned on her bed lamp, and decided to read herself back to sleep. She had picked up her childhood Bible from her night stand, had turned to St. Paul's letter to the church in Rome, and had read the eighth chapter in its entirety. When she had reached its conclusion, she had spoken the eloquent King James phrases aloud, softly: ". . . neither death, nor life, nor angels, nor principalities, nor powers, nor things present, nor things to come, nor height, nor depth, nor any other creature, shall be able to separate us from the love of God, which is in Christ Jesus our Lord." And with that, she had returned the Bible to the night stand, turned off the light, and fallen into deep, restful, dreamless sleep.

Now, continuing to pace slowly through her room, she thought again of the newest arrival to the mansion, Matthew Clark. She had not been satisfied with her reactions and responses to him. At the gate, she had recognized from the first moment that he was taken by her appearance, despite her being clothed in her mother's ill-fitting (even on Elisabeth herself) housedress and low-heeled work shoes. Rebecca had come to grips long before with the fact that boys . . . then men . . . were likely to be occupied by her beauty. At first, in her teens, when she had reached her physical maturity, her nascent Christianity had led her to assume that it was her duty to regard herself as plain, regardless of others' reactions to her. But Elisabeth, accustomed in her youth to similar responses, had persuaded her daughter early on that her Christianity should imply no such thing. She was beautiful, tall, intelligent, and broadly talented. As a Christian she should acknowledge all of those as portions of God's blessings on her, and be thankful to Him for them. God's help should be sought, her mother had urged, not in denial of the fact of these God-given qualities, but in a purposeful, disciplined foreclosure on *obsession* with them: a refusal to use them for her own gain; a refusal to exploit others by means of them; a refusal to invest money, time, and energy to accentuate these gifts in a thousand superficial ways.

Above all, a refusal to credit herself for possessing these advantages . . .
a refusal to feed her pride with them . . . a refusal to create an "imagined
self" in her mind and then to dwell on this fictional being and its
imagined power and glory . . . *these* were the dangers, and they were
eternally deadly in their potential impact on her soul.

When Rebecca had seen Matt Clark's stunned reaction to her, she had
concentrated on responding to him as unaffectedly as she could, and had
readily succeeded, in part because this was her long-practiced discipline.
Her first real difficulty had come in warding off the compulsion to assist
him physically. He had been so conspicuously flustered, embarrassed,
confused, and miserable, that her natural inclination was to put her hand
on his arm, or his shoulder, or even to embrace him in his abject helpless-
ness, as she would a tearful, pitiful child in her classroom in London. She
had not, because she knew how any of these physical displays would
exacerbate his torture and, at the same time, introduce sexual ingredients
into an emotional mixture that as yet did not contain them.

Her mother had been of immense help, years ago, in leading her to
see that when one "falls head over heels" in this way, the last thing one is
looking for at that moment is sex, unless, perhaps, one party to the relationship presses (even unintentionally) in that direction. Instead, the
stricken individual, her mother had explained, wants above all to be
permitted to continue to *think* about the beloved. It is an all-consuming
desire to contemplate her being, rather than to experience her body. In
this instance, Rebecca was not certain that she should even have shaken
Matt's hand in formal greeting. Even that level of touching had not truly
been necessary. Courtesy had not absolutely required it, and it had probably been inadvisable. She shook her head at herself. She had had enough
experience with this to be better at it than she had been with Matt Clark.

And now, of course, Matt was going to be there—with her—at the
mansion, for what might turn out to be an extended period. That meant
that she would soon face the question of whether or not to talk with him
about this very subject, one that contained so many layers of potential
misunderstanding that successful conversation on the topic almost defied
possibility. She sighed. It was too bad. There was so much going on right
now that demanded her best . . . everyone's best . . . that this distraction
might require harsher handling than charity would seem to require.

And then, of course, there was the far larger threat. And that was the threat to her soul. Already, recalling Matt's blushing face and stricken expression, she could feel her pride responding, trying to take her beyond the factual acknowledgment that she was attractive, to the pride of self-regard, of smug self-congratulation, and of the desire to luxuriate and languish in an image of her own beauty. This, she knew, was the Legion at work in her. *This* part of her conundrum, in contrast to the first, was uncomplicated. It was simple Evil. There was nothing about *this* that was difficult to work through intellectually. And she heard herself actually speak, in a low voice, the Lord's crushing dismissal: *"Get thee hence, Satan."*

She had seen how Matt had relaxed, once she had introduced him to her parents and to Dr. Sutton, and how he had spoken rather easily about his sense that he "ought" to come here to Birmingham. She smiled when she recalled his studied composure in the face of her parents' quick objection to his disclosing even the slightest detail about his mother's diaries. They agreed with each other that that discussion should be held as a part of an opening session with Drs. Sutton and Ashford, as soon as the latter had been transported to the mansion by Luke Manguson, and as soon as he, Dr. Ashford, had been given time to relax and recuperate from his escape from Yorkshire. And Rebecca could see how comforted Matt had been by the concern and solicitousness of the three older adults at the news of his parents' disappearance. They provided the emotional and physical consolation that she herself was, by her own reckoning, in such poor position to supply.

Matt had, thought Rebecca as she took a seat once more in her chair, been graceful in accepting the judgment that his report could be given only after Dr. Ashford's arrival, though she knew he was desperate to focus upon his parents and on some formulation of a plan on their behalf. And she knew he must also have been at least somewhat bewildered at the two men's repeated, overt, acts of deference to Elisabeth Manguson, as though she were the chief member of the group and the others were there to serve at her pleasure. She smiled to herself at the recollection of Matt's simple acceptance of it all, whether he understood any of it or not. It was going to be hard not to like him; she just wished the romantic theme did not have to play through the relationship. It could be such a nuisance.

Rebecca's impatience for the upcoming session was mounting, but there was no way to guess exactly when her brother might return with Dr. Ashford, nor to estimate how long the elderly scholar would need to recover from his trip. She took one more look out her window, lingered there, smiled to herself in gratitude, and reached down to remove her mother's shoes. She moved to her wardrobe, took from it her "escape clothes" and running shoes from two nights previous, and prepared to go for a run inside the perimeter wall. It would quickly become repetitious, circling the property on the small path that traced the interior of the eight-foot barrier. But her excitement was building to the point at which, she knew, she needed to expend some of her energy. Perhaps when she returned, her brother would have arrived.

Meanwhile, Matt Clark entered the small upstairs guestroom to which he had been escorted by the gracious Elisabeth Manguson. Her very presence comforted him; her friendship with his mother, after all, predated Matt's birth by years. Her distress over his parents' disappearance matched his own, though she clearly dampened her emotional response so as not to allow her sense of alarm to feed his own. He thanked her, closed the door, and collapsed on the bed, his feet dangling far beyond the footboard. A sense of well being enveloped him again, as it had intermittently from the moment this sense of "direction" had come over him during the flight to London. Improbable though it most certainly was, he had crossed the North Atlantic and traveled to a place about which he had known virtually nothing only a few days previous, and had done so for reasons that would have seemed preposterous then. Yet here he was. The nearly transporting comfort he had received from the Mangusons and even from Thomas Sutton, coupled with an undefined aspect of the place itself, suggestive of sanctuary, had filled him with a still stronger certainty that he had done right.

And then there was Rebecca Manguson. Involuntarily, he covered his face with his hands at the recollection of his behavior at the gate. Mortifying, and worse. Horrible to remember, except when he stopped thinking of himself and of his own awkwardness and, instead, thought of her. His heart raced at the reintroduction of the memory of the woman's face. Where was she now? For all he knew, she could be in one of the adjacent rooms, perhaps just a few feet from him. Would she be thinking of him? If so, what might she think? He cringed. He knew what she would think. That she had rarely seen such infantile behavior from an adult, and that she hoped never to see it again. If only one could just erase such an episode entirely from both individuals' memories. But, he thought, to his credit, he had recovered in superficial ways. He had managed one ungarbled statement to her, while still at the entrance, and then had spoken with reasonable articulateness to her parents and to Dr. Sutton in Rebecca's presence. What would he do when next he saw her? Should he tell her how he felt? How should he tell her?

He shook his head in hopes of clearing from it this hideous obsession with someone whom he had just met. Surely, *this* was not why he was here. And, since not, his job should be to set "this" aside and concentrate on . . . what? Perhaps coming to some kind of understanding, in this evening's promised discussion, of the nature of this place and of the people and of the "emergency" that seemed imminent? And, somehow, beginning to work his way from that understanding toward some sort of plan of action, either alone or with one or more of the others, regarding his parents? It was as much as he could hope for now. And it was as much as he wanted to try to think about.

He reached to his night stand and picked up his copy of Merton. Pushing his pillow against the head of the bed, and sitting up just enough to see the book as it rested on his chest, he turned to the first page, something, he realized, that he had not yet done in his haphazard thumbing through the book. There he read the opening words: "On the last day of January 1915, under the sign of the Water Bearer, in a year of a great war . . . I came into the world. . . . That world was the picture of Hell, full of men like myself, loving God and yet hating Him; born to love Him, living instead in fear and hopeless self-contradictory hungers." He read the passage again, slowly. He raised his eyes from the book and thought about his life and his plans. But his plans for himself seemed impossibly distant now, and without a shred of importance. He closed the book to think, his index finger marking the place. His eyes closed as well.

Matt, dreaming restlessly of a tall, elegant, dark-haired angel who seemed sympathetically to be observing his hapless efforts to balance a ball on the end of his nose, struggled to come awake to the sound of persistent knocking. After what may have been some time, his head cleared enough to make out the words that accompanied the rapping: "Matt . . . Matt . . . It's Elisabeth Manguson, dear. Do you want to come down for dinner with us? Or do you want to go back to sleep until Luke arrives with Dr. Ashford?"

"Oh . . . I . . . I'd like to come down, Mrs. Manguson. Thank you."

Matt pulled himself to a sitting position, feet on the floor. As he allowed himself to awaken gradually, he thought of his mother, thirty years ago, struggling with those dreams. Struggling, it would seem, with the universe itself. He missed her. Where was she now? What was she doing? Was she . . . was she still alive?

At that exact moment, his mother, still very much alive, was looking hard into his father's eyes, questions flying at him from her angry expression and rigid posture. Jonathan Foster had just left the two of them alone in the upstairs parlor after nearly three hours of . . . she supposed it was conversation. Mostly, the two men had talked to each other. No portion of the session had been satisfactory from the viewpoint of any of the three. Martha Clark, for her part, had simply said, many times and in a number of different ways, "I have no permission to tell you anything about what you call my 'special dreams.' I will not tell you about them. I will not tell Mr. Lancaster about them."

Paul Clark, on the other hand, had tried throughout the episode to enter into some kind of bargain, first with Foster, then with Martha. His hope, it seemed, was to negotiate some satisfactory middle ground between Foster's seemingly desperate need to learn about Martha's dreams, on the one hand, Martha's unyielding refusal to comply, on the other, and, complicating everything, Foster's oblique threats, first, directed toward "Matt," as he familiarly called their son, and, later, toward Martha and Paul themselves. Though Foster's ingrained, politically adept, circuitous language and logic often softened his message, each time giving Paul hope that some common ground could be found, such common ground never materialized.

From Foster's perspective, talking to Paul gave him almost continual encouragement that he was making progress. There was much nodding of heads, of eye contact implying agreement in principle, of sober restatements of the other's position. But always there was the demure figure to his left, sitting erect, sending daggers into his very soul. Foster even had the startling thought at one point that, if Martha Clark were in possession of a loaded firearm at that moment, she might well aim it in his direction and pull the trigger without hesitation or compunction. In any case, it became increasingly obvious that Lancaster had got it wrong. While it was true that his threat to their son had gripped the Clarks and had obviously shocked them, Mrs. Clark was most surely not moved, as Lancaster had promised him, to disclose anything about her dreams. Foster recalled Lancaster's confident words: ". . . she will be yours. You'll have no trouble at all." On the contrary, her transparent contempt for him . . . no, her obvious *hatred* of him had at times nearly taken his breath away, so that, several times, he had found himself entertaining thoughts of helping them somehow . . . even of rescuing them, if he could. . . . But each time, he told himself that such reckless thoughts would bring final destruction, swift and terrible, upon him. Twice, catching himself thinking of helping the Clarks, he had wondered how such thoughts could even form themselves in his mind.

What was happening to him? How could he lack his usual clarity at a time like this? And so he burrowed on, determined to exhaust every imaginable possibility of striking some compromise that would suffice for Lancaster's purposes. When at last he had been forced to concede, he had left the room, already beginning to feel ill, resigned to a night of "correction."

Paul Clark, now alone with his wife, gestured to Martha helplessly. "I couldn't just ignore the chance at some reconciliation, you know. *One* of us had to be civil . . . had to try to work something out."

Ignoring her husband's appeal, Martha stated with the breathtaking fearlessness of a mother whose child faces the final danger: "We are leaving this house tonight, Paul. I don't care what it takes, and I don't care if they kill us in the bargain. We are going to warn and save Matt. Tonight."

"Martha . . . shhh . . . There may be microphones hidden here," Paul whispered.

"I don't care, Paul. Don't you understand? Matt's ship was due in Norfolk Friday. This is Monday. Matt is processing out of the Navy right now. Or, he may already have finished with that. He could be driving from Norfolk to Charlottesville this minute, for all we know. Or the New York police may have contacted him by now about us. Either way, he's a *civilian,* Paul. He is completely vulnerable."

"Martha, I just don't see how we can help. What can we do? We can't escape this place."

"What makes you say that? How do you know that?"

As if in answer to her question, they heard doors closing and being locked up and down the hallway outside the parlor. Then came the clatter of the parlor door opening, followed by Lancaster's face, materializing as it had every evening of their stay, and his voice speaking to them brightly. "Good night, you two. I'll drop by in the morning on my way to the House of Commons to see if you've changed your minds about anything. I'd say it's likely to be the last time I'll inquire about that. Time's up, you know, Mrs. Clark.

"You'll both be sure to remember there are friends here with you, inside and outside of the house. And the boys do like to use their guns, so sit tight. Cheerio."

And he was gone.

Paul looked at Martha, as if to say, "Are you answered?" without daring actually to ask.

Martha rose and began collecting the few things of her own with which she had arrived in England: handbag, hairbrush, small notepad. She walked to one of the windows, paused, and watched while the black Mercedes rolled slowly down the driveway until it began the steep descent from the hilltop, disappearing into the wooded slope. Paul sat still, watching her, his stomach in knots. "Martha, we can't do this," he said. "We've no chance . . ."

"Stop talking, Paul. It's dusk. There is one man sitting in his car out front. We know that the young man who serves us is downstairs, probably getting something together now for our dinner. Is it really your preference to sit here tonight and wait to be executed tomorrow morning? Is it really your opinion that Meredith Lancaster will not do what he threatens? And shall I even raise the question of duty and obligation with you? Our son is in mortal danger. Even that fact apparently does not move you to action."

Martha tossed her hair back over her shoulder in a gesture of disgust. "I shall be leaving, Paul, as soon as full nightfall is here." She glanced out the window again. "In ten minutes, I should say. And no, I do not have a plan. But I am going to leave. You may do as you wish."

Paul Clark knew his wife was right in every particular, but his brain seemed unable to respond, paralyzed once more by the physical cowardice that had plagued him most of his life. He ran his hands through his hair, leaned forward in his chair, and heard himself moan softly in an agony of shame.

Martha was at his feet in a flash, kneeling in front of him, her hands on his knees. "Darling, I know you want to do what's right. You always do. This is no different from the countless times you've faced down your opponents in college. You must stop thinking that it is. Yes, the stakes are higher. But it is the same *kind* of choice that you have made so well for so long."

Paul's head remained down. He shook his head.

"Paul, look at me." She clutched at his hands with her own. "Paul! *You can do this!* Think back, darling. We faced them before. This is not our first war . . . not our first battle. They *had* to be faced then, and we did. *You* did. *We* did. It was just as dangerous then as now." She paused. She placed her cheek against his and spoke into his ear.

"Paul . . . you . . . can . . . do . . . this. . . . Take my hands, darling. Look at me."

She smiled into his face, gripping his hands in hers, still on her knees in front of him as he leaned forward in his chair. Slowly, she rose to her feet, pulling him to a standing position. Then she wrapped her arms around him, pressing her face into his chest. She looked up, pulled his face down to hers, and kissed him. "Darling, we *must* leave. If they stop us and hurt us . . . or even take our lives . . . we will have died the Christian death . . . we will have died *for* something . . . *for* someone."

She stepped back, still squeezing his hands in hers, and looked up into his eyes again. "But, Paul, I don't think we will die tonight. I don't think I've been given my dreams again in order to die not having been permitted to warn the others. Think about it, darling. Why would I be given the dreams, if not to transmit their contents? We are not alone here, Paul. We have not been abandoned. If we try, we will be helped. We *will* be helped."

Her husband, captivated and inspirited as he had been for most of his adult life by his wife's fearless confidence, finally nodded his head. Slowly, looking into her eyes, he pulled her hands to his lips and kissed them. "I know, Martha," he whispered. "I know."

Turning from her, Paul gathered his few belongings and walked to the window. Darkness was upon them. He peered into the night and considered. He knew that he remained terrified to the point of near incapacity, but he also knew that Martha's words were working in him, as had so often been the case in their history together. She was, of course, right. He *had* once faced the enemy, with capture and death imminent. And he had lived. They had lived. And the hopeful note that Martha had struck, that she would not have been given her dreams again merely to die with them still in her brain, had had its own powerful effect on Paul, a fact that would have surprised Martha.

Paul was a believer, but his belief had never in itself made him strong. He turned to Martha, gathered her in his arms once more, and kissed her.

Without further conversation, holding hands, they turned and walked slowly to the parlor door, which had remained unlocked throughout their stay to provide free access back and forth to their small bedroom, opened the door quietly, and stepped into the hallway. Moving with care, they crept to the top of the stairway and listened. They heard distant sounds from the scullery, but nothing else. After a full minute, as Martha placed her foot on the top step, she drew back with a start and an involuntary "Oh!"

A man's shout and a violent, concussive thud seemed to vibrate through the very walls of the old house. There followed muffled, indecipherable voices—men's voices—and the noises of unconstrained, desperate struggle. Pots and pans crashed, rolled, and clattered at a distance . . . far in the rear of the house.

Martha looked up at Paul. "They're fighting each other!" she whispered.

He nodded.

Together, running down the stairway as fast as they could while still trying to tread softly, they reached the main floor, glanced back through the house, saw nothing, pulled open the front door which stood nearly adjacent to the foot of the stairs, and stepped onto the porch. Through the darkness, they saw, faintly illuminated by the house's interior lights, the car in which a guard had been sitting moments ago. Now they saw no one. Turning away from the car and the driveway, still holding each other's hand, they ran across the side yard toward the tree line. In contrast to the twins' graceful, gliding run through the streets of London two nights earlier, Martha and Paul Clark, a full generation older than Rebecca and Luke Manguson and never very athletic nor well-conditioned themselves, moved in bursts of three or four ragged, running steps, alternating with hurried, stumbling, walking steps.

Under different circumstances it would have appeared comic. But, even though burdened with this awkward and exhausting gait, they managed to reach the first of the trees before they heard shouts behind them. On they went, tripping over tree stumps and vegetation, in darkness that deepened as they moved further into the woods. Martha fell, but scrambled lightly to her feet, still holding Paul's hand. Both gasped for breath.

A searchlight probed the woods around them, casting strange shadows in their path and making more uncertain their efforts to find footing and avoid the surface roots and ubiquitous small declivities.

Shouts drew nearer. Paul struck his head on an overhanging branch, staggered, tripped, and fell heavily, twisting an ankle. Martha stopped, pulling at her fallen husband.

"Martha," he said, "go on. Please. I can't. Please. Go."

Chapter Eight

LATER THAT SAME EVENING, HOURS AFTER MARTHA AND Paul Clark had begun their hopeless flight from Meredith Lancaster's Cambridge headquarters, Elisabeth Manguson sat erect in the subterranean meeting room of the Birmingham mansion. She and her husband and others had, decades before, converted the elaborate 1930s-era bomb shelter into a four-room complex containing, in addition to the meeting room, two dormitory rooms and a small chapel. Sited along the west side of the main structure's foundation, the underground hideaway could be accessed via a hidden doorway in the basement of the mansion itself, or from an outdoor hatch covered by heavy undergrowth. The complex was self-sufficient, utilizing much of the original bomb shelter's infrastructure: ventilation, heating, cooling, refrigeration. Renewable batteries could provide power independently of the mansion's when necessary. The underground complex had been in regular use by the Mangusons from the very first, even in times of relative calm.

Elisabeth formally called the session to order. Present were her husband, their twins, Lawrence Ashford, Thomas Sutton, and Matt Clark. Purring loudly in Elisabeth's lap was the family's calico cat, Penelope. Curled at Elisabeth's feet was Mildred, the three-legged border collie that Rebecca and Luke had saved from a dog pack more than a decade ago.

Elisabeth began by turning to Matt. Smiling at him, stroking Penelope, and, her right foot out of her slipper so that she could scratch Mildred with a bare toe, she seemed to embody everything that the word "nurturing" ought to mean. And yet Matt found himself for the

92

first time in her presence feeling a certain tension. "Nurturing" Mrs. Manguson obviously was, but she was also obviously in command here, and suddenly Matt found himself placed in mind more of his warships' commanding officers than of anyone's mother.

"Matt," she was saying to him, "I need to begin by explaining several things to you. I want to do this in the presence of the others because we are a special group with a special name and a particular charge. When we are present together and in official session, I am required to act in certain ways, as are they. Please listen closely, and ask questions when you have them."

Matt nodded to her. "Yes, ma'am," he said. He found himself sitting erect in reflection of her own posture, and in a manner consistent with the sudden military tone of the transaction.

Elisabeth began. "We are the *Legati*. The Latin term means *ambassador* or *envoy*. We are ambassadors chosen specifically for missions which are both dangerous and holy. Your parents have made you aware of something that we called the Cambridge War. Your own contribution as a teen was to rename it the Prayer Book War. You intended that as a joke, but we, after we laughed, found it a better term than our own.

"We are Christians. Other than that, we know of no reason why we were chosen to become combatants in this ongoing conflict. And, in truth, we do not need to know. The fact that we were chosen is enough.

"Our charges—both the original, issued nearly thirty years ago, and the newest one, given fewer than thirty days ago—are delivered to us by a class of Creature with which you are not, so far as I know, explicitly familiar. The Creatures are supernatural. They may be *angels*, though we ourselves are so very unclear on the question of angelic varieties that we do not generally use that term. The term that the Creatures themselves have given us is *Nuntiae*. The singular of that Latin plural is translated *she that announces*, or *messenger*.

"Do you wish to ask me anything yet, Matt?" she asked, still smiling, still stroking the animals.

"No, ma'am," he replied, but added, "but I hope you'll let me ask a few questions about the . . . the . . . *Nuntiae* after you've explained further?"

"Of course," Elisabeth replied. She paused, reflecting on something. Then she continued. "In the Cambridge War, Matt, the *Nuntiae* appeared to my husband, not to me. They appeared to him while he was in prayer alone, and they issued to him a specific instruction. He complied, and that is how the *Legati* came into existence as an entity with a divinely initiated mission. The original group comprised your parents and those you see here, and Dr. Ashford's lovely wife, Arianna, on whom be peace. You and the twins, of course, were yet to be born. Thus, we were three couples and Dr. Sutton.

"Our charge from the *Nuntiae* was supplemented by a series of special dreams which were given your mother, Matt, usually while she was awake. We assume that the *Nuntiae* generated her dreams, but the fact is that we do not know that. We know so little about *how* the Holy Spirit operates on this planet, Matt, and, in truth, we do not need to know much. We just need to be receptive to His messages in whatever form they may be given. And then we must obey."

Elisabeth stopped and looked even more closely at Matt. She smiled again at him, and he realized that he felt somehow that she loved him in the same way that she loved her own two children as they sat with him in the meeting room. And yet she knew him only through his parents. After a pause, now leaning toward him, she asked, "Matt? What were you thinking just now?"

He returned her gaze, astonished. He looked down, searching for a way to respond. Finally, he looked up and, speaking carefully, he replied, "It seems to me . . . I really think . . . that they . . . or He . . ." He stopped, flustered. After a pause during which Elisabeth Manguson continued to smile gently in his direction, and the others respectfully awaited his reply, he tried again.

"I think that I've been given a charge, too, Mrs. Manguson. It happened while I studied my mother's diaries back in New York and, later, on the plane to London. I tried to say something about that to Rebecca, when she met me at the gate this morning, and I tried to say the same thing to you and Mr. Manguson when Rebecca introduced me to you.

"I don't know enough to say that I've been receptive to the . . . the . . . the Holy Spirit . . . but I've certainly felt that I *should* come here. There really isn't any other reason for my having come, Mrs. Manguson," he concluded. "I just grew more and more confident that this is where I ought to be."

"Yes," she replied, "and that is exactly why I have asked you to be present with us tonight, Matt. You made sufficiently clear to us this morning that you, too, have been given orders. We do not, you see, ourselves select the membership of the *Legati*. Members are selected by God's own actions. You are required by God's actions to be here, as are we. Each of us has her or his own version of the same tale. We are chosen, Matt, but we can decline. Granted, we can decline only at the greatest possible risk to our souls, and to the strength and vitality of the Christian church—the Body of Christ—here on earth, but we can certainly decline. We have chosen not to do so. And so have you."

Matt nodded. "Yes, ma'am," he said again. He could think of nothing to add, and so he set his mind simply to attend to Elisabeth Manguson as she continued her explanation. He briefly noted to himself, and with some satisfaction, that his Navy experience had prepared him nicely for this: respond when spoken to; listen with the greatest intensity; remember *everything*.

"Matt," she continued afresh, lifting the mildly protesting Penelope and placing her on the floor beside Mildred, then brushing casually at her skirt, "several weeks ago the *Nuntiae* appeared to me in the underground chapel just next to this meeting room. There and then I was given an explicit charge from them. And, as in the first instance, that charge roughly coincided with the onset of your mother's *special dreams*. She and I communicated immediately, not about the content of the charge or of Martha's dreams, but about the fact of both.

"And I began to form plans to reassemble the *Legati*. Since the *Nuntiae* appeared to me this time, rather than to my husband or to someone else, I am required to be in command, just as Jason was so required in the Cambridge War. Neither of us sought the position; we were each ordered to assume it.

"My most recent letter from Martha arrived last week, Matt, on Wednesday. It had been mailed from New York on the previous Saturday. And so we had no idea that anything had happened to her and Paul until you arrived this morning and told us. We should have anticipated something, but we were not careful enough . . . or quick enough. I accept the full responsibility. Had I assembled our group as quickly as I should have. . . ." Here Elisabeth stopped, faltered, and looked down at Penelope and Mildred. The cat made a small, sympathetic noise. The dog looked up at her, deep concern in her solemn eyes. She smiled down at them both.

"In any case, Matt," she continued, her voice strong again, "as this meeting continues, I will explain our specific charge from the *Nuntiae*. Then we shall hear, please, from you, on the subject of your mother's recent diary entries. Finally, we shall hear from Rebecca and Luke regarding their own special experiences. That is the first part of our agenda. The second is to begin to form our plan of action."

Elisabeth stopped and looked around the room, her eyes stopping briefly at each face. Turning again to Matt, she asked, "So, Matt, what more might we tell you by way of background. Are there questions?"

Lawrence Ashford cleared his throat, and was the instant object of rapt attention. Dr. Ashford had not spoken since his arrival, except in brief greeting to his old friends, and to the three young people whom he was meeting for the first time. His voice was weak, and quavered, but he was determined to speak in the context of Elisabeth's presentation to Matt. His lifelong experience as a teacher told him that young people could not be trusted to ask the right questions, and so he was in the longstanding habit of answering the unasked questions that should have been asked. The Mangusons and Thomas Sutton knew that Lawrence Ashford rarely missed the mark in such judgments.

The old man looked at Elisabeth. "Permission to speak, please?"

She nodded, smiling.

Dr. Ashford turned his face toward Matt. "If I may say so, Mr. Clark, the universe is, to understate, quite a large place . . . *quite* a large place. Between our infinitesimally small selves and the Almighty God of the universe there are more layers of supernature, good and evil, than you and I might be able to count in our lifetimes. In the Incarnation of His Son, God parted the curtain for us, and made it possible for us to . . . accept the salvation that He has made available for us, if we will but do so, but He parted the curtain only so much as we needed and could comprehend. The stage behind the curtain is vast beyond imagination. We have been given a narrow glimpse, albeit a glimpse of precisely that portion of the stage that we most needed to view. He was by no means giving us a look at everything; we are not adequate examiners of data of that magnitude and complexity. There may be, for example, dozens or hundreds or thousands of classes or categories of these *Nuntiae* to which we have been, through Elisabeth and Jason, introduced, but we apparently do not need to know of them.

"In this era, Mr. Clark, on this planet, in this particular corner of this universe, human beings have, with assistance and prompting from the Dark Masters who form the real opposition to any form of Christian endeavor, determined to conduct their affairs as if nothing supernatural existed in the whole of the universe. An astounding premise, in view of the fact that *most* of what exists in the universe, and *all* of the root causes of *everything* in the universe as a whole, *is* supernatural. And please note my choice of the word *premise*. To *conclude* that there is no supernature, one must start with the *premise* that there is no super-nature, since that *conclusion* cannot be drawn from observation of any data in any class or category.

"Here, on our planet, we choose to operate in utter blindness. It is an arrangement in which the Dark Masters can take justifiable pride, as I am sure they must. The unhappy world of violence, depression, confu-sion, lust . . . the incessant search for *entertainment*, material wealth, unfettered power . . . all this and more . . . is the result, young man. And we have richly earned it."

Matt was struck by Dr. Ashford's phrase, ". . . more layers of super-nature, good and evil, than you and I might be able to count in our lifetimes. . . ." But Elisabeth Manguson was speaking again, and he pulled himself away from the direction in which his thoughts yearned to go.

"And so," she was saying, "as I said before, Matt, during my morning prayers in the underground chapel on Saturday, three weeks and two days past, they came again."

Every eye was riveted on Elisabeth Manguson. It seemed to Matt that the room held its collective breath.

"The *Nuntiae* came to me. As they approached, and while they were with me in the chapel, I did not think I would live. When they left me, I still did not think I could survive. When Jason found me, I was at the altar, unconscious.

"The sensations that I experienced were nearly indescribable, but I want to try. It may be that Jason can help me.

"It was as if my brain had been laid open for deposit. I felt powerful electric shocks . . . repeated shocks that seemed to fill me and empty me at the same time.

"Their faces were visible, but they were visible only in periphery, not directly ahead in my line of vision." She paused and looked toward her husband.

"Yes," said Jason. "You Naval officers will recall being trained to look to the side of anything you're trying to see in near-darkness, rather than directly at the thing? And then, when you do, you actually begin to see your target even though your eyes are slightly averted?"

Matt and Luke nodded in unison.

"Same idea," he continued. "We've no clue, of course, how they are formed in the molecular sense. We only know that they can make themselves apparent to us visually if they choose, but only obliquely to our line of sight." He turned his eyes back to his wife, and she continued.

"Since the faces are visible only in periphery, one can never actually *grasp* the features in detail. I would not, for example, be able to distinguish the face of one *Nuntia* from another if they *did* appear directly in front of me. . . . Further—and I know this must sound so strange to you all—they are . . . well . . . actually *golden* in color. Golden faces, set to the side of one's view . . . but perfectly visible in that mode." She stopped and looked at her husband, then at Drs. Ashford and Sutton. "What else should I be saying, gentlemen?"

"I believe, Mrs. Manguson, that you might profitably review the auditory sensations that you and Jason have encountered and, at times, in Jason's three-decades-ago experience, encountered even in the complete absence of the visual?" suggested Lawrence Ashford.

"Oh, of course," said Elisabeth. "I hadn't thought to mention that part because, compared with the visual images of the *Nuntiae,* their auditory *style* is . . . well . . . almost ordinary. They simply say words . . . and in English . . . at least, when speaking to us. They say very little, please understand. Usually three- and four-word commands. Very terse.

"The striking thing is the pitch of their voices. Imagine the lowest possible note that a piano can produce. Then try to imagine a note that would be perhaps two full octaves lower . . . yet, somehow you still hear it. It's something like that." Again, Elisabeth paused and looked to her husband.

Jason nodded. "Yes, I was struck in my long-ago experience by how biblical their voices seemed. For example, you know the passage in St. John—the twelfth chapter, if I am not mistaken—where we read, 'Then came there a voice from heaven. . . .' And some of the people say an angel spoke, but others say that it *thundered*? For me, their speech always sounded exactly that way, such that, if you had listened with the slightest carelessness to this stupendously deep, rumbling noise, you might have interpreted what you heard as nothing more than the reverberations and echoes of prolonged thunder."

Nearly half an hour passed in the subterranean meeting room while the four original members of the *Legati* sought to answer a variety of questions from the young people. Some questions could, in fact, be answered; others could not. At length a pause ensued, and faces began to turn back to Elisabeth Manguson.

This time she did not address Matt Clark specifically, for she was about to report what no one had heard except her husband. She came directly to the point, knowing that the preliminary discussions had served their purpose.

"On that morning," she began, "*Nuntiae* came, as I have said, in such strength and with such force that I was overwhelmed. I was on my knees at the altar in our little chapel when they appeared, and their strength seemed to turn my muscles into water, and I found that I had collapsed on the altar, face down, helpless to move. Nothing hurt, you understand; I was not in pain. The shocks that I mentioned did not hurt me. They . . . *enlivened* me at the same time that they subtracted from me. I simply had no strength available in the usual sense. I have said to you that it seemed that my mind was laid open to them. Yes. That will have to do. I know these words cannot give you a sense of the experience . . . but words cannot. We do not have words for this.

"In any case, my eyes were closed and I saw them as my husband once did: golden faces in the periphery . . . perhaps five or six . . . strong, bright, beautiful, feminine. . . .

"And then the words came . . . deep, thunderous, fearsome, masculine. . . .

"And the words were spoken in groups of three.

"And this was the first group: '*Assemble the Legati.*' Thus, my immediate notification to Martha and Paul in New York, and to Dr. Ashford in Yorkshire, and to Dr. Sutton in Oxford. My mistakes were two: I failed to call us together immediately; and I failed to realize that you, Rebecca, and you, Luke, and you, Matt, were to be included as members of the *Legati* this time. Subsequent events have shown that I was mistaken on both counts. I am so sorry."

Here she paused, and looked toward her daughter.

"And this was the second group: '*Attend the dreams.*'"

In the silence that followed before Elisabeth Manguson spoke the final portion of the message, Matt felt his heart race at her words, a reference, in his mind, only to his mother. And before he planned it, he found that he had said a prayer to himself on his mother's behalf and in thanksgiving to God. He was surprised at himself. This was all so very strange. Perhaps he *would* be able . . . But Mrs. Manguson was speaking again.

"And this was the third." Here she paused and reflected . . . remembering. And then she spoke the words: "'*Protect the saint.*' I can only assume that this was a reference to something in the dreams, and that it is we ourselves who are ordered to take the action implied by our analysis of the dreams."

Rebecca felt her own heart race at the second and third parts of the cryptic message. "Yes! Thank you!" she prayed to herself. "Thank you, Father." She reached for her brother's hand as he reached for hers.

No one spoke for minutes after Elisabeth Manguson completed her statement. Rain had begun to fall lightly just after the evening meal, and had now become heavy, so heavy that it could actually be heard overhead in the underground meeting room, drumming on the ground.

Suddenly Luke's head jerked up, eyes tense. After a moment he leaned over to his sister. "The warning light just began to flash," he whispered to her.

Rebecca turned her head and saw the indicator, then, quickly, with a movement of her hand, called her mother's attention to the small device high on the wall near the meeting room's only door. Elisabeth Manguson stood quickly and spoke rapidly. "There has been penetration of the perimeter wall. Luke, take Rebecca and Matt on reconnaissance. We will seal the underground system as soon as you leave. Luke, I am not allowed to place the senior *Legati* at risk; you will not be able to enter the underground either from the mansion's interior entry or from the overhead entry once we have sealed the system. If you determine that the situation is benign, use your key to disable the alarm system. If we see that the light has stopped flashing, we will unseal the entrance from the mansion's basement, though we will keep the overhead entrance sealed.

"Is that clear, Luke? Godspeed."

Matt rose quickly and followed the twins out of the meeting room and down the short passage to the hidden doorway into the mansion's basement. He waited while Luke manipulated the sliding entryway, then moved quickly into the mansion proper. Jason Manguson closed the door behind them. Matt heard the metallic slides and clicks of the system sealing itself off. The doorway covered itself automatically as the intricately programmed mechanism completed its swift series of preset maneuvers.

They were unprotected now, on their own.

Matt had little time to process anything that was happening. His mind played rapidly over the previous day's discovery in London that he had been followed, perhaps all the way from New York, and by at least three men. What could possibly have led him to think that he had eluded them simply because he had stayed overnight at The Commodore and then taken a cab all the way to Birmingham? *How stupid*, he thought to himself. He had exposed the entire group to assault and capture, or worse, through his own carelessness.

By now the threesome was on the main floor of the mansion. Luke turned to face Rebecca and Matt. "Rebecca," he said, "come with me to the south grounds. We'll move into the woods and begin a patrol of everything between the house and the main gate. Matt, do the same on the north side; go all the way to the north entrance where we left the

Alfa. The family entrance itself is hard to see, but the car is parked no more than twenty-five feet from the gate.

"And Matt," he added, his hand now on Matt's arm, "this is reconnaissance. We'll take no weapons and, if we have to engage, it should be only if we think we can gain a captive. No heroics . . . at least, not yet. Understood?"

Matt complied at a run, loping along the mansion's hallways and through its great rooms. As he ran, he acknowledged to himself that he had no idea of the nature of the threat he might encounter, nor of appropriate action in case intruders were evident. How would he "gain a captive" without a weapon and without "heroics"? He only knew that the Manguson family's response was clearly one designed to cope with hostile visitors. He was determined to do his part, whatever that might be.

His hand on the interior door to the north porch, he realized that the porch light was on. He stepped back, switched it off, then switched off the lights in the anteroom. Returning to the door, he turned the handle slowly and, his eye pressing against the emerging crack in the doorway, stopped the door after two inches of movement. He waited for his eyes to adjust to the darkness, peering across the porch and through the gusting rain into the shrubs and gardens of the mansion's near north grounds. After counting off sixty seconds, he opened the door wide enough to allow passage for himself, stepped onto the porch, closed the door softly behind him, glided quickly across the porch, and, without pausing, exited the porch and stepped off the side of the steps into the hedge. He was immediately drenched both by the gusting rain and by torrents of water cascading over the gutters of the porch roof.

There he waited.

As he prepared to move across fifty yards of open frontage between the porch and the tree line, Matt saw in the corner of his eye a hooded figure emerging around the northeast corner of the house. He was astounded at the sight. Not for a moment had he actually expected to encounter intruders, and yet, in defiance of all probability, he was facing exactly that from a distance of twenty-five feet and closing.

Adrenaline surged into Matt's bloodstream. His breathing quickened. Muscles in his hands, arms, shoulders, chest, and legs tightened in preparation. He waited only another five seconds, as the hooded figure neared the porch steps, its hands pulling its cowl as far forward over its face as possible to close off the driving rain. Matt sprang forward, planting himself on the porch steps, and launched his six-foot-four-inch, 215-pound frame in a headlong leap directly into the figure's unprotected midsection. Matt's left shoulder and upraised forearm smashed into his enemy's sternum, producing a satisfying, splattering noise of bone on fabric, mediated by water. The intruder went down hard on its back, emitting an unintelligible "Uhh!" as it struck the soft earth. Matt fell on top of his enemy with all his weight, then planted his right knee in the ground, grasped the figure's left bicep with his right hand, and lifted and pulled the man so as to force him over onto his face and chest. Matt succeeded with surprising ease, then, continuing to move as rapidly as he could before his stunned enemy could recover his senses and begin some sort of counterattack, Matt grasped the left wrist, brought it up behind the man's back, and rode the wrist far up through and beyond its maximum rotation. Then, placing his free hand on the man's neck and his left knee in the small of his victim's back, he growled through gritted teeth, "Who are you? How many are there?"

Receiving no answer, he pulled harder on his hammerlock, pressed his knee into his enemy's lower back with still more force, and reached around the cowl to grasp a handful of hair. Placing great force on all three points of pressure, Matt repeated his question. When he realized that the figure was trying to speak, he relaxed his grip on the man's hair, reduced the pressure from his knee, and brought his face down close to the enemy's. Through the roar of wind and water, he was able to hear a guttural voice, straining to speak through the excruciating pain produced by the all-points violence of Matt's assault. But his victim's pain did not bear itself out in the words that came to Matt's ears, for they were words spoken not only without hostility but with irrepressible good humor: "You wanna get your knee outta my back, kid? I'm a little old for this. Y'know what I mean?"

Chapter Nine

FEWER THAN FIFTEEN MINUTES AFTER REBECCA, LUKE, and Matt had rushed from the subterranean meeting room, the senior *Legati* found themselves witnesses to an unexpected procession. Preceded by an openly astonished Jason Manguson, who had unsealed the basement entryway shortly after the alarm signal had ceased flashing, came Rebecca and Luke, rain-soaked and beaming. Behind them, arms around each other, weeping and laughing as one, Matt Clark and his mother entered, speechless in amazed joy. Just behind them came Paul Clark, grimacing and limping, his head heavily bandaged. And finally, several paces behind him, there entered a stooped, rumpled, mud-caked gnome. He slunk through the doorway furtively, appearing to search in some desperation for a place to hide himself.

When those who waited had finally grasped the miracle, bedlam erupted. Elisabeth Manguson and Tom Sutton flew from their chairs into the arms of Martha and Paul Clark, nearly sending the latter to the floor in his damaged condition, everyone exclaiming and crying at once. Tom, seeing Lawrence Ashford struggling to rise from his chair, rushed back to his side, threw one arm around the older man's waist, and escorted him slowly toward the melee.

Mildred ran from cluster to cluster, jumping and exclaiming in canine ecstasy, falling silent only when she reached the final visitant, then pausing to sniff and stare with perhaps justifiable skepticism. Penelope arched her back, alone in feline exasperation at the complete absence of decorum.

Gradually the din subsided, more chairs were brought forward to the circle, and Matt, realizing that he was the person who should be

104

introducing the stranger, began to do so as best he could. Seeing that Sid Belton's response was to drift toward the doorway as attention was drawn to him, Matt walked all the way back to the hallway door, tenderly gripped one arm—the one Matt had nearly dislocated minutes before—and pulled the reluctant detective toward the others. He concluded his introduction with, "I don't know how the detective did this, but he did, and I'll be grateful every day for the rest of my life."

"We offer you welcome, Detective Belton, to England and to Birmingham," said Elisabeth Manguson. "Can we persuade you to stay with us this evening?"

"Well . . . no thanks, ma'am," replied the detective. "I gotta start back to London. I figure I can grab a spot on a New York flight in the morning. Got stuff to do back home. I'm not lookin' forward to tryin' to drive on the wrong side of the road from here to Heathrow, but I'm gonna give it a shot. Thanks anyway."

Startled, Martha Clark realized for the first time that the detective intended to leave the mansion immediately. She rose quickly, crossed the circle to stand with him and her son, locked her elbow tenderly inside the detective's free arm, and said, "With your permission, Elisabeth, I will not allow the detective to leave tonight. He has saved our lives: Matt's, Paul's, mine." Pausing for a moment to wipe bits of grass and mud from Belton's craggy brow with a tissue, she added, "And he has been treated, shall I say, extremely roughly just now." She leaned around the detective and looked at her son in loving accusation.

"Do stay, sir," added Elisabeth immediately. "Jason will find you a nice room upstairs. Let us take care of you for at least a little while."

"Well . . . all right, all right," said the little man, the crooked grin displaying itself for the first time, "if somebody'll promise to keep the kid here from throwin' me on the ground and stompin' me before bedtime."

While the detective, still trying to repair himself and his clothes after the one-sided fracas with Matt, took his seat at the extreme outer edge of the circle, Jason Manguson inquired of his wife, "Liz, after we have heard something about how on earth the Clarks have been rescued, and from what, should we postpone further work until tomorrow morning? The Clarks must be exhausted, as, surely, is Detective Belton."

"No!" Martha Clark virtually shouted. "We must begin tonight. We have little time, I fear. Paul and I know the source of the danger, but nothing about the exact nature of the threat, and there are so many complexities . . . please, let's go as far as we can tonight."

Elisabeth and Jason exchanged glances, then Elisabeth turned to the group. "Good, then," she said. "Why don't we take several moments to hear of the Clarks' rescue, and then, while Jason and I gather some biscuits and tea, Lawrence and Tom can apprise the newcomers of what has happened here thus far. By then, we shall perhaps have refreshed ourselves enough to complete our business. Does that seem satisfactory to everyone?

"Martha? Paul? Detective Belton? Will one of you begin?"

Seeing Sid Belton decline with a wave of his hand, Paul inquired, "Shall I start, Martha?"

Martha, who had not completely stopped crying since her arrival, gave her ascent and leaned once more into the arms of her son, who had pulled his chair over to his mother's, chair arms touching.

Dr. Paul Clark, having been given the floor, found that, as usual, the *raconteur* in him came to the fore. Immediately expansive, he found that the further he went with his description, the more he relished his own narrative. He began by explaining that he and Martha had decided to go out for late breakfast and uptown Manhattan shopping a week ago, on Monday, a day on which Paul did not, during this early summer term at Columbia, have pupils scheduled. At about half past eleven, they had decided to return to their apartment by way of Central Park. When, on one of the park's more lightly used roadways, a limousine with heavily tinted windows had pulled beside them and slowed, Paul had assumed that its driver would be asking for directions. He and Martha accordingly stepped nearer the vehicle and suddenly found themselves violently pulled and pushed into the elongated passenger compartment, and made to lie face down on the floor. Nothing was said, then or ever, until, having been flown overnight in a private aircraft from somewhere in New England, Paul thought, to an airstrip in the Cambridge area, he now assumed, they had arrived Tuesday noon at the farmhouse from which they were, nearly a week later, finally rescued.

He paused, noting to himself with satisfaction that the group not only hung on his every word, but that several had actually edged forward in their chairs as he prepared to reveal, they hoped, the identity of the kidnappers. "We were then taken upstairs to a parlor, where we were served quite a pleasant meal. Even then, no one had said a word to us since the moment we were snatched from Central Park. And Martha, although at her most furious and indignant, was not able to goad these men into a response."

Everyone, including Martha herself, smiled at this. "I found myself at first wondering," she added, having gradually recovered her composure, "whether or not they spoke English. Eventually, since they never spoke a word to us *or* to each other, I decided that they were simply under orders to maintain silence under all circumstances."

"In any case," Paul resumed, "late that first afternoon, a gentleman came into the parlor, smiled at us as though we were his long-lost friends having finally come to visit him in his home, and introduced himself. He said his name was Meredith Lancaster."

Several gasps were audible. "I gather some of you know this man's name?" asked Paul.

Jason Manguson replied, "Actually, Paul, you and Martha know this man's name, too. You've just forgotten. He and Jonathan Foster were junior members of the opposition in the Cambridge War. Ah! I see the light turns on! Yes, Lancaster was at Cambridge in some minor role at the time, just a junior fellow, while Foster was just getting into administration at one of the institutes that Bradford was starting back then. They were, you'll recall, the two who were *not* on the death train that night.

"Since then, Lancaster has become prominent in church affairs, city politics, academic policy disputes, and more. He's been at the fore, both as an author and as an organizer, of a number of efforts to 'bring the Gospel up to date,' as he puts it, and to 'enhance the inherent rationality of the Church of England prayer book,' euphemisms which, of course, echo those of his senior colleagues in the Cambridge War. I'm surprised, actually, that his name has not been splashed around in the *New York Times*, or even on your television networks, Paul. But nothing, I suppose?"

Lawrence Ashford again cleared his throat and began to straighten his slight body. Heads turned. "Really, Jason," he said, "you shouldn't be surprised. Lancaster's notoriety is of that consciously diminished sort, at this juncture, that brings his name and his face to prominence only in this country and, even here, only among those actually engaged in or, at least, concerned about, those areas you listed. He carefully selects, each time, both his opponent and his forum. Even now, as far as I can determine, he works only the midday BBC interviews and the Cambridge, Oxford, and Canterbury news reporters and their editors. It's just the right balance for a true subversive.

"I'd make the guess that even our young twins know neither his face nor his name. They're teaching all day, which is when he does his interviews, and they'll not find him, as yet, splashed across the international news summaries that they doubtless review to stay abreast of worldwide developments." Here he glanced at the twins, each of whom, with their parents' easy forthrightness, nodded their confirmation of Ashford's speculation about their lack of awareness.

"But rest assured, Jason," Ashford concluded, "Meredith Lancaster will have not just the *New York Times*, but every other major North American and European news organ in his sights before long. And after that, the world. His agenda, and that of his Masters, is global."

Silence followed. Paul Clark, seeing this, prepared to continue his narrative. As he opened his mouth to speak, Thomas Sutton motioned with his hand to Elisabeth Manguson. She nodded, and Clark stopped before the first syllable had emerged.

"Lawrence," began Sutton, addressing the older man, "I find I'm struggling with this. I've spent half a lifetime running up against these blokes, as have you, but I still cannot grasp the . . . ah . . . mechanism for their effectiveness. I *see* the effectiveness, but I admit I cannot *understand* it quite the way I'd like."

"If you read Lancaster's books or hear his lectures, whether on theology or history or something outside his fields," responded Ashford quickly, "you'll never get the impression that the man wants to destroy the faith or anything else. You'll simply get drummed into your brain, and quite skillfully and compellingly, I might add, the main implicit ideas: that Christianity is a *philosophy;* that Jesus Christ was a great *moral teacher;* that Christianity, rightly understood, will bring us an enhanced *social order.* All of which can be somewhat true. And since it can be *somewhat* true, none of it seems pernicious, does it? But when you've finished examining that approach to the faith, if it can be called that, and when you realize that he is trying to convince you that those ideas comprise the *heart* of the matter, you'll find you're left with a small, cold plate of ashes, my old and young friends. Ashes that disintegrate between the tips of your fingers as you try to lift them from the plate."

Here Lawrence Ashford paused for breath, sat up as straight as he could in his chair, and, his face suddenly contorted with anger, brought his conclusion: "The *raging fire* of miracle, of salvation, of eternal life . . . of a Christ whose love and severity *challenged* everything . . . of a Christ whose sacrifice and resurrection *changed* everything . . . all gone. And gone without your ever having realized that Mr. Lancaster was doing anything but stoking the Christian fire. He is cunning, you see. It is *his* career that has convinced me more than that of any other in my lifetime, in this country, that the most effective Evil is that which is very nearly Good. That the most effective Lie is that which is very nearly True."

With that, Lawrence Ashford sank back in his chair, drained by the passion aroused in him by the name and image of Meredith Lancaster.

After waiting a moment to make certain that Ashford had said all that he wished, or all that he could, Paul Clark spoke again. "My thanks to you, Dr. Ashford, and to you, Jason. I do, as you noticed from my reaction, now remember Meredith Lancaster's name from the Cambridge days. Odd that I remembered Foster, but not Lancaster. But the truth is that, when Lancaster walked into the parlor and introduced himself to us last week, I had no recollection of ever having heard his name in my life.

"I was so absorbed in trying to comprehend the nature of the situation that we faced, that I only understood a few things that day: that it was Martha that Lancaster really seemed to want, that he assumed that her *special dreams* would have begun once more, and that he wanted to encourage her, as he put it, to 'share her stories' with him."

Seeing Elisabeth Manguson suddenly sit even more erect in her chair and turn her eyes toward Martha, Paul Clark stopped and inquired, "Elisabeth? What is it?"

Elisabeth turned her face back to Paul Clark, apologized to him for the interruption, and then faced her old friend again. She spoke excitedly: "Martha, I just realized that you are, I am quite certain, completely unaware of something that will amaze and delight you. Something we learned about only yesterday when the twins arrived here." She paused and turned her eyes to her daughter. "This time, my dear Martha, you are not the only dreamer."

First puzzlement, then astonishment, and finally joy sprang to Martha Clark's face. She turned to Rebecca and clapped her hands. "Rebecca! How wonderful! Now I shan't feel quite so . . . alone . . . and so . . . strange."

Uncharacteristically, she jumped from her seat, rushed to the younger dreamer, and embraced her. Rebecca, rising to meet her mother's lifelong friend, towered over and enveloped Martha's slight figure, so that, to Sid Belton's eyes, seated behind Rebecca, the object of his rescue effort earlier that evening disappeared completely from his view.

One pair of eyes within the circle watched this embrace with mounting confusion. Matthew Clark stared, uncomprehending. Not only his mother, but this woman with whom he had been so forcibly smitten earlier that same day . . . *Rebecca, too?* He looked down at his feet. So much to absorb. So much to comprehend. What had Dr. Ashford said to him earlier? Oh yes . . . the universe is *quite* a large place. So much to try to grasp. So much that he had never imagined before. He shook his head. Things were so different than what he had always thought. Than what he had always imagined.

He stirred himself again. Elisabeth Manguson had started to speak.

Still smiling at the impromptu embrace of her daughter and her friend, each chosen as carriers for the extraordinary series of visions that had served to inform the *Legati* for three decades, Elisabeth addressed the group. "I want us to hear the rest of the Clarks' story now, please; there is a great deal more we must consider this evening if we possibly can." She then nodded to Paul Clark, who moved to his conclusion.

"Each day that we were there, at the farmhouse," he began, "was more or less the same until today. That is, we were alone most of the time. We were fed well. Our rooms were comfortable and clean. And Meredith Lancaster would visit us at least once each day, though briefly. He always asked the same questions, inviting Martha to describe for him the content of her dreams. Each time, Martha said she 'had no permission to do that.' Each time, Lancaster became a trifle less gracious, a little less courteous, somewhat more insistent. Today, this very afternoon, he sent Jonathan Foster to us to try to accomplish the same, thinking, perhaps, that Foster's skills of persuasion would somehow alter things enough to produce a different outcome. When it did not, Foster . . . no doubt at Lancaster's insistence . . . threatened us."

Here he looked at his son. "He threatened us, and he threatened Matthew, saying he knew just where Matt was. Since we knew that Matt's tour with the Navy was scheduled to come to a close this very weekend, we feared that Lancaster's American associates could indeed find him unprotected and do something to him. And that's where the detective comes into the story."

Paul looked at Sid Belton. "Sir?" he said, "would you like to explain how you got to us?"

Belton, looking down at the floor, shook his head. "You're doin' good, professor," he said, seeming to address his own feet. "And you've *got* the story, anyway. You just go ahead."

Paul Clark began by explaining how he and Martha had extracted the story from the detective during the drive from Cambridge that evening. "The detective was not at first forthcoming," said Paul, "but he eventually became . . . ah . . . resigned . . . to Martha's insistence that she be given every detail, from the first telephoned notification of our disappearance to our rescue this very evening." Here Clark glanced at Belton for validation.

The detective looked up at Paul. "She's good at browbeating, if that's what you're tryin' to get at, professor. Seemed to me I'd get no peace until I just laid it all out for her." Belton, still cleaning his muddy hands, looked at Matt. "Your mom can be a real irritating person, kid."

At this, the entire room dissolved into laughter. Martha Clark's was the brightest and longest lasting of all. She loved the detective's bluntness. It had, she had noted as she had gotten to know him, not the slightest trace of unkindness. On the contrary, his forthright observations were delivered somehow with a full measure of both respect and love. And humor. A remarkable man.

Paul Clark then resumed his story, explaining carefully and, he thought, quite well, how Sid Belton had "cashed in" some of the favors he had performed over the years on behalf of his Scotland Yard counterparts. Having obtained both their permission and, if needed, their active cooperation in the search for the Clarks, he and three of his "boys," in plainclothes, had obtained last-minute seats on Matt's flight to London. On an airliner the size of a 747, Belton had had no trouble keeping himself far removed from Matt's section of the plane. The detective had his own agenda in mind, but hoped to provide Matt a measure of protection at the same time.

However, after having assigned his three men to follow and, if necessary, protect Matt, the detective had found it necessary to modify his plan when "the kid," as he insisted on calling him, had realized in Kensington Gardens that he was being watched. At that point, the policemen had abandoned their efforts to shadow Matt and had rejoined the detective. Thus, Paul explained, whereas the detective's original plan had been to travel north to the University of Bradford alone, the four American lawmen entrained for Yorkshire together.

The detective and his men had arrived there sometime after midnight on Sunday . . . actually Monday morning . . . with the intention of questioning Dr. Jonathan Foster as soon as he might arrive at his office that morning. The detective had concluded, explained Paul Clark laboriously, that, of all the still-living people described in Martha's diaries—Meredith Lancaster's name appeared nowhere in them—only Jonathan Foster was likely to have any kind of villainous interest in the Clarks. When the detective's hastily arranged conversations with his Scotland Yard friends supported his inferences, Scotland Yard having itself connected Foster to a series of suspicious events, he needed nothing more.

At this point in the tale, Paul Clark took pains to note that Belton had considered, among his options, requesting a Federal Aviation analysis of private (non-commercial) air traffic during the period in question, with the hope of identifying the aircraft on which the Clarks might have been smuggled into England, but had concluded that the process would be far too slow for his purposes, and was likely to yield nothing conclusive in any case. The more he had examined the data, the more confident he had become that the truly promising starting point was in an intensive questioning of Jonathan Foster.

The detective's actual discovery of Foster early that same morning and, consequently, his arriving in position by dusk to rescue Martha and himself, had been a near thing . . . a *very* near thing, Paul explained to the group, looking slowly around the room to make certain that everyone understood just how close they had come to facing execution the next morning. Of the four New York lawmen, only Belton himself had been more hungry than exhausted at daybreak. So it was he who had been walking the streets near the institute, eating an apple and casually checking on the location of Foster's office, when, to his surprise, Foster himself walked briskly out the institute's gate and turned toward the train station five blocks away. Belton, who had studied carefully the good photograph provided him by Scotland Yard, stopped a sleepy student to ask if that was indeed Dr. Jonathan Foster walking down the other side of the street, then had raced back to the lodge, dragging his subordinates from their beds and giving them two minutes to be out the front door and on the run to the station.

So it was that when Foster took his seat on the 8:12 to Cambridge that day, he was accompanied by four disheveled New York City lawmen, each sitting within just feet of him. And later, as Foster had browsed through Cambridge shops, then quickened his pace to Magdalene College for his rendezvous with Meredith Lancaster, he had been shadowed every step by Belton and his operatives. And when, after the dramatic clash on the pedestrian bridge over the Cam, Lancaster and Foster had been spirited from the city in the black

Mercedes, Scotland Yard had long since arranged for a police helicopter to be standing by. At length, once the black Mercedes had arrived, conspicuous from the air, at the hilltop farmhouse outside of Cambridge, the local police had supplied their American counterparts, in just minutes, with two unmarked automobiles for a trip to the obscure property.

Paul Clark then described how, just as he and Martha had been moving from the upstairs parlor to attempt their desperate escape on Matt's behalf, they had heard fighting in the scullery. Having assumed from the noise that the guards were fighting with each other, they had run for their lives, but, especially in his case, had done it badly. Here he looked over at his wife. "I hit my head and twisted my ankle all at once. Martha refused to leave me. And suddenly we were, we thought, recaptured. It was one of the worst moments of my life."

Martha rose from her son's side, walked to her husband's, and stood over him, a hand on his shoulder, looking down at him with the eyes of a wife who knows her husband better than he knows himself. She looked up and said to the group, "Imagine our amazement at hearing these familiar New York City accents from our pursuers, and our trying to fathom being saved at the very moment when all seemed lost." She kneeled beside Paul and, again, they held each other, the tears once more beginning to come from both.

As the Clarks comforted each other, joined quickly by Matt, the detective, perhaps seeing a chance to complete the story and send the focus of the session elsewhere, spoke for the first time on his own initiative. "There wasn't much to it, really. My buddies at Scotland Yard get all the credit. Them and Mrs. Clark, that is, for keeping such an outstanding log for all this time. The only thing that worried me a little was that we weren't allowed to bring our guns with us from New York, and I figured we were gonna run into somebody that was armed, sooner or later. That's why I picked those particular three boys to come with me. They're pretty big and tough. If you'd tried to tackle one of them instead of me a few minutes ago, kid, you might be tryin' to put yourself together sorta like I am. Know what I mean?"

"Don't remind me, Detective," said Matt ruefully. "I'll be trying to live that down for quite a while."

"Anyway," Belton continued, "I sent the boys back to Cambridge to return one car, and told 'em to head back to London tomorrow on the train. And I explained to the Clarks that I was pretty sure, from what the kid had told me back in New York, that his destination was the Mangusons' place.

"I thought Mrs. Clark was gonna faint dead away when she heard that. Then, when Mrs. Clark said that that was where she had to go anyway, to report on her *intelligence*, and that she knew the Mangusons' address and roughly how to get there, we jumped in the other Cambridge car and headed this way. Mrs. Clark drove us, since the professor is hurt, and since *I* sure wasn't anxious to drive in England if I didn't absolutely have to do it. Mrs. Clark even knew enough to find that special family entrance to the property, since we didn't like our chances of gettin' past your security boys at night and without passports for the Clarks.

"I had no trouble with the lock on your family gate, Mrs. Manguson. I figured I might be settin' off some alarm, but I just hoped somebody wouldn't shoot us without findin' out who we were. The kid here sure found me in a hurry."

There was a fresh, relaxed silence while each member of the new *Legati* tried to assimilate all that had been said. Jason Manguson finally spoke, slowly and thoughtfully, to his wife. "Is this our starting point, Elisabeth? Do we start with Meredith Lancaster, and with Martha's and Rebecca's dreams?"

Elisabeth Manguson responded with a regal forcefulness that Matt Clark recognized as the voice of total authority. And indeed, as she spoke, her bearing and demeanor *were* those of a commanding officer or, perhaps, he thought to himself, of a queen: "The *Nuntiae* have answered, my dear husband, before you have asked: 'Assemble the *Legati. Attend the dreams. Protect the saint.*'"

Chapter Ten

AFTER REFRESHMENTS AND A PAUSE WHILE DRY clothing was furnished the rain-soaked members, the late-night session resumed with fresh teacups perched on knees and tables throughout the underground meeting room. Elisabeth Manguson, exhibiting, thought Matt Clark to himself, the first trace of discomfort that he had seen in her, called the meeting to order and immediately turned to the detective: "Detective Belton," she began, "while I have no wish to appear ungrateful to you for all that you have done, I am required to establish the appropriateness of your further participation in this counsel."

The detective looked up, swallowed a bite of biscuit, and replied, "I just wanted to have a little somethin' to eat, ma'am. Your husband has already shown me where my room will be. I'd like to be goin' off to bed, as soon as I finish my tea, if you don't mind."

"Oh, but I do mind, Detective Belton. We would very much benefit from your keenness and, especially, from your experience in penetrating mystery. Since, however, this is not a worship service, to which, naturally, all would be supremely welcome, but a counsel of war, I must know that you serve on our side or, at minimum, that you can provide legitimate and trustworthy advice to our side even while not serving on it.

"And so I ask, sir, whether or not you are a Christian."

Belton, fingering his teacup uncomfortably and studying his lap, spoke so softly in response that only those nearest heard the deep and throaty, almost muffled reply. "I missed mass only four days in the last year, ma'am, and two of those were yesterday and today."

116

"I beg your pardon, Detective?" said Elisabeth, leaning toward him.

Rebecca, seeing him hesitate, turned to her mother and answered for the reluctant defendant: "The detective said, Mum, that he has missed mass only four days in the last year, yesterday and today among them."

The brief silence following Rebecca's translation was broken by the still softer voice of Lawrence Ashford, whose rich, fragile words seemed to create a hush through which his syllables passed, clear as high bells. "As a Roman Catholic myself, good sir," he said to Belton, "let me anticipate Mrs. Manguson's more formal welcome with my own. We will be delighted for you to serve with us. And I will put your soul at rest," he continued, smiling gently, "by observing that Tom or Luke will no doubt be pleased to see that you arrive at St. Mary's tomorrow morning at seven o'clock. My best, please, to Father Johnstone, if you have the opportunity."

At this, Belton looked up at Dr. Ashford, smiled his crooked smile, and said, "I appreciate that, sir. Three missed days in a row would be hard to take."

Elisabeth Manguson, about to speak to the detective, hesitated, paused, and turned now in the direction of Martha Clark. "Martha, dear," said she with obvious concern, "is something wrong? Do you not feel well?"

Martha Clark glanced up at her closest friend with a look of great discomfort. "Liz, it's just that . . ." and here she turned her eyes toward her son. "It's just that . . ."

"Mom," Matt said, interrupting his mother's embarrassed stammer, "before you and Dad arrived tonight, I tried to explain to everyone that . . . well . . . something happened to me while I was studying your diaries back in New York and, especially, on the flight to London. I'm . . . well . . . I'm not quite the person I was this time last week, Mom. I'm different. And I'm *supposed* to be here."

"Martha," said Elisabeth, "we're quite comfortable with Matt's presence in these counsels. I'm sure that you and Matt and Paul will want to speak further on this subject tomorrow, in private."

Sitting back and addressing the whole group once more, she then added with a trace of formality, "Both Matthew and, now, Detective Belton, are to be considered full members in the *Legati.*"

Martha Clark sat back in her chair, looking first at Matt and then at her best friend. Her adult lifetime of shared friendship and motherhood with Elisabeth, and the radiant clarity on her face, told Martha all that she needed to know for the moment.

There was a longish pause. The room grew quiet. Even the animals seemed unusually still. Finally, apparently satisfied with the stillness, solemnity, and, perhaps, the holiness present in the room, Elisabeth Manguson turned, picked up her copy of the Anglican prayer book, and opened to a previously marked page. She glanced up. All heads were bowed. And then she read:

> Almighty God, King of all kings . . . Save and deliver us, we humbly beseech thee, from the hands of our enemies; abate their pride, assuage their malice, and confound their devices; that we, being armed with thy defence, may be preserved evermore from all perils, to glorify thee, who art the only giver of all victory; through the merits of thy only Son, Jesus Christ our Lord. *Amen.*

Her prayer concluded and the stage now prepared for the core business of the evening, Elisabeth looked up, first at Matt and then at the detective. "Gentlemen," she said, "I want you to understand as do the rest of us that without God's protection, by which I refer to His literal, physical protection of the sites on which the *Legati* have met, first near Cambridge, decades ago, and now here, we would never have been able to function at all. The mere facts—that this site itself is somewhat isolated; that when we are closed to guests, we station private security at St. Martin's entrance; that the property has a *secret* entrance from a seldom traveled roadway on the north side; that the property has a perimeter wall that is physically imposing and electronically alarmed; that the perimeter wall has a *family entrance* that is difficult to negotiate even if one does discover it; that the mansion has this virtually impregnable subterranean shelter that itself can be sealed completely in seconds—are themselves of less than no importance in the face of the Evil that we have been required to confront. Without divine protection we would have been eliminated, that is, murdered, long, long ago. Do not think we are in this fight alone."

She paused once more, then turned to Martha Clark. "Now," she said, high expectancy in her voice, "I think we are ready, dear. Will you begin?"

Martha took a deep breath, closed her eyes for a brief moment, and then, opening her eyes and fixing them on Elisabeth, began to speak in her high, confident voice. "There are really only two aspects of my dreams that are completely clear to me. Each dream has had other ingredients, and I will try to say what they are, but I shan't do well with those other parts, I fear.

"The first clear thing is the face of Meredith Lancaster. His is the centerpiece, each time. I did not know that it was he until he came into the farmhouse parlor last week when we arrived there, and introduced himself to us. As Paul has said, we did not recognize the name, either from the old days or from his current notoriety. I'm sure Dr. Ashford is right when he tells us that the level of his fame is somewhat moderated at the moment through his own choice. Later he will choose differently. That is, if we fail to stop him."

"Martha," interrupted Elisabeth quickly, "please forgive me, but I must ask you simply to describe what you saw in the dreams. I will remind everyone that these dreams are messages. They provide us with facts on which we must act. We must focus on the data."

"Yes, Liz, I'm sorry," said Martha. Thus admonished, she went on to describe in minute detail the face of Meredith Lancaster. Rebecca and Luke listened, alike stunned, thrilled, and humbled, as Martha described feature for feature the shifting eyes, grimacing mouth, disconcerting goatee, and lift of the chin by now so familiar to Rebecca and, through her description, to her brother. But when Martha endeavored to describe the other two figures, she could not say more than to report the fact that two more figures were present, and that one seemed to be placed in danger by the ever-multiplying lethal image and intent communicated by the Lancaster emanations. And Martha could say even less about the vial and about the background structures, though she could acknowledge that there was a small, peculiar container of some sort, and a shapeless, purplish mass in the far corners of her field of dreamed vision.

"But regarding the scroll or parchment," she continued, "the text of a message presented itself to me in increasing detail as my dreams went on, over several weeks, back in New York. Eventually I was able to write the whole thing into my diary, word for word. The trouble is, I don't know this language, or even if it is a language. At first, Meredith Lancaster's multiplying images crowded the words aside. But in my last several dreams before we were captured, it was the strange words themselves that crowded Mr. Lancaster's images aside. It was as if the words pushed back and won out over his face. And I've had no dreams at all in the last week, since we were kidnapped from Central Park."

She turned to her son. "Matt said, almost as soon as we found each other tonight, that he brought my current diary with him to the mansion." He nodded in response, and reached under his chair to retrieve the small kit containing his copy of the Merton book and of the diary. The diary passed from her son's hands into Martha Clark's, and she cradled it tenderly as though it were her child.

Then, looking up, she asked of Elisabeth, "Shall I show the text to Dr. Ashford now, Liz? It may be that he can identify the language, if it is a language, even if he cannot read the passage."

In response to Elisabeth's affirmative, Martha rose and walked to Lawrence Ashford's side. Kneeling beside his chair, she opened the book to the same strange text that had confounded not only Martha herself, but her husband, her son, and the detective, when each had examined it in New York. Jason Manguson moved the nearest floor lamp to the old scholar's elbow. Ashford, adjusting his spectacles and holding the diary on his knees and under the light, bent over the manuscript. Martha's precisely lettered reproduction of her dreamed message, complete in every letter, accurate—that is, conforming to the dream—in every punctuation mark, fell under his eager scrutiny. Once again, an uncanny hush enveloped the room. At length, he looked up at Martha, an odd, vaguely amused look on his face. "Mrs. Clark," he said, with his soft, elaborate formality, "exactly how many years did you pursue your language studies as an undergraduate?"

Puzzled, Martha replied after a moment. "Well . . . three years altogether, Dr. Ashford. Is this a language that I should know?"

Ignoring the question, he continued, "And in all that time, young lady, am I to understand that British educators failed so much as to *introduce* you to the historic languages that are spoken to this day on this very island?"

In the vaguely uncomfortable silence that followed this query, a guttural voice rose from somewhere behind Rebecca. *"It's Welsh."*

"What?" Jason Manguson said, fairly shouting in Sid Belton's direction.

The detective looked over at Dr. Ashford, who by now was again smiling in quiet reproach at Martha Clark. Seeing that Ashford appeared content to let him go on, Belton explained. "Yeah. *Welsh.* When I showed the boys back in New York a copy of Mrs. Clark's . . . ah . . . transcript, it didn't take 'em long to figure it all out. They're pretty good, those fellas. Sorry not to have said somethin' earlier, just now. I was afraid I'd just make a fool of myself. All of you folks seem so smart, y'know? I figured maybe the fellas back home were just kiddin' with me, tellin' me it was Welsh. They do try to do that with me sometimes. But when Professor Ashford said what he just did to Mrs. Clark, I figured it must be just like they told me back home. So, yeah. No kiddin'. *It's Welsh."*

Jason, still stunned, turned to Ashford and asked, "Do you mean to tell me that our dreamer has dreamed in a language that is historic and contemporary and *local?* That we could travel a few miles west, show Martha's transcription to any schoolchild we might come across, and have the thing translated for us?"

"That would depend, sir, on the community in which you found yourself," said Ashford, smiling impishly, "but once you'd entered Wales, Dr. Manguson, you'd certainly have no trouble finding translators, of all ages, ready to help."

"Ohhhhh," said Martha. "I am *so* embarrassed."

"Oh, don't be too hard on yourself, Mrs. Clark," replied Lawrence Ashford kindly. "I just wanted to poke a little fun in your direction. The fault is entirely our own. We in education still put far too little emphasis on our neighbors in every direction, I'd say. But I'll note for everyone here, that the mere fact that the detective and I know what language we are seeing in Mrs. Clark's diary does not for a moment mean that we can translate more than a handful of these words.

"Or am I wrong, Detective? Have I underestimated *your boys*? Did they also manage some sort of translation for you?"

Sid Belton, just finishing his tea, put his cup down rather noisily onto its saucer, and once more treated the group to his unique, rumbling, New York City rasp, the words as usual directed toward the floor: "Well . . . yeah . . . actually, they did manage to translate enough of the thing to give me the source. So, I can tell ya' this much. What you got here is parts of..." and here the detective looked up at his wide-eyed companions . . . "parts of . . . ah . . . the *Nicene Creed*. Not all of it, you understand. Just certain pieces of it. They didn't tell me which pieces. They just told me what it came from."

Jason Manguson responded incredulously. "Portions of the *Nicene Creed*? In Welsh? Dr. Ashford, what could this *possibly* mean?"

Ashford shook his head. "Jason, I am as mystified as you. I hardly know where to begin."

Young Rebecca Manguson, displaying none of her elders' stunned consternation, spoke up quickly and forcefully, addressing her mother. "Mum," she inquired, "do you know whether or not the mansion's library still contains its copy of the Welsh *Book of Common Prayer*?"

"Well . . . it might, dear. I admit I don't know."

"May I do a quick search, then?"

"Of course," replied Elisabeth. "Jason, dear, would you go with her to unseal and reseal the doors?"

But both her husband and her daughter were already on their feet, moving at a near run from the meeting room.

Rebecca entered again carrying a small volume, her father just behind her. She placed the book carefully in Lawrence Ashford's hands and took her seat quietly. Ashford examined the book briefly, looked up at Rebecca, nodded his thanks, and leafed slowly through the pages near the front of the prayer book. At a particular place he stopped, looked up again, this time at Martha Clark, and asked her to assist. She moved swiftly to his side, knelt again beside him, and held her open diary in her hands, its pages touching the edge of the Welsh prayer book in Ashford's. Then, together, the two began to compare her handwritten transcription of her dreamed text, line by line, to the *Credo Nicea,* as printed in the prayer book.

And the two of them saw, both in Martha's fluid longhand and, intermittently, in the bold typeface of the prayer book:

> . . . *unig-genedledig Fab Duw,*
> *cenedledig gan y Tad cyn yr holl oesoedd,*
> *Duw o Dduw, Llewyrch o Lewyrch, Gwir Dduw o Wir Dduw,*
> *wedi ei genhedlu, nid wedi ei wneuthur,*
> *yn un hanfod a'r Tad,*
> *a thrwyddo ef y gwnaed pob peth.* . . .

> . . . *ac esgynnodd i'r nef,*
> *ac y mae'n eistedd ar ddeheulaw'r Tad.*
> *A daw drachefn mewn gogoniant i farnu'r byw a'r meirw:*
> *ac ar ei deyrnas ni bydd diwedd.*

> . . . *sy'n deillio o'r Tad a'r Mab,*
> *yr hwn gyda'r Tad a'r Mab a gyd-addolir*
> *ac a gyd-ogoneddir,*
> *ac a lefarodd trwy'r proffwydi.*

Ashford looked up at Sid Belton. "Your colleagues are to be congratulated, Detective, as is Mrs. Clark. Her transcription is *verbatim.* Even her punctuation matches perfectly. Martha has been given in her dreams lines . . ." and here he paused to scan the lines with his finger, ". . . lines five through ten . . . lines eighteen through twenty-one . . . and lines twenty-four through twenty-seven."

Rebecca, who had had her Church of England *Book of Common Prayer* open for several minutes, asked with her eyes, first of her mother, then of Lawrence Ashford, to speak. "The format of the creed as printed in our prayer book may not match the *Credo Nicea*, Dr. Ashford. If I read slowly, can you tell us where each of Mrs. Clark's dreamed segments begins and ends?"

"Yes, Rebecca, I think so," said Ashford. "Read *very* slowly."

Rebecca began. As she reached each dreamed portion, Ashford indicated such with a gesture and a nod. And so she read, from start to finish:

I believe in one God
the Father Almighty,
Maker of heaven and earth,
And of all things visible and invisible:
And in one Lord Jesus Christ,
the only-begotten Son of God,
Begotten of his Father before all worlds,
God of God, Light of Light,
Very God of very God, Begotten, not made,
Being of one substance with the Father,
By whom all things were made:
Who for us men and for our salvation
came down from heaven, And was incarnate
by the Holy Ghost of the Virgin Mary,
And was made man,
And was crucified also for us under Pontius Pilate.
He suffered and was buried,
And the third day he rose again
according to the Scriptures,
And ascended into heaven,
And sitteth on the right hand of the Father.
And he shall come again with glory
to judge both the quick and the dead:
Whose kingdom shall have no end.
And I believe in the Holy Ghost,
The Lord and giver of life,
Who proceedeth from the Father and the Son,
Who with the Father and the Son together

is worshipped and glorified,
Who spake by the Prophets.
And I believe one Catholick and Apostolick Church.
I acknowledge one Baptism for the remission of sins.
And I look for the Resurrection of the dead,
And the life of the world to come. Amen.

Rebecca stopped, looked up, and closed her prayer book, returning it to the pocket of her mother's loose smock, one of three such that Elisabeth had loaned her daughter the day previous. After several moments, Ashford raised his eyes from the texts and said quietly, "I confess, Mrs. Manguson, that at this early juncture I cannot form so much as an hypothesis. I do not know whether these *particular* lines are to be seen as significant, or if the mere fact that this is the Nicene Creed is the operative signal, or, further, whether or not the Welsh versus English aspects are irrelevant or of fundamental importance."

Following an uneasy, confused discussion conducted among individuals sitting around the circle, Elisabeth Manguson raised her hand for silence, looked toward Rebecca, and nodded. "Please begin," she said simply.

As soon as she began to speak, Rebecca could no longer sit still. She rose—commandingly, thought Martha Clark to herself admiringly—and began to pace back and forth, outside the circle, conscious of Lawrence Ashford's weak hearing, thus, speaking in her "teaching voice." Her grace, energy, and power to transform herself and, indeed, the entire room, left her mother and father, among others, astonished. Only her brother, of those present, had ever seen *this* Rebecca. A heretofore contemplative, though athletic, young woman had become suddenly an utterly arresting public presence, so dominant that it seemed impossible not to be consumed by her every word, gesture, expression.

Matt Clark, for his part, simply avoided looking in Rebecca's direction at all, knowing that, if he did, he would be unable to concentrate on what she said and, in the bargain, that his face would change in ways that would announce irrevocably his feelings for her. He still held out an unexamined hope that, thus far, no one had noticed. He even clung extravagantly to the still more irrational wish that Rebecca herself might have "forgotten" his earlier foolishness and clumsiness. He tried to follow her words as she paced behind and around him, but at times she passed so close to the back of his chair that he could actually *feel* her nearness. He leaned forward, holding his chin in one hand and determinedly staring a hole through the floor.

"And so," she was saying, "tonight, as soon as Mrs. Clark described the dreamed countenance and spoke the name, I saw that Meredith Lancaster was my haunting, too. Each time it has been, I now know, Mr. Lancaster's emanations that have turned my dreams into horrors, and far more than any other aspect.

"But I have been given other details, as well. There is the benign appearance of someone, apparently a bishop, and, far more striking, a rugged, charismatic, full bearded man standing to the side of my dream stage, exuding great force of intellect and of will, and positively *radiating* charity. . . . At times it has seemed almost as if this person *were* charity. And not the *insipid charity* we talk about so carelessly. No, not that, definitely. This was *charity* . . . the *force* that converts love to action." She paused in her description, though still pacing with her soft, gliding steps and her erect, shoulders-back posture, her thick, black tresses swinging softly out and away from her face and shoulders each time she spun to pace in the reverse direction. Her hands remained active throughout, caressing and shaping the air in front of her, appearing to mould her words physically as she spoke them, her gestures often providing punctuation for those who could see her across the circle. She moved from one extreme corner, near her mother, all the way round to the other, again near her mother on the opposite side, before pivoting to retrace her path once more.

Now she continued, her voice low in pitch, strong in volume: "My dreams always pressed on me the idea that this threat, as *incarnate* Evil, wished to bring itself to bear directly on this bearded figure of . . . pristine charity and . . . as silly as it seems . . . also on me . . . the dreamer. And—I don't quite know how to explain this—the threat from Meredith Lancaster's emanations was somehow, yet clearly, far, far more serious and more certain than mere death . . . to either of us. I can't say in what way."

Her parents exchanged glances with each other, and then with their son. He returned their gaze, nodding to them slightly with the confidence of one who by his very nature does not allow threats to fulfill their promise. One whose innermost being expects to defeat, with God's help, any threat that can be identified, especially a threat to one of God's own.

Rebecca had resumed. "Prior to last night, the other features of my dreams were small and less distinct than were the three human figures. There was, each time, a vial, and a scroll or parchment on which a few—in my dreams, very few—words appeared from what we now know was the *Credo Nicea*. And, finally, there was in deep background, a massive ruin, with purplish tint, as Mrs. Clark said . . . a medieval fortress, perhaps . . . or even a cathedral.

"Then, last night, in my room upstairs in the mansion, I was given another dream. It had all the components of the others, but something new, as well. The same vial appeared, but, this time, it was quite cleverly hidden—or, more precisely, someone *wished* it to be hidden. It was hidden, though not from me, within the cut-out pages of a hymnal. Hidden so that, with the hymnal closed, the book appeared as any other hymnal. Only if it were opened could one see that the interior of the pages had been cut and removed to allow placement of the vial, a vial that contained poison, or so I assume. A skull and crossbones design was emblazoned on its side and on its cap.

"And there was still more to this new scene, as it grew. The hymnal, with its vial of poison, was given a setting. The setting was a church, or cathedral, or chapel. Since I could only see the altar and the first row, I don't know how large the enclosure might have been. But I was shown the altar, the wall behind the altar, the flooring, and the first row in detail, and I would know it, I feel certain, if I were to see it in waking life. I remember being struck by the height—the lack of height—of the two entrances I could see, one on each side of the sanctuary. They were arched, and seemed extremely short, no doubt made, I remember thinking, in an era when people were simply smaller than they are today . . . surely medieval, or older."

Though she continued to pace, Rebecca fell silent. The group waited, knowing that she remained deep in thought . . . deep in memory. Finally, she came to a halt behind her own chair. Placing her hands on her chair back, she raised her eyes to her mother's. "I can think of nothing else, Mum," she said.

Her mother nodded, and Rebecca stepped around her chair and resumed her seat. Elisabeth Manguson allowed the thoughtful silence to continue for several minutes. Satisfied that no questions were to present themselves for Rebecca or Martha, she then turned to the detective and smiled at him.

"And Detective Belton," she said, "do you have questions or observations for Martha, Rebecca, or the rest of us at this juncture?"

Belton stared down at his—actually, Jason Manguson's— gardening shoes for some time before he answered. The others waited with obvious respect for their new colleague while he considered the invitation. Still looking down, he began, "I got a pretty good bit of what Mrs. Clark described for us out of my study of her logs, back in New York, so I've been expectin' some unusual stuff here. If I wasn't, y'know, a Christian fella myself, I'm not sure what I'd think of any of this. But I have been, y'know, all my life. And I've been around the block a few times, too, in my day. I've seen for myself, lots of times, over and over, what the Chief and His troops can do if they feel like it. So I'm *interested* in the *special stuff* we've been hearin' about tonight, but I'm not really *surprised* by any of it. Not a bit. I've been around. I've seen . . . well . . ." The detective's voice fell away, and he seemed lost in recollection. After several moments, he resumed.

"But, y'know, what does get my attention is . . . I don't hear anything from any of you about the regular news . . . I mean, your newspapers . . . your television . . . your radio. I mean, for sure this dirtbag Lancaster is manipulatin' the news just about every day, right? Why aren't we talkin' about that in this meeting? Don't we gotta put all that stuff together with the *special stuff* to get it all figured out?

"I feel like we're talkin' so much about our *special* evidence that we aren't payin' attention to our *regular* evidence. A lotta times in police work, the clues that really get you to the end of the story are just right there in front of your eyeballs. You just gotta look." Only then did the detective lift his eyes from his feet. He searched the faces around the room. "Know what I mean?"

Somewhat sheepishly, Jason Manguson reached behind his chair and pulled out several sections of the Sunday *Times,* and one section of Monday's just-received edition as well. "Detective," he said, "you couldn't be more correct. The papers and TV reports have been filled with this gentleman's—that would be the aforementioned 'dirtbag,' you understand—with this gentleman's hints and allusions for quite some time. You see, he is a member of Parliament, and many other things as well. Consequently, he can access, manipulate, and exploit for his Masters' ends any number of forums: political, scientific, educational, commercial, religious. And he can draw upon untold numbers of powerful contacts, both here and abroad."

"Jason," said Paul Clark, speaking for the first time since completing his narration of the escape from the farmhouse, "that reminds me . . . when Lancaster popped in to say his good-byes to Martha and me earlier this afternoon . . . could it really have been *this* afternoon? . . . and, of course, to deliver his final threat . . . he said that he would stop by the farmhouse tomorrow morning on his way to the House of Commons, and that it would be our last chance to give a response to him."

"Yes, of course," replied Jason, "he has been filled with forecast for several weeks now, with cryptic allusions to a . . . 'revelation,' as he sometimes puts it . . . that will . . . ah . . ." and here Jason held a section of the *Times* to one side of his chair, more directly under light from the nearest floor lamp, searching for a particular passage. He adjusted his eyeglasses and raised the newspaper closer to his face.

"Here. He is quoted as saying, 'In a specially arranged press conference just before the House session on Tuesday afternoon . . .'—tomorrow, then—'I will provide for the public the exact site and time of our impending announcement. As I have said in numerous interviews, this revelation will lead both Christians and non-Christians to an enhanced understanding of Our Lord Jesus Christ and of His true nature. Further, we shall be rewarded with an exciting new glimpse of the development of our Christian heritage.'

"Elsewhere," Jason Manguson continued, "he has used phrases such as, 'you'll understand how reluctant I would be to introduce anything that might seem to *diminish* Our Lord and our traditions.'"

"So," said the detective, "you're tellin' me that tomorrow he's gonna give us the time and place of his big announcement." Jason nodded, and Belton briefly resumed his study of his gardening shoes before adding, "If I've got this guy figured out a little, I'm guessin' he's gonna tease us tomorrow . . . give us a little bit to chew on, y'know . . . while he holds back the really big stuff 'til later. And I figure . . . I figure that Mrs. Clark's bits and pieces from the Nicene Creed will not turn out to be some random bunch of lines tellin' us to be alert for somethin' about that creed. I figure she and the young lady here are bein' given exact words . . . exact *ideas,* really . . . that we gotta pay attention to . . . and I figure that Mrs. Clark and young Miss Manguson, too, saw those words in Welsh for some reason that is supposed to make a difference in how we should look at all of this.

"In fact," continued Belton, straightening himself in his chair as he warmed to his own line of analysis, "I doubt very much if anything in these ladies' dreams is . . . well . . . sloppy . . . y'know? I think we'd make a big mistake if we . . . uh . . . underestimated the Chief and His allies . . . *our* allies . . . here. If they give us particular lines from a particular creed in a particular language, I don't think we oughta get too far away from those specifics. I'd guess those specifics do matter . . . a lot.

"And if this . . . ah . . . *gentleman* . . ." and here he smiled his crooked smile at Jason Manguson, "decides to tease us a little tomorrow with his announcement, I figure we're gonna get at least somethin' to work with, people. I keep thinkin' about this young lady's dreamed bishop, for example, and I keep thinkin' about that purple fort . . . or church . . . she keeps seein' in the background when she dreams, and I keep thinkin' about this tube of poison she sees hidden in a hymnal, of all places. We got some *very* specific factual material here, folks. *And* . . . we got . . . Mrs. Manguson has got . . . a *face-to-face visit* from about the most impressive *angels* I've ever heard of, this side of the Bible itself, comin' right here to this place, to the room right next to this one we're sittin' in, and givin' her . . . givin' us . . . some orders.

"And I just wanna say that second order—*attend the dreams*—is not sloppy, either, any more than any of the rest of this special evidence is. If an angel says, '*Attend the dreams,*' then, let me tell you, I, for one, am gonna *attend the dreams,* folks. I'm not foolin' around, because I don't think we're bein' fooled around *with.* We got, right here, from these three ladies, Mrs. Manguson, Mrs. Clark, and Miss Manguson . . . *direct orders* from angels . . . and an image of this Lancaster guy . . . and exact words from the Nicene Creed, in Welsh, no less . . . and an image of a bishop . . . and an image of a saint, maybe . . . and some poison hidden in a hymnal . . . and a church that the young lady can identify from the inside, which, I'm beginning to think, may be the same purple building that both ladies have dreamed from the outside. . . . We got a *mountain* of special evidence, and it is *very, very specific,* folks.

"And if this . . . *gentleman* . . . is the . . . *dirtbag* . . . that I think he is," and here his crooked grin spread out across his craggy, crinkled face, "he may just give out enough rope to hang himself tomorrow. I hafta tell ya' . . . I'm pretty excited, people. I like our chances. I like 'em a lot."

Belton looked again at Jason Manguson. "Is there some way we can get Lancaster's full announcement tomorrow afternoon? Or do we gotta wait 'til next morning and read about it in the newspapers?"

"There is a television set here, Detective Belton, in one of the reading rooms. Surely we can listen to a summary on the BBC evening news tomorrow," suggested Elisabeth.

"Dear," said her husband, "we can do better than that." He looked at the detective. "We can have the announcement *before* he speaks it, Detective Belton. We have several reliable friends in the London press corps, and Meredith Lancaster's staff routinely provides the press with advance copies of his formal remarks, usually quite early on the morning of the day he expects to give them.

"Luke, if Tom doesn't mind taking Detective Belton to early mass in the morning, rather than your doing that, I'd ask that you start off at about daybreak in our automobile for London. I'll get on the phone later in the morning, about eight o'clock, with . . . which do you think,

Liz . . . Smythe or Preston? Preston, then . . . and set up a rendezvous for you at the Westminster underground station at . . . let's say . . . ten o'clock. You can park our auto at the High Barnet station and take the underground into center city from there. Give me a call here at the mansion as soon as you arrive at High Barnet, and I'll be able to tell you if there is a change in the arrangements. If all goes well, you'll have the advance copy of Lancaster's text at mid-morning, and can have it back here at the mansion by one o'clock, I should think, probably a few minutes before Lancaster actually speaks. In the bargain, we'll gain the advantage of being in position to study the full prepared statement, rather than needing to sort it out from the television or newspaper summaries.

"What do you think, Liz?"

"I think," she replied somberly, "that I wish the children didn't need to go back into London just now, Jason. That was a very well-organized effort to capture them just two nights ago."

Her husband nodded, and smiled at his wife understandingly. "Yes, it was, my dear, but . . ."

Elisabeth Manguson looked down at her hands as they rested in her lap. "I know," she said, a sadness in her voice. "I know . . ."

And, slowly, she raised eyes laced with anguish to the face of her only son.

Chapter Eleven

NEXT MORNING LUKE MANGUSON DROVE AWAY FROM the mansion at daybreak, bound for London as scheduled. His mother and sister escorted him to the family gate in the perimeter wall, watched him squeeze the family sedan through the narrow opening, and returned to the north porch holding hands, not speaking, alone with their thoughts and prayers. In part to keep her worries at bay, Elisabeth began, after her devotions, elaborate breakfast preparations, while Rebecca, for similar reasons, went for another run on the interior perimeter pathway. Elisabeth, joined by her husband in the scullery, timed her preparations to coincide with the return from mass of Sidney Belton and his chauffeur for the morning, Thomas Sutton.

As breakfast dishes were being cleared, the detective, unusually talkative, chatted amiably with the others. "Dr. Sutton took good care of me," he noted. "He's a Church of England fella, of course, but he says he never misses a chance to go to worship services, no matter what kind of church he happens to be near. 'Course, I think he came in with me partly to make sure nobody made fun of me in Mr. Manguson's clothes."

"Oh, I don't know, Detective," Matt Clark observed, "I think they might have been more likely to make fun of you if you'd worn your own clothes."

Belton turned to look at Martha Clark, rather than at her son. "Did your boy pick up his endearing personality from you, or from your husband, Mrs. Clark?" Not waiting for an answer, he had then faced Matt and, speaking through the general laughter and pointing his fork in the grinning young man's direction, he added, "I tell you I'm fed up with you, big fella. If I'd known what kind of character you really were,

I'd have beat you to a pulp out there in the rain last night. I'd have whipped you into butter. Wish I'd done it, now."

"Boys, boys," Martha interjected, "if you don't behave I'll send you both to your rooms for the day."

Not only were the members of the new *Legati* feeling happy and rested, they were conscious of their having advanced a very long way during the previous night's eventful and exhausting session, and they were similarly aware that there could be no substantive work until Luke returned from London in early afternoon with the advance copy of Meredith Lancaster's announcement. So, it had been a relaxed and lively group that had chatted and laughed its way through Elisabeth and Jason's substantial breakfast, lingering at the table long after the last scraps had been consumed. As the clatter of freshly cleaned dishes being placed in cupboards had begun eventually to die away, the Clark family moved quietly and without prearrangement to the north porch. Sitting in the rising warmth in comfortable silence, appreciating the plain fact of their being together again under such unexpected circumstances, they contemplated the utter improbability of it all, thankful in their own individual ways for their being at the mansion, and alive, and, for the time being, safe.

Finally Martha spoke. "Matt, will you tell your father and me more about . . ." and she stopped, seeing he was already smiling and nodding his head.

"Sure, Mom. I read your diaries. I'm sure I read things you did not expect another person to read, but I was desperate for anything that would provide clues about your disappearance. But the more I read, the less I found myself reading for specific clues, and the more I got . . . caught up in what you'd experienced here in England, in the Cambridge War, with the Mangusons, and the Ashfords, and Dr. Sutton, before I was even born.

"Now that I think about it, in fact, it seems to me that I started getting caught up in your . . . your *Christian* story . . . *before* I picked up your diary box. Something seemed to be happening to me as soon as I read from one of the passages you had marked in the prayer book that you keep on your desk at home. That prayer for armed services personnel? I started to *feel* different while I read that, imagining you . . . kneeling there beside your little desk, reading that prayer, thinking of me. . . . I can't explain it, Mom. I just felt so different.

"And when I read . . . and reread . . . all that you wrote in your diaries about your long-ago Christian experiences, I just *believed* that what you had found . . . or, I guess, what had found you . . . was real. I became surer and surer of it.

"I just think I've become at least *sort of* a believer, Mom, though I can't quite say *exactly* what it is that I believe . . . at least, I don't *think* I can say exactly what I believe. I can tell you that I bought Thomas Merton's book . . . the one you wrote about in your diary. . . . In fact, I woke up early this morning and read in it for nearly two hours before breakfast. And I have found that, when I am reading passages from that book, from Merton's descriptions of what he experienced while *he* was gradually becoming a Christian, I actually recognize some of what he is describing. It seems to me sometimes that . . . I don't know . . . it seems to me that . . . I know *exactly* what he means, Mom. Can you imagine that?"

Matt had been looking out over the north lawn as he spoke. When he finished, he turned to look at his mother. Her cheeks were streaked with tears, but she was smiling, eyes closed. He moved to her quickly and hugged her awkwardly but happily, reaching down over her trim, small figure with his long, heavily muscled shoulders and arms. "I'm so thankful that you and Dad are okay, Mom," he whispered.

As he stood again, holding his mother's small left hand in both of his own, his attention was diverted by a movement to his right. Looking beyond the east end of the long screened porch, he saw in the distance the movement of a small wire, its length interrupted by . . . clothespins, he decided, on second look. Releasing his mother's hand and stepping forward to change the angle of his view, he saw the tall, athletic figure of Rebecca Manguson hanging her freshly washed running clothes, and a variety of garments presumably belonging to others in her family, on a clothesline partially obscured by shrubbery and two young trees nearer the house. He found he could not take his eyes from the distant figure. The figure repeatedly reached with, he thought to himself, an athlete's efficiency and a ballerina's elegance into one of two wicker baskets resting on the wet grass, rose to shake out one piece of clothing after another, and swiftly pinned each item onto the gently flexing line.

He thought he had never before seen such a masterpiece of dance. He found himself taking a step closer, when he was actually startled to hear his mother's voice.

"Exactly *whom* are we observing so *intently*, Matthew?" she said, the playful tone revealing to him in a flash of embarrassed understanding that *everyone* knew his secret. There *was* no secret. He was such a fool to think that his infatuation did not display itself like a second sun in the morning sky. He spun around to face the direction opposite, away from Rebecca and away from his parents, and brought his hands to his head.

"Oh . . . oh . . . she's . . ." he stopped, shaking his head.

Martha stood, stepped forward, and looked for herself. "Why don't you go help her, Matt? I'm sure she would be delighted to have your assistance."

"Mom!" replied Matt. "I'm not an adolescent any longer, you know," he protested, sounding very adolescent indeed. "I can handle this just fine," he added, knowing that there was literally nothing he was in fact less able to handle at the moment.

Martha turned toward him, her arms crossed, an exaggerated solemnity on her face. "Oh, I can see you have this in hand, Matthew. Nothing adolescent about the way you're . . . um . . . *handling* this. Wouldn't you agree, Paul?"

"Oh, Martha," replied her husband, who had himself finally risen to glance across the east lawn. "Matt is miserable enough. At least let him be miserable in private." Then, affecting a stage whisper and cupping his hand next to his mouth in clownish concealment, he added, *"Go help her with the clothes!"*

Matt rolled his eyes, shook his head again, and, without quite knowing how it happened, found himself passing through the outside porch door and walking toward Rebecca Manguson, who appeared busily oblivious to the attention she had attracted from the Clark family.

Twenty minutes later, Rebecca and Matt sat across from each other in the east reading room, just off the main living room on the first floor of the mansion. Two empty clothes baskets sat on the floor, one near each. No teacups were at their elbows, one party not wishing to prolong the impromptu tête-à-tête with that stylized invitation to extended conversation, and the other party having no idea how to prepare hot tea or serve it. Matt, struggling to appear bright and casual, had nearly exhausted his repertoire of questions and impressions about the Birmingham region and the English weather.

Rebecca was struggling, too, and with two specific and closely related aspects of the situation in which she found herself. First, she was distracted by the fresh realization that, on her morning run three hours earlier, she had had flashes—forecasts—in her mind of this very conversation, of sitting in this chair in the east reading room, facing Matt Clark. What could that mean? Should she understand this to belong to the same classification of phenomena as her dreams? But to what purpose? This simple foretaste of a morning chat struck her as a parlor trick, as little more than a gratuitous preview of something altogether inconsequential, particularly in contrast to everything she believed she knew about her . . . and Martha Clark's . . . "special dreams." And the first distraction flowed into the second. Could it be that she was to understand this chat with Matt to be something *not* inconsequential? Something related to the larger purposes for which they had been called together as a group? She realized suddenly that Matt had been speaking to her again, that she had heard nothing that he had said, and that he had stopped, apparently awaiting a response from her.

"Oh, Matt, I am sorry," she said, her left hand idly toying with her hair as it fell just forward of her right shoulder, a habitual movement during moments of reflection. "I have so much on my mind, I'm not likely to be good at polite conversation right now, I'm afraid."

As soon as she had said that, she reproached herself for the incompleteness of the statement. It was not untrue. But it was far from fully true. She thought for a moment about Matt's bravery the previous day at the perimeter wall, when he had screwed up his courage to tell her exactly why he had come, despite exposing himself to possible ridicule in the telling. Before he could repeat his statement . . . or his question . . . she said, "No, wait . . . there's more." She brought her eyes back to his, hers having drifted elsewhere during her reflection. She moved both hands to her lap and leaned toward him, her legs crossed at the ankles, her hair falling forward and framing her cheekbones.

"On my run this morning, I foresaw this conversation. Here. In this reading room. I foresaw it in the same way that I have foreseen things in my dreams. Yet it was no dream in the usual sense. I was awake and running. I've been trying to think what that should mean for me . . . for us . . . for the *Legati*.

"I was on my second circuit of the perimeter, thinking about last night's discussions, when, in an image marked by the same kinds of sharp edges that I see when I am having the dreams, I saw us, here . . . the two of us, in this room, talking about . . ." her voice trailed off. "Talking about . . . you, Matt."

Matt resisted the quick temptation to interpret Rebecca's words as flirtation, or even to take pleasure in the notion that she had been thinking of *him*, as he so often was of her. It was clear to him that this was not the usual man-woman disclosure, but something far different. Something that he had already begun to recognize as pregnant with the unmistakable shape of the supernatural.

Both of them had been silent for several moments, he, because she did not appear to be finished, and she, because she continued to struggle with what she considered to be her duty under these discon-certing circumstances. Finally she continued, still uncertain. "Matt, it simply cannot be the case that even such a small, odd vision as this one would have been placed in front of me as a method of forecasting a talk between two people about English weather and geography. I have no doubt that our supernatural allies—those responsible for your mother's dreams and mine—are joyful creatures, but I cannot fathom their being . . . well . . . frivolous . . . at least, not in their interventions with humankind.

"Since I am also skeptical that it would be appropriate for the two of us, without my mother's permission, to attempt to wrestle with your role, or mine, in facing the *Legati's* core issues, I'm inclined to think that our conversation should conform, in the simplest possible way, to this odd vision that was presented me this morning . . . that we should talk about you . . . about you as a believer. Nothing else makes sense to me about this.

"So, tell me something, Matthew Clark. Something serious. Such as, what goes through your mind when you think about belief . . . yours . . . your mother's . . . mine . . . Dr. Ashford's . . . the detective's? I do understand from what you said last evening that you are newly believing . . . in something. Let's talk about that."

Matt was astonished, relieved, overjoyed. All at once. He was being offered the chance to engage the *topic* most on his mind, and to do so with the *person* most on his mind. He felt as if a gate to heaven itself had been opened for him. He sensed immediately that it would be impermissible for him to pose, or entertain, or disguise. He was being invited to speak his soul, if he could. He smiled at her, no longer anxious to the point of incapacity, his mind suddenly free of the fog that her presence had continually induced in ways great and small until this moment. He leaned forward, his elbows on his knees, and began, "Okay, Rebecca, I'll try. Well . . . here at the mansion," he said, "it has seemed to me that Christianity—that is, what I think of as Christianity—is quite obviously true. I have trouble even forming a doubting thought about it, and have felt that way, consistently, since arriving here yesterday morning.

"And Christianity," he continued, "seemed almost as obviously true when I was buried in my mother's diaries, back in New York, and on the flight to London, the more so as I sensed the conviction that developed in her when she was locked in the Cambridge War with your parents and the others.

"But there have been many times in my life, and not so long ago, when Christianity has seemed certainly false. A complete sham. A preposterous fabrication. At most something for the children, like the Easter bunny and baskets of colored Easter eggs . . . or reindeer on the rooftop at Christmas.

"It's just so weird . . . that I could have such absolute certainties at opposing ends of a spectrum, and in such a brief time span. I know I haven't asked a question yet, Rebecca, but, I think, if I could form one, the question would be, 'How can a person be sure of anything when he experiences such polar opposite certainties within just days of each other?'"

"Let me ask you something first, Matt," Rebecca replied. "When you say that Christianity has, at times, over the last few days, seemed 'obviously true,' can you tell me what that means to you? What is it exactly that has become so obvious . . . and true?"

Matt found himself successfully fighting off his practiced inclination to respond in the way most likely to impress the other party to a conversation, particularly a party toward whom he felt such powerful attraction. It was another facet of his new self . . . a better Matt, it seemed to him, than the usual one. He answered as honestly as he could. "I think . . . I think what seems obvious and true to me is that God exists . . . and that He . . . ah . . . *works here on earth,* so to speak. And that, of all the things He has ever done that we can actually know anything about, it was Christ's coming that was the . . . ah . . . the *Great Work on Earth* . . . the *Greatest Work of all His Works on Earth*. . . . I think I would say that is what seems obvious and true . . . that God works here on earth, and that there was a Great Work among the Great Works . . . and that it *is* Christianity, and that it is both obvious and true. I wish I could say it better."

Rebecca nodded thoughtfully, then asked, "And when you think of this Great Work on Earth . . ." here she smiled, very nearly destroying Matt's concentration as a result, and she commented to him, as an aside, "I *like* that, Matt." Then she started again. "When you think of this Great Work on Earth, what exactly do you think? What seems critical . . . central . . . to you about Christ, Matt? Can you say? And please understand," she added, "that I ask so that we can go back to your question . . . your question about your opposing certainties . . . and perhaps do justice to that question."

Matt looked down and thought, and he saw immediately the answer that seemed honest, and so he spoke it to her. "I don't know what I would have said about that before Dr. Ashford addressed us last night, when he was so angry at the thought of Meredith Lancaster, but, once he said what he did, everything seemed pretty clear to me.

"The way I remember it, he talked about how Lancaster was good at pushing the *rational* aspects of Christianity, and Dr. Ashford implied that there were plenty of rational aspects that anyone might reasonably study and learn and be thoughtful about. But he was so absolutely clear on the main point in Christianity: not the rational, but the *miraculous* aspects of Christ's life . . . and death . . . and resurrection. . . . All those aspects that make people most . . . well . . . uncomfortable. Those parts of Christ's life that you're not supposed to talk about in polite conversation . . . or, at least . . . in *intellectual* polite conversation."

And here a new thought presented itself to him, and, again, he spoke it to Rebecca as soon as he understood it.

"It's the Christ that the Nicene Creed gives us, now that I think of it. I was struck when you were reading the creed last night . . . reading it slowly for Dr. Ashford's benefit and, as it turned out, for my benefit, too. I was struck by how the creed goes right to the heart of the miraculous in Christ's life. I think I must never have considered the creed as an adult. But last night, when I did, and now, when I think of it again, it seems to me that there's nothing at all in the creed regarding the *content* of His teachings. I mean, *absolutely nothing.* The creed is entirely about who He *was*, not what He *said.* Isn't that right?"

Rebecca smiled again and, Matt noted fleetingly, his mind was not instantly derailed by the mere fact of her face, which, he was nevertheless also aware, was alarmingly near his own. "Alarmingly near," that is, from Matt's point of view. An independent observer would have calculated a distance of at least six feet between the two young faces, as each of them leaned toward the other from their upholstered reading chairs.

"Well," she replied finally, "you certainly have it *mostly* right, Matt."

And after another pause, she continued, "So, then, when I think of the question you asked me about your feeling such opposite convictions within such a short time . . . your feeling that Christianity is obviously false one day, and obviously true the next . . . here's what comes to my mind. Please forgive me if I sound preachy, but I want to remind you of several things you already know.

"You and I live in a strange time. Since it is a *time*, as one of my favorite writers always reminded his readers, we can be confident that it will be looked back upon as odd, or interesting, or striking, or some other way of saying that times are by definition replaced by other times, and that the only time that looks normal—and, therefore, not like a time at all—is the one that happens to be contemporaneous. In this era, in most advanced countries and in many *unadvanced* countries alike, materialism, laced with pervasive unbelief, dominates. It dominates, in other words, whether a given people is among the *haves* or the *have nots*, and so, looks to us normal and correct and not at all like just another oddly skewed perspective of a particular time. Acquisition. Wealth. Possession. Power. Influence. None of it ameliorated, conditioned, softened by the sort of built-in belief systems so prevalent throughout much of world history. In our time, *materialism unbridled* dominates us from almost every source, including, sometimes, the church itself.

"You've heard the adage, 'The rising tide lifts all boats'? Usually that metaphor is used in reference to something considered a general good, like a thriving economy. But if you'll agree that our era's most obvious rising tide is materialism unbridled by belief systems, then you'll get a nice sense of why, for most of us, rowing our small boats hither and yon and bobbing about like corks on this rising tide, it is just so difficult *consistently* to look at things from a Christian perspective, no matter how intellectually clear we may be on its truth. Or for us to *feel* consistently that Christianity is *obviously true*, as you've said you do here at the mansion, rather than, at least at certain moments, merely to *know* intellectually that it is true because we have *decided*, at some different moment, that it is true, and that it remains objectively true regardless of how we may happen to *feel* about things at a given moment.

"To recapture the metaphor, one might imagine our stepping out of the small boats altogether, to swim and wade about in directions that we understand to be the right ones, using a Christian chart of the waters in which we find ourselves. Looking back at our boats, we see them moving away on the tide, largely at its mercy. The boats *do* appear quite safe and secure when we are aboard one of them, and, after all, they were constructed just for us by the secular boat builders of a particular *time*. But the boats may look quite different to us as we wade or swim in some direction not so much at the mercy of the tide, a direction that we ourselves have charted, perhaps a course that we have set for a different harbor, based upon Christian data concerning these waters.

"In fact, Matt, the boats are coffins. There is a certain kind of transitory safety to be found in them, but no Joy, no Truth, no Eternity."

Rebecca, whose gaze had drifted to one side as she considered the limits of her metaphor, looked back to Matt and smiled again. "When you used those lovely phrases, Matt . . . God 'works here on earth,' and God has provided us a 'Great Work on Earth,' you were making statements about how Christianity looks, *intellectually,* to Christians, all of the time and, beyond that, how Christianity feels, *emotionally,* to Christians, some of the time. The real test for most of us is to sustain our Christianity, our sense of Christian purpose and commitment to what we have decided is true, through the swirl of routine materialism, professional setbacks, personal difficulties, and, hardest of all, in the face of our greatest successes. The milieu in which we live, don't you see, will often make it quite hard to *feel* the Truth to which we have committed.

"And some of us gain perspective in this by keeping in mind the fact that the Dark Masters that Meredith Lancaster serves do not comprise some masterful, elaborate reification. They are as real as anything else in all of supernature. As unpopular as the notion is today, in the midst of all this materialism unbridled, and as unsophisticated as it sounds even to mention this with any seriousness, devils and demons are not fantasies to frighten or intrigue the children, Matt. When St. Paul—in one translation that I admire—writes that, '. . . neither angels nor demons . . . will be able to separate us from the love of God that is in Christ Jesus our Lord,' he's not using clever metaphors to represent good and evil . . . metaphors that we moderns can toss aside safely merely because two thousand years have passed. What could possibly lead us to think that we have a superior platform from which to view Reality, as compared with the platforms from St. Paul's era? How are our lifeless, empty, grasping, desperate, secular cultures somehow steeped in a *true* picture of Reality, as compared with that of the first century? Or the fifth, B.C.? Or the tenth, A.D.? And what is two thousand years to an angel or a demon?

"Right now, here at the mansion, you are in protected territory, but you and I can expect to live out most of our lives in enemy territory. Attacks will be frequent. Discipline will be demanded of you, if you are to live as a Christian, no less than it was of you in the military from which you've just come. But it is a joyous and joy-filled discipline, infused with wonder and with Eternity." She paused, then began again.

"One more thing, Matt, and then I should go. We . . . all of us . . . are, or will be, in danger. I don't mean spiritual danger, although there will certainly be some of that, always. I mean in danger of losing our lives. I don't yet know what will be required of us. But you may be wounded or killed in this conflict, as may I . . . as may we all. Your parents would in all likelihood themselves be dead by now, were it not for Detective Belton, Scotland Yard, and whatever assistance he and they received from our special Allies, who, no doubt, are taking their own considerable interest in all this.

"There is nothing abstract about what we are about to face. Whatever it is that you *feel* here at the mansion, and whatever certainties you may *feel* about Christianity while standing within this protected territory . . . prepare yourself to be tested under very, very different circumstances, Matt.

"I will help you all I can."

With that, Rebecca rose from her chair, placed the two clothes baskets one within the other, and looked again at Matt, who had risen with her. "I hope that the conversation we've just had was consistent with . . ." and here she looked away, searching for words that might fit the extraordinary conditions under which the conversation had occurred, ". . . with the charge that I was apparently given in that odd vision that I saw during this morning's run. This has been the only kind of conversation that I can conceive as worthy of such a charge."

Matt nodded. "This has been of immense help to me, Rebecca. I want to thank you for moving the conversation to this level. I have a lot of trouble speaking coherently around you, as you may have noticed." Matt tried to give this a jocular turn, and laughed aloud, awkwardly, in his effort to appear breezy and unperturbed. Then, having thus clumsily introduced the subject, and being uncertain how to extricate himself, he staggered on. "Do you think we might . . , sometime soon . . . have a discussion about . . . about our relationship . . . yours and mine, I mean?" His face began to change color as he spoke the words. He wished as they escaped his mouth that he could get them back, knowing he had gone where he had not intended, and certainly where he had not been invited.

Rebecca turned toward the doorway, and Matt thought for an instant that she was going to walk out of the room without so much as a comment on his new idiocy. But she had simply turned her back to him, had thought for a moment, and had then faced him again. "When you say 'our relationship,' Matt, you mean something different from our inherent relationship as the children of parents who have been best friends for decades. But that *is* our essential relationship, don't you see, and it is a wonderful, though unearned, relationship."

She paused, still holding her clothes baskets against one hip, still fixing him with her incredible, penetrating gray eyes, and, thought Matt to himself, crushing him—no doubt inadvertently—with the plain weight of the rejection that he knew was building in her mind and in her words. He struggled to breathe.

"You *do* mean," she continued, "when you say 'our relationship'— unless I am confused—a *romantic* relationship. Or am I wrong, Matt?"

He looked away. Rebecca's response to his blundering question had devastated him. She had not, he knew, meant her reply to be unkind, but its effect was to place "romance" in a context in which it appeared as out of place as some hideous weed in a garden of roses.

She was right, of course. Placed next to the richness of what she termed their "inherent" relationship as children of best friends, the notion of a romantic relationship seemed in comparison a fool's self-indulgence. This time, no words came to his mind. And in this instance his silence was less a consequence of infatuation and proximity than of sheer humiliation at his own myopia and selfishness. He kept his eyes averted.

Sensing his devastation, Rebecca spoke again, with difficulty resisting the urge to place her free hand on his arm. "Matt," she said, smiling at him, "next time you go up to your room, look at the Bible that Mum and Dad have placed on the night stand in each room. Take a moment to read Ecclesiastes, the start of the third chapter . . . the first eight verses. And *don't* read rejection into what I just said to you. And don't read acceptance, either. Just read the start of Ecclesiastes 3, and know that *that* is the only reply I can give you just now." She smiled again.

And then she was gone.

He stared at the floor at the spot on which she had last stood. Her presence was still strongly with him, and he felt bathed in her essence. As he remained there, unmoving, his mind turned to Ecclesiastes and, as it did, a faint smile began, unbidden, to take shape. She had cited one of the very few scriptural passages that he actually knew somehow, at least in its broad shape, and, in bits and pieces, *verbatim.*

And so, his smile broadening without conscious invitation, he silently formed the phrases that he could remember from some childhood memory assignment, the King James language seeming as natural and as welcome as love itself: "To every thing there is a season, and a time to every purpose under the heaven: A time to be born, and a time to die . . . A time to weep, and a time to laugh . . . a time to embrace, and a time to refrain from embracing . . . A time to love, and a time to hate; a time of war, and a time of peace."

"A time to love. . . ."

Matt turned and walked over to the window of the reading room. He looked out over the east lawn at the clotheslines, swaying with their brightly colored fabric burdens. His eyes moved beyond, to the fields and woods, and on to the horizon. He was consumed by something he recognized as joy, and he knew that this joy went beyond . . . and above . . . his attraction to a woman. There was holiness in this joy, holiness that transformed *this* attraction to a woman, and made it larger, stronger, of more weight than mere "romance."

He turned, crossed the small room, closed its door, and returned to the window. There he knelt and, unskilled and uncertain, composed his prayer of thanksgiving.

Chapter Twelve

ELISABETH MANGUSON STOOD ON THE NORTH PORCH, about half past noon, and stared toward the woods at the small opening which marked the private driveway's emergence. Her husband, stepping onto the porch from the anteroom behind her, approached quietly and took her hand. "He'll be all right, my dear. If anyone can take care of himself, it's Luke. Come in and have a bite to eat. Once he arrives, you'll take us right into meeting and you won't have a chance to get something until tea time."

Not quite fifteen minutes afterward, Elisabeth and Rebecca, the only ones to hear the faint grumble of an automobile engine struggling with the north slope, together pushed back their chairs from one of the small dining tables and ran for the door. The two women fairly tackled Luke as he closed the car door and turned toward the mansion.

"It was fine," he said reassuringly to his mother and sister, returning their hugs and kisses indulgently. "Mr. Preston was actually waiting for me, even though my train was a few minutes early getting to Westminster. He sends his best regards, Mum, to you and Dad.

"I got a cab to swing by Paddington to pick up Matt's bag and Mrs. Clark's lock box from the space he'd rented at the station; then, once I'd got back to our car, stopped at a stationer's about halfway home and had copies of the press release made for everyone. The statement is only three pages."

In just minutes the *Legati* had assembled in the subterranean meeting room. At his mother's signal, Luke provided for the group his brief summary of the uneventful trip to and from London and his rendezvous with Preston, then distributed the copies of Meredith Lancaster's press release. Each member read silently; the room was still.

Advance Press Release
Date: June __, 19__
Heading: Meredith Lancaster Announcement of Public Event
Welcome: *Ad lib,* Mr. Lancaster
Acknowledgments: *Ad lib,* Mr. Lancaster
Complete text to be read by Mr. Lancaster:

Five days from today, on Sunday, June __, 19__, I will be granted the unrivaled privilege of reading, from the pulpit of St. David's Cathedral, Pembrokeshire, on the rugged and magnificent coast of Wales, a document of immense historic significance. [pause] It is no less than a new creedal formulation, one that I am able to attribute with complete confidence not only to the sixth century, but to the patron saint of Wales himself, St. David.

[lengthy pause]

This new creed, which, pending formal ecclesiastical action, I have christened "The Creed of St. David," has been lost from view for fourteen centuries, passed along orally and in secret, from generation to generation, by those charged with its sacred perpetuation. This creed—*the true creed*—has been hidden through the centuries due to a legitimate fear on the part of the initiates that church authorities [pause] would condemn and suppress the creed. The Creed of St. David, when revealed on Sunday in the saint's own cathedral, will at last stand before the world in its spare elegance, seen finally and truly as *the essential Christian statement of belief*, a statement that will immediately be understood to underlie *all* traditions, to inform *all* doctrinal approaches, to define *all* churches' polity and theology, and to influence and ultimately to determine *all* Christians' conceptualisations of their faith commitments.

The Creed of St. David, as you will all see for yourselves on Sunday, will, in its brevity and simplicity, strip away in a single stroke most of the pernicious accretions that have fatally misled and misguided the church and its worshippers for so many tragic centuries.

Brought now to light through my corporate-funded research efforts, in cooperation with reserachers from the University College of Wales in Aberystwyth, the Creed of St. David will be revealed on the holy ground on which the cathedral stands, in the company of a distinguished and international congregation, and with the cameras of BBC television transmitting this revelation to viewers throughout the world.

[pause]

As we make our slow approach to the end of the second millenium, I can state with the utmost confidence that the Creed of St. David will at last become the theological foundation stone for Christian belief and worship throughout the world.

In my message from the pulpit of the cathedral, I will explore in more detail the full range of implications of this discovery. Those implications are far-reaching indeed, and will prove a challenge to all those who, with me, urge the continual updating of our Christian message in response to the failure of contemporary society to construct the spiritual, scientific, and governmental underpinnings necessary for the fullest development of peace and prosperity for all people.

Those who will join me at St. David's, and who will stand with me on this unforgettable Sunday morning, will lend their not inconsiderable weight to what will surely become a worldwide movement stimulated by, and on behalf of, the Creed of St. David.

Those leaders expected to be in attendance at St. David's from our churches, from our seminaries, from our institutions of higher education, from our governments, from our scientific communities, and, as well, from our corporate and industrial elite, include the following:

[List to be distributed separately in an addendum at the conclusion of the announcement.]

[Addendum will also include complete list of corporate sponsorships provided in financial support of the research effort that has produced the new creedal formulation.]

After some time, Elisabeth looked to Lawrence Ashford. "Dr. Ashford," she said, "would you like to begin?"

"St. David's . . . of course . . ." he mused, seeming to speak almost to himself. "The Welsh *Credo Nicea* coupled with the purple stone of the background structures in both dreamers' visions should have been enough." Ashford looked up, almost as if awakening to the fact that others were straining to hear him. Looking alternately at Matt Clark and at Sid Belton, he continued in his soft voice. "The cathedral was constructed eight hundred years ago, my friends. It was constructed of the purple stone, locally quarried, which you can see in the savage cliffs jutting from the sea, just one mile south of the town of St. David's. It is an otherworldly hue, whether you view it at the cliffs or as it is set into the cathedral walls. Those walls are lichen-encrusted, battered by eight centuries of North Atlantic wind, rain, salt, and sun. The purple stone of the building has been weathered as if to expose its very soul. A *magnificent* soul." He seemed again to drift away, remembering. The group held its silence, waiting.

Speaking once more in the small, distracted voice with which he had begun, now nearly whispering to himself, he added, "Yes . . . its soul is exposed, but not in shame. In triumph. The cathedral rests on the holiest ground in Great Britain, my friends. It has no equal. Almighty God has been worshipped every day on St. David's grounds for nearly one and a half *millennia,* first in the small church built there by David himself . . . eventually in the cathedral."

Suddenly and alarmingly, Ashford's face flushed bright red, and he struggled bolt upright in his chair. "How *dare* these brigands corrupt the *holiest ground . . . the holiest structure . . . those degenerate monsters . . . those brazen purveyors of Evil. . . .*"

He stopped, halted by Martha Clark's hands on his shoulders. She had moved so swiftly from her chair to kneel in front of him that he had not known she was there. She gripped the bony shoulders gently, firmly. Her face was close to his. "Dr. Ashford . . . Dr. Ashford," she repeated softly. "We will not allow it. *We will . . . not . . . allow it.*" She turned her head and glanced at Matt, indicating something with her eyes. He grasped her meaning, quickly stood, and moved his mother's chair so close to Lawrence Ashford's that the chair arms overlapped. She rose from her knees, keeping both hands on his shoulders, and slipped sideways into the chair. The room remained silent, every individual leaning toward the two, prepared to assist.

After several moments, Tom Sutton rose from his chair and moved slowly to his old comrade. Luke, seeing the movement, quickly seized an extra chair and held it there for the physician, who took his place on Ashford's other side, facing Martha. In the most tender of medical scenes, Sutton first checked the pulse of the heavily breathing, perspiring patient, then, as Rebecca retrieved the stethoscope and blood pressure cuff from his medical bag near the door, he continued to minister with powerful hands and lightning intellect, processing the physiological data as rapidly as it could be transmitted.

Moments later, Luke and his father, having quietly left the room as Tom Sutton began his ministrations, returned carrying a cot, small but easily able to accommodate Ashford's skeletal frame. So many hands assisted the struggling warrior onto the cot that it was difficult to say that anyone in the room had not. Positions of chairs were adjusted so that the physician sat next to his recumbent charge, with Martha Clark remaining close to the patient on the other side. The circle of chairs was by now completely reconfigured so as to face the small cluster formed by Elisabeth Manguson, Tom Sutton, Martha Clark, and the prone Lawrence Ashford.

Just as Elisabeth was about to speak, Ashford's voice rose eerily from the cot, soft and clear, seemingly undisturbed, confident, and compelling. "I want to add," he said as if nothing untoward had transpired, "that I've been thinking all morning about the creed. Those Welsh passages that Martha dreamed . . . they can only be *subtractions* from the creed. They do not stand alone. They modify and explicate and enrich the core ideas. Lancaster wishes to remove those explications. This document . . . this *fraud* . . . that he calls 'The Creed of St. David' will, in likelihood, conform in its core expression to our Nicene Creed, using similar phraseology.

"Yes . . . the counterfeit creed will give us the core of the *Credo Nicea*. But we shall have it *sans* the dreamed phrases, *sans* all the fullness and subtlety of concept that makes the Nicene Creed what it has always been to the church universal.

"And—hear this clearly—it will not be merely those particular church traditions which have incorporated this formulation into their regular worship services that will be affected by this fraud. Lancaster himself has accurately forecast the impact in the press release. The phrases still echo: these concepts 'underlie *all* traditions . . . approaches . . . polity . . . theology. . . .' *Every* church body today, whether its members are aware or not, has been shaped in its doctrines by the ancient creed. And *every* church body . . . *every* believer . . . will be affected by this monstrosity that will spring upon the world on Sunday.

"The Nicene Creed, keep in mind, was adopted mid-fifth century. This fictitious creed, since the liar wishes to attribute it to St. David, will supposedly, then, have been developed at least fifty years later. Lancaster will contend, no doubt correctly on this one point, that St. David knew the Nicene Creed. The essence of the lie will be that David, knowing the Nicene, therefore must purposefully have removed the phrases that Martha has given us, in order to . . ." and here Ashford turned his eyes upward from his cot, and to one side, to inquire of Martha.

She turned her head, quickly glanced at the press release on the small table beside her, and provided the quotation that Ashford sought. "In order to . . . in order to eliminate . . . 'the pernicious accretions that have fatally misled and misguided the church and its worshippers for so many tragic centuries.'"

To the astonishment of every person in the room, Lawrence Ashford at this point actually fought his weakening body to a semi-erect position, propping himself precariously on one elbow, now half facing Martha, whose efforts to prevent this exhausting maneuver had brought a scowl to his face that had stopped her in a heartbeat. "I want you to hear this, *everyone*," he continued with such comparative force that Dr. Sutton rose completely out of his chair to lean over him, one hand on his wrist, feeling for the pulse, the other against his upper back, helping to support him.

"Do you understand, *everyone*, that this abominable, revolting vomitus that the voice of Evil wishes us to call 'The Creed of St. David' will *subtract* these phrases from our creed and, thereby, *from . . . the*

. . . seminal . . . traditions . . . honored . . . by . . . all . . . believers . . . everywhere." And here began, in Ashford's tremulous, quavering voice, a recitation in English of the subtracted Welsh phrases that froze every member of the *Legati* in a horror of fresh understanding: *". . . the only-begotten Son of God, begotten of his Father before all worlds, God of God, Light of Light, Very God of Very God, begotten, not made, being of one substance with the Father, by whom all things were made. . . ."*

". . . and ascended into heaven, and sitteth on the right hand of the Father; and he shall come again with glory to judge both the quick and the dead; whose kingdom shall have no end. . . ."

". . . who proceedeth from the Father and the Son, who with the Father and the Son together is worshipped and glorified, who spake by the Prophets. . . ."

Ashford, his slight voice catching in his throat as he spoke the concluding phrase, fell back onto the cot with a moan just larger than a sigh. His eyes closed in exhaustion.

Thomas Sutton continued to hover feverishly over him, his stethoscope moving swiftly from point to point over the thin chest. And yet, still again, opening his eyes, the failing scholar spoke in a whisper that only Sutton and Martha Clark could hear. When he fell silent once more, Martha sat up, turned her face to Elisabeth and Jason, both now standing at Ashford's feet, and said softly, but loudly enough for all in the room to hear, her voice faltering, tears welling, "Dr. Ashford asks that one of you summarize for the group the meaning of these subtractions."

As the Mangusons stepped back reluctantly to their chairs, the group saw Martha whispering directly into Ashford's ear, and then saw her move her own ear to his lips to listen for the response. None could hear their words to each other. But some saw Ashford's hands unclench, his jaw relax, his eyes close once more. After several moments, Dr. Sutton resumed his seat, Ashford's hand clasped in his. Martha gripped his other hand tightly from her side of his cot. Then Martha looked toward the Mangusons and nodded, saying, "Please do speak loudly. Dr. Ashford does not wish to *miss* anything."

Elisabeth and her husband exchanged looks, and it was she who, having taken her seat again, stood to speak in obedience to the old man's request. She spoke clearly and with volume, her eyes on the pallid face of Lawrence Ashford.

"Mr. Lancaster has fabricated a creed which he wishes to attribute to the patron saint of Wales. He would like the public to believe that the fraudulent creed represents St. David's planned, carefully considered revision of—that is, a set of subtractions from—the Nicene Creed. His lie will include an argument that his 'Creed of St. David' would have been suppressed, with severe repercussions for those advocating and professing it, had it not been kept *secret* for fourteen hundred years. He will produce his *original* in the language in which Martha and Rebecca dreamed of it, although their dreamed phrases will, of course, since they comprise subtractions, be exactly those that will *not* be contained in the false creed."

Elisabeth paused, held up her copy of Lancaster's press release for a moment to review something, then continued. "I infer from the wording of today's announcement that he will try to get around the fact that what we call Welsh today would have been a form of . . . I should imagine . . . Brittonic Celtic fourteen hundred years ago by presenting the document not as a fourteen-hundred-year-old parchment, with all the physical verification difficulties that that would have introduced, but as a more contemporary document rather lately penned. The Welsh of his 'Creed of St. David' will be presented simply as the language in which the formula would finally have been reduced to paper, since he will allege that it was recorded in Wales, and supposedly, I should think, in the twentieth century. Thus, Mr. Lancaster will invite us to conceive his fraudulent belief statement as having been passed along through the centuries by a tiny handful of Celtic and Welsh initiates, from generation to generation, using language contemporaneous to each era. A secret *oral tradition,* then, with its origins in St. David himself.

"The document that Mr. Lancaster will give the world on Sunday . . ." she stopped, looked directly at her daughter and son, and corrected herself. "The document that Mr. Lancaster *expects* to give the world on Sunday . . . may actually be a few months old, or it may be fifty years old or more. The age of the document itself will be of little interest, since age-of-document is not the basis upon which the claim is being made, and becomes, as a result, scientifically and historically uninteresting. One of the really clever aspects of this is the idea of a *secret* oral tradition, unlike the early gospels, for example, that were transmitted via a *public* oral tradition." Elisabeth paused, and looked inquiringly at her husband, who rose to stand at her side.

"I think that Lawrence's and Elisabeth's analyses are breathtaking," said Jason. "With an allegedly secret *and* oral tradition in hand, Lancaster's allegations in support of his creed's authenticity cannot be disproved by the absence of an ancient original, or by the absence of parallel historical and independent references to it. Thus, you can see the utility, for him, of this vast and gullible menagerie of opinion-makers that he has doubtless marshaled to his cause in advance of the disclosure. It will be extremely difficult to slow, and eventually to reverse, the momentum of support for this creed once it is announced, given the impossibility of establishing a *prima facie* case against it, and given the preeminence of the dignitaries whose support, without question, Lancaster has garnered."

"And, in addition, Jason," Elisabeth added quickly, "Mr. Lancaster will play to the legitimate national and historical consciousness of the Welsh people by attributing his *great discovery* to St. David himself, and by naming the false creed after their saint."

He nodded, and acknowledged his wife's point. "Yes. Yes, I hadn't actually thought of that part, Liz. . . . That's still another buttress in support of the whole edifice, isn't it.

"In any case," he continued, "this alleged creed will, then, appear to retain the Nicene Creed's core ideas, probably using somewhat different language just to help establish its own purportedly authentic *sound*, but nonetheless appearing to reinforce fundamental Christian concepts: God as Creator, Jesus Christ as His Son . . . but, notice, without any defining phrases crystallizing the meaning of Sonship . . . and Christ as crucified and risen. It will still make reference to the Holy Spirit . . . but, again, without definition or embellishment.

"As Lawrence reminded us last night, Lancaster's genius, inspired by those he serves, rests in his emphasis on partial lies, rather than on whole lies. His lies appear true because there is so much of truth in them. It's *profoundly* effective." He stopped and turned his face to Elisabeth.

"And so," she added, "what the false creed will take away may not *seem* particularly significant to many Christians. And that is why Mr. Lancaster can, as we have seen, evince such confidence that he will be able to gather widespread support for the lie, right from the start."

She paused, looked to her husband, thought for a moment, and added, "The more one considers these subtractions, the more obvious it becomes, doesn't it. This counterfeit creed actually subtracts the Trinitarian concept from our belief statement, and manages to do it . . . *unobtrusively.* It's just an amazing *coup.* The heart of the Trinitarian formulation simply vanishes from sight."

Silence followed this. Then Jason responded.

"I think you and Dr. Ashford have hit it right in the center, Liz," he said. "The concept of God in the counterfeit creed is made to be both primitive and attenuated. This *God* would not intervene in human experience and, as I think about it further, *could not even be prayed to.*" He thought for a moment, and then concluded, "Altogether, Lancaster and his Masters have cobbled together as destructive a package as I can imagine: a secret oral tradition impossible to disprove; the identification of their fraud with a revered and sainted historical figure; and a seemingly innocuous series of subtractions from an accepted belief formula, leaving us with a creed that encourages belief in a distant, impersonal, *unjudging and, thus, unloving* Deity that will leave us alone to do as we wish . . . that will leave us alone to face the eternal consequences of our decisions and our actions." He shook his head. "The best adjective to apply to the whole show is the one that is truest: the entire fabrication is simply and purely *demonic.*"

Elisabeth took her husband's hand, squeezed it, and with him stepped to the foot of Ashford's cot. His eyes were closed. Elisabeth, glancing first at Tom Sutton, then leaning over Martha to place her hand high on Ashford's fragile shoulder, asked softly, "Dr. Ashford, was that satisfactory? Did we make mistakes?"

Seeing his mouth working, Martha again brought her ear to the old man's lips for several long seconds, then sat back. "He pronounces your combined recitation satisfactory, Elisabeth . . . and Jason. He judges it 'quite comprehensive and clearly organized.' And he adds that he wishes you now to cite appropriate references from the fourth Gospel, in support of the true creed, in support of authentic Christianity within *all* traditions, as a reminder to us of the staggering *violence* of the fraud."

Elisabeth, still standing beside Martha, smiled down at her friend, feeling pleased, almost as though she were a child again, by the professor's favorable evaluation of her and her husband's summation. At the same time, she was mildly nonplussed by the insistence that they provide references from John's Gospel. The juxtaposition of Ashford's precarious, even desperate, physical condition, the acuity of his analysis, and his demand for academic rigor under near-death circumstances filled the members of the *Legati,* herself included, with a palpable mixture of astonishment, amusement, admiration, humility, and outright fear.

Jason, having resumed his seat, opened the King James Bible that Luke had quickly retrieved from the nearby bookcase, looked to Elisabeth, and, receiving her nod, read the familiar opening passages from John's Gospel: *"'In the beginning was the Word, and the Word was with God, and the Word was God. . . . All things were made by him; and without him was not any thing made that was made. . . .*

"'And the Word was made flesh, and dwelt among us. . . .'"

He stopped and looked up.

After a brief silence, Rebecca unexpectedly spoke, clearly and, it seemed to some, with a sense of triumph. *"'Before Abraham was, I am.'"*

Seconds later, from her chair beside the cot, Martha joined the recitation of Christ's words initiated by Rebecca, adding in a glad, strong voice, *"'. . . with the glory which I had with thee before the world was.'"*

And then, a moment later, Elisabeth spoke in a hushed, prayerful voice: *"'. . . for thou lovedst me before the foundation of the world.'"*

Finally, after another lengthy silence, once more came the strong, modulated voice of Rebecca Manguson, as if in benediction: *"'I and my Father are one.'"*

Elisabeth, still standing beside Martha, looked down at Lawrence Ashford. His eyes were open. The smile of an angel illuminated his face.

Then Elisabeth, seeing Lawrence Ashford's beatific smile of satisfaction, looked up from his radiant face and addressed the group. "With our documentary analysis complete for the moment, I am ordering Dr. Ashford to the dormitory room across the hallway for the rest of the afternoon and night. Dr. Sutton, would you be good enough to remain with him? Interrupt us immediately if there is anything we should know, or anything we can do."

With that, the group quickly organized itself to transport Ashford, three members on each side of his cot, their collective grip fixed so as to carry the featherweight burden as smoothly as possible. Thus assisting him to bed, they reluctantly left him, having smothered him with their tender words and bathed him in loving caresses of his pale forehead. Tom Sutton stayed behind with him in obedience to his orders.

The session resumed with Elisabeth's simple announcement, words that sent a thrill down the spine of her daughter: "I want to move now to a consideration of the actions that are required of us. Jay? Please?"

"The command," Jason responded without hesitation, "of the *Nuntiae* is unequivocal: *'Protect the saint.'* Clearly, given this press release, we are to protect St. David from the false attribution to him of a corrupt and counterfeit belief statement. If we can succeed in that, we shall have succeeded as well in protecting Christianity itself from the attempted corruption. We must not permit this to go forward. If anything has become clear to me in the last quarter hour, it is that this is not about the Church of England, but about Christianity worldwide, in every form that it has ever taken, on every continent, in every era.

"In hurling this 'Creed of St. David'—this vulgar and outrageous fraud—at the church universal, Lancaster seeks to capture a lightly defended ridgeline that *must* be held. Loss of the ridge will certainly result in loss of the territory that it protects, so that, in short order, civilians—that is, believers everywhere—will stand before the onslaught utterly unprotected by the battlements that have always comprised mainstream Christian belief."

Jason paused.

"But as for *how* we may foreclose Lancaster's plan. . . ."

As her husband's voice trailed off, Elisabeth was already beginning to speak. She was, though seated, animated and restless in her chair. She went straight to her daughter's dream. "I want to know in what way Rebecca is threatened by something 'worse than death'.

"I want to know why we have the dreamed threat of murder, including the vial hidden in the hymnal. Whose murder? The dreamed bishop? And is he the bishop of St. David's?

"And who is the murderer? Meredith Lancaster? How? Why? He seems to have what he wants—the announcement and likely public acceptance of a fraudulent creed, one with potential to visit immense damage on Christianity itself, throughout the world—and without further recourse to violence beyond that which he has already attempted against Martha and Paul, and against Rebecca and Luke."

Here Elisabeth stopped and looked at Sid Belton across the circle. "Help me, Detective. I have more questions than I have answers."

The detective uncharacteristically replied immediately, looking not at his feet but directly into Elisabeth's eyes. "I've gotta be careful here, Mrs. Manguson. My lieutenant told me I could stay in England as long as I need to, to work on the Clarks' case. Well, we *got* the Clarks, but the only thing I'm supposed to be doin' now is, with Scotland Yard, tryin' to identify the people back in the States who were involved in their kidnapping.

"The reason I say that first, Mrs. Manguson, is that you've only got four days to do somethin' about this situation. And . . . here's the thing . . . *doin' somethin'* is probably goin' to mean doin' somethin' *illegal.* Know what I mean?

"Mrs. Clark said earlier to Dr. Ashford that we 'will not allow' this Lancaster guy to make his big announcement on Sunday . . . that we won't allow him to corrupt the Christian faith with this fraud he's cooked up. And we have angels' commands, for goodness sake, to protect St. David. Well, how are we gonna accomplish any of that, y'know, without breaking a law or two? And maybe some pretty serious laws, too . . . not just a little *breaking and entering* here, or a little *petty theft* of a fraudulent document there. People could get hurt in this, y'know? How're you gonna get this accomplished without goin' around the law?

"Anyway, Mrs. Manguson, that's what I mean when I say that I gotta be pretty careful here. I shouldn't be givin' advice about how to get around the law of the land, much less givin' assistance to any of you who might actually *do* somethin' illegal. Know what I mean?"

A long, disturbed, restless silence descended on the group.

Elisabeth, having risen to pace behind her chair, now turned again to face the detective. "Detective Belton," she said, "I respect your professional dilemma. I will not ask you to participate in any action, of any kind, that we feel compelled to undertake. And I will not ask you to provide advice and counsel regarding specific actions. I will, however . . . and I do . . . ask that you continue to assist in the analysis. We have, as you, yourself, have emphasized more strongly than anyone present, an unambiguous charge from, using your perfectly apt term, the angels themselves. That charge has priority for us beyond England's laws.

"And so, indeed, does the moral law that underlies all Christian thought and action. Consistent with that moral law, you will understand, I am not allowed to be *too* clever, or *too* calculating, or *too* Machiavellian in developing our own plan of action. I cannot allow our group to begin to conduct its affairs using the premises and methods of our enemies. I cannot preempt our enemies' maneuvers by devising maneuvers of *ours* that, if undertaken, would be consistent with *theirs*. To speak plainly, I cannot order Luke to find Meredith Lancaster and kill him. I *can* order Luke to attempt to find the vial of poison that our dreamers have shown us, in order to prevent a murder. And if, in the process of finding and removing the poison, Luke were to find himself forced to defend himself physically, or to defend another member of our party physically, or to defend any other innocent physically . . . so it must be. Our evidence is *special evidence* on which, we all agree, the police cannot act. Only *we* can act upon it. And so we must. And so we will."

"Yes ma'am," said Belton in quick response. "Everything you just said is completely true, and it is, by the way, a good description of how I've always tried to conduct myself as a law enforcement officer. I've never actually had to hurt somebody beyond a little arm-twistin', but I've always known it could happen . . . it coulda happened in any of a hundred different scrapes I've been in.

"Ma'am, I'll provide assistance to you right up to the point . . . to the point where I find that I'm about to advise you to break a law. I'll need to stop there."

"It is all that I can ask, sir. Thank you." Elisabeth resumed her seat and leaned forward. "Help us, Detective. What are your thoughts now?"

"The thing about the press release, ma'am, that got my attention more than anything else," replied Belton immediately, "was the mention of some *researchers* from that college in Wales. My years in learnin' how to deal with guys like this Lancaster tells me that those researchers can compute their life span in days or hours right now. They're technical experts. He brought 'em in to help him get this fraud put together, probably by threatening their families. Now they know too much. He doesn't need 'em anymore. They're done. So, I figure you gotta find out who these guys are that Lancaster used to help him create the fake document.

"Then, get to 'em somehow. Save 'em, if you can. Once they're saved, if they're smart . . . and they gotta be smart, or Lancaster wouldn't have picked 'em in the first place . . . they're pretty likely to spill the beans, y'know?"

Seeing several blank stares, Belton added, "Y'know, *spill the beans . . . squeal . . . let the cat outta the bag. . . .*"

"Yes, yes, Detective, we know," said Jason, smiling, "but we have no information about these people at all. Where would we begin?"

At this, Belton stared directly into Jason Manguson's eyes and smiled his crooked smile. Then, after several moments, the detective rose from his chair, turned to Elisabeth, and said, "Mrs. Manguson, it's time for me to step aside. If there's somethin' else I can help with, call me. I'll go down the hall to the other dormitory room and make a few notes for myself."

As Sid Belton left the meeting room, Elisabeth spoke thoughtfully. "We need more information, then, from some source other than the ones we have used until now. We need to know who these researchers from the University College of Wales are. . . . We need to know where the fraudulent creed is being held. . . . We need to know what the bishop's role might be, and whether he is, in fact, the bishop of St. David's . . . and whether or not he is in danger. . . . Oh! There is so much we don't know, how can we begin to decide what action to take?"

Rebecca stood abruptly and walked rapidly away from the drawn-in circle of chairs, her path tracing the perimeter of the long rectangle formed by the meeting room. Her hands worked against each other in front of her chest as she paced, her head bowed in concentration, thick, black tresses falling over the contours of her face and down over the front of her mother's dark blue dress. The room was once again silent.

At length coming to a halt near her mother's chair, she addressed the group in her commanding voice. "Luke and I must go now, this afternoon, to Cambridge, to the farmhouse where the Clarks were held. I don't know if the detective will feel that he can give us the location, since our purpose would be, as he put it, to 'break and enter.' But we can ask him.

"We may find that we need to wait until nightfall in order to enter the house, but, somehow, we must enter and search Mr. Lancaster's offices for information. That's all we can do. It's the only source available, and we must move quickly since, as the detective has said, the Welsh researchers are likely to be in grave danger right now."

Luke responded. "I agree, Rebecca, and have been thinking the same thing. There is an issue, though, beyond merely finding the farmhouse. In order to gain the information we need, and yet prevent Mr. Lancaster from developing a counter to whatever plan we then form, we need to gather the information in such a manner that he will not know that we are moving against him. We want him to think that he can move forward just as he has planned. If we ransack his offices to find what we need, he may alter his plan in any number of ways, none of which we could anticipate. For example, he may either move the Welsh researchers somewhere we cannot know about, or he may go ahead and execute them summarily and secretly.

"I have been concerned since last night about the mere fact that the Clarks escaped the farmhouse. I am, obviously, thankful that they did, but their rescue may already have prompted Mr. Lancaster to make adjustments that we cannot anticipate."

Rebecca, the only member of the circle standing, looked toward the doorway, a surprised look on her face. "Detective?" she said. "Can we help you?"

Sid Belton leaned against the door frame, his grin apparent to the group even at a distance. All faces turned to his, curious at his almost immediate return from his self-imposed absence. "Well, folks . . . I couldn't do it . . . couldn't leave you . . . didn't even get all the way down the hallway."

Still slouching against the door, he continued. "Luke, you got a good point about Lancaster's reaction to the Clarks' escape. We were careful not to give the impression that we were police, and we sure didn't show any interest in anything except the Clarks. So, we're hopin' he'll just figure somebody there—one of his henchmen, or a cook, or a cleanin' person—let it slip in a pub that some people were bein' held there, and somebody that hates Lancaster . . . I figure there's *a lot* of those around . . . decided to mess him up.

"But we're just *hopin'* that, Luke.

"Fact is, he knows by now not only that the Clarks are gone, but that his boys didn't manage to capture Miss Manguson, Luke, or the kid. He can't be too happy about any of this, y'know what I mean?"

The detective stepped inside the door, his hands deep in his pockets, his eyes on the floor, concentrating. "Even so, Luke, I think your sister's idea is right. Go to the farmhouse now, look in Lancaster's offices. See what you can find. He'll have his fake creed and any directly related stuff in a safe, but what you need is not gonna be in his safe . . . it's the kind of thing he'll have in file cabinets or even laid out on his desk: schedules, calendars, files full of internal memos and letters, address books . . . everything we look for whenever we're tryin' to figure out what a crook might do next.

"Luke . . . Miss Manguson . . . I've still got the map the Cambridge police gave me, with the route to the farmhouse marked clearly. I can't really give it to you, but I might accidentally drop it outside my door, once we go back to our rooms this afternoon. Oh . . . and you'll find that the windows along the front porch of the farmhouse are probably just as badly secured tonight as they were last night. People put good locks on their doors and ten-cent hardware on their windows.

"But be careful dealin' with anybody Lancaster might have stationed there to guard the premises, young folks. He's lost his two prisoners, but, if he's got all his documents there in that office like we think he does, he's gonna provide a rough welcome for anybody that tries to get in that farmhouse again.

"Luke's right, y'know. He'll be on the alert now, even more than he was before. He may change some of his plans and, regardless, he's gotta be mad.

"Last night, those people that my boys tossed around at the farmhouse . . . they were amateurs. But the thugs he had watchin' and chasin' Miss Manguson and Luke in London sound pretty professional, even though she made 'em look silly in that little Alfa Romeo. I figure he may have that farmhouse guarded now by those same characters that were tryin' to get the young people in London. They'll be tough, and they'll be well armed, and they'll be ready."

The detective half-turned, sidling back toward the door. Not turning his face back toward his audience, he added, "And, I hafta tell ya', I'm worried, too, about Lancaster tryin' to get inside this perimeter, right here. It's not foolproof . . . and, even though we can hole up here in the dungeon for a long time, it's not gonna do us any good to be stuck down *here,* when we got orders to stop Lancaster from doin' his worst out *there.*

"I know you've explained to me, Mrs. Manguson," he added, turning to face Elisabeth from the doorway, "that we got special protection here, in the mansion, and that accounts for why all of you weren't wiped out long before now. And I know you're right about that. I just hope Lancaster is so convinced of that, too, after all these years, that he decides to put all his efforts into beefin' up the protection level at his headquarters, and at St. David's this week-end, and then sits back and dares us to do anything about it."

The detective paused briefly, and then added.

"And one more thing, young people," he said, addressing Rebecca and Luke specifically. "My boss in New York let me bring along two of his new palm-size cameras. He likes toys like that.

They're made especially for photographing documents. They're loaded and ready, and I've got extra rolls of film. I might be clumsy enough to drop those outside my door along with the map and a couple of pairs of the gloves we use to handle evidence. With these cameras and gloves, and if you're careful about how you put everything back, you can leave the place just like you found it."

The detective said these last words as he shambled out the door, hands in his pockets, head down. The *Legati* listened as his footsteps retreated down the hallway.

Chapter Thirteen

MATT WAS NERVOUS. HAVING JUST UNFOLDED HIS LANKY, long-muscled frame from the compact front passenger seat of Elisabeth and Jason Manguson's sedan, now standing beside the car to stretch his cramped limbs, he ran his hand over the fine, textured wood of the stock of Jason Manguson's hunting rifle. Uncomfortably, he watched in bright moonlight as Rebecca and Luke stepped quietly from the vehicle, Rebecca from behind the wheel and Luke from the right rear seat behind her. Both of them were clad in their dark "escape clothes," as they cheerfully called them, and both seemed much more at ease in this extraordinary situation than he, dressed in a pair of ill-fitting but at least dark colored trousers, shirt, and cap, all belonging to the shorter and, in places, wider Jason Manguson. Since only Matt's "police civies" were packed in the luggage that Luke had retrieved from Paddington Station, and since nothing suitable for *this* occasion was contained therein, only the shoes on his feet were actually his.

He knew that the twins' appearance of relaxed, yet focused, comfort was a result of more than the mere fact that they were once again in their own clothing. And he knew that his impetuous act of volunteering for a genuinely perilous intelligence gathering mission was prompted by pure bravado, and that he had regretted the act almost from the first moment he had asked Rebecca and Luke, and then Elisabeth Manguson, for permission to accompany them.

Unlike Luke, his experience and training as a Naval officer had included almost nothing that could contribute to the success of this planned incursion. The one exception was his having twice qualified as a Sharpshooter in the use of military rifles and side arms in enclosed

166

firing ranges. But, in his mind, of greater concern by far were the appalling uncertainties inherent in the endeavor. They would conduct this raid without advance knowledge of the enemy's dispositions, his strength in firepower, or his strength in numbers. They did have at least some knowledge of the character of the enemy, but it was not encouraging, in that it underscored Meredith Lancaster's propensity for selecting henchmen from those who had served time in British jails for the commission of violent crimes against men, women, and children.

For their own part, they were two men and a woman, carrying one rifle, Luke's set of knives of varying size and purpose, several coils of multi-purpose line and rope, two miniature document cameras, two pair of binoculars, and *accoutrement* appropriate to the mission. They had no information about the documents the photographing of which formed the purpose of the raid: Lancaster's calendars, schedules, memoranda, and the like.

Further contributing to Matt's remorse at his hasty decision to volunteer was his uncertain view of himself. He knew that the *Legati* assumed divine protection as a matter of course in all their endeavors. If a thing had been ordered, then one simply threw oneself into it, planning in as much detail and with as much care as possible, and executing the task with all the vigor, resourcefulness, and courage that one could muster. Beyond that, it seemed that one was to proceed without extended contemplation of the likelihood of the mission's overall success, and—here was the daunting aspect to Matt—without consideration of personal consequences. He felt inadequate as a new and "provisional" Christian, unworthy of this venture and, especially, unworthy as a comrade-in-arms for Luke and Rebecca.

The drive to Lancaster's Cambridge-area headquarters had been routine. Rebecca had navigated the assortment of roadways leading out of the Birmingham region with such skill and aplomb that Matt had soon stopped attending to the vehicle's passage entirely, allowing his thoughts to alternate between the joy of sitting inches from Rebecca's left arm and hand as she moved the sedan's shift lever continually through its gears, and his own questionable emotional and spiritual condition.

Upon reflection, he saw with a sort of detached curiosity that he harbored no doubts at all regarding the divinely commanded nature of their mission. He had seen enough and felt enough in his experiences with his mother's diaries, with the members of the *Legati,* and with his own formative ventures into prayer to feel confident in the reality of their charge. To his surprise, he felt this no less, now that he was approaching enemy territory, than he had while still back at the mansion. The fact that, in his case, none of this seemed to translate itself into the self-confident, self-assured demeanor that he saw in Rebecca and Luke formed itself into a hard core of uncertainty around which his sense of inadequacy threatened to grow to overwhelming proportions.

Rebecca and Luke had said little on the drive. The talking and planning had been completed at the mansion, in the presence of Sid Belton, who had abandoned his initial reticence. The detective and Luke had taken the lead over Rebecca and Matt in the planning process, a reflection, in Sid Belton's case, of his experience with police assault units and, beyond that, of his familiarity with Lancaster's farmhouse headquarters and its terrain; and, in Luke's case, of his specialized training with the Royal Navy in organizing and leading boarding party actions, a form of high-risk embarkation onto hostile decks often resulting in hand-to-hand combat both close and sanguine.

The rules of engagement had been made clear by the senior Mangusons during the final presentation of the proposed plan of action. Luke would be in command of the raid. His father's old, bolt-action hunting rifle was the only firearm that would be allowed, and Luke's versatile set of knife blades the only other weaponry of any kind. In addition, the Mangusons gave strict orders that the weapons could be employed only under direct and lethal threat, to save the life of any person, including their own, and that the weapons were to be employed, if at all, in a non-lethal manner wherever possible. These constraints were not merely noted in the midst of a litany of instructions; they were explained in detail and then extensively reinforced through a series of hypotheticals posed by Elisabeth and Jason. In response to each hostile scenario offered, the three members of the raiding party were required to formulate oral responses consistent with the specified rules of engagement. Matt found the planning and, especially, the presentation to, and the testing by, the senior Mangusons exhausting. He had, thus, felt himself enervated by the time they departed, but now, as the three gathered themselves for the moonlit climb to the hilltop farmhouse, the excitement and dread of the actual events were upon him.

Leaving the automobile in a tangled knot of scrub one hundred yards from the narrow roadway, near the base of the ridge on which the farmhouse property rested, and slightly more than a mile of straight-line, sloping distance from the farmhouse itself, they moved wordlessly through the mixed underbrush and clusters of young trees that populated the lower spurs of the ridge. The bright three-quarter moon made artificial light unnecessary for the moment, though gathering, fast-moving cloud cover would soon threaten.

Matt trailed the twins, the loaded hunting rifle at port arms, its safety switch on. He found himself mysteriously awash in thoughts unrelated to the objective. At times he recalled yet again his mother's oldest diaries and her unshakable commitment to Christianity in the midst of similar danger. At other times, as the threesome moved steadily and silently upward through thickening vegetation, Matt looked up at the moonlit black-clad woman just in front of him, her hair swinging hypnotically from side to side in the action-ready ponytail she favored for tennis and running. Mostly he fought the urge to move to her side, to place his arm around her shoulders, and to reassure her that he would protect her at all costs. At one point his thoughts raced ahead even of that fantasy, and his imagination saw him throwing himself between her and a stream of machine gun bullets, then dying slowly in her arms as her tears fell on his face and she confessed her love for him. He shook his head violently, as if in hopes of physically tossing the lunacy out of his brain.

And he thought of fear and Christianity. It seemed to him that the twins' calm certainty in their Christianity and in the eternal life that Christ had promised infused them with a courage that was itself super-natural. They did not seem to need to steel themselves to face danger, as he himself was continually attempting to do. They seemed only to need to understand precisely where their Christian duty lay, and, once that was clear, they simply moved in the direction of that duty. If that direction happened to be routine or unchallenging, then they accepted that and engaged the task. If that direction happened to be extraordinary or danger-laden, then they accepted that and engaged *that* task.

And that put him unexpectedly in mind of a gripping sentence from the Merton book, one that his mother had shown him just before they departed the mansion, in a private farewell before they walked together to the car. "Our duties and our needs," he had written in *Mountain*, "in all the fundamental things for which we were created, come down in practice to the same thing." That sentence had immediately become still another treasure in his mind amidst a storehouse of treasures from his mother, coming, as had so often been the case in his life, at a moment when his duties had seemed too much for him to face.

With his mother's help, Matt had decided that he actually *felt* like a Christian, in that he acknowledged intellectually and emotionally the belief that had been growing in him. But he also knew that he had little of the settled, rationally developed certainty that Rebecca and Luke displayed, and perhaps none of the paradoxically humble and relaxed assurance borne of prayerful experience that, he was learning, seemed to move a Christian's focus outside himself, and toward others . . . toward duty . . . toward joy . . . toward perhaps the only sustainable happiness that human beings can reliably embrace.

Suddenly he looked up. Rebecca and Luke had each dropped to one knee, and Luke's hand was raised behind him, palm toward Matt. Almost at the same instant all moonlight was extinguished by low, scudding, black clouds that reduced the landscape in seconds to a close-in mass of ghostly shapes and the disembodied hand signal from Luke, some ten feet ahead. Just over Luke's barely visible hand, Matt then saw in the medium distance the lights of the farmhouse. He realized that the clearing must be no more than a few feet in front of them, the same clearing, he thought to himself, over which his parents had attempted to flee just twenty-four hours earlier.

Luke dropped his hand and Matt, cradling the rifle, crept forward to a position on Luke's right. Rebecca was on her brother's left. She had slipped her backpack from her shoulders and, in a silent gesture dimly visible in the new darkness, inquired of the men as to whether or not they wished the binoculars. Both assented.

Rising to a high kneel, Luke and Matt, field glasses to their eyes, scanned the first and second floor lights, the front porch, and those portions of the open lawn made visible to them by the interior lighting. They saw three dark sedans, one of them a black Mercedes. They whispered to each other the count of men they could see through the windows, and agreed after several moments that there were at least seven who could be counted to that point.

The men lowered the field glasses and relaxed, and the three now maneuvered themselves into sitting positions with small trees or, in Matt's case, a flat outcropping of rock at their backs. The plan had been formed on the assumption that, as was the case during the Clarks' captivity, a skeleton crew would remain on guard at the farmhouse overnight. Sid Belton expected a different, more professional, more violent, and probably more ruthless group of men than those he and his "boys" had so easily dispatched the previous night.

Their plan also contained the assumption that, if the guards could be evaded or subdued successfully, Rebecca and Luke would busy themselves photographing documents while Matt would create the appearance of burglary by moving small objects of value—vases, paintings, and the like—to the basement or the attic. The point of this simple ruse was to induce Lancaster, seeing no theft of his documents, to conclude that the same parties who freed his prisoners the night before had now returned to steal whatever valuables had caught their collective eye at that time.

Rebecca had protested that Lancaster was, in her view, unlikely to follow such a diversion under circumstances in which his fortress headquarters had been forcibly penetrated twice in twenty-four hours. She made clear that, in her mind, it was more likely that he would conclude the truth: that his Dark Masters' old nemesis, the *Legati,* had been resurrected and had somehow produced both a rescue and a second mission that tried, but, it would appear to him, simply failed, to discover and steal the "Creed of St. David" that he had announced to the world earlier that same day. Lancaster would, said she, view the "theft" as the ruse that it, in fact, was.

Belton's reply had been generous. "You could be right, Miss Manguson," he had admitted. "But remember this. In the end, it won't make any difference what guesses Lancaster might make about these two raids on his farmhouse. He'll find his 'Creed of St. David' right there, undisturbed, in his safe. He'll find that his office looks just like it did when he left it. He'll think about the fact that everything went well for him in London today, and that the Sunday announcement is ready to go; and he'll remind himself that he'll have all kinds of security forces, both private and state, working for him at St. David's. He and his Masters aren't likely to worry much that an outfit like ours, even if they decide that there *is* an outfit like ours, can mess up this scheme he's cooked up. And, when you look at the kind of preparation he's made for this, ma'am, you gotta admit that our job is not gonna be a piece of cake. It's gonna be harder than anything you've done in your life so far, I'd be willin' to bet. But, like I said before, miss, I do like our chances. I like what I see of you young people. And, more than anything else, I like the fact that we got angels—real, honest-to-God angels—lined up with us. We got *real* good help on our team, people."

For Matt, in the warm darkness of the hilltop, the minutes passed slowly. After a time, he began, strangely, to feel himself growing sleepy. He peered through the darkness at his comrades. He could not make out any detail of Rebecca's face at a distance of perhaps fifteen feet, but he could see dimly that Luke, only half that distance from him, was rubbing his eyes and stifling a yawn. Just as Matt began to form the general shape of a thought regarding this improbable torpor, he saw Rebecca creeping forward to a position midway between the two men.

"Luke! Matt!" she whispered softly but sharply. "Something is happening to us. Do you *feel* the lethargy? Fight it! It's *them!* It's their Masters. Fight them!"

Matt saw Luke shake his head and swiftly pull himself forward into a low crouch. As he did, he looked toward the farmhouse and whispered, "Rebecca . . . Matt . . . look . . . they're moving."

The men raised the field glasses and trained them on the front porch. There they saw a group being addressed by . . . unmistakably . . . Meredith Lancaster. His face was turned toward the clearing across which the raiding party crouched just beyond the edge of the tree line.

He was speaking rapidly, gesticulating expansively and decisively, the others in his party arrayed in a silent semi-circle around him.

"I count eight of the henchmen, plus Lancaster," whispered Luke to Matt. "Look at the size of those characters. Looks like a prison rugby team."

Matt responded softly. "Yes. Eight, and Lancaster."

Matt extended the field glasses toward Rebecca, who declined with a small gesture of her hand.

As they watched, most of the men began to move toward the vehicles. They saw Lancaster and two others climb into the black Mercedes and, moments later, four more step into a second sedan. The two vehicles rolled forward, made a wide turn, and, the Mercedes leading, exited the broad clearing by the single driveway, passing well to the right of Rebecca and the men as the two sedans started down the long, switch-back roadway which would take them eventually within one hundred yards of the Mangusons' car, hidden in the trees, and then to the highway back to Cambridge.

Matt and Luke, still peering through their field glasses, observed the two remaining men in conversation with each other for several moments. Then, to their disappointment, a third figure, even more physically imposing than his rough-hewn colleagues, stepped onto the porch carrying two powerful automatic rifles, handed one to each, and stepped back into the farmhouse. Immediately, the two newly armed men left the porch. One took a position in front, near the remaining automobile, and faced the driveway as it disappeared from his view not too far distant from the spot in the underbrush where the threesome waited. The other moved round the house and took a position near two enormous chestnut trees, their trunks just visible at the fading edges of the weak light escaping the rear windows. This sentry, too, was able to face the driveway's exit from his position to the rear and side of the farmhouse, so that both guards were looking generally in the raiding party's direction, their automatic rifles at the ready. Matt found this disconcerting in itself, even though he was confident that he and the twins could not be seen from their hidden positions in such complete blackness. He realized, nonetheless, that he very much wanted to drop to a prone position and crawl away from the clearing as fast as possible.

He resisted that temptation with more difficulty than he wished to admit even to himself.

Luke was whispering to them both. "Don't take your eyes from the windows. We still can't assume that there is but one additional guard."

A full fifteen minutes afterward, Luke motioned in the darkness for both Rebecca and Matt to move to his side. "I'm satisfied," he whispered quickly, "that we'll face only what we've seen: two outside and one inside. I want us to take the next hour to move at least three hundred yards straight back down the hill, then, clockwise, round the hill to positions 180 degrees from here, then back up the hill to the opposite edge of the clearing. We'll move on them from there."

Without further conversation, Rebecca placed each pair of binoculars in her backpack, Matt checked again the safety switch on the rifle, and they moved, at first creeping, then, after fifty yards, standing and walking softly, back down the ridge. As Luke had directed, they reached a point less than a quarter mile from their initial reconnaissance position, turned to their right, and moved laterally round the hill. Since the hill was actually part of an extended ridge line, the lateral movement included one short, steep climb, far in the rear of, and still below, the farmhouse, and a corresponding descent. After roughly forty-five minutes of maneuver, they turned again to their right, moved up the hill to a position generally across the clearing from their original post, and repeated the process of examining the objective, the men using the field glasses to study the positions and readiness of the outside guards, whose backs were now exposed to the raiding party.

At length, Luke drew his comrades to him and whispered, "It looks as if it's Plan C for us. Agreed? Right, then . . . Matt, we'll eliminate the rear sentry first . . . Rebecca? Ready?"

In the intense darkness, Rebecca, her face inches from her brother's, nodded, then turned, and produced something from her backpack that Matt could not at first see. Moving behind the men so that they were between her and the farmhouse, she switched on one of the hooded flashlights that she carried in the pack, and, her hands nestled deep in the low underbrush, gave the flashlight to her brother, who, with Matt, had turned toward her. The men moved their faces so near to hers that all three heads nearly touched, and, with the beam from the flashlight illuminating the pages of her little Anglican prayer book, Rebecca read in a soft whisper:

> O most powerful and glorious Lord God, the Lord of hosts, that rulest and commandest all things . . . Stir up thy strength, O Lord, and come and help us; for thou givest not alway the battle to the strong, but canst save by many or by few. O let not our sins now cry against us for vengeance; but hear us thy poor servants begging mercy, and imploring thy help, and that thou wouldest be a defence unto us against the face of the enemy. . . .

She closed the book, placed it in her pack, took the darkened flashlight from Luke, returned it also to her pack, then reached in the blackness for both men's hands. She held their hands—Luke's left and Matt's right—against her face, her eyes closed. She then kissed first one hand and then the other, squeezed them tightly, and whispered softly, "Amen."

Then, releasing their hands, she removed from her pack a small can of shoe black. She opened it and held it while Luke smeared his face with the substance. He then held the can for her while she did the same. She returned the can to her pack, produced a pair of tight-fitting, dark leather driving gloves, and helped her brother slip them snugly onto his hands. She and Matt then waited while Luke removed the set of knives from his belt holster, slid the longest from its sheath, and snapped the huge, terrifying weapon into its universal handle, a steel handle large and heavy enough in itself to serve as a formidable blunt instrument.

Rebecca and Luke then nodded their readiness to each other and to Matt, who slowly turned toward the farmhouse again, dropped carefully to his chest in the prickly undergrowth, and, still cradling the hunting rifle, crept forward to the very edge of the clearing. He then switched the rifle's safety to the off position, raised the stock to his right shoulder, and, left elbow driven hard into the soft ground, sighted down the barrel onto the rear sentry's broad back.

He felt Rebecca at his side, on his left, and heard her voice in his ear. "Ready?" she whispered.

He nodded, not taking his eyes from the sentry. He heard her quiet, slow movement away from the clearing, angling back down the hill and to Matt's left, and then, nothing. He felt Luke at his right side. "We'll give her ten minutes, as planned," he whispered to Matt. "Relax your muscles. Breathe."

They waited.

Ten minutes exactly passed, Luke checking his watch periodically. He then whispered again to Matt, "Now."

At this, Matt resumed his previous level of taut readiness, barrel again trained on the rear sentry's spine, left elbow anchored firmly in the ground. He took a deep breath. "Now," he whispered.

He heard Luke also draw a deep, full breath. Then he heard him exhale, long and slow. Matt saw in the corner of his eye, as Luke rose to a crouch, the huge knife blade in his left hand. And then he was gone.

Luke, running with amazing speed in a half crouch, held the knife near the ground, his head up. He ran just to the right of Matt's line of sight, giving Matt a clear target should the sentry wheel to fire the automatic rifle at this onrushing visitant of death. Simultaneously, Matt heard crashing noises deep in the woods at the front of the clearing; it was Rebecca, he knew, distracting the front sentry in concert with Luke's rush at the rear.

As Luke, now racing at top speed, closed to within ten yards of the unsuspecting guard, his opponent heard him and turned, frozen by the sight of blackened face and glint of steel, his high-velocity weapon unready to fire and already useless for the hand-to-hand encounter now but a microsecond away. The knife still in his left hand, Luke, now virtually flying, drove his open right hand upward, the rock-hard base of his palm smashing into its intended target with the force and impact of a sledgehammer. Struck at the base of his nose by this thundering apparition, the sentry's head snapped back, his nose broken. He collapsed as a felled tree, unconscious from the instant of contact, Luke falling on top of him, the flat of the knife blade against the anterior carotid artery at the side of the exposed neck.

Matt, seeing the astounding force of the collision, raised the rifle barrel slightly and cut his eyes all the way to the left. He saw the front sentry, his rifle raised and his hand on the trigger, moving warily but rapidly away from the farmhouse, peering intently at the edge of the clearing opposite the site of Luke's successful rush. Matt was satisfied with this glance that Rebecca's diversion had succeeded. He moved his eyes back to the scene at the rear of the farmhouse and saw that Luke had already begun to truss the unconscious sentry's hands and feet with the coils of line that he carried on his belt. With lightning speed, Luke secured the hands and the ankles, used a short, separate length of line to secure these two knots to each other so that there was no possibility of the man either using his hands or, upon regaining full consciousness, trying to rise to his feet. Matt saw Luke then, with equal speed, blindfold the victim and drag the limp form from the dim light at the rear of the house to a position well beyond the circle of accidental illumination that it cast.

As the incapacitated sentry was removed from Matt's sight, he swung his rifle to the left and trained the barrel on the other guard, who was now backing slowly toward the farmhouse, continuing to stare in the direction of Rebecca's distracting activity, the automatic rifle still at near-firing position, his hand on the trigger. At the extreme right periphery of his vision, Matt then saw Luke reappear from the shadows of the large chestnuts at the rear of the farmhouse, once more in his half crouching run, now circling the near side of the farmhouse, ducking low as he moved past each window. Reaching a point near the front porch just forty yards away from, and behind, the second sentry, he paused to position the knife once more in his left hand, and held the blade aloft briefly, this to permit Rebecca, far off across the clearing, to see his readiness, and to ensure with this signal that Matt's rifle was now trained on the new adversary. This time Matt saw rather than heard Luke's long, slow inhale and exhale, then heard the indistinct, animal-like crashing noises in the brush far off to the left, and, at the same moment, watched the sentry bring his rifle to his shoulder and move forward again toward the front of the clearing as Luke sprang from his crouch and closed from behind at his swift, terrible run.

The next few seconds remained forever confused in Matt's mind. As Luke closed on the sentry, again covering the final yards at his top speed, Matt saw a movement from the front porch and immediately swung the barrel of the hunting rifle to his right, sited the barrel at this new target, and without hesitation pulled the trigger.

Matt felt the stinging recoil of the rifle against his shoulder. The bullet exploded from the muzzle a full second after the third guard opened fire at Luke's sprinting figure. The guard, having blasted through the front door onto the near side of the porch, had crouched quickly to fire at Luke's flying form with a huge, long-barreled handgun held at eye level and aimed professionally with a two-handed grip. Matt's single rifle shot was precise, the bullet appearing to strike the enormous man on the side of his left kneecap. The impact sent him sprawling and crashing wildly onto the porch steps, careening head first, screaming obscenities, the monstrous pistol flying off into the darkness. Without waiting to assess any of this, Matt found himself on his feet and running toward the writhing, cursing gunman, working the bolt action on the old hunting rifle in readiness for a second shot.

As he approached in his loping sprint, Matt saw the man, still venting a continuous stream of unintelligible oaths, roll completely off the porch steps and onto the ground, holding his shattered knee with both hands. Quickly, Matt braked to a halt and pivoted to his left, swinging his rifle in the direction of Luke. He found his comrade on the ground, engaged in a violent, rolling struggle with the front sentry. Pausing only long enough to confirm that the sentry's automatic rifle was not in his possession, but on the grass some six feet from the furiously grappling combatants, Matt turned again to his right and ran several strides past the wounded guard, looking in the weak light for the long-barreled handgun.

Finding it quickly in the short grass to the side of the steps, he gripped the heavy pistol in his right hand, his finger on its trigger, and, now holding the hunting rifle mid-barrel and at the vertical in his left hand, ran toward Luke, the pistol raised to fire. He arrived seconds before Rebecca, herself a startling figure with her face blackened and her ponytail flying out behind her at the end of her long sprint from the perimeter. Still running, Matt dodged around the wrestling figures only long enough to place the hunting rifle in Rebecca's hands as she brought her sprint to a stop. He then wheeled into the fray, still holding the pistol at the ready. He found the sentry rising from the ground, fighting free of Luke, who, Matt sensed, seemed somehow not to be moving normally. As the sentry stretched toward Luke's knife which, Matt now saw for the first time, was no longer in Luke's hand but lying in the grass just beyond his reach, Matt hurled himself into the man, at the same time driving the butt of the heavy handgun into his temple. The sentry fell with a thud, unconscious.

Matt, his body fully extended at the instant of impact, rolled onto the ground, having fallen almost on top of his opponent. Matt quickly confirmed the sentry's apparent unconsciousness, stabbing the man's unprotected abdomen hard with the pistol barrel, using enough force to elicit a sharp muscular and respiratory response from any conscious person. He found the sentry inert. He then rose to one knee and looked immediately back toward the farmhouse. There he saw the third guard, now silent, curled into a ball, his face turned away and buried in his chest, rocking back and forth almost under the front porch, and still holding his fractured kneecap in both hands.

Matt then turned back to his comrades and saw that Rebecca had hurriedly picked up the sentry's automatic weapon and had placed it, along with the hunting rifle, some twenty yards from the men, barrels facing away, and was starting back toward them in her graceful sprint. She ran straight to her brother, and she and Matt together bent over Luke, who remained prostrate, face buried in the coarse grass. As Matt had suspected from Luke's dogged but unexceptional performance against the second sentry, he had been hit by at least one of the shots from the porch.

Wheeling to pick up the long knife, Matt moved nearly astride Luke and swiftly sliced his left trousers leg from waist to knee, exposing two wounds. A single round from the powerful handgun had passed through the muscle of Luke's left thigh. The entry and exit holes pulsed blood at an alarming rate and volume. Matt then cut away the left trousers leg entirely, sliced the fabric into two strips, and, with Rebecca's assistance, applied both a tourniquet wrap at the top of the thigh and a staunch wrap directly over the twin bullet holes. The effects of the double wrap became obvious in just seconds as the blood flow diminished to an almost imperceptible seepage.

No sooner had Matt completed the second wrap and sat back on his haunches to breathe for a moment than he heard Luke's whisper, insistent, hissed through gritted teeth. "Get blindfolds on these blokes right now, Matt. I don't want them to see Rebecca, or anything else. *Move now!*"

Fewer than twenty frenetic minutes later, Rebecca, having donned a pair of the detective's evidence gloves, pushed fully open the half-closed door to Meredith Lancaster's second-floor office. She flicked the light switch and surveyed the enemy's inner sanctum. She could hear in the late-night silence the distant sound of Matt's tread, as he moved around the first floor rooms, removing art objects as suggested by the detective and gingerly carrying them down the basement steps to a remote storage recess that he had quickly found after the two of them had entered the farmhouse.

Luke remained on the porch, sitting with his back against the outside wall, one of the captured automatic weapons across his lap and the other, along with the hunting rifle, beside him. Although in obvious pain from his wound, he had not relinquished command of the mission, and had given explicit instructions to Rebecca and Matt regarding the disposition of the sentries prior to allowing the two of them to enter the farmhouse.

Matt had begun by dragging the wounded guard, blindfold in place, his bleeding leg and knee wrapped in a fashion similar to Luke's, across the twenty yards of open ground to the remaining vehicle. There, with assistance from Rebecca, he had lifted his victim, hands bound behind his back, into the rear seat. In accordance with Luke's instructions, Matt left both rear doors open, so that the injured man's movements, if any, could be seen from the porch. Matt and Rebecca had then placed the front sentry, blindfolded, trussed, and still unconscious, on the ground near the vehicle. Luke had been confident that the rear sentry would be unable to move even an inch from his position behind the chestnut trees at the rear of the building, should he manage to regain consciousness while the raiding party remained on the premises. Luke then sat watching the second and third guards, but remained on maximum alert primarily against the return of Lancaster and his still intact corps of convicted murderers, torturers, kidnappers, and armed robbers.

Rebecca, her gloved hand lingering near the light switch, scanned Lancaster's spacious office. She sensed, rather than saw, framed art work of a macabre genre prominently displayed on all four dark-colored walls, including the front-facing wall that overlooked the porch roof and the front clearing. Her eyes traveled back to a large desk with a high-backed chair, then to two enormous tables, each covered with documents, files, and boxes apparently awaiting packing. She saw between the two tables a blocky, metallic green, waist-high safe with its black combination dial protruding from the center of its door. The rest of the office seemed to hold nothing of interest to her: a few pieces of badly upholstered furniture, more empty boxes resting on the dark carpet, and several wheeled lift carts and metal briefcases, all appearing to await packing. Meredith Lancaster was ready to move.

Rebecca fought an insistent urge to rush her assignment. She desperately wanted to fly down the wooded hill to their auto, bring the car at best speed up the twisting road to the farmhouse, lay her wounded brother onto the seat, and drive him away toward Birmingham and Dr. Sutton's ministrations.

Working against this in her mind was Luke's stern reminder, issued just minutes earlier, to remember that the success of the larger mission depended almost entirely upon the thoroughness with which she examined and photographed Lancaster's documents. Forcing herself to move deliberately, she stepped to Lancaster's desk and began at once to move methodically through his papers. Returning each to its place before moving on, she efficiently photographed item after item, finishing in just five minutes those on the desk and then turning to the two large tables. Although she did not take time actually to read the material that she photographed, she found herself increasingly pleased. It seemed that much that she recorded with the document cameras was indeed the sort of thing the detective considered critical: schedules, agendas, calendars, diagrams, maps, memoranda. After nearly forty more minutes of intense activity, she heard heavy footsteps on the stairs and then Matt's voice, soft, but purposely loud enough for her to recognize at the first syllable. "Rebecca? Rebecca? It's me. Just coming to see if I can help."

He stopped at the door and she turned to him. She was aware of the sinister image created by her blackened face in Lancaster's dark-walled office. "I'm nearly finished, Matt. How is Luke doing?"

"He's fine, Rebecca. He must be in great pain, but he is, to say the least, alert, and ready for anything with that arsenal he has in his lap."

"Please tell him I won't be fifteen minutes more."

"I will," he replied, and turned to go.

"Matt?" she added, and he stopped and looked back at her. "Thank you. You saved him, Matt. You saved us all."

He nodded, smiled at her, and moved away, down the corridor past the second floor parlor which, he realized vaguely, must have been the room in which his parents had been held captive throughout the week preceding. Starting down the staircase, he worked at pushing away the self-congratulatory edifice that he habitually built in his mind after any pronounced success and, even more, after any such pointed acknowledgment of his success as that just supplied by Rebecca. This simple expedient of pushing prideful indulgence into a mental corner brought a quiet smile to his face. Before his extraordinary series of experiences that he had begun to categorize nonspecifically as "Christian," it would not have occurred to him to make this small internal gesture. But it now truly seemed to Matt that the more he placed his confidence in God— especially in the divine protection that the *Legati* so clearly assumed—the more capable and resourceful he somehow became.

He stopped near the base of the staircase. "No," he thought to himself. That really wasn't it.

He considered for a moment. What was it, then? And he knew.

The more he placed his confidence in God, the "truer" his thoughts and actions became. That *was* it. And then he realized that it was precisely this which would allow him honestly to acknowledge that, in point of fact, he *had* done exceptionally well in that night's fierce combat with the three guards. Just as Rebecca had finally understood with her mother's help years earlier that she was allowed to acknowledge her own beauty and talent in a certain way, Matt had now begun to understand tentatively that a Christian was not required, in the name of humility, to pretend that something done well had not, in fact, been done well. He was allowed to acknowledge excellence in himself in the same way that he would acknowledge it in someone other than himself. And he could, in that way, experience the same unbiased joy in his own performance as he would in Rebecca's, or Luke's, or his mother's. It was a matter of acknowledging the Source, and of knowing where the "credit" actually lay. It was a matter of learning to live in the only true joy: the joy of "real Reality." He smiled again, almost laughing aloud at the elegance and simplicity of it all. He took the final three steps quickly, and walked onto the porch to relay Rebecca's message to Luke.

Luke looked up at Matt, all three rifles still crowded around him within easy reach from his seated position. "Good show, Matt," he replied. "If you'll help me up, I'll take a look at your *faux* thievery in the main rooms before we go."

Within five minutes of Matt's departure from Lancaster's office, Rebecca stepped back from the second of the two document tables. It seemed to her that her mission was complete, but she wanted to move back to the doorway to survey the room from that longer perspective before leaving. She wanted to be certain that there were no photographic targets that she had missed from the close range at which she had worked since her arrival, and to confirm that there was no obvious trace of her having been present. She reached the entrance to the office and turned back to survey Lancaster's dark lair for the last time. Avoiding the distraction of the disgusting framed art on his walls, her gray eyes moved systematically around the room. She had almost completed this visual sweep when her eyes came to rest on a small mahogany table beside one of the upholstered chairs, a chair situated directly under a brass floor lamp. She realized then that a single file folder had been placed on the table by someone who had chosen to sit in that well-worn chair, rather than at his desk, to review its contents. As Rebecca stepped to the small table to remove the folder, the thought flashed through her mind that this file perhaps contained something that Meredith Lancaster wished to reflect upon at more length than the sort of routine memoranda that he handled at his desk. She reached the table, took careful note of the folder's position so that she could place it again at just the same angle to the chair, and carried it to one of the long tables in preparation for photographing the contents.

Document camera at the ready, she opened the folder to scan the heading:

Confidential Report to Mr. Lancaster: June __, 19__
Subject: Rebecca Jane Manguson

Stunned, her eyes moved directly to the text as if drawn by Forces infinitely stronger than herself.

Overview: This twenty-six-year-old is a woman of staggering beauty, physical gifts, and intellectual capacity. Of all the young adults in England on whom we should concentrate in order to move them to our side, Sir, she is absolutely of the first rank. This would be the case, we wish to emphasise, even without her possible foretelling capacity. [We place some stress on this, Sir, because, if she were to serve with us, that particular capacity, made available to her by the Enemy, would, we think it prudent to assume, no longer be available to her.]

If she could be converted to the cause, she could reasonably be expected to carry forth the banner of our new creed as its leading spokesperson, not merely in the UK, but in the USA and around the world. Since she has not been in any way associated with the development of the creed, she would speak with an apparently "impartial" and "unbiased" voice, the voice of one converted to the truth of the new creed by the purity and authenticity of its content and history. There could be no more compelling image for our project than this articulate young woman, a gifted and forceful public speaker who demonstrates a most persuasive and attractive conviction to audiences of all types and sizes.

With the political, corporate, and media platform that we would readily provide for her, she could in a moment's time come to be seen internationally as the face of the Creed of St. David. It is our considered view, Sir, that, other than yourself, of course, no more dynamic, vibrant, and persuasive face could be found to lead in the promulgation of our creed to the millions who would be drawn inevitably to her and, through her, to our creed.

Miss Manguson's striking, captivating image on the covers of newsmagazines in all major markets, in newspapers around the world, in televised interviews in all English-speaking nations, and, once we have used our most persuasive forces with our agents in California, in motion pictures or, perhaps better, in a series of motion pictures, first in the USA and then. . . .

Rebecca stopped reading, placed her camera on the page, removed her gloves, and stepped back from the table, hands perspiring, pulse racing. She turned her back on the Confidential Report on Rebecca Jane Manguson and raised her eyes to the front wall of Lancaster's office. She found herself staring at one of the framed prints that she earlier had missed. It was unlike the others. It portrayed a young woman with striking gray eyes and long, flowing, black hair, physically prepossessing, beautiful and seductive, moving toward her on billowing clouds of glory.

Rebecca's chin lifted ever so slightly, suggestive, had there been an impartial observer to see it, of Meredith Lancaster's most characteristic mannerism. The Confidential Report's phrases coursed rapidly and dramatically through her mind: ". . . striking, captivating image on the covers of newsmagazines in all major markets. . . . a series of motion pictures. . . ." It was preposterous. It was ludicrous. And yet, despite herself, in that Evil-filled room, she found her mind indulgently fondling the idea of such influence, such power, such *worldwide* fame. . . .

Suddenly Rebecca felt a vise-like grip on each of her shoulders. She turned her head first to one side and then the other, but saw nothing. The pressure built in seconds to levels that seemed to her superhuman, driving her inexorably toward the floor. Sound escalated in her ears . . . a howling, screaming cacophony . . . a deafening, horrifying clamor in the silence of Lancaster's office . . . nausea rising inside her abdomen and throat. . . . She understood dimly that she was now on her knees and being pushed forward onto her hands. The weight increased steadily with grinding inevitability, forcing her forward and downward. Her face neared the dark carpet, and she turned her eyes first to one of her own hands and then the other. She saw the veins on the back of each hand standing out from the skin surface, muscles straining against an Irresistible Force. Steel bands seemed to have formed around her chest, tightening with such inhuman demand that to breathe again was impossible.

For an eternity of seconds, she remained unmoving on her hands and knees, her face two inches from the floor, her black ponytail falling down the right side of her neck and curling darkly into the carpet, rivulets of sweat now beginning to pour down her blackened face to fall to the carpet from her nose and chin. Low groans from the physically devastating effort now began to issue from deep in her chest. She became aware that the muscles in her upper and lower arms and in the back of her neck had started to quiver uncontrollably from the unremitting strain of sustained maximum effort. She heard sounds from her own throat as if an animal's— strange, strangled, rattling, inarticulate. Then, in a convulsion generated from the core of her Christian being, Rebecca forced from her agonized center a moaning, scarcely audible cry: *"Father . . . help . . . me."*

The next sensation Rebecca experienced was impossible: She heard her name. She heard her name pronounced, but she knew it had not been spoken. The shape of her name had been transmitted to her, not formed by human mouth, throat, and lungs. Her name came to her as a thunderous rumble of such depth and power that the howling cacophony was silenced in the same instant in which the first syllable of her name reached her.

And she knew in that instant what, if not who, had shaped her name. She knew that triumphant supernature had driven her Attackers from her, and that only the *Nuntiae* could have acted in instantaneous and overwhelming response to her desperate cry, acting in uncompromising and everlasting opposition to the Dark Masters who had held her until the moment of that cry.

And she also understood in a flash of recognition precisely what each of her dreams had foretold. She saw that this was the threat that her dreams had warned of . . . the something worse than death . . . not the universal and inconsequential certainty of physical, earthly expiration . . . but the active and perpetual horror of Death Eternal.

Later, she would not be able to remember when, after her desperate plea to God the Father, she had been able finally to relax her burning muscles and blessedly to lower her body and her face the remaining inches to the floor. But Rebecca would remember for the rest of her life her own desolate appeal from the edge, and the force of supernature's response, and the corresponding and immediate certainty of salvation from the Voracious Evil of Meredith Lancaster's infernal Masters. And she knew that all this had come in no more than a few swift seconds of earthly time . . . and in no time at all by eternal measure.

She remained unmoving for two more exhausted minutes, breathing, not thinking. Then, still prone, she brought her powerful hands to her face and prayed aloud, softly and urgently, now beginning to sob quietly, tears flowing into her open palms, "Father, forgive me . . . Father, please forgive me. . . ."

Gradually, her weeping began to diminish. Still prone, she wiped caked tears and salt perspiration from her blackened, smeared, still-wet face with her ungloved hands. After two deeply drawn breaths, having pronounced her quiet *Amen,* she pushed herself carefully up from the floor, first to a kneeling position, then, after a pause, to her feet. She turned slowly to face once more the document table on which the Rebecca Jane Manguson file still lay.

Unsteadily at first, she stepped back to the long table, donned her evidence gloves, removed the camera from its place on top of the Confidential Report, closed the file with a shiver of mixed outrage and disgust, and carried the folder across the room. She placed it carefully on the mahogany table in the exact position in which she had found it, and strode back to the doorway.

She turned once more and faced Meredith Lancaster's office, eyes clear, head high. She pulled the door half closed with one gloved hand to approximate its original position, then switched off the overhead light with the other. In the nearly complete darkness she then perceived in her eyes' periphery the golden faces of the *Nuntiae:* beautiful, feminine, powerful.

Rebecca removed her gloves and carefully slipped them into her pack with the rest of the equipment. Then, in a gesture compelled by the visual presence of the great *Nuntiae,* she bowed her head, raised folded hands to her lips, and murmured softly, "Father, I give Thee thanks for commissioning Thy Messengers to my rescue in my time of greatest failure, in my time of greatest temptation, in the time of my soul's greatest and most eternal danger."

Her folded hands still at her lips, she raised her head, and, with glistening eyes, allowed her mind to concentrate on the beautiful faces, the Rescuers that had, in response to her cry to God the Father, removed the Enemies' claws from their deadly insertion points deep in her eternal soul. And Rebecca smiled: a small, shy smile.

Then she stepped back from the doorway, turned, and was gone.

Chapter Fourteen

REBECCA SWITCHED OFF THE IGNITION IN THE SMALL hours of Wednesday morning, having driven fast and hard to Birmingham from enemy headquarters. As she opened the car door, she saw both sets of parents already emerging from the mansion, the mothers in front, running. Rebecca stood quickly and spoke loudly and strongly in words designed to convey both reassurance and urgency: "The mission succeeded. Matt and I are fine. Luke is wounded in the thigh. He'll need Dr. Sutton at once."

No other words were spoken. Paul Clark, just stepping from the porch, and Jason Manguson, trailing Martha and Elisabeth, reversed course instantly, diving back into the mansion to return in moments with a cot-and-stretcher apparatus similar to the one used hours before with Lawrence Ashford. Luke had been weakening for some time, partly from physical and emotional exhaustion after the violence of hand-to-hand combat with the sentries, but more from intermittent loss of blood en route to Birmingham. Matt, squeezing himself into the narrow space between the auto's front and rear seats while Luke reclined insofar as was possible, had been forced to loosen and retie the tourniquet repeatedly so as to allow at least some blood flow to the leg, despite the hemorrhage produced each time by the maneuver.

As members of the group gathered around him and as he was helped onto the stretcher, Luke permitted himself to be handled as a battle casualty despite his contempt for the role—his inbred desire to thrust assistance aside. His apparently indulgent attitude toward the "handling" was a result of Rebecca's explicit warning, delivered just minutes before arrival at the mansion: "Luke," she had said firmly, "I

189

know you can't tolerate anyone's making a fuss over you. And Dr. Sutton, of course, will not; he will simply treat your wound and your pain. But Mum and Dad and everyone else will hover and smother. Let them, Luke. I mean it. Don't waste your energy explaining that you'll be fine with a little sleep. They won't believe you. Don't push them away from you. You'll just seem mean."

Luke had groaned at Rebecca's forceful directive. "Yes, Mother," had been his flippant response. But he knew that she had meant what she said, and he set his mind to follow her instruction with as much good cheer as he could summon. Where he and his sister were concerned, orders were both given and received without question, each to each; their respect for each other allowed roles to turn upside down in an eye blink. Either of them could be the other's equal, leader, or follower, all within a single conversation, all without either of them so much as noticing or attending to the change. Such is the nature of respect rightly conceived.

Tom Sutton approached his wounded patient as Rebecca had forecast: with brisk professionalism and distant courtesy. Within half an hour of their arrival, Luke's wound had been cleaned, treated, and dressed, and Jason Manguson had returned with the pain medication that, despite the post-midnight hour, Dr. Sutton had been able to order from an apothecary with whom the Mangusons had dealt for years, and whose discretion was beyond question. The physician administered the pain solution by injection, allowed the patient to decline the sleeping pill offered him, and sat by him until he slept.

Meanwhile, despite the hour, Elisabeth Manguson convened an emergency session with the six *Legati*, herself included, who were able to attend. The absent included Dr. Sutton, still at Luke's bedside, and Martha Clark, who now assumed the vigil with Lawrence Ashford.

The meeting began hastily in a tension-filled atmosphere despite which Rebecca, Matt, Paul Clark, and Sid Belton agreed quickly with the senior Mangusons that, as soon after sunrise as practicable, the detective and Paul, both amateur photographers, would take the film shot by Rebecca to a small nearby development lab that could be made privately available to them. Rebecca had protested that the detective would be thereby unable to attend mass for the third time in four days. He had responded to her with a seriousness of expression that she had not seen from him. "Miss Manguson," he had replied, "you're movin' heaven and earth on behalf of us and on behalf of everything that's good. You've already put your life on the line in service to God Almighty and all His angels, and there's more to come. You're takin' risks that I wouldn't allow my bravest men to take. I've never seen anything like it in my whole life, and if I can't miss mass one more time in order to help you just a little, I oughta just. . . ." His voice trailed off. He shook his head.

Analysis of the filmed documents, all agreed, would begin at the mansion as soon as the detective and Paul Clark returned with the developed film, probably by late morning. Allowing four to six hours for document analysis, a planning session—what the Mangusons preferred to call a "war counsel"—could begin at sundown. This would allow forty-eight hours of planning and preparation prior to, as everyone now grimly assumed, a Friday night sortie from Birmingham, and a Saturday night strike into the Welsh town of St. David's on the coast of Pembrokeshire. The raid would necessarily be conducted, all had come to realize, without its natural leader. The supreme, and possibly sacrificial, gesture, in fulfillment of the charge from the *Nuntiae—Protect the saint*—could ultimately be offered only by the two uninjured *Legati* having sufficient youth, stamina, and strength to make the attempt.

Everything would finally rest in the hands of Rebecca Manguson and Matthew Clark.

Some six hours later, as a shaft of the June sun's morning rays coursed through the filmy aperture created by the twin curves of her room's flowered curtains, Rebecca was awakened by the sound of persistent tapping. Sleepily, she forced her mind to attend to the muffled words seemingly spoken from a great distance: "Rebecca? Rebecca? May I come in, dear?"

Still more asleep than awake, Rebecca managed a weak, "Yes, Mum," and watched through half-closed lids as the doorknob turned.

Sleep had not come easily or quickly when she had collapsed into her bed earlier that morning. Her mind had churned crazily along through the overwhelming fatigue, its agitation surprisingly not driven by the effects of the supernatural battle for her soul from which she had emerged so narrowly. She had found, in fact, that her rescue by the *Nuntiae* and her overpowering sense of divine forgiveness had not only sanctified the experience for her, but had placed such a muscular benediction upon it that it seemed to her to have been almost a sacramental encounter. Those several most humiliating, terrifying, and elevating moments of her life had already been consigned by her memory to a place of quiet, blessed thanksgiving.

No, she had been kept wakeful by the gritty, grisly image of her brother's pulsing wound . . . by the blindfolded anguish of the sentry who had shot him, himself the immediate victim of Matt's rifled counterstroke . . . and by the astonishing, raw violence of the action even before shots had been fired. Until she had fallen into bed, there had been no time to process the sequence of events that she had faced at the farmhouse. She had had to remain focused, first, upon the photographic mission itself, and second, upon the mechanics of the fast, difficult drive from the farmhouse to the mansion.

But in the solitary darkness of her small bedroom, Rebecca had seen in her mind the rushing, roiling chaos of desperate hand-to-hand action, of gunfire, and of gunfire's wrenching flesh-and-bone carnage. With a suppressed moan, she had physically recoiled in her bed at the memory of the third guard's bursting onto the porch, raising his handgun to eye level, and opening fire at her brother as he hurtled, knife in hand, toward the unsuspecting sentry whom she herself had distracted. "No!" she had then cried from the dark and tangled thicket from which she had watched.

And in her bedroom in the small hours of that morning, she had spun onto her back, her gray eyes opened wide in the darkness as she saw herself running across the clearing toward the grappling combatants, unable to ascertain whether or not Luke had been wounded, and, if so, whether superficially or mortally. She felt again the wave of terror that she had fought into submission as she ran, her mind flying ahead of her racing feet in hopes of seizing upon a course of action that would save her brother's life. And she remembered the shadowy image of Matt's running figure, crossing first in front of her, near the porch, then sprinting toward her as he and she converged upon Luke, grappling in the dirt and grass with his adversary. And she brought to her mind in memory the utter calm that had seized her as she took the hunting rifle from Matt, stooped to lift the sentry's automatic weapon from the ground, turned to place both weapons at distance from the fighting men, then turned again to face . . . what?

It was at that point that she had sat up in her bed and switched on the light on her night stand. She had reached for her King James Bible, and instinctively had turned to the twenty-third Psalm. Though she knew the entire psalm by heart, she had read the lines aloud, softly, as was her wont, taking comfort not just from the reading of the familiar words themselves, but equally from the fact of their ancient origin, a fact made stronger and more concrete by the feel of the leather covers and the texture of the pages in her hands and the sound of the phrases made audible. She had let the psalmist's prayer wash over her, and in the process had felt herself strengthened again, cleansed in memory and steeled in anticipation:

> The Lord is my shepherd;
>> I shall not want.
> He maketh me to lie down in green pastures:
>> He leadeth me beside the still waters.
> He restoreth my soul:
>> He leadeth me in the paths of righteousness for
>> his Name's sake.
> Yea, though I walk through the valley of the shadow of death,
>> I will fear no evil:
> For Thou art with me;
>> Thy rod and Thy staff they comfort me.
> Thou preparest a table before me in the presence of mine enemies:
>> Thou annointest my head with oil;
> My cup runneth over.
> Surely goodness and mercy shall follow me all the days of my life:
>> And I will dwell in the house of the Lord for ever.

Now she felt her mother's gentle fingers moving across her face, carefully lifting her dark, confused tresses, at last freed from the constraints of the action-ready ponytail, away from her still half-closed eyes. And then once more the soft maternal voice. "I so much want you to sleep, darling, but I promised you that I would wake you early so that you could look in on Luke. He's sleeping, my dear, and Tom thinks he is unlikely to wake before noon. May I let you sleep until then? If he wakes earlier, I'll get you right away."

But Rebecca was already beginning to push herself into a sitting position. She rubbed her eyes slowly and shook her head. "No. I want to talk to you, Mum. Let me brush my hair and throw some water on my face. Can you stay? And will you call Dad?"

Fifteen minutes later, Jason Manguson arrived at Rebecca's room with a tray, hot tea, and three cups, in response to Elisabeth's request. He filled each cup, offered milk and sugar to the women, took his own, then looked inquiringly at his wife. "She'd like to speak with us both, dear, about last night," said Elisabeth. "I'm afraid we have taken the only chairs. Will you bring one for yourself from down the hallway?"

When her father was seated comfortably, Rebecca began: "I'm sure that some sort of action report will be necessary at this evening's session. My thinking is that the report should be kept abbreviated, so that we can all bring our best to the document analysis that Detective Belton and Dr. Clark will offer us. If you will let me tell you the details now, then perhaps the two of you can, some time during the day, decide how much needs to be presented tonight, and by whom. I'm hoping, I'll admit, to tell the story just once . . . and to you, rather than to all. I'm hoping that one of you might simply provide a summary this evening for the group, and that it will be sufficient."

And so she began. Rebecca felt herself oddly detached from the story as it unfolded from her lips. She omitted nothing that her memory could recover, knowing that her parents would be more reliable judges than she of which oddments might or might not have salience for the evening war counsel. When she reached the final scene at the farmhouse, the supernatural battle for her soul in Meredith Lancaster's office, she hesitated. The humiliation of her response to her great temptation, though laid to rest in her memory and in her soul through her prayers for forgiveness, rose again at the point of confessing her failure to her parents. Shame dropped like a veil in front of her face. She fell silent, her eyes at her feet.

Rebecca felt her mother's hand on hers. Then she sensed her father's movement from his chair, and realized he had moved around Elisabeth and had fallen to one knee in the small space between his wife and daughter, covering both their hands with his. The parents respected the daughter's silence, and did not themselves speak. Finally, Rebecca began again, and, with repeated pauses and lengthy searchings for language adequate to account for the phenomena, described her experiences following the discovery of the Confidential Report on Rebecca Jane Manguson. Each time her voice would catch in her throat and her hands clench in her lap, she would feel her parents' hands encompassing hers with theirs, adding their own layer of human, parental forgiveness to that divine pardon already granted.

At length she reached the conclusion to the high drama in Meredith Lancaster's office. She did not pause at that point, but continued rapidly to describe her long run to the car and then the demanding drives, first back to the farmhouse to retrieve Luke and Matt, then finally with her wounded and weakening brother from Cambridge to the mansion.

Rebecca stopped. She looked up at her mother. Elisabeth's eyes were ablaze with a mother's furious indignation, and Rebecca knew at what before Elisabeth spoke.

"How *dare* they!" said Elisabeth, her jaw clenched tight, muscles working in her face. "How *dare* they think that they could corrupt you to their cause! Do they understand *nothing* about their Opposition? Did they actually expect a mature Christian woman to toss away everything that is good and right and holy and eternal in order to get her face into newspapers and on *television?* What is *wrong* with these . . . these . . ."

"But Mum," Rebecca protested, "don't you see that I was indeed tempted? I was *not* immune. I was *not* above it all. I did, in fact, begin to imagine myself wearing that appalling cloak of fame and power and prominence. If it had not been for the great *Nuntiae* . . ."

"*No!* Rebecca," said her father, his voice unexpectedly loud, "that's *not* it."

His hands tightened around theirs. He looked away for several moments, and the women waited. When he resumed, his voice had softened, but only a little. "It's true that in that particular spot, in Meredith Lancaster's headquarters, Evil was so packed and wedged and compressed into that small space that the force of temptation was multiplied infinitely. And so your indulgence in the report's suggestion of Rebecca Jane Manguson's fame and power in the service of Evil proved all that the Dark Masters needed for their ambuscade. They had laid the trap as only they can, and the surprise of the onslaught drove you to your knees, figuratively and literally.

"But the point is that, even in a locus of Evil perhaps beyond any that exists on the entire planet at this moment, they could not prevent your calling out to Almighty God. Even then, even there, with every advantage that could possibly accrue, they *could not separate you from the love of God that is in Christ Jesus our Lord.* They could not do it. And they cannot do it. And that is the eternal point. You were *saved,* my darling daughter, through *your* decision to call upon the Lord, and *no* opposing Power could prevent it."

Matt shook himself mentally from his reverie. The evening war counsel had begun as Elisabeth Manguson often required, with a lengthy, silent preamble during which human and animal and super-natural creatures alike prepared themselves to consider their next steps in response to divinely commanded service. To Matt's mild surprise, Luke was present from the start, lying on his portable cot, his head elevated by pillows and his eyes flashing with anticipation. And Lawrence Ashford, too, had been allowed by Elisabeth to attend. He sat, looking pale and small, in a winged chair brought down into the meeting room from the first floor reading room by Matt and his father. Dr. Ashford was again flanked, Matt had noticed with a smile, by his mother and Dr. Sutton, their chairs touching his. And Matt had seen that Mildred had immediately curled herself at the feet of Sid Belton, whose scent and *persona* had attracted her so intensely from the moment of his arrival. Penelope had quickly settled with her usual assurance and possessiveness into her private spot in Elisabeth Manguson's lap.

But when Elisabeth had begun to speak, providing the group with an overview of her agenda for the evening, Matt's mind had drifted away from her words, caught up helplessly in thoughts of the woman whose presence so inevitably arrested him. He had, from the moment he had finally awakened shortly before noon that day, found himself amazed that he had actually functioned so competently on the Cambridge raid, despite working throughout in such proximity to Rebecca. How had that been possible? Was it this "Christian thing" at work? Was he somehow infused with Something that made him better than he knew how to be? Less self-conscious. Less fearful. More focused. Even more courageous. By concentrating on duty and purpose and obligation, he had indeed behaved courageously. And he could actually say that to himself, acknowledge the fact, and move on unaffected to the next thought.

But what of the upcoming mission to St. David's itself? Obviously Luke would not be able to participate. It would be just the two of them: himself and Rebecca. How could he possibly journey half a day to the west, to the coast of Wales, alone with this overwhelming presence, then commit himself, with her at his side, to a venture quite possibly more dangerous than the one just undertaken? And how, if they were still able, could he make the return journey to Birmingham with Rebecca—*Rebecca!*—sitting inches away from him in an automobile, and without her brother with them to soften the edges of Matt's raw emotional tension? A very few minutes alone with her in the first-floor reading room, after the clothes-hanging episode, had, after all, nearly undone him. How would he cope with her solitary presence for hours at a time?

Just last week, he mused, he was a United States Naval officer, preparing to process out of the military and head for graduate school. How on earth had he gotten from Virginia to England, from security to peril, from secular materialism to Christianity, from no romantic attachments to . . . this? In spite of himself, he raised his eyes and looked across the small circle. He beheld Rebecca's face. Her gray eyes were fixed on her mother, who continued to speak.

Rebecca was again clad in one of her mother's loose dresses, and her face presented itself to him in partial profile. Her hair glistened darkly, coursing down the side of her face as she leaned forward in her chair with her head turned toward Elisabeth Manguson. His eyes drank in the geometry of the junction of her hair with her mother's oversized rectangular belt buckle. His mind capitulated as usual, lost in the sight of her. Any view, any sound, any scent would do. This time, he had been inexplicably and hopelessly captivated by the gleaming tresses that descended to a neatly trimmed arrow just inches above her hands as they rested in her lap. As he stared at her, she slowly leaned back in her chair, her eyes still fixed upon the speaker. As she straightened in her chair, the neatly trimmed length of hair lifted away from her hands and from the belt buckle, appearing now to flow upward toward her face. The left hand released the right and came up from her lap to toy absently with randomly selected strands of hair as they fell across her right shoulder.

Suddenly, without seeing how it happened, he realized that Rebecca was looking back at him. Otherwise she had not moved. Her hand still absently fingered her hair, and her face still directed itself toward her mother. But her eyes had moved, and had affixed his with a stare of their own. For what seemed minutes but was in fact seconds, the two young warriors, fresh from one fight and preparing for a second, looked into each other's eyes. Her expression did not change. He felt as though she were staring through him and into his soul, and he felt an indescribable thrill race in an electric movement from his eyes to his chest to his groin to his toes. It was a look she had not previously granted him, and it seemed to melt his entire body. He felt absolutely stunned. He wanted to look away, and he wanted never again in his lifetime to look away. He found in the end that he had not. Finally, after a period of time that he could never recreate for himself because it seemed time had actually stopped, she smiled, just a little smile, and abruptly returned her gaze to the speaker.

Matt knew his face was red, but for once he didn't care. What was there to hide? He loved her, whatever that might mean in some taxonomy of the affections. He loved her, and he wanted just to look at her and think about her and imagine a life with her and . . . and it was then that he sensed that someone else had been staring at *him*, perhaps for some time. He shifted his eyes and found himself looking into an older and very different face, though perhaps no less beautiful than Rebecca's. It was his mother's. And Martha Clark's eyes delivered the same message that they had silently transmitted to him a thousand times: the unmistakable look that says more effectively than words, "Would you please stop immediately what you are doing? Would you please do immediately what you are *supposed* to be doing?"

Matt looked down at his feet and smiled. A small chuckle actually escaped his throat. And he knew somehow that he had never been happier than he was at that moment. All in the fragment of time that we call one week, he had become someone utterly different than the person he had spent his first twenty-six years trying to be, and the change had been completely unsought. After the passage of mere days, he knew that he now saw the world through the eyes of a Christian. And, beyond that, and, he knew, because of that, he loved. He loved Rebecca Manguson. And she had just told him something with her eyes that he knew he would hold in his mind for as long as he might live. She had not told him that she loved him. No, not that. Perhaps never that. But she had told him that she knew he loved her, and that it had become an acceptable thing to her. It was astonishing: he had just received permission to court her. And the permission had been given as clearly as if he had knelt in front of her and begged for the permission, and then received a note in her own handwriting with her father's endorsement and seal affixed.

And he reflected that he even knew with perfect clarity why she had given permission to him. He understood that she had seen in the wild events of the previous night that he could respond to duty and obligation with selflessness and courage. He had shown the capacity, by the grace of God, to function as a person. *My life for yours:* the Christian's most fundamental transaction, had been evident in much that he had done. He knew that. And he knew with equal clarity that none of that had he done on pretense; he had committed to a Christian obligation and had been given the strength to do it. It had been actually quite simple. The unanticipated, unsearched for outcome had been the beginnings of respect from the woman he loved.

When he looked up again, he did so with a purpose. He was aware that at some point Elisabeth Manguson had stopped speaking and Dr. Ashford had begun. Very well, his job was to attend. And prepare. His duty was clear. Rebecca, certainly, was busy with the same job: attending and preparing. She had given him permission to court her. But on that subject she had not dwelt for long. There were infinitely more important issues before her now. And before him as well.

The old scholar's voice was accepted gradually into Matt's consciousness: ". . . and so, in the twelfth century, on the same ground on which St. David had constructed his sixth-century church, the cathedral was begun, using from the first the purple stone from the local quarries that gives the structure such an otherworldly cast. And you must not imagine the usual setting for a cathedral, perched on the highest ground in the territory, visible for miles around. No, the Cathedral of St. David is set in a dramatic declivity, hidden not only from the raiders who plied that forbidding coast and who would have had no difficulty whatever finding and bombarding such a huge building set only a mile from the water, but also hidden, incredibly, even from marauders who might travel by horseback on the main road itself."

Ashford paused, his eyes far away, remembering. "Even today, one can stand very nearly adjacent to St. David's Cathedral and have no idea that there is holy ground anywhere near. On my first visit, years ago, I walked down the hill from the Cross Square in the center of town, did not notice that the cathedral had become visible on my right, and passed under the only remaining guard tower, assuming that I must still be a great distance from it. I cleared the guard tower, walked not ten steps more, looked to my right, and there, perhaps one hundred yards from me, stood the entire structure, *completely* visible, and yet, seconds before, *completely* hidden. An astounding experience in itself. Why, the main tower alone is so high and of such bulk, that to conceal it from view has required a remarkable surprise of nature: a geological pocket sudden enough and large enough to accept St. David's Cathedral and its accompanying Bishop's Palace, and to protect both from coastal weather, to some extent, from troops and marauders, for the most part, and, until now, from any truly great Evil."

Dr. Ashford paused again, a frown passing briefly across his brow. Tom Sutton and Martha Clark watched him intently.

After a moment, Dr. Ashford seemed to brighten. "And the greater history! Imagine Celtic missionaries passing through and around these headlands. Imagine Irish evangelists crossing from their island and stopping here on their way to a pagan Europe. Imagine St. David himself establishing his monastic community, building his church, farming the land. . . . I wonder what he would think of his cathedral, of his place in Welsh history. . . . I wonder how he faced the Meredith Lancasters of his day. Certainly they were here on earth then. Certainly they are here on earth now."

At this last, his face began to change, and Elisabeth Manguson spoke quickly. "Lawrence, I cannot allow you to risk yourself again tonight. Take Martha's and Tom's hands, and think about the cathedral again. Tell us something about the interior. Rebecca and Matt, especially, and all the rest of us as planners, will need a sense of how it appears inside."

Lawrence Ashford complied immediately. He paused and thought for a moment, then continued. "One enters the cathedral from the south porch and finds himself almost immediately at the west end of the nave itself. Looking to the right, to the east, one sees in the interior distance the altar and the pulpit, but only for a moment, because one's eyes are drawn immediately upward. And there, unless one has been carefully prepared for the experience in advance, one simply cannot believe what he is seeing. One doubts his senses, looks down and away in disbelief, then inevitably up again. And then he accepts the fact: those massive pillars, and more so at the west end of the cathedral than at any other point—right over one's own head, in other words—lean outward at such an angle that the initial impression is that one must have entered in the very midst of the complete collapse of the entire structure. And then one understands the meaning of something he perhaps read long ago, that an earthquake in mid-thirteenth century shifted the entire cathedral, forced those pillars outward, and left the east end of the building nearly *fifteen feet* higher than the west.

"Now, if you would, try to imagine the experience at Holy Communion. You rise from your knees at your pew. You move to the center aisle. You have been immersed in the worship service, sitting in your pew, not thinking now of the fact that the front of the church is substantially elevated. You begin to walk forward toward the altar, as thousands upon thousands of Christians have done over the past eight hundred years. And it comes upon you in your first steps, with an impact that drenches your body and soul like the waters of a river baptism, that you are *climbing* toward Holy Communion. On the holiest ground in Great Britain, ground on which worship services have been held every day since St. David built his first church there on the banks of the Alun, you are walking upward in obedience to our Lord's command to 'Do this in remembrance of me.' If you ever experience it, you will never forget the impact, no matter how many years pass . . . even when the one with whom you had the experience has gone on before you. . . ."

The room fell completely silent as the image of Arianna Ashford formed in the minds of those who had known her, and, indeed, indistinctly, even in the minds of those who had not. Ashford started to speak again, stopped, looked down, and began once more. "But whether you are there for a worship service, or are simply there as a visitor at some other time of day, there is an absolutely unmistakable Presence that you will sense from the moment you enter. You will remove your hat. You will not speak loudly. You will tread softly. And everywhere you look, you will—and I don't pretend to have a vocabulary adequate—you will be looking *through* something that you know is floating between you and the object that you are considering from a distance: the pulpit, the altar, those vast columns, the intricate ceiling, the rose window. The entire cathedral is suffused with some sort of uncanny, unearthly light that seems to bathe everything inside. I don't know if it is the purple stone, or something beyond that. But you'll sense the Presence. And you'll be reminded afresh of what the word *awe* should properly mean.

"I don't know what will be required of Rebecca and Matthew, but the cathedral has received numerous additions over the centuries, and, particularly at night, I should think, it would quickly become a maze of crannies and corners and unseen and unseeable objects. There are three enclosed chapels, for instance, each capable of seating perhaps thirty to eighty people. There are side aisles that run the entire length of the building. There is the choir area. There is the library. There is the vestry. There are tombs. . . . The cathedral is an enormous, complex building. But I do have one thought that might be helpful in our planning.

"When Rebecca recounted the dream that she experienced here at the mansion on Sunday night, she described something beyond the massive purple edifice that we now are certain was St. David's Cathedral, the structure that had already appeared both in Martha's and in Rebecca's earlier dreams. Rebecca was able to provide details of the vial-and-hymnal vision, and something of the room in which those were set." Dr. Ashford looked toward Rebecca now as he spoke, the teacher in him searching for an indication of ascent or disagreement from her. He saw ascent.

"She said, as I think, that she could see an altar and the first row, and, this I remember distinctly, she recalled being struck by the height—the lack of height—of the two entrances she could see, one on each side of a sanctuary. She noted that those entrances were arched and presumably built when people were simply smaller than they are today."

Seeing Rebecca's nod, he continued. "That could only be one room in St. David's Cathedral. Holy Trinity Chapel is the only worship center in the entire cathedral that has opposing doorways, and they fit Rebecca's description exactly. That small chapel is near the extreme east end of the structure, and has much more width than depth. Its width is, I'm quite sure, the full width of the main structure between its north and south aisles, but its distance from front to rear cannot be more than, I should think, twenty or twenty-five feet. At the times when I have visited, Holy Trinity Chapel had but two rows of seats. I think the back row, against the chapel's west wall, had fixed seating . . . probably benches permanently installed. But the other row, just in front of the benches, comprised individual, movable chairs, each with its own rack on the rear surface of the chair, a rack designed to hold a hymnal and a prayer book."

Seeing Rebecca lean forward, Ashford stopped, and she spoke. "Oh, Dr. Ashford, I had not remembered that detail until you said it. The hymnal and vial in my last dream were indeed held in a wooden rack on the chair back of an individual seat, and that seat was placed in the midst of a long row of such seats. That's *just* how it was."

Ashford nodded, then looked at Elisabeth Manguson. "Elisabeth, it would seem that we may have placed the toxin rather precisely within the cathedral grounds. But are we getting too far ahead of the detective's report? Is it time to hear from Detective Belton and Dr. Clark?"

"Not yet, Lawrence," she replied. "Having heard their preliminary report two hours ago, I think that we will find that what you have given us regarding the cathedral, its history, and its setting, coupled with your having placed Rebecca's dreamed vial-and-hymnal in Holy Trinity Chapel, altogether will provide an excellent context for their full report. But there is still another statement that I wish all to hear and consider before that."

"This morning," continued Elisabeth, "Rebecca provided Jason and me with a detailed action summary of last night's strike at the enemy's headquarters."

Here she turned to face her daughter more directly. "Although I realize that it is your wish, Rebecca, that your father or I summarize the entire action sequence for the group, I must ask that you yourself provide the description of those final moments in Mr. Lancaster's office. Your father and I will speak to the events before and after, but those moments provide us, more than anything that has happened since the crisis began, with the clearest picture of the nature of our Enemies and their designs upon us all. Those moments will serve to remind us that, in the end, both our Lord and our Enemies are interested ultimately only in individual souls, and have concerns about creeds and organizations and political movements and wars only insofar as those help move individual souls either closer to One or to the Other. Those moments that you, Rebecca, will describe for us will also include the second appearance of the *Nuntiae* during this crisis, and that fact alone demands more than a superficial or second-hand account. No, it must be you, Rebecca."

Rebecca nodded. "I'll be glad to try, Mum. It may be that I'll need help from you or Dad at certain points, but I will certainly make the best attempt at it that I can."

Matt, at Elisabeth Manguson's reference to Rebecca's final moments in Lancaster's office, and at her allusion to the *Nuntiae*, turned, confused, first to Rebecca and then to Luke. Neither of them returned his inquiring glance. He looked away, puzzled. What had happened to Rebecca? How could he not have known? Then he realized that Elisabeth was speaking again.

She and Jason in turn provided a summary of the night's action, occasionally looking to Rebecca, Luke, and Matt for confirmation, correction, or addition. Their summary placed greatest stress upon the extent to which enemy headquarters had been fortified and defended, clearly to prepare the group for the likelihood that St. David's would be even more so.

With her mother's concluding words, Rebecca was on her feet and pacing, her hands working against each other as she circled the group, reversed course, and circled again. Her description was as complete as it had been for her parents, with additional commentary regarding the dream fulfillment aspects through which the "something worse than death" had indeed materialized in Lancaster's Evil-dominated lair. In her account of her rescue, she again found herself nearly overcome with the emotion of the recollection. Near the end, she stopped, turned away from the circle, and collected herself before she could continue. When she turned again to face the *Legati,* she concluded: "I can hardly bear to acknowledge the truth, even to myself, that I was so tempted by our Enemies' solicitation that I gave them license to invest themselves with such force in my mind and body and, I'm sure, in my soul. But the truth is that I was. And they did.

"Mum and Dad helped me this morning to attend to the real point: that even in that place—that horrible place—I was not alone. I called upon our Father and He sent my Rescuers and I was saved."

Matt had listened to Elisabeth, Jason, and, now, Rebecca, at first with a sort of bemused detachment at what sounded, nearly twenty-four hours later, like exploits relayed from a movie plot. It hardly seemed possible that they were describing something in which he had played a major role, or any role at all. But when Rebecca drew them into the narrative of the Dark Masters' assault in Lancaster's office, he found himself anguished, first by the description of her agony and then by a sense of his own guilt. He felt sick. How could such a calamity possibly have occurred just seconds after he had been in that office with her? How could he possibly have failed to realize that supernatural danger lurked in that room, and that leaving her alone was supreme folly? Never mind that her ability to resist Evil was many times his own, he, a Christian beginner. He could, he screamed inwardly at himself, have done *something*. He should have. . . .

Suddenly, without forethought, Matt was on his feet, had wheeled around his chair to reach Rebecca's side as she stood behind and to one side of him, and there, before anyone had realized what had happened, he had crossed in front of her, faced her, and had taken both her hands in his. He stared down into the gray pools that had captivated him from the first moment he had seen her: "Rebecca, I am *so sorry*. I didn't know. I would gladly have given my very . . ."

In a flash, she pulled her hand from his and covered his lips with her fingertips, preventing his completion of the sentence. "I know, Matt," she whispered softly. "I know."

In a long silence they stood unmoving, in full view of their colleagues, her right hand cradled in his left, her left hand on his lips, their eyes fixed on each other. Time passed. Then she moved her hand slowly from his face, pulled her other hand carefully from his gentle grasp, took her eyes from his with apparent reluctance, and walked around him and across the circle to her chair. Matt remained for a moment with his back to the circle. Then he turned and watched her take her seat.

Martha Clark stared at her son's face in disbelief. For the first time in his life, in her presence, he had exhibited public affection . . . deep, quiet, moving, public affection . . . and yet there was not so much as a trace of blush on his intense face. He seemed, in fact, conscious neither of himself nor of the others who observed him. He seemed conscious of nothing and of no one except the woman herself.

Rebecca sat down, erect, placed her hands in her lap, looked back across the circle at Matt, and smiled. It was another smile that she had not until then awarded him. And its message seemed to him unambiguous. It said to him, "I like the person you are, and are becoming. You and I are going to know each other well. I will look forward to the experience."

As Matt finally lowered his eyes and began to move to his own chair in the lengthening silence, he sensed indistinct struggling movements from his right. He turned his head just as he was sitting down and saw Luke Manguson pulling himself to an upright position on the cot. Grimacing in pain from his wound, Luke leaned in Matt's direction, then extended his right hand as far as he could reach. Matt quickly rose again, stepped toward Luke, and took the hand that was offered. Matt was stunned both by the iron force of Luke's grip and by what he read on his face. His eyes burned into Matt's, and he said, his jaw set, emotion thickening his voice: "I couldn't hope for a better companion for her than she'll have on this raid. You're everything I could possibly wish for, as her comrade-in-arms . . . and more. I will expect you both back here on Sunday night, Lieutenant. I'll expect you both right here. Whole."

CHAPTER FIFTEEN

AT ELISABETH MANGUSON'S NOD, SID BELTON AND PAUL Clark rose and brought to the center of the circle a long, portable table that they had earlier carried to the subterranean complex from the first-floor kitchen. The table's surface was covered in document photographs, organized meticulously.

The detective began at once. "Professor Clark and I need to keep this summary of our analysis as short and tight as we can, because Mrs. Manguson wants to leave as much time as possible for our planning session. Miss Manguson was able to get photos of just about everything we could realistically hope for, and I think we're in pretty good shape, so far as figurin' out what this rat is tryin' to do.

"Professor Clark is gonna give you the list of what we've decided we know and don't know, after he and Mrs. Clark and I spent most of the day studyin' everything. Mrs. Clark said she'd just as soon listen to us give the results, and she'll chip in whenever she wants to. Professor?"

Paul Clark stepped up to the table and cleared his throat.

Martha mentally rolled her eyes in embarrassment. "Why can't Paul just relax and *converse* with a group as small as this?" she said to herself. "Why can't he leave his pomposity at college?" And in the same instant she reproached herself; she had over the years mostly succeeded in letting go of her yearnings to reconstruct her husband's mannerisms. This was one of the last to which she seemed still to cling. She began to attend to his words.

". . . and the detective was certainly right that virtually everything that can materially assist us was in plain view of Rebecca's cameras," said the professor. "And so, here is our best summary after repeated

208

analyses and several early and tentative reports during the afternoon both to Elisabeth and to Jason.

"I'll start with this. We readily found correspondence to and from the researchers at the University College of Wales in Aberystwyth. There appear to be but two of them involved. Mr. Lancaster has scheduled them for television interviews on Sunday morning, so, whatever danger they may be facing, it is not likely to descend upon them between now and then. They are, in any case, already sequestered by Mr. Lancaster's forces, and there's no possibility of our reaching them. There are memoranda between Mr. Lancaster and the head of his security force that provide a suspicious amount of detail regarding the two men's scheduled drive, alone in their automobile, from St. David's to Aberystwyth just after a luncheon on Sunday. In sum, however, we have nothing except Detective Belton's speculation and these memoranda referencing their departure that imply their endangerment. Detective?"

"That's about it, sir. I was disappointed to find we can't get at 'em between now and Sunday. But we can't. And there's nothin' we can use, really, except that info about their drive home."

Jason Manguson quickly inquired of Belton, "Do you still believe they are at risk, Detective?"

"I believe they are dead men, sir."

A shocked pause ensued. Paul Clark waited. Then he turned to his wife. "Martha? Anything to add on this?"

She shook her head. "No. There's clearly nothing we can act upon, and nothing we might induce Scotland Yard or the regular police to act upon, insofar as these two people are concerned. And it may be worth remembering that nothing about them appeared in my dreams or in Rebecca's."

"And your best guess, Martha, regarding their safety?" Jason asked.

"Oh, I think Detective Belton is right, Jay. Mr. Lancaster cannot afford to let them live. He will not be willing to leave himself exposed to blackmail or worse. I fully expect him to murder these accomplices, albeit unwilling ones, immediately. He'll allow no survivors among those privy to the hoax, other than his own henchmen, and perhaps not all of them. I am actually a little surprised that he apparently will allow the researchers to live until Sunday morning. Something will happen to them on that drive home on Sunday. Personally, I've no doubt of that."

Paul Clark looked around the room. "Other comments, anyone? Questions?"

Several heads shook slowly. Other faces stared unhappily and impassively at him. The atmosphere was somber. Mildred whimpered quietly at Elisabeth's side, the spot to which she had moved as soon as the detective had risen.

Clark began again. "While we're on the subject of the university researchers, I'll note an interesting historical quirk, one that we had not expected. It really makes no difference to anything, and, as with a good deal of our material, we have nothing completely solid on it, nothing that would allow us to go to the police or even to the newspapers. But here it is.

"We have a document that references what seems to be the original creedal statement underlying the entire fraud. According to an early bit of correspondence from the Welsh researchers to Mr. Lancaster, they stumbled across a box in some basement storage bin at the university, and, in sorting through what seems mostly to have been early students' personal effects, came across what they referenced in their letter as a 'shortened creed.' The thing seems to have been penned—in Welsh, of course—soon after the university was founded in Aberystwyth, which would place it mid-1870s. Martha, Detective Belton, and I eventually decided during the afternoon that the researchers probably contacted Mr. Lancaster innocently enough, hopeful that his recognized influence with publishers and editors in virtually every category of print media—religious journals, scientific journals, historical journals, popular newsmagazines— might lead to a serendipitous enhancement of their resumes.

"They got more than they bargained for. It seems likely to us that Meredith Lancaster developed his entire plot on what was originally an innocuous inquiry by a couple of history scholars. And it also seems likely to us that the original document may well have been nothing more than some poor student's work in confirmation class, some young man or woman struggling to commit the Welsh *Credo Nicea* to memory, writing drafts as a sort of self-test, and, in the draft that happened to survive, failing to remember several segments of the text. Or, perhaps equally plausible, the student's having been a native speaker of English, not Welsh, and having trouble with translation, rather than plain memory. In either case, it is, we concluded, quite simply a case of Lancaster's having had the genius to turn the thing into this monumental fraud that has got the attention of half the English-speaking world, all of the Welsh-speaking world, and all the company of heaven besides. It is corruption built upon innocence, and, in that sense, I think we probably would all agree, the conventional formula for the greatest Evil.

"Of course, as we've noted among ourselves previously, the core of the successful deceit has, from the first, been Mr. Lancaster's wholly original concept of a secret *and* oral tradition, allegedly passed along for fourteen hundred years by a sequential handful of initiates. And thus, a tradition impossible to disprove by the ordinary methods of examining historical cross-references or of scientifically establishing the date of an ancient document."

Matt got his father's attention with a move of his hand, and asked, "But Dad, isn't there anything in that correspondence that a newspaper editor could use to expose this fraud in print? After all, 'HOAX EXPOSED' would make a nice headline in London's newspapers Friday or Saturday morning, wouldn't it?"

His father replied, smiling, "Yes, and an even better headline in a Cardiff newspaper, I should think. But no, Matt, the correspondence is too vague on all points. We can draw these inferences because of the special access and insight that we have through your mother's and Rebecca's dream sequences. But since we can make no credible allusion to the dreams in any report or request we might make to police or to newspapers, our hands are bound, son."

"And that, we assume," added Martha, "is why we have involvement of the *Nuntiae* in the first place. Without these special reports of our own, Mr. Lancaster's plot would be unassailable. And that is why *we* are given the charge to *Protect the saint.* It is only we who *have* the special information, and only we who are in position to comprehend and believe it, and, in the end, only we who are in position to act upon it."

There was another pause. Paul Clark, in his element as presenter and discussion master, looked carefully around the room, and once more cleared his throat to signal resumption of his presentation.

"Let's turn, then, to other data, shall we?" he said in his formal manner. "Regarding the bishop whose appearance has been prominent in the dreams of both Martha and Rebecca, I'm afraid that, as with the researchers, there is nothing direct here, either. Nothing that would allow us to go to Scotland Yard or to the news editors. However, the three of us have concluded that the clerical figure in the dreams must indeed be the bishop of St. David's, and that Mr. Lancaster's plot almost certainly includes his murder—or, at the least, his incapacitation—as well as the researchers' murders.

"The basic evidentiary datum is Rebecca's dreamed vial with skull and crossbones design, hidden in the hymnal which Dr. Ashford has placed for us in Holy Trinity Chapel, deep inside the cathedral. Supplementary evidence is, of course, inferential, and stems primarily from exchanges of memoranda among Mr. Lancaster, the chief of his security force, and the University of Bradford's Jonathan Foster. It becomes clear in the reading that Mr. Lancaster is greatly concerned about, and sorely angered by, the good bishop who, reasonably enough from our standpoint, has insisted upon being the one who reads *all* the fraudulent material—not that he has the faintest idea that there is fraud involved, of course—on Sunday morning. He insists upon reading both the historical background narratives and, of course, the 'Creed of St. David' itself."

At this, the detective bestirred himself and, sensitive to his audience's every movement, Paul Clark paused to acknowledge his colleague. From his seat near the evidence table, Sid Belton said, "We don't want you folks to have the impression that even Lancaster would kill the bishop of St. David's just because the bishop wants to be the one to stand up in the cathedral and read the fake creed and all the fake histories they've fudged up to go with it. It's more than that.

"But, when you get right down to it, folks, it's not *much* more than that. Lancaster wants control of everything, see. As long as the bishop is alive and well and insisting on being . . . well . . . the bishop, Lancaster really doesn't have the absolute control he wants over . . . what he calls in some of his memos . . . his 'marketing plan.' Lancaster is obviously the great salesman. He could sell you the Brooklyn Bridge as a way to get from New York to London and back. But he's also the great manipulator. And great manipulators can't stand somebody else having a say in the grand plan, whatever the grand plan may be.

"Now, Professor and Mrs. Clark think it's possible that the dreamed poison vial might just be knock-out drops of some kind. Y'know, just enough to put the bishop outta commission Sunday morning, so that Lancaster will be in complete charge of everything that happens in front of the TV cameras. But everything I know about scoundrels like this guy tells me that he wants the bishop dead much more than he wants these two researchers dead. Never mind that it makes no sense to us. It's control, first . . . he *has* to have it, and I mean *all* of it, and it's . . . what's that word you used this afternoon, Professor Clark? 'Hubris,' that's it. It's control, first, and it's *hubris* second. Lancaster has such *hubris* that he honestly thinks he can get away with murder. And not just one, but three, and all on the same day."

"As the detective notes, however," Paul Clark quickly interjected, "both Martha and I are skeptical on this point. Our conjecture is that even Meredith Lancaster would hesitate to be quite that brazen."

"Yes," added Martha, from her seat beside Lawrence Ashford, "Paul and I can't quite feature Mr. Lancaster having the bishop of St. David's killed within hours of his big announcement, in part because the murder would detract from the main show, from the hoax itself. It just seems too much of a stretch to us."

After a brief silence, a new voice was heard.

"How old is the bishop of St. David's, Detective?" asked Rebecca.

"We don't know exactly, ma'am, but we found a sheet that will be part of the materials distributed to the press on Sunday morning that goes back at least forty years, just on the man's professional career." Belton's crooked smile materialized for the first time that evening. "I think I know where you're goin', Miss Manguson. Go ahead, ma'am."

"I have two thoughts," she replied, remaining seated. "One is that there surely must be poisons that kill without trace, and in such a way that, at least in the immediacy of this Sunday morning extravaganza, give the impression of death by natural causes in a distinguished older gentleman. That would produce quite a different impact than would death by murder. I suppose one might even contend that the Sunday services would take on a memorial cast that would heighten the solemnity of the announcements in ways that Mr. Lancaster would see as beneficial to his overall objectives.

"My other thought is this. My dream's skull and crossbones image was altogether clear, Detective. And more than that, the Evil that I encountered in Mr. Lancaster's office was clear, too, to say the least, and tells me that, to the Evil Ones whom we now face, *unexpected* death is the best kind for their purposes.

"I mean no unkindness toward the bishop of St. David's when I say that to take a man's life moments before he expects to become internationally famous may well be, in the minds of these Evil Ones, the most propitious moment of all. Their interests are, after all, eternal. Their chances of capturing the souls of most priests or ministers must be quite poor. But taking the bishop by surprise under circumstances in which he will have perhaps been guilty, as was I, of beginning to imagine worldwide fame and fortune. . . .

"I don't know, Detective. Perhaps I am wrong. I hope I am. But I fear for the bishop of St. David's. And I do not want us to underestimate the willingness of Meredith Lancaster and his Masters to seize the chance to surprise a good man at a bad time with unanticipated death. There is, I should think, nothing they would relish more. And, as we have noted already, they, just as our Lord, would view policies and procedures and documents and fanfare primarily as opportunities to bring individual souls into their camp.

"I think they may see this as their chance." Rebecca sat back, a sadness subtly recasting her features into a different sort of beauty. Yet, while Matt—and, to be fair, all others in the room—watched her face, it gradually hardened into its more familiar aspect, no less beautiful, but faintly suggestive of threat, too. No one needed to guess the object of her studied wrath.

The brief silence was broken by Sid Belton.

Suddenly he slapped his forehead with the dramatic exaggeration of a vaudeville actor, and with enough force to startle both of the animals and several of the humans. Simultaneously he jumped to his feet. "By George!" he exclaimed. Then he began scrambling through one of the stacks of document photographs, obviously looking for a particular one.

Finally he raised a document photo to his face, and nodded with grim satisfaction. He turned toward Elisabeth Manguson.

"Mrs. Manguson," he said, "it wasn't until your daughter mentioned poisons that kill without trace that I remembered somethin' that I've read ten times today without having given a single thought to it. Can't believe I'd be that slow. But here it is, in one of the memos from Lancaster to the head of his private security unit. It says this: 'Bring the potcy container to the cathedral with the Saturday midnight delivery of the document box. Secure it in the lock box as discussed previously.' That's *potcy container*, ma'am, spelled . . ."

Dr. Thomas Sutton, speaking for the first time, interrupted him excitedly. "Yes, Detective! Yes! I know how it would be spelled. Mr. Lancaster is planning to import *potassium cyanide* into the cathedral."

Silence followed this astonishing announcement. The silence was soon broken by Tom Sutton himself, his initial excitement now tempered. "But I have an immediate doubt, Detective Belton," he said. "You're suggesting that our enemy plans to use potassium cyanide against the bishop of St. David's. But you're aware, no doubt, that that particular poison does not fit Rebecca's suggestion of a toxin that kills without trace, or one that kills in such a way that death from natural causes might be inferred. If the dose is large enough, and administered orally, the bishop will undergo disorientation, nausea, vomiting, fainting, and convulsions. He may be dead within sixty seconds, and that death will not closely mimic heart attack or any other natural event."

"I do know those things," Belton replied. "But I think this, sir. First, I think that Lancaster will *arrange* for this to take place, and in such a way that someone else will be set up as the murderer. In fact, I think I might even know who that is likely to be. Second, I think that the schedule Lancaster has put in place for Sunday morning—and we have it right here—makes it easy for this murder to take place well before the time the television cameras get rolling. And third, I don't think he'll view the bishop's murder as a distraction at all. I think he'll view it as a chance for himself to prove to the whole world how Meredith Lancaster can rise above the chaos from any disaster and not only carry on in ways that will lead people to say things like, 'that would have made the bishop proud,' but also to show that he can even point the finger at the murderer—the person he will set up to take the fall for him. I think he will *like* the spectacle. I think he will relish every moment of this: pageantry, murder, confusion, distress, police, media, fraud on a grand scale, the whole thing. It's gonna look so much like Hell that he'll feel right at home from the first minute. He'll view every aspect of this as perfection, looked at from the viewpoint of Evil. And he will rise above it all, sanctimonious to a fault. That he will.

"I do think, though, that he will make those two researchers' deaths look accidental. He won't want more than one obvious murder in a given day. Confuses the media's story lines. He'll have 'em bumped off in such a way that it'll hardly seem interesting to the public in general. They'll still be mired in the big stuff. Y'know what I mean?"

Another prolonged silence ensued. Then Elisabeth Manguson nodded her head, thoughtfully, and looked first to her husband, and then, systematically, around the meeting room. One by one, each head returned her nod. In the end, she returned her gaze to the detective with a small smile on her face.

It was Matt Clark who finally spoke. "Detective," he said inquiringly, a mischievous grin on his face, "exactly how many serious crimes have you ever failed to figure out?"

Belton met Matt's grin with his own lopsided smile. "If you mean in the years since I've been twice as smart as you, kid, none at all. Not one."

Dawn on Thursday found Rebecca already well into a two-mile run, circling the perimeter on the walking trail that traced the inside of the wall. Clad in her black "escape clothes," the ponytail swishing rhythmically behind her head, she marked the halfway point in her run as a splendid June sunrise began to unfold. Consciously, she began to increase the pace as her muscles and lungs, earlier protesting mildly, began finally to accept heightened demand and to rejoice in their own refinement and power.

As she ran, Rebecca continued to sort through details of the planning session that had ended late the previous evening. She thought about its implications for herself and for Matt, and she thought once more of its surprising ending. She mused at how swiftly everything had seemed to fall in place following the detective's masterful analysis. The original three-part command from the *Nuntiae,* the long trail of Martha's and her own dreams, the rescue of the Clarks after their kidnapping from New York, the raid on enemy headquarters and the perilous photographing of Lancaster's documents, the subtleties and intricacies of the data analysis . . . all brought up hard against Lancaster's concrete schedule of events, had in the end yielded a picture of remarkable clarity.

Shortly before midnight on Saturday, just two days hence, Meredith Lancaster and his security force would arrive at St. David's Cathedral with a small metal file box under lock and key. The file box would contain the original "Creed of St. David" and the text—prepared by Meredith Lancaster and the two university researchers—of the bishop's address to the congregation and to an international television audience. Lancaster, determined that no copies of his "creed," his fabricated history of the creed, and the creed's hoped-for implications for Christianity and its churches would be in any hands other than his own, had insisted that the core documents remain locked in the safe in his headquarters. And he insisted now that they be transported personally by him to St. David's Cathedral.

At that point, Lancaster's security corps, having assisted him in the delivery of the material to the cathedral, would remain on guard from midnight until five o'clock Sunday morning, when law enforcement officers from St. David's and other communities in Pembrokeshire would relieve them. Lancaster himself or his head of security presumably would, once inside the cathedral, swiftly remove the "potcy container" from the lock box, carry it to Holy Trinity Chapel near the east end of the cathedral, and place the vial of potassium cyanide, nestled in the cut-out pages of its hymnal, in the designated hymnal rack.

The cathedral would not be open to television crews until 6:45, and not to the public until 7:45. Mr. Lancaster himself, however, together with a dozen other dignitaries who would be involved in the television interviews, would arrive by 6:00 for a special Holy Communion service, organized by the bishop especially for them, in Holy Trinity Chapel. It was obvious to the *Legati* that the hour between 5:00 and 6:00 provided ample opportunity for the cyanide to be moved from the hidden vial to the communion wine prior to the 6:00 service. The communion wine would have been brought to the chapel well before the service, probably by 5:15, by the bishop's assistants. Holy Trinity Chapel would be unoccupied for nearly forty-five minutes prior to the dignitaries' arrival. The bishop and his assistants would process into the chapel at precisely 6:00.

One of the distinguished guests, arriving perhaps by 5:15, his credentials and his briefcase checked by the police at the door, would be free to walk the length of the cathedral, to enter darkened, hushed Holy Trinity Chapel, to remove the cyanide vial from its concealment, to lace the communion wine with an overwhelming dose of the lethal toxin, and to retire until time to return just before the service. The bishop of St. David's, presiding at the service, would be first and, given the speed of the toxic effects, last, to drink the wine. The murder was straightforward.

Television interviews and reports were to begin at 7:00. The first regularly scheduled Holy Communion for the public would be held at 8:00, as always. The special combined service would begin at 9:30, and would be conducted both in Welsh and in English, broadcast internally to the overflow crowds which would occupy all three of the smaller chapels in addition to the main sanctuary, and telecast via network worldwide. For the 9:30 service the drama had been choreographed in detail, having been written by Lancaster and eventually agreed to, after numerous refusals, vetoes, and forced changes, by the bishop. It would begin with Meredith Lancaster's ceremonially transporting the lock box to the pulpit, unlocking it in public view, and handing the documents to the bishop of St. David's for his reading of them. The bishop was scheduled to read in both Welsh and English.

The bishop's "interference" had been apparent in much of the photographed correspondence and documentation. In addition to his refusal to yield his pulpit to Lancaster, it was he, for example, who insisted upon regular police security from five o'clock on, rather than Lancaster's private unit. And it was he who insisted that none of Lancaster's security men would be allowed within two hundred feet of the cathedral itself during their midnight to five guard tour, except to transport the lock box into the cathedral before midnight. And it was the bishop who insisted that he himself would be there to unlock the main cathedral door at the south porch, to oversee Lancaster and his men's coming, and to observe their going. He would lock the door behind them at midnight, confident that no one remained inside, and secure in the knowledge that the new creed had been placed safely in the cathedral.

Altogether, there was more than enough evidence to support Sid Belton's conclusion that the bishop was far too authoritative to be allowed by Meredith Lancaster to coexist alongside him at this fraudulent celebration, or at any time thereafter as the hoax moved through its carefully planned stages worldwide. The bishop was a threat because he insisted upon control. Very well, he would be eliminated.

As Rebecca began the final quarter mile of her run, her breath hissing in and out of open lips and dilated nostrils as she drove herself onward, she tried to recall her own words to the group. She had been hoping to convey to them the grotesque pleasure that Lancaster and his Masters would take in their own cruel stroke. What was it she had said to her colleagues? Yes: ". . . to surprise a good man at a bad time with unanticipated death." Right. She *knew* them.

Increasing her pace still further and delighting in the demands placed on all her systems at once, her long, sculptured legs reaching for purchase as she completed this final lap of the perimeter, she thought of the session's final moments. Her mother had just reached a conclusion that she then had presented the group with obvious reluctance. She had said, in clipped tones: "Now that we have been given the fullest picture of what must transpire, my decision is this: I cannot permit Rebecca and Matt to attempt a penetration of the defended cathedral perimeter unless there is complete overcast of the expected full moon or, better, actual precipitation. With Luke leading the raid, I think I could have authorized the risk. Without him, no. Neither of our healthy young people has Luke's specific incursion training, his highly developed infiltration skill, or his consummate physical prowess. Rebecca and Matt have, to be sure, established their courage, their stamina, and their strength. It is not enough.

"And, as a separate but no less critical point, I must make note of the obvious: two is fewer than three.

"Without the blackness of an overcast night, they will be easy prey for Mr. Lancaster's professionals, who will be at least as well armed as at the farmhouse headquarters and, given what happened there on consecutive nights, readier than ever to take aggressive action."

She stopped and looked around the room, her eyes stopping at Matt.

"Matt," she said, "Rebecca will be in charge."

She waited for a response from him, and he nodded to her immediately: "Of course."

She then continued: "Rebecca, I will, with your father, your brother, and the detective, give more explicit instructions Thursday and Friday, but now, tentatively, let me emphasize that I want you to make your decision as late as possible, probably when the two of you are within a mile of the St. David's perimeter. Without the requisite overcast, you must turn back. We will be forced to *Protect the saint,* as we have been ordered, but after the fact. We have been commanded to act, but that does not give me license to send our flesh and blood to their certain deaths. We will, in the event, be forced to do whatever work we can after the announcement has been made, after the bishop has, in all likelihood, been murdered, and after the researchers have themselves met their deaths.

"It is all that I am allowed to do. You must accept it."

Now Rebecca, her arms pumping hard as she moved into full sprint, focused her attention entirely on running itself, concentrating on the uneven surface. She crossed the unmarked start and finish point of her run, slowed gradually, and then continued at a relaxed jog through the woods to the clearing in front of the mansion's north porch. Still breathing deeply, hands on hips, she began to walk toward the porch itself.

She thought now of the meeting's final moments. Her mother had just explained to the suddenly depressed group that, on Thursday and

Friday afternoons, there would be specific briefing sessions for Rebecca and Matt regarding the details of the driving route, the coastal hiking route, the physical environs of the town of St. David's, and the details of the cathedral's interior, as well as the specific order of battle once inside. She scheduled Rebecca and Matt to meet with Lawrence Ashford and Jason Manguson first, early on Thursday afternoon, since those two knew the Pembrokeshire coast better than anyone else, and with Luke, Sid Belton, Jason, and herself thereafter, for detailed planning for the raid itself.

It was at that point that, once more, the strange, raspy, guttural voice had raised itself seemingly from nowhere.

"*I'll go with 'em,*" the voice had said.

Rebecca, now walking more slowly and breathing more easily, lifted her towel from the porch railing and, continuing to walk, began to wipe the perspiration from her face and neck. She smiled at the recollection.

Elisabeth Manguson had fastened her eyes upon the detective. At first she had said nothing. She shook her head slowly at the detective, the radiance of her face contradicting the movement. "Detective Belton . . . Detective Belton . . . I cannot allow . . ."

"Please excuse me, ma'am," he had interrupted, emboldened by the transparency of her response. "I've been thinkin' about this hard. And I brought it with me to my prayers, too. I'm clear on what I'm supposed to do, ma'am. I mean, I'm either on our side or I'm not. And if I am, there's no point in my tryin' to do this halfway. Y'know what I mean? I know where my priorities are, or, at least, where they're supposed to be. I know that what we're doin' here is authorized at the highest levels. Angels and archangels and all the company of heaven are waitin' for Sid Belton, New York City detective and, so he claims, Christian human being, to do his duty here.

"I don't know what the consequences for me will be, so far as my police department is concerned. But I know that I'm just not allowed to think about that right now. I have to go. I'm *supposed* to go, ma'am.

"I know I can't do the things Luke can do. I couldn't do 'em even when I was his age, and that was twenty years ago. But I know I can pick the lock to that big cathedral door in ten seconds, and Miss Manguson and Matt can't do it at all. And I know I can get into that lock box that has the core documents in it, and in not many more seconds than that, and these two young people can't do that, either. And I know I can carry one of your husband's or Luke's old military side arms, and I know how to use them just as well as young Matt does.

"And one more thing, ma'am. I know that if we run into somebody other than Lancaster's thugs on this raid, my New York City detective's badge just might mean something.

"Please ma'am, let me go. I won't slow 'em down much. And if I do, Miss Manguson is plenty tough enough to make the decision to leave me behind and get the mission accomplished. *Protect the saint,* ma'am. That's the charge. With me there, we have a decent chance to do that whether we've got moonlight or overcast or rain or all three. I'm a lot better than nothin', ma'am. And I'm *supposed* to go, Mrs. Manguson. I know I am."

Rebecca, her face and neck now dry and her breathing restored nearly to its normal rate, turned to face a glorious sunrise, then stopped and raised her face upward into the sun's early rays. And then she gave her thanks to God for the new day. With her glad *Amen* she laughed aloud with happiness. Sid Belton was wonderful. And so was someone else.

As she turned and began to stride up the short sidewalk to the screened door that opened from the north porch, she realized that a figure had been standing just inside it. The figure was six feet, four inches tall. It opened the door for her and it said softly, "Good morning, Miss Manguson. How was the run?"

"Delightful, Lieutenant Clark," she replied. "The run was delightful."

Chapter Sixteen

THURSDAY AFTERNOON TEA HAVING BEEN LEISURELY completed, Rebecca and Matt moved into their second meeting of the afternoon, as scheduled, this one with Elisabeth and Jason Manguson, the detective, and Luke. The group assembled in the small reading room on the mansion's first floor. Luke had become mobile thanks to Tom Sutton, who, working throughout the morning with materials scavenged from Jason's basement workroom, had fashioned a pair of crude but serviceable crutches that allowed Luke to maneuver freely from room to room and even up and down the mansion's several staircases.

Rebecca was speaking. "I find that it is so easy to confuse our priorities. I *feel* that saving the bishop's life by finding and removing the cyanide is the critical step, and that nothing else really matters much. But I *know* that neither the charge from the *Nuntiae* nor Martha's and my dreams imply any such idea. The essential thing is to secure and destroy the fraudulent documents; anything else we may accomplish is secondary to that."

Jason nodded at his daughter's words. "Yes, I know exactly what you mean, Rebecca. I find myself doing the same thing. But of course from the divine perspective, there is no comparison between the two, as the bishop of St. David's himself would doubtless agree. He would be the first to insist that, compared to a hoax with potential to distort and diminish Christian belief itself for millions of people and for hundreds of years, and, in the bargain, to corrupt the memory of the Welsh saint, his own life and death is of no importance."

"I understand that part, but I wish, Mr. Manguson," said Matt, "that I could be more confident that the destruction of the false documents will, in point of fact, derail the whole plot. Even after we get into the lock box so that we can get rid of those fabrications before anyone other than Lancaster and his associates see them, it seems to me that there is at least a fair chance that Lancaster will still be able to push his lies in front of the public.

"We can embarrass him on Sunday by ruining his big announcement, sure. If we're successful, the bishop will be alive and well at the 9:30 service, and he'll find himself reading what we will have substituted in the lock box, rather than this 'Creed of St. David' and its fake histories. And Lancaster will, I suppose, be sitting there wondering how on earth the bishop is looking so hale and hearty.

"And, as well, Lancaster will be trying to fathom how it's possible that what's being read aloud to the world is simply the true Nicene Creed and the *Credo Nicea,* together with the authentic history of the creed, and of St. David himself, and of the cathedral.

"But I can imagine Lancaster forcibly gaining the floor, right there during the service, to accuse persons unknown—or even the bishop himself—of sabotaging everything. It worries me a lot. We can save the bishop and we can spoil the ceremony for Mr. Lancaster, but there is still a lot of damage, it seems to me, that he can do."

"That's right, Matt, there is a lot he might still do," responded the detective. "But my thoughts on this are partly the same as yours and partly different. Where my thoughts differ, it's because I think this guy is gonna have a real tough time comin' out of this with his master plan still up and runnin'. When you're dealin' in fraud the way he is, and when one of your main weapons has to do with your reputation and your credibility and your smoothness and your polish, you really take a hit when you're made a fool of in front of the world. Nah, he's not gonna get up and confront the bishop or anybody else under these circumstances. The bishop will be *in charge* once that service gets underway. There's no way Lancaster gets up and tries to take the service away from the bishop of St. David's. Later, after he works on things a bit, he may give it a shot.

"Sunday at 9:30, since he's gonna find the bishop alive and presiding, Lancaster will have to go along with the *scheduled* agenda, meaning that he'll have to walk up to the pulpit with the lock box, get out his key with his trademark flourish, unlock the thing personally in front of the whole world, pull out the folder that he *thinks* contains his fake creed and his fake histories, and hand 'em over. That's what the bishop has clearly agreed to in their correspondence.

"Picture how that's gonna go, Matt. The bishop hasn't seen any of Lancaster's documents. He'll just read right through the pages that Lancaster hands him, at least for a time, readin' each line word for word, just as your Mom is writing them for him right now: the *real* Nicene Creed, first in Welsh, then in English. Then the *real* histories that she's typin' for him, alternating in Welsh and in English.

"But, on the other hand, Matt, I agree with you that what we're doin' on Sunday may not turn out to be enough. You're right about that. The best thing we've got goin' for us right now is that Lancaster has been too clever for his own good. And too thorough. And too suspicious.

"He's gone to so much trouble to make sure that there are no copies of the fake creed anywhere, and no copies of the fake histories, that he's gonna have nothin' he can turn to for help. Every document he'd like to have will have been pulled out of his lock box by you and Rebecca, thrown in the sea, and ripped apart by the breakers and the Pembrokeshire rocks, hours before the service even starts.

"But at some point in this presentation, the bishop is gonna become so conscious of the fact that what he's reading is ancient, familiar material, and so certain that he's reading nothin' like what he'd been led to expect, he'll just come to a stop. *And then he'll do something.* And I don't know what. And that's when we'll find out if what we've done is gonna be enough. Y'know what I mean?"

Matt nodded, as did the others, while the detective cast his eyes around the small room. After a moment, Belton continued, the familiar crooked grin beginning to creep across his face. "*But*, my young friend, if I can get Mrs. Manguson's permission, I've got somethin' else up my sleeve. And this is the part that really gets at your question, Matt."

The detective turned in his chair to face Elisabeth Manguson. "I've been thinkin', ma'am, that, since Lancaster and his boys don't know me by sight or in any other way, I oughta stay behind, in the town, after your daughter and Matt make their getaway with the documents early Sunday morning. We'll have removed the cyanide, and we'll have replaced the fake documents with our own legitimate documents, and the two young people will have scattered those fake documents in the sea. Okay, that's fine. That part's done. We'll have accomplished the things we were sent to do.

"But I'm thinkin', ma'am, that if I can hang around town all morning, and if I can just be a member of the congregation that attends the 9:30 service, I might be able to get to the researchers in the confusion that's gonna follow the bishop's reading of the documents. We don't know how anything is gonna look at that point. We do know that, as Lancaster tries to figure out what happened with his lock box, these two researchers are gonna be his prime suspects. Lancaster may decide that these two guys had an attack of good conscience and somehow made substitutions in the lock box, y'know?

"But here's the thing: They'll *know* they're his prime suspects. Who *else* is he gonna suspect?

"I see these two guys tryin' like crazy to get outta there, and I see me havin' a chance to get at 'em while they're in their panic."

"Well, I don't get it, Detective," said Matt. "That sounds like such a long shot to me. You're taking a huge risk, and I can't see that, even if you're successful, it will stop Lancaster from trying to undo our damage."

"A risk it will be, Matt," replied the detective, nodding his head. "But they're gonna be so scared that I like my chances, if I can just get to 'em. Think about it. I'll tell 'em that I'm a New York detective—that's where the badge comes in handy—and that I understand exactly what's happened. Never mind *how* I understand what's happened. And that it's gonna be a *real* good idea for them to turn themselves in to the police and to Scotland Yard just as soon as they can, for their own protection.

"I'll tell 'em that their careers, and probably their lives, are over, unless, maybe, they are willin' to talk to police and help get Lancaster behind bars for conspiracy, fraud, attempted murder, and other stuff. And, I'll tell 'em, if they do that, they just might live nice, long lives with their careers intact. Any other approach, I'll say, and they're seriously done for, and in more ways than one."

"You still see them as the key to the complete fulfillment of the charge, don't you, Detective?" asked Elisabeth. "You think that, to

Protect the saint in the long run, those researchers have to survive and confess. Is that right?"

"Yes, ma'am, that's right," Belton responded. "And that's why I'm gonna stick around Sunday morning, with your permission, ma'am. When it's all over, I'll get a ride back this way with one of the police units, and then I'll get in touch with you to get a ride all the way home.

"In the end, Matt's point is good," he added. "We can save the bishop from murder, and mess up Lancaster's ceremony real thoroughly. But unless we get those research guys to talk, to the police or to the press or both, we may still lose out. I'd have given a lot to be able to get at 'em today or tomorrow or Saturday. But those guys are hidden away too good. This looks to me like the only chance."

The detective looked again at Matt. "And kid, I hafta say this one more time. Even if everything I just said turns out to be wrong, and even if nothin' I'm thinkin' now turns out to be true, and even if everything we're plannin' goes bad, I expect us to prevail anyway. Do you really think that the angels that showed up in Lancaster's headquarters to save your girlfriend are gonna stand around and watch us fail Saturday night and Sunday morning? I tell you, kid, what the Lord requires of us is to get outta our chairs and *try*. If we've got the courage to go *at* it, we'll get help, son. Count on it."

The detective, satisfied, sat back in his chair.

Gradually, he became aware that Rebecca Manguson was staring at him with an expression on her face that he did not recall seeing before. And he became aware that the others in the group seemed to be looking at Rebecca, and, he thought to himself, somewhat apprehensively. "What is it?" he asked, looking first at Rebecca and then at the others. "What's the matter?"

Rebecca leaned toward him, her expression enigmatic. "Matt's *girlfriend*, Detective? I'm Matt's *girlfriend*?"

Sid Belton's face sagged. "Oops," he said. "Ah . . . ah . . . how much trouble am I in, ma'am?"

"A very great deal indeed," she replied, an affectionate and amused smile beginning to spread across her countenance and strongly suggesting otherwise. "I think you should be punished. Don't you agree, Mother?" she added, looking toward Elisabeth, who nodded vigorously.

Seeing that Rebecca's response was good-natured, Belton said, with obvious relief in his voice, "Well, ma'am, you and the kid here stood in front of everybody last night, holdin' hands and lookin' at each other in ways that sure made *me* think I was lookin' at a girlfriend and a boyfriend. And I hafta tell you, Miss Manguson, I was pretty pleased with what I think I saw. If there are two better people to get together, I can't think of 'em. I give the kid here a hard time, Miss Manguson, but I think he's top of the line.

"Of course, I'm sure girlfriend is not the right word. I hardly ever say anything with the *right* word. Y'know what I mean?"

Rebecca reached over and patted the detective's knee. "You say things very, very well, Detective. There's hardly anyone I'd rather listen to.

"And," she added mischievously, "speaking for my *boyfriend* and me, I want to say how thankful we are that you will be with us at St. David's this weekend." At this, her face changed. "And I mean that as seriously as I can mean anything, Detective. We need you. We're very grateful."

The evening meal finished and dishes put away, Rebecca and Matt walked together to the north porch of the mansion and sat down beside each other on the outdoor couch. The others studiously moved in other directions.

After a moment, Matt inquired, "Are you cold? Can I get you a wrap?"

"No," she replied. "Thank you, Matt. I think this is a wonderful time of day, just at sunset, and I like the feeling of the temperature dropping. I don't want to miss it by putting on another layer."

There was a pause. Rebecca's eyes were far away, looking north through gathering darkness toward distant, gray ridges still faintly visible in the fading light. Then she turned her face to him and said, "I meant to ask you this earlier, Matt. Did you read Ecclesiastes after we talked before?"

He smiled in reply. "Yes, but you'll be surprised to know that I didn't really need to. That's one of the few passages I actually know—not the whole thing, but most of it—pretty well. I knew what you meant, Rebecca, before I looked it up. But I liked reading it, knowing that you'd asked me to."

Another pause ensued. Both sat watching the June colors transform themselves into a narrow spectrum of indistinct and fleeting variations on black and white. And they watched comfortably and patiently while their long view to the northern ridge line shortened itself rapidly and became a compressed view of the mansion's northern tree line, then finally a view that included just the porch on which they sat. It was as if a director had set the stage, prepared the theatre, and brought the lighting down to a tight spotlight on the two players whose time had come to open themselves. The audience waited expectantly.

Rebecca broke the silence. "I want to say something to you now, Matt, because tomorrow will be filled with preparation for our evening departure, and, after that, who knows. . . ."

She paused again.

"If we both live through the raid, Matt, I want the two of us to have a conversation about . . . us. Luke and I have, in the last several years, felt an increasing vocational pull into teaching. And at this moment, I don't know anything about your plans for your post-military life, or your thoughts about vocation at all. But before our relationship goes very far, Matt, I'd want us both to understand its context. And for me, that means vocation, and service to community, and much, much more. I don't want to make it sound hard, or too formal, or too intellectual. But neither do I just want to start *having a relationship* with you, without having come to some understanding about what a relationship has to be built upon. Do you know what I mean, or is this nonsense to you?"

Matt looked at her. "I do know what you mean, Rebecca."

"Do you, Matt? Let me say this as bluntly as I know how: I think that you think you love me. And you may. I think perhaps I *could* love you. But—and I know this sounds strange—I will refuse to allow that unless I am satisfied that such a loving would . . . well . . . become an integral part of my Christianity. And yours. We can be great friends and enjoy being with each other for as long as we are together, but if there is to be more than that. . . ."

She stopped and searched his face in the soft light provided by the table lamp just inside the nearest window. Matt smiled. "Don't misunderstand this, please, Rebecca," he said. "But the truth is that I already knew everything that you've just told me. I *know* who you are. And yes, to use your cautious words, I do indeed *think* that I love you. But I know that for us to move forward together, I will have to understand my own Christian frame better than I possibly can at this moment, so soon after that frame has been put into place. And I know that mine would have to match yours somehow . . . or, better, would have to *complement* yours.

"But, Rebecca," he added after a short pause, "I want you to know that I really do accept the way that the detective puts things. I don't mean the dialect, of course," he said, chuckling aloud, "but his insistence that certain things are . . . um . . . *authorized*. And I don't think any of this . . . uh . . . this attraction I have for you, or your . . . well . . . your *acceptance* of my being so attracted to you . . . is accidental in the least. And I'll be very surprised if, as I've tried to put it, our *frames* don't match pretty well, once we've examined them, side by side."

She nodded. "Thank you," she said quietly.

And after a moment, she spoke again. "We may die at St. David's, Matt. We could easily have been killed on the Cambridge raid. We just weren't. Like the detective, I do expect our *mission* to succeed. I think that, through God's grace, we will do what we must. But none of that means that we will live through the experience. If we do not, then we will remain God's servants, in a different realm, and in ways we can't imagine. If we do return alive, then we will simply remain God's servants here on earth. And perhaps together.

"And, either way, Matt, if *not* together . . . then something better."

She stopped and looked again into his eyes, and he, into hers. She reached for his near hand, his left, with both her hands, and, her eyes dropping to follow her own hands' movements, she brought the hand to her lips and kissed it softly. Then, closing her eyes, she brought his hand to her right cheek and held it there. Entranced, he studied the beauty of her face, their hands entwined against its pale softness. Transported, he felt the strength of her hands and the smoothness of her cheek on the surface of his skin. Then, without the slightest uncertainty as to whether it was permitted, knowing, in fact, beyond doubt, that it was, he leaned toward her, cupped her face in his right hand, pulled her to him, and placed his lips in the soft, sweet blackness of her hair.

Friday evening had arrived too quickly. Good-byes had been said, most of them tearful. Rebecca, having waved once more to her parents, moved their nimble sedan into gear and felt the car, with which she was by now very much at home, begin to roll forward toward the secluded family gate. Matt was beside her in front, while the detective sat awkwardly, perched on a sofa pillow, in the center of the rear seat. He'd made clear that he liked to sit in the back, but that he also liked "to be able to see where we're goin' and who might be gainin' on us."

The day had been filled with activity. Some of that activity had included target practice with Jason and Luke's military handguns. Once more, the rigid rules of engagement had been reviewed and rehearsed with the combatants. These were unchanged from the Cambridge raid, but the three members of the raiding party had to undergo the same elaborate question-and-answer testing as on the previous occasion.

In mid-afternoon, Luke, standing in the east yard on his crutches, had given all three of them instructions in the use of his knife array, including horrifying but non-lethal uses of the two largest blades in the set, such as cutting a would-be killer's tendons behind an ankle or a knee. And he had overseen brief target practice sessions with the handguns, sessions that included Rebecca, herself a novice with any firearm.

But the only uncomfortable and disconcerting moments for Rebecca had come during a mid-morning session. Her mother, assisted by her father, had explained to her, Matt, and the detective, that Rebecca, as the designated leader, would, prior to their departure that evening, be given information that would be withheld from the other two. The rationale had been stated as follows: "One or more of you may be captured during this engagement. If it is you, Rebecca, then you must trust to your faith and courage that you will be able in the face of torture to keep silent regarding *anything* having to do with the *Legati,* including any elements of the St. David's attack not already obvious to your captors. If it is you, Matthew, or you, Detective Belton, you will have the same constraints. The difference will be that certain aspects of the St. David's raid will simply not be known by either of you gentlemen. Consequently, in the event, you will be able truthfully to say, 'I do not know,' in response to some questions."

Though Rebecca had been extremely discomfited by this, neither of the men seemed in the least perturbed. The detective had explained. "See, Miss Manguson, the kid and I just don't care. He's just spent five years in the military, and I've been in the military and on the police force for five times that long. We're accustomed to this sort of thing, ma'am. We've never *expected* to be told everything about everything. So, not knowing everything about this is just standard procedure for us. Right, Matt?"

"Right, sir," Matt had replied. "Of course, Detective, if it were *you* who were being given the secret information, I'd have to sing a different song."

"Hey, kid," Belton had said, "if it were *me* with the secret information, we'd be in so much trouble, we might as well not go any further than the front porch."

As she moved the sedan into the downhill roadways leading away from the mansion, Rebecca turned on the headlamps and settled into her "driving set," a state of heightened alertness in both mind and body via which the driving activity was handled much as she had handled tennis competition throughout her life. It allowed her to remain supremely alert, whether driving on a roadway that demanded continual action from eyes, hands, and feet, or little other than to hold a steering wheel straight and steady while rolling at speed down the center of a multi-lane motorway. And for this trip, unlike those undertaken with her brother, she knew she would be the only driver. Neither of the Americans wanted to experiment under these circumstances with piloting a right-hand drive automobile along the left-hand side of unfamiliar motorways crowded with mysterious road signs, clockwise roundabouts, and, once they reached the smaller roads near land's end, ancient rock walls turning already narrow passages into one unforgiving meeting situation after another.

Early in the drive, the detective chatted away about New York City and some of the high and low points of his long career. But his companions were not talkative, and soon he moved his cushion to one side of the rear seat, curled into a very compact ball, and slept. Matt, too, nodded in the front passenger seat, occasionally reaching over to touch Rebecca's arm and to ask how she was. Each time he did this, she touched him back and thanked him. She appreciated his solicitousness toward her. She had seen from the first that it was never based on a presumption that she was so fragile as to require special treatment. No, it was obvious to her that it was simply a function of how love translated itself through him. She smiled to herself at the thought.

For Rebecca, driving with her accustomed trance-like concentration, the trip passed swiftly, and, ninety minutes after their departure from the mansion, she pulled the sedan onto a secluded street in a suburb of Cardiff, the Welsh capital city. Arrangements had been made hastily by her parents and Tom Sutton for the three to be lodged with a couple that could be trusted under any and all circumstances. The wife was a physician and former medical resident with Tom, and the husband once a junior faculty member at Cambridge with Jason. The two were reliable beyond question, and their home was isolated.

The total distance from Birmingham to St. David's was not nearly so great that the drive needed to be done in two stages. But the members of the group had been unanimous in their view that a movement to Cardiff on Friday night would allow a more rested threesome the following night. The Cardiff-to-St. David's drive would take perhaps another two hours, and the threesome would depart soon after dark on Saturday.

Photographed memoranda from enemy headquarters had shown that the two approaches to St. David's—actually a single numbered roadway, the A 487, which twice stretched to the St. David's promontory by nearly doubling back on itself—would be closed off by Meredith Lancaster's security forces as early as Thursday noon. Thus, the A 487 into St. David's from due east, and the A 487 into St. David's from the northeast, would be blocked to all except St. David's residents, authorized dignitaries, and members of the media until early Sunday morning.

This step, memoranda had made clear, would allow tight security within the town of St. David's itself, and would force visitors flocking to the town for the 9:30 Sunday service to find lodging in Haverfordwest, southeast of St. David's, Fishguard, northeast of St. David's, or in other, mostly smaller communities. Some, of course, would simply arise early enough on Sunday to drive from their homes, even those facing three- and four-hour journeys.

All of this meant that Rebecca, Matt, and Sid Belton would drive the Mangusons' sedan from Cardiff, on Saturday night, only as far as Solva, approaching on route 487 from due east. There they would sequester the automobile by ten o'clock, would move on foot to the Pembrokeshire Coast Path, and would follow the path, in the darkness, directly west for four miles, trekking high above the pounding waters of St. Brides Bay, at most points well over one hundred feet of precipitous, purpled cliff below. They would arrive due south of the town of St. David's near midnight. From that point, near St. Non's Chapel, they planned to swing north for the final three-quarter mile stretch to St. David's itself. They would be ready to move on the cathedral by one o'clock Sunday morning.

The threesome would seek to penetrate a perimeter held by Lancaster's heavily armed cathedral guard unit, the group required by the bishop—according to internal memoranda—to remain at least two hundred feet from the cathedral itself. And they would attempt to broach the perimeter regardless of the weather conditions.

Drenched by rainfall, buffeted by coastal winds, cloaked in the blackness of overcast, or bathed in bright moonlight, they would move to the perimeter, through it if possible, and ultimately on to their objective: the cathedral's holy, and wholly dangerous, interior.

Chapter Seventeen

TWENTY-FOUR HOURS AFTER HAVING REACHED THEIR Cardiff safe house, Rebecca, Matt, and Sid Belton stepped from the Mangusons' auto again, this time hard by St. Brides Bay on the coast of Wales. The powerful scent of salt water infused their senses immediately with a new reality. No longer encapsulated within the vehicle, they drank in the supercharged sights, smells, and sounds of the Welsh coast. Their muscles and their minds sprang to highest alert.

Rebecca had pulled the car off on the right, or landward, side of the A 487 in tiny Lower Solva, nestling the vehicle carefully between two others, its license plate not visible from the roadway. Quickly she and the men crossed the darkened highway and gained the Pembrokeshire Coast Path which, at that point, ran close to the road as the two squeezed themselves between the slopes of the Solva hills and the waters of the town's harbor. In just seconds of purposeful walking the threesome lost all sounds from the highway as it took its own, separate path, well inland, up into the hills and toward St. David's, an adventurous, twisting 3.5 miles by auto.

As with the Cambridge raid four nights previous, bright moonlight shone, but was to be threatened, they knew, sometime that night by the solid, jet-black overcast that they could see, even now, moving inland from the southwest, far off to their left as they swung westward after clearing Solva's long harbor.

Matt adjusted his stride to fit the pace that Rebecca had set from her point position, and, as well, to adapt to the detective's disconcerting style of walking. He appeared to have a built-in limp as part of his normal gait, and Matt took several moments to gain confidence in the likelihood that Sid Belton was not on the verge of collapse, but was, in fact, making steady headway.

Once satisfied that the detective was, at least at this early stage, able to handle Rebecca's swift hiking pace, Matt let his mind play back over the long Saturday. He had slept as late as he could, knowing that this night would provide no sleep at all. But by mid-morning he had been too wide awake to remain abed, and had gone downstairs in the unfamiliar house to find his two partners just finishing breakfast with their hosts, all chatting amiably as though on holiday. He had tried to join in the apparent carefree spirit of the group, and had failed utterly, eventually giving up and returning somewhat sullenly to his room, there to read his Merton and doze throughout the day. He ignored someone's whispered invitation to tea, certain that it was not Rebecca's, and remained in his room until time for the evening meal. Even then, his mind was too preoccupied with the impending events of the night to be good company for anyone. Embarrassed, he had apologized to Rebecca after they had thanked their hosts and returned upstairs to dress for departure.

"I'm sorry I've been such poor company today, Rebecca," he had begun.

She had interrupted him with a smile and a touch on his arm. "No, Matt, don't even think about it. I've found it *very* hard to be social today, and have even regretted the arrangement at times. It was a wonderful gesture for them to play host to us on short notice, but I'd so much have preferred to be alone in a hotel today. It's even occurred to me that it would be like asking the marines—yours or ours—to spend a day chatting with new acquaintances in the hours just before storming ashore on some well defended beachhead. Actually, I think you've been commendably civil, Matt. I think perhaps we've all struggled today. I'll just be glad to get started."

Indeed it had been an enormous relief to get back on the road and to start westward from Cardiff. There had been even less conversation among the three on this second stage of the drive than on the previous evening's. Each was alone in private thought or solitary prayer.

Near Newgale, just five miles short of Solva, Rebecca had pulled the car to the side of the road and engaged in her customary final preparation. Turning to face them, she had again read from her prayer book, reciting in her strong, sure voice the prayer suggested before a fight "against any enemy." This was the same prayer she had read for Matt and Luke just before they had moved against the headquarters guards. Matt had been especially struck that night by a particular phrase, one that had stayed with him since then. He waited expectantly to hear it again, and nodded grimly, his eyes closed, as Rebecca spoke the phrase: ". . . Thou givest not alway the battle to the strong, but canst save by many or by few." Then once more, having completed the prayer, she had taken both men's hands in her own and pressed them against her face, her eyes closed. She had kissed first one hand and then the other, squeezed each hand before releasing it, and spoken her strong *"Amen."*

Now Matt looked up at her from his trailing position in their westward moving column. She was by now thirty feet ahead of him, the familiar ponytail swishing from side to side in the moonlight. The detective, however, had at some point begun to fall further behind her with every step and was now little more than arm's length in front of Matt. Seeing the older man struggling, Matt called to Rebecca over the rising wind. She turned her head, saw the distance to the detective, and immediately slowed. Nothing else was said.

Some time later, Matt estimated that they had covered nearly two miles along the Coast Path and, thus, were about halfway to the point just south of St. David's at which they would turn north to move to town's edge. All three were clad darkly, and each carried a waterproof backpack. Rebecca wore the same dark blue and black tennis warm-up clothing that she had donned in her London apartment for the escape from the city one week previous—though it seemed, she had acknowledged to Matt earlier, months ago. But both Matt and the detective wore new clothes purchased, along with the three waterproof backpacks, just two days ago by Elisabeth and Jason, shopping locally, as they not infrequently were asked to do, for guests of the lodge. Their new clothes were lightweight and a dull black in color, as was their new footwear. Further, each backpack contained both a change of clothing and black, hooded waterproofs for use in the expected and hoped-for coastal storm later that night. Rebecca's pack also contained Luke's knife set. Each man's pack held one of the military handguns, with one extra ammunition clip for each.

Sooner than he would have expected, given their markedly slowed pace, Matt became aware that they had reached the south-jutting point of land that marked the dividing point between two small bays, Caerbwdy and Caerfai, and that they were probably no more than twenty minutes' walk from St. Non's Chapel, the point at which they would turn toward the waiting enemy. He began to rehearse their planned penetration in his mind for the hundredth time.

They hoped that Lancaster and his henchmen would interpret the bishop's prohibition against their standing guard within two hundred feet of the cathedral itself as meaning that they should simply take positions at the entrances to the walled perimeter: the guard house high above and near the building's east end; the driveway entrance from the southwest; two secondary driveways located on the other side of the narrow, swift-flowing Alun; and the smaller gap, on the cathedral side of the Alun, leading down to the flying buttresses of the north cathedral wall. If, in fact, the guards were to confine themselves to these five widely spaced entrances, then long stretches of the partly ruined walls would be left unguarded and unwatched.

Matt knew that Rebecca, her parents, and her brother—the senior planners—had developed three different approach options, and that she would make her choice depending upon the guards' actual dispositions, the weather conditions, and other variables. And Matt bore in mind, too, Elisabeth Manguson's unambiguous statements to him and to the detective that Rebecca would have information and instructions regarding the details of this raid that would not be shared with either of them. With so many possible scenarios, and with some of them presumably known only to Rebecca, the utility of mental rehearsal was, Matt knew, open to some question.

But he had, over the past forty-eight hours, developed a way of rehearsing that he thought helpful and appropriate. His approach had to do not so much with his projected physical movements and reactions during the raid as with the posture of his mind and spirit. He had practiced an internal gesture of placing himself in obedience to Rebecca, in specific obedience to the supernatural charge that animated them, and in general obedience to the Lord whom they served. And so Matt rehearsed again as they closed on St. Non's Chapel, visible in the moonlit distance. He placed himself in readiness to do what would be required to *Protect the saint,* to save the bishop, and, he felt impelled to acknowledge, to protect the woman. This last was something for which he admittedly had no explicit charge, and yet he had felt strongly that Luke's iron handshake three nights earlier in the war counsel had served as an informal commission, given to him personally.

Protecting Rebecca was, he had become certain, part of his role here, not because she was in need of such, but because it was she who had been chosen as his mother's successor for the dreamed visions. And it was she who was the authorized leader of this mission. And it was she whom he loved. Looking up again, beyond Rebecca's rhythmically moving figure, he saw the chapel of St. Non's now surprisingly close at hand, not more than a hundred yards off to the right. Their time had come.

Having climbed the narrow, sloping, three-quarter mile access road that connects St. Non's Chapel with the town's southern edge, the three turned right onto a local footpath that took them eastward for a few yards along the edge of fenced pastureland. The massive weather front, precisely on cue, swallowed the face of the moon at the very second they made this turn. Immediately Matt felt himself struck by the thudding percussion of the huge raindrops carried in the bowels of the front. Rebecca stopped and the three quickly pulled from each backpack the black hooded waterproofs that would shield them from the rain and, in their dark, ample shapelessness, disguise the raiders as they moved through the town.

Hoods in place, they reached an opening in the fence line, and Rebecca turned abruptly left. She glanced behind at the men, and broke into what, for her, was a slow jog onto a paved street, the beginning of a tiny residential section along the town border. Sid Belton tried to match the new pace, struggled for a few steps, and slowed to a walk. Rebecca, watching him carefully over her shoulder, stopped, waited, and continued, now walking briskly again.

"Sorry, ma'am," Belton muttered.

In response she simply touched his arm.

Street lights, in the rain, turned the residential neighborhood into a streaky blur. In moments they had made two more turns and had come to a halt at the north-south pedestrian alleyway connecting the residences to the A 487 as it moved west into the town. Here, the highway traveled under the name of High Street, and had but one block to run before its right angle-plus bend to the northeast.

In response to a gesture from Rebecca, each man removed his handgun from his backpack. Each keeping his pistol nestled within its holster, safety lock in place, first Matt and then the detective tucked the gun-and-holster unit into the back of his trousers at the point where the lumbar spine creates enough curvature to allow the makeshift arrangement.

Each nodded to Rebecca his readiness, and she turned and strode the length of the alleyway, stopping at its entrance to High Street. The men waited behind her while she stepped onto the sidewalk and looked carefully through the slanting rain. After several moments she turned, walked back to where they waited, and moved her face close to theirs. In the lee provided by the alleyway, she spoke quietly.

"I can see hooded figures everywhere, mostly in groups of two and three. It appears that Lancaster has placed roving patrols out in the streets, in addition to his perimeter guards. Ready?" she said evenly. She turned and the men followed, hoods in place over their heads.

This was the eventuality for which they had most hoped. The weather had forced Lancaster's guard units into a uniform of sorts and a manner of patrolling that could be replicated by anyone who has ever tried to move on foot through a coastal storm. The tactical response for the threesome was simply to patrol the streets in exactly the same manner as the guards themselves, dependent entirely upon the hooded waterproofs and the violence of the wind and rain to provide cover. The great difficulty for the threesome was accepting the necessity to saunter through enemy-occupied territory under circumstances so perilous that, at least for Rebecca and Matt, running would have seemed easier, more natural, and, in one sense, but not all, safer.

They had stepped out into the narrow thoroughfare of High Street without hesitation. And, fewer than twenty terrifying yet leisurely minutes later, they swung their packs off their shoulders and sat down, their backs against the ancient rock wall that formed the northeastern perimeter of the cathedral grounds. They had walked unimpeded through the heart of the town, visible to at least half-dozen two- and three-man guard units, once actually waving back at their *faux* comrades. They had crossed to Quickwell Hill Street, which had taken them down into the cathedral's geological declivity, well north of the perimeter, then had crossed the wet, grassy terrain leading to the left bank of the Alun. Following the rushing stream in the blackness to the point of its penetration of the perimeter wall, they had sat down to prepare for the final stage of the cathedral approach.

The planners had decided that, given the Alun's strategic course through the very center of the cathedral perimeter, the waterway provided the best entry and exit regardless of weather conditions. The storm's welcome arrival had greatly reduced the dangers in crossing to a position upriver of the cathedral, for the gale-force downpour had pounded roofs, pavement, guard units, and raiding party without slackening during their transit. As he sat down and moved his pack to his side, Matt realized that as yet he had not so much as glimpsed the cathedral, and yet he was at a point fewer than one hundred yards from its north face.

For five full minutes, they sat motionless, recovering from the excruciating tension of the movement through the town and preparing silently and individually for what was to come next. Because the gale blew from the southwest, and since the wall at that point ran northwest to southeast, they remained for the moment dry and wind-sheltered. During those minutes, Matt knew that Rebecca was praying. He guessed that the detective was, as well. Matt felt exhausted, and yet he knew that he had expended little energy. The exaggerated slow-motion walk through the town under scrutiny of the enemy had drained him more than he would have imagined.

Now, following the lead of his companions, Matt put his face in his hands and tried to pray. He found that he could form no coherent prayerful thought. Then he remembered what Rebecca had told the group on Wednesday night about her prayer, generated *in extremis,* as she had lain helpless in Meredith Lancaster's headquarters the night before. And so he prayed those simple, evocative words of urgent petition: *"Father, help me."* And then he prayed them again.

And yet again.

While sitting thus, under his hood, deep in exhausted, desperate prayer, Matt had heard nothing over the constant roar of the storm for the five minutes that had passed since they had stopped in the lee of the wall's stony comfort. And so, at length, he was surprised to feel two strong hands pulling his own hands from his face. He opened his eyes to find Rebecca's face almost touching his. She cupped his face in both her hands and spoke to him, their hoods forming a single bridge of fabric and affording an uncanny sense of privacy, even of isolation. "Matt," she said, "I need you to be strong. Can you do it? Are you ready? *Will* you do this?"

Matt stared into the beauty of this rugged femininity, this indomitable softness, this woman that he loved. Her mouth was inches from his. And, in wordless reply, he moved his hands to her face and pulled her lips slowly and carefully to his, holding her face gently enough so that, had she not wished to be kissed, she could have stopped the movement.

She did not stop the movement.

Thus, surrounded by violent enemy and raging storm, he kissed the angel. And he felt his kiss returned: soft, delicate, lingering, all at once. When the kiss ended, Matt drew her cheek alongside his and continued for long seconds to hold her. He could hear and feel her breath in his ear. "Yes, Rebecca," he whispered into hers, "I am ready. I *will* do this." Then he carefully moved her face away from his, just far enough to fix her eyes with his once more. Cradling her exquisite face in his long, muscular hands, he brushed his thumbs lightly across her white, rain-wet cheeks.

Finally he nodded his head. "Let's reclaim our cathedral," he said.

She looked steadily at him, the penetrating gray eyes unwavering, a faint smile on her lips. Matt watched her take a long, deep breath, the same movement he had seen and heard from her brother in the final seconds before his darkened runs toward the headquarters sentries. Then he saw her move back onto her haunches, move to Sid Belton, and lift his hood from his face. He looked up at her. "Are you ready, Detective?" she asked, forcing her voice through the wind.

At first he did not move, dropping his eyes from hers. Then he shook his head, looking away. Matt had turned his head to see him, and, at this unexpected response, he moved immediately, alongside Rebecca, to a position that brought them both in front of the little man. "I'm whipped," he said weakly. "I shouldn't have tried it, ma'am. The hike was too much. I don't have anything left for what we gotta do now. I'm sorry, ma'am."

Rebecca and Matt looked at each other. Matt took her near hand and spoke rapidly. "Rebecca, let me change places with you on the run in. You go in first, and I'll come in after you and carry the detective. If you can take all three packs, I can bring him with me." He nodded at her in reassurance. "We can do it."

She nodded in return and, without consulting the shivering detective, they began preparations. Matt and Rebecca removed their hoods and helped Sid Belton to remove his. Then they did the same with their shoes. The two handguns were returned to their packs, and the largest knife blade removed from Rebecca's pack and fitted into its universal handle. With hoods, handguns, and shoes secured tightly in the waterproof packs, and with the huge knife, wrapped in a cloth, now clasped in Matt's teeth, Rebecca quickly applied shoe black to her face and to the men's, and they were ready.

Wordlessly they went over the wall, which, near where they had crouched, had deteriorated over the centuries to a height of only four feet. As they had expected, they found that the cathedral's spotlights and walkway lights shined nowhere near the river's own, as it were, private entrance into the perimeter. Now on the cathedral side of the wall for the first time, they moved quickly back to the left bank and crouched at river's edge. Matt helped Rebecca position the three packs, one high and one low on her back, the third on her chest. She looked at him once more, he nodded, and she immediately turned and plunged powerfully into the rushing blackness of the water.

As the Alun passes through the cathedral perimeter, its waters are constricted severely by steep-sided concrete retaining walls. The tightness of the forced constraints gives the water both depth and force, even in seasons when total volume is low. Matt watched Rebecca's disappearance downstream, her black hair and ponytail briefly visible. Without waiting further, and still clasping the weapon in his teeth, Matt turned to the miserable detective, placed his hands on Belton's shoulders, and turned him around. Matt then encircled him from behind with long, muscular arms, locking his hands together over Belton's sternum. Then, crouching at water's edge and clasping the detective's lightweight figure tightly, Matt slid into the Alun on his back, arching immediately to kick downward, thereby keeping the two of them high in the water as the current swept them toward the cathedral.

The waterborne journey was brief. In fewer than twenty seconds, Matt found himself passing through the brightly lit area just west of the main cathedral doors, and he knew he must be nearly to the concrete bridge that spanned the narrow river near the cathedral's entrance. He twisted his body, still holding the detective high in the water, saw Rebecca reaching for them, and, holding Belton with his left arm and grasping the bridge's support structures with his right, he stopped them under the bridge, fighting, with Rebecca's help, to hold position against the current's insistence. Swiftly Matt and Rebecca helped the detective to a secure handhold on the steep retaining wall, still positioned well under the bridge. Matt then swung himself, now using both hands, to the upstream side of the bridge and pulled himself up, high enough to survey the immediate area. Through the driving rain, he looked carefully in all directions and saw no one. It appeared that, as they had hoped, all guard units were stationed at the perimeter entrances or on roving patrol through the town. The interior of the perimeter was deserted, in accordance with the import of the bishop's directive.

Matt, still suspending himself with both hands, lowered himself far enough to make eye contact with Rebecca. He nodded down at her. She reached up, took the knife from his teeth, and, sheathing it quickly, placed it through a loop on the outside of the pack that rode across her chest.

They knew that these last few yards were riskiest of all, in that there could be no protection and no deception. They would have to move from the underside of the bridge to the south porch door, at the near end of the building, a distance of perhaps thirty yards. Anyone looking toward the cathedral itself from the perimeter entrances, though each entrance was at some distance from the building, would have no trouble, even in the storm, observing their movement. And it would be obvious that such an approach was unauthorized.

They knew that one moment was as good or as bad as another for the maneuver. And so, as soon as they could gather themselves, Matt and Rebecca scrambled up from the bridge, pulled the detective up after them, and, supporting him from each side as he walked unsteadily between them, moved to the south porch. Once they were within the shadows cast by the porch's overhanging stonework, they were relatively safe from observation, but they wasted no time. Still supporting the detective between them, they placed his small tools in his trembling hands and waited patiently while he worked the mechanism. True to his promise, the door yielded within seconds and they were inside. The massive door closed behind them and they were embraced in the holiness of the Cathedral of St. David.

Once inside, Matt and Rebecca immediately helped the detective into a complete set of dry clothing, and fed him one of the candy bars that he had insisted upon bringing. Then, crossing to the north side of the cathedral, they seated him in a softly lighted area behind one of the outward leaning pillars. There, the detective and Rebecca each donned a new pair of the evidence gloves with which Sid Belton always traveled, and Matt stayed beside him while Rebecca, gracefully genuflecting at the head of the center aisle, moved swiftly and soundlessly to the front, near the altar. There she removed Meredith Lancaster's lock box from the elaborately adorned table on which it had been placed by Lancaster himself at midnight, and brought it to the detective. Using another set of small tools, he unlocked the box in seconds. Rebecca opened its lid and found inside the spectacularly beautiful, leather-bound document binder that they had seen described in the memoranda.

Moving quickly but with great care, Rebecca and the detective worked the temporary binding open, removed the fraudulent documents, and inserted Martha Clark's handwritten copies of the Nicene Creed and the *Credo Nicea,* followed by her typed histories of the creed, St. David, and the cathedral. They placed the false documents inside the large envelope from which they had drawn the true ones, fastened it tightly, and returned the envelope to Rebecca's pack. The authentic documents now encased in the leather binder, they returned the binder to the lock box.

Then Rebecca, still moving with her customary speed and efficiency, left the two men sitting together behind the westernmost north aisle pillar, moved to the center aisle, strode to the front, and replaced the lock box on its table in front of the altar. Without pausing, she then moved directly back to the north aisle, turned away from the men toward the east end of the cathedral, and walked swiftly back to Holy Trinity Chapel. Stopping at its north side entrance, Rebecca took a deep breath. She looked through the arched entryway into the chapel. Unsurprised and yet amazed, she observed the exact configuration given her in the dreamed vision: the identical arched entryway on the south side of the chapel, its altar, its row of fixed benches, and its front row comprising individual chairs. Stooping to allow her six-foot frame to pass through the arch, she strode swiftly to the third chair from the center, on the right side facing the altar, leaned over the back of the chair, and pulled out the hymnal that she found, as expected, in the rack. Then she dropped to her knees facing the chair, placed the hymnal on the chair surface, and opened the book. Grinning skull and macabre crossbones met her gaze. She felt a tingling sensation in every nerve as, before her eyes, dream became reality. Pulling a plastic bag from a pocket, she removed the vial with her gloved hands and inserted the vial into the bag. Then she stood, lifted the now-empty book, reached over the chair back, replaced the hymnal, and moved quickly back to the cathedral's north aisle. Now breaking into her soft, gliding run, she was at the men's side in seconds.

She knelt beside them. Sid Belton took the plastic bag from her, removed a small rubber evidence holding container from his pack, and placed bag and vial therein. He snapped the lid in place. Their work was done. There was a pause while Rebecca mentally worked through their task list up to that point, and reviewed their options for the next steps. Satisfied, she spoke.

"Detective," she asked, "how do you feel?"

"Much better, ma'am. The dry clothes and the candy bar brought me back. Don't worry about me, now. You two just get outta here in one piece and get these damned documents in the sea. I'm fine."

Rebecca and Matt helped him to his feet, then escorted him east along the cathedral's north aisle. Stopping just outside the Chapel of St. Thomas Becket, they bid him good-bye. "You two get goin'," he said to them again with some urgency in his voice. "The storm could ease off any time now. Get out while people still can't see much and are spendin' most of their energy tryin' to stay dry and warm. I've got my dry clothes on. I've got five more candy bars. I've got a thousand places to hide myself at five o'clock when things start up inside the cathedral. By the time those researchers get here, I'll be at my sneakiest best. Don't worry about me. I'll get the last part of the mission done."

Rebecca stepped to him, hugged him tightly, and turned to go. Belton looked at Matt. "Don't *you* be tryin' to hug me, kid. I'll pop you one."

Matt laughed, reached out, and touched his arm. "We'll see you at the mansion tonight, Detective."

Chapter Eighteen

AS REBECCA AND MATT CROSSED TO THE SOUTH PORCH of the cathedral where they had entered half an hour earlier, they stopped at the head of the center aisle and looked toward the sanctuary. They wanted to hurry away, but they also felt compelled to remain, at least for moments. Exchanging glances, they moved into the rearmost pew and knelt together. Then, eyes closed in prayer, they allowed fourteen centuries of daily Christian worship on this ground to wash through them. Indescribable sensations ran through them both, sensations that made meaningless the facile verbal distinctions between awe and fear, joy and gratitude, love and obedience, judgment and forgiveness. And both knew that the Presence with them in that place was larger and greater than any of those that they had yet encountered in this week of otherworldly comings and goings and interminglings with their own kind. And they also knew with greatest certainty that Eternity awaited them, singly or together, whether on this night or in sixty years. And they knew that it was time for Eternity to tell them which of those was to be. They rose from their knees.

At the cathedral door they stopped and put on the shoes that they had placed in their waterproof packs for their approach in the river. Then Matt extracted his handgun and placed it again against the small of his back. The knife remained sheathed in the outside loop of Rebecca's pack, now set high and tight on her back. The hooded waterproofs remained rolled tightly inside the packs.

Rebecca's preferred escape route from the cathedral perimeter was to cross the lighted area back to the concrete bridge, duck below the bridge, remove their shoes again, place them and the handgun in the backpacks, then float the Alun to the river's exit at the opposite side of the perimeter from which they had entered. But she wanted their shoes on and handgun and knife available as they stepped from the cathedral, in case the enemy's dispositions now eliminated the river as escape vehicle. She wanted to be ready for any eventuality, and, she thought, she was indeed ready for any that could reasonably have been planned for.

They checked each other's packs once more. Then Matt pushed the door open wide enough for the two of them to slip through. It closed and locked behind them. Even before they looked, their ears told them that the rain had ceased in the half hour since they had entered that door, and that the wind, if not calm, had dropped to little more than a light coastal breeze. Then, turning to peer out from the shadows onto the south lawns and walkways of the cathedral grounds, they were stunned to see, perhaps fifty yards from them, a huge black Mercedes, its doors open. And beside the Mercedes stood a man clothed, like them, in black. In his hand he held an enormous, elongated object that appeared, improbably, to be an umbrella. Yet, both to Rebecca and to Matt, at first glance, the massive object seemed much more weapon than rain protector. The man was looking directly at them.

Time stopped. No one moved.

Then, with no need to signal each other, Rebecca and Matt wheeled to the right, running. They sprinted back across the west face of the cathedral, following the left bank of the Alun, swiftly retracing the route by which they had floated through the perimeter. Matt fell in behind Rebecca, astonished at her speed. She cleared the cathedral's outlying structures and turned sharply to the east, away from the river.

Rebecca could never remember exactly how they managed to extricate themselves from the perimeter walls. She knew that they had sprinted up the steep hill, still within the perimeter, that dropped so precipitously from the town itself to hide its treasured cathedral, running and climbing mostly on grass, and that during the running climb they had vaulted more than one wall. The last of the walls was part of the outermost northeastern perimeter, and so immediately they had found themselves crossing Nun Street, wheeling right again, racing past the square, across High Street, and into their pedestrian alleyway. They had heard shouts throughout their climbing, scrambling run. Twice they flew past clusters of still-hooded guards who, startled, had stared at them unmoving until too late. They had heard no shots behind them.

As she raced back through the residential neighborhood along the south edge of town, Rebecca realized that Matt was no longer at her shoulder. Looking back, she saw him, struggling, twenty-five yards behind her. She slowed, then stopped. He reached her and stopped beside her, hands on knees, gasping. They looked behind. They saw no one. They heard no shouts. But they did hear a new sound, seemingly near at hand. It was thunder. Looking up through the residential street lights, they saw that, while the rain associated with the front line of the storm had moved on, the heart of the storm was actually overhead. Lightning had begun to play spectacularly around the town, its cathedral, and its coastal cliffs. The noise of its thunder seemed to come from all directions.

Matt's breathing gradually slowed and, finally standing erect again, hands on hips, he took in and released a deep breath. "Okay," he said. "Sorry. Let's go."

They turned and, side by side, jogged slowly to the end of the paved street and turned west along the footpath that would carry them to the three-quarter mile north-south paved driveway to St. Non's Chapel near the cliffs. Reaching the drive, they turned south and continued, their way illuminated by near-continual lightning that seemed both to link the storm front with itself and to connect it to the land and the sea. With a quarter mile still to go, jogging comfortably toward St. Non's, headlamps suddenly fixed them in their glare and they heard simultaneously the howl of a Mercedes engine. Instantly they returned to sprinting speed. Immediately in danger of being left behind again, Matt labored to stay abreast of the flying Rebecca, his long strides keeping him just behind her right shoulder, so close at times that the long ponytail actually brushed against his face. Then, as the desperation of their plight became obvious to him, he fell back a half-stride and moved directly behind her, his running shadow now completely covering her image within the headlamps' glare. There, in that position, he remained.

Reaching a dirt and gravel parking area on their right, Rebecca turned off the pavement, flew across uneven ground, and, without slowing, raced across the treacherous unevenness of pasture terrain. Somehow they passed over a chest-high, three-rail wooden fence line without pause, circled to the left around the small ruin of St. David's legendary birthplace, situated just yards from St. Non's Chapel, and then wheeled right again, knowing the cliff line loomed just in front of them. Rebecca had, without breaking stride and while still sprinting along the pavement, pulled her backpack to one side and removed the envelope containing the fraudulent documents.

Now, approaching the cliff line, sprinting hard, she moved the envelope to her right hand and prepared to hurl Meredith Lancaster's lies to their death in the churning surf at the foot of the Pembrokeshire cliffs. But in the instant that, still running hard, she drew her hand back in preparation for a discus-like throwing movement, she heard the same unmistakable sound that had played over in her mind countless times in the days and nights since their Cambridge headquarters raid. It was the report of gunfire, the noise of human violence reaching her ears in the form of a pathetic attempt to mimic the majesty of the thunder under which the gunfire issued.

Within the same moment in time, the two sounds too close together to separate, Rebecca heard another noise, this one horrifying beyond any that she had theretofore experienced. And she knew what it was, though she had never heard the sound before. It was the unique sound of large-calibre bullets ripping through fabric, flesh, blood, and bone. The ripping, slapping noises were coupled with the involuntary vocal response demanded from the human being whose body was torn by the bullets' impact.

Rebecca never forgot the timbre of Matt's deep groan, the awful shape of the uttered sound, the indistinct yet powerful "Uhhh" as he fell. Matt, she had known without looking back, had been, almost from the moment the Mercedes' headlamps illuminated them, running directly behind her, lining his body up with hers. He was four inches taller, at least that much wider. And from that position, shielding Rebecca with his body, his flesh willingly accepted—no, welcomed— the bullets that would have been hers. He crashed, tumbling and rolling, into the grass, dirt, and mud. And, in this cacophony, Rebecca heard still another sound, this one altogether as sickening as the last. She heard the appalling thud of his skull smashing into one of the rocky protuberances that dotted the landscape of the cliff line.

Allowing the document envelope to fall from her hand to the path, Rebecca dropped and spun to the ground, reaching across Matt's back for the handgun even as he continued to roll, his body completely inert. Bullets whined overhead and ricocheted off the dirt and rocks around them. She quickly freed the pistol, flicked off the safety, and, following her brother's careful instructions over the previous two days, squeezed off three rounds in the direction of the gunfire, aiming high. The immediate result was that which Luke had promised her. Firing ceased as Lancaster's guards, surprised, took cover.

She looked to each side of her. There was no cover for them. She looked back to the fence line from which the bullets had flown, and estimated the distance. It was, she guessed, eighty to one hundred yards. Her chances of hitting anything with the handgun at that range, under those conditions, were poor, but she knew that she and Matt were well within accurate range of whatever weapons were being trained on them.

Lightning continued to flash from almost every direction, and the thunder, if anything, seemed louder and nearer than ever. It was almost as if daylight conditions obtained; she could not hope for darkness to provide assistance. She did not know how long the respite would continue, but she was certain that her life expectancy and Matt's, if indeed he lived even now, likely should be calculated in seconds, not minutes. Matt had fallen and tumbled into a position in which he lay on his right side, his legs sprawled generally toward the cliff line, his head toward Lancaster and his gunmen. Rebecca crawled up beside his prostrate form, pushed him gently onto his back, and lay across his chest and neck. Her left forearm braced itself hard into the dirt, serving as a cradle for her right hand and thereby for the handgun, and at the same time forming a thin shield of flesh and bone between Matt's head and the muzzles of the automatic weapons she faced. Her right index finger caressed the pistol's trigger. She took aim at the wall behind which her assailants crouched. She knew she had five rounds in the pistol now, and a second clip in Matt's pack which would yield eight more. "Father," she said aloud, "into Thy hands we commit . . ."

At that moment three men, satisfied from their visual assessment that they faced only a single handgun and at a range far exceeding its accurate capability, stood up, side by side. In the glare of nearly continual lightning flashes, Rebecca could look down the barrels of automatic rifles aimed at her by both gunmen who flanked the man in the center. That man was dressed in black, and he raised with one arm the huge, ominous umbrella that she had seen from the cathedral door. But now she saw that the umbrella was not. Stripped of its fabric disguise, it had become an outsized large-calibre rifle or shotgun. She could not tell which from this distance and, she knew, it made no difference.

For she saw that Meredith Lancaster had no intention of using the gun to kill her. He might use it to shred her corpse and Matt's, once his two gunmen had riddled them with automatic weapons fire. But for now, he was not even aiming it in her direction. Instead, he held the monstrous weapon at the vertical with his right arm, positioning the instrument straight over his head, muzzle pointing to the sky, his left hand on the metal swinging gate just in front of him. His gunmen stood nearly shoulder to shoulder with him, one on each side, awaiting his command, their rifles trained on her face. Lightning played behind, over, and around them, and she saw him beginning to shout in her direction. The wind was still light, so that, in the fleeting intervals between the nearly deafening concussions of thunder, she could hear Lancaster's screams. The screams were not the inarticulate imprecations of a madman. No, he screamed at her with words and in language, and she knew without question that it was not human language. It was the language of his Masters.

Now Rebecca, conscious of the limited range and performance of her handgun, took aim just above Meredith Lancaster's forehead. Her intent was to get off as many rounds as she could before the gunmen opened again on her, thinking that if she could so much as wound him, they, who doubtless hated Lancaster almost as much as they feared him, might desist. Her finger tightened on the trigger while Lancaster, still raging at her through the fury of flash and shudder of thunder, his weapon still pointing straight to the sky, prepared to end her life with a word to his men.

Then her hand was stayed.

She sensed that something had begun to happen within the storm cloud directly overhead, a boiling, churning eminence now so low that it seemed almost to enclose them. She raised her eyes from Lancaster's twisted, bulging face, and she saw the cloud begin to separate even as she watched. Incredibly, and as though it had suddenly transformed itself into a savage animal, it began to form a vast, sweeping, menacing, sinewy vortex within itself, an inverted tornado of apocalyptic scale. For long seconds, Rebecca stared transfixed. Then, pulling her eyes away from the spectacle above, she told herself that she must hesitate no longer. The automatic weapons could open on her and Matt at any second. She returned her eyes to Lancaster, and readjusted her visual focus to the line of her handgun's barrel with the spot just above Lancaster's forehead at which she would fire. And still he screamed. And still he held his weapon straight skyward, its muzzle now aiming directly into the vortex that swirled above his head.

Again she prepared to fire.

Again her hand was stayed.

In one second there was above them only one black, tightly circling cloud. In the next there appeared a red eye of light in the center of this cyclone. In the next the red eye of light seemed actually to begin to pulse, and to pulse purposefully, as if it were a Mind. It pulsed directly downward . . . once . . . twice . . . three times. And with the fourth came a magnificent, majestic shaft, not of lightning in any natural sense, but of a golden fire hurled from somewhere deep within the living, pulsing eye. The shaft struck Meredith Lancaster with all the force and power and judgment of Almighty God.

Rebecca's eyes reflexively squinted, but did not close at the preternatural roar and intolerable brightness of the darting, blinding shaft which seemed to throw out subordinate, probing, horizontal beams in all directions and along all points of the main shaft. And she saw that it had descended, faster than vision could follow, from the eye in the vortex to the upraised muzzle of the weapon that Lancaster had held pointed to the heavens. And she saw, in seconds that ticked past like centuries, that the golden fire was inexorably consuming Meredith Lancaster, his weapon itself, and the two who flanked him at this, his execution. Even from her eighty-plus-yard distance Rebecca could see the incandescent rod of fire and light eating . . .melting . . . dissolving . . . every aspect of Lancaster's face, his torso, his extremities. Yet somehow Lancaster and his two gunmen, already dead men, were allowed by the awful force of the shaft to remain erect even as the shaft consumed them. And when this mighty rod of light finally, at length, withdrew back into the red vortex of divine vengeance from whence it had come, the three consumed figures began, quite slowly, to disintegrate before Rebecca's eyes, literally becoming, first, granular, salt-like, insubstantial, nearly transparent. And then, moments after, in a protracted gust from the persistent coastal wind, they simply blew away to their reward, the gray Hell of the eternally damned.

Rebecca did not know how long she lay there, her pistol still poised in readiness, her chest still resting on Matt's, her forearm and body still positioned to prevent his being riddled by more bullets than the number that had already torn him. But at length she felt light rainfall on her hands and face, and she began to waken to her new reality. Meredith Lancaster was dead. No, more than dead. Meredith Lancaster had been deemed worthy of divine destruction. Some word stronger than *dead* would be needed to represent what he had finally become. As she wakened to the reality of Lancaster's execution, she wakened as well to the fact of the wounded man who lay beneath her, unconscious and bleeding . . . and perhaps, himself, already dead.

She raised herself, at first unsteadily, to her knees. She switched on the safety mechanism for her handgun, and, holstering it, placed it carefully in Matt's pack. Then, in dread, she looked at his ravaged face. The rock on which he had fallen with such force had horribly distorted his left temple, which now bled steadily from a maze of lacerations. She could not tell from visual inspection if his skull was fractured, and knew that, if it were, there would be nothing she could do in any case. She looked at his body and realized that, in his black clothing, soaking wet from storm and river, she could not see the extent of his injuries. Extracting the knife from its sheath, she sliced his shirt from neck to belt and pulled it back in both directions. Then, rolling him toward her, she reached behind him with the knife, under his still-attached backpack, and slit the full length of his shirt from behind. Quickly peeling the shirt's remnants down over each arm and hand, she viewed his unclothed torso. She saw horrible exit wounds in and around his left shoulder, upper left arm, and upper chest. She rolled him toward her again, and leaned over him to view the entry wounds behind the shoulder, stifling a groan at the catastrophic destruction of tissue and bone. She returned him gently to his back and, shifting her position, slit the outside seam of his trousers on both legs. Peeling back the fabric, she saw no wounds below his waist.

She reached into one of the packs for the dry clothing, and pulled out a garment at random. Slicing it into strips, she bound the bleeding shoulder and upper left chest in every way possible, tightened the strips as much as she could, and then bound his head lightly, not wanting to increase the pressure on his damaged cranium. She sat back once more and looked up. The rain was starting again in earnest. She looked down at Matt. Leaning over him, she hesitantly pressed her index finger into the side of his neck and felt for a pulse. It was there. She did not know for how long.

Then, in response to an insistent impulse, she looked over her shoulder in the darkness and saw dimly the document envelope, lying where she had dropped it when the gunfire began, just feet from the precipice. She picked up the knife again, strode to where the envelope lay, then knelt and drove the knife through the entire sheaf, the "Creed of St. David" and the fraudulent histories that Lancaster had prepared to accompany it. Then, still holding the knife by its heavy universal handle, she walked to the edge of the cliff, looked out over the dark sea, and hurled the thing entire—knife, envelope, documents—as far as she could into the uniform blackness of night and sea. Then she waited, her eyes on the boiling surf, and seconds later was rewarded by the sight of the small splash that, for the briefest of moments, interrupted the water's surging rhythm.

She ran again to Matt, knelt beside him, and once more rolled him onto his side. She opened his backpack, still securely in place, removed several items, and replaced them with some from her own pack. Placing all unneeded items in hers, she walked back to the cliff and threw her pack into the sea. Returning to Matt for the last time, she leaned down, placed her mouth near his ear, and spoke to him quietly. "Matt, we're going now. It's my turn." Then she placed her lips on his blackened, dirt-encrusted cheek.

She rolled him forward onto his chest and checked the security of his backpack. Then, moving on her knees, she gently pulled his arms, first the right and then the horribly mangled left, to positions above his head. She returned to his side and lay down on her back at a right angle to his body. Inching toward him until the top of her head was against his side, she reached over her head, forced her hands and arms under his chest and thighs, and, groaning with the effort, lifted and dragged his two-hundred-plus pounds across her face, as she wiggled her own body further and further under him, until, finally, he rested across her own chest. Then, her body under his, she rolled, in stages, onto her stomach, so that both of them lay face down on the ground, his body draped across hers at his waist in transverse aspect. Then, almost delicately, yet with immense muscular effort from her powerful arms, back, and legs, Rebecca began to raise herself. First she came to a fully kneeling position, and then, after extending one foot in front so that she rested now on but one knee, she rose from the ground in a mighty upward thrust that drew from her a prolonged moan of maximum effort. And now she stood erect, Matt's helpless form draped around her neck and shoulders. Staggering briefly, she looped one arm behind his knees, and with her other hand she gripped the uninjured arm at the elbow.

For several seconds she remained stationary, giving her muscles time to adjust to the weight and balance of the burden. Then, still breathing heavily from the continuous exertion, Rebecca turned carefully and faced the sea. She moved hesitantly, still learning the muscular techniques required, toward the cliff, straining to remain erect. At the terminus of the small footpath, where it found its final intersection with the east-west Pembrokeshire Coast Path, she stopped.

Solva and her waiting automobile were four tortuous miles to the east. And she knew that, in all likelihood, the guards stationed on the A 487 between Solva and St. David's would have been notified by radiotelephone of their raid. From their blocking position on the highway, those gunmen would have to move but a short distance south, on foot, to cut off her escape route to Solva. The thing seemed impossible. She could neither cover four miles of trail with Matt's dead weight on her shoulders, nor, in any case, cope with the armed enemy that she would certainly meet along the way.

She thought about the black Mercedes parked in the darkness two hundred yards behind her, near St. Non's Chapel. If she could walk at all with Matt's body on her shoulders, she could surely cover that much ground. But she knew that, in all likelihood, none of the three men just executed had been the Mercedes' driver. At least one of Lancaster's men doubtless waited there, with the vehicle. And even if not, the only vehicular escape route from St. Non's was the short roadway down which she and Matt had just sprinted. The Mercedes could extricate itself from St. Non's only by moving directly back into the teeth of the enemy forces that swarmed through the streets of St. David's.

Rebecca stood for another long minute, thinking.

And then painfully, carefully, she turned to her right, away from Solva. Bearing her crushing burden, she set her face to the west, toward land's end.

After five minutes, moving westward on the Coast Path, Rebecca felt that her shoulders would break. Still she walked on. After fifteen minutes, every muscle in her body screamed at her for relief. The pain had become excruciating. It was at that point that her prayer had begun again: *"Father, help me."* She could think of nothing except that prayer. Though the rain had again ceased, the overcast remained and she could scarcely see well enough to follow the intricate turns of the Coast Path as it traced the irregularities formed by eons of warfare between sea and cliff. And still she walked on.

She knew that if she were to lower Matt to the ground it would be impossible to lift him again. And she knew that if she stumbled and fell, she herself would not be able to rise. And she knew, further, that Matt might by now be dead. But she acknowledged to herself that whether she carried a living man or a dead one, both her duty and her wishes were unchanged. She was no more willing to leave his corpse behind than she was willing to abandon the living man who had loved her and sacrificed himself for her.

After nearly forty-five minutes of agonized movement, her pain long since having become so much a part of her being that she no longer identified it as a sensation separate from sight or hearing, she rounded *Trwyncynddeiriog*, the Mad Point, so named because of the gale-force winds that beset its face even under relatively calm conditions elsewhere. She had decided early on that she would not leave the Coast Path even if she heard pursuit behind her. Leaving the Coast Path meant turning inland, and at nearly all points that meant crossing fences or climbing embankments that ranged from a few feet in height to more than twenty. She knew that she could not step upward a single foot, and that even to try would result in a fall, and that it would be the end.

It was now after three o'clock on Sunday morning. Though Rebecca was chilled by the wind coursing through her still-wet clothing, she knew she was becoming dehydrated from loss of fluids. She had perspired steadily from the moment they had bolted, running hard and climbing fast toward the perimeter wall, from the cathedral steps. Now she gasped for air through cracked lips completely caked with salt from her own body and from the sea spray. And still she walked on.

There were times when she felt she was losing consciousness. There were times when she felt the approach of delirium. There were times when she screamed into the darkness and wind in agony and in despair. But there was no time when she did not repeat, at times to herself, and at times aloud, the plea that for Rebecca was infused both with desperation and with a visceral, uncompromising confidence: *"Father, help me."*

And still she walked on.

Half past three o'clock came and passed. She had now been walking for more than seventy-five minutes and had covered perhaps one mile. The Coast Path had just brought her into another tight turn to her right when she stopped, confused. She saw something, but could not interpret what she saw. Then she realized that it was the act of seeing itself that had confused her. The swift-moving overcast was beginning to break up in places, and scattered rays of moonlight had begun to play across the landscape and seascape. And as she turned her head to the right, or inland, side, and as she looked down from the new vantage point provided by the pathway's sharp bend to her right, she observed several small objects glistening against water.

In a flash of recognition she realized that she had reached Porth Clais, the sliver of inlet that had served St. David's as harbor from at least the time cathedral construction had begun more than eight centuries ago. She stood for long moments, looking down at the small fishing boats below her. Then carefully, uncertainly, Rebecca crept forward, feeling with her toes before shifting her weight forward to the next step. The Coast Path was descending to harbor platform level—just eight feet above water level itself. She could see in the uneven light that the descent was quickly to become precipitous. And she could see dimly that, to reach the tiny harbor, she would be required not only to negotiate a series of steep slopes, but what appeared from a distance to be steps cut into the slope as well. Neither of those things could she do with Matt on her shoulders.

Then, as she studied the descent, the moon was covered once more, and blackness overwhelmed the scene.

Now, afraid to allow herself, but knowing that she must, she raised her eyes from the harbor and turned her face to seaward. She searched for something, and, her heart sinking, at first found nothing. But then, scanning the blackness again, she saw in the distance, she thought, a tiny red light. Was this a channel buoy? Were there channel buoys at all at Porth Clais? As her eyes strained toward the elusive pinpoint of redness, she sensed interruption—or was it movement—in the speck of light itself. Was she simply imagining both her dread—the blinking light of a stationary marker—and her hope—the movement of a small boat's running light?

Shaking the ridiculous question from her mind, she then acknowledged to herself that it actually mattered no more whether the light was moving than it did whether Matt, lying across her shoulders, was now alive or dead. That is to say that in one way, it mattered more than anything to her; in another, it made no difference because the action required of her was the same in either case. Whether Matt were alive or dead, her duty and her joy was to carry him away from the violent men who had pursued them from St. David's. And now, whether this tiny red light moved or did not move, her next action must be the same, regardless.

Keeping her face to the sea and her back to the embankment that at that point rose nearly vertically behind her, she began to edge back toward the bank. Feeling with her heels, and covering just inches with each cautious step, she eventually felt the rocky wall of earth behind her foot. She then slowly straightened her back and raised her shoulders as much as she could, muscles screaming in pain at this new demand. But she was rewarded by the feel of Matt's body making contact against the embankment. Next, keeping her back straight, she began to bend her knees, imperceptibly lowering him, inch by inch, toward the uneven ground. When she had finally reached the point at which her buttocks rested on her heels, she could see by turning her head that Matt's head and shoulders were beginning to touch the ground on her left, as were his feet on her right. With a supreme effort, she arched her back, pushed his body up and back with her hands, and slid from under him.

Freed from his weight, she fell forward in exhaustion. She caught herself with her hands, her face almost over the side of the cliff. She pushed herself away from the edge and, on her hands and knees, turned back to Matt. Taking a deep breath, she reached toward his neck and pressed her index finger again into the carotid artery. She kept her finger there for a long time.

Fighting panic, she probed slightly deeper and higher, bending closer as though her eyes could somehow help her fingertip detect a pulse. And then, her heart leaping, she sensed the faint impulse that she sought, slow, weak, and irregular, a signal both of life and of the nearness of its end.

Fighting the desire to lie down beside him, to cradle his wounded head in her arms, and to rest forever, she pulled him toward her, far enough so that she could unzip the backpack. From it she pulled two objects. The first was a dry sweater. She rolled it up, lifted Matt's head from the ground, and gently lowered the side of his face into the sweater's softness. The second object was a strangely configured device that she handled with great care. Turning to face the open sea, she pulled an extender tube on the device to lengthen it, drove its base hard into the Coast Path, directed the elongated cylinder toward open water, and, turning her head away, pressed a release mechanism near the base. There was a loud hiss and a shower of sparks. She turned to follow the flight of an iridescent green flare. It seemed to slow a quarter mile out over the water, then to drift down in smaller, but still brightly burning, fragments of light.

The moon was still hidden from view. Rebecca peered through the darkness on her knees, searching again for the diminutive point of redness.

Finally finding it, she held her breath, clasping her hands tightly under her chin. For long minutes there seemed no change and no movement, and she became certain that the light was indeed a channel buoy. She turned and moved back to Matt's side on her hands and knees. She bent low to speak to him, not knowing or caring whether he could hear her. "We've made it, Matt," she said softly, her lips near his face. "We've saved the bishop. We've destroyed the documents. Meredith Lancaster has been . . . executed. . . . I don't know if we will live or die tonight, but we've done our mission, Matt. And you saved my life. You saved my life again."

Now dehydrated and hypothermic nearly to the point of unconsciousness, Rebecca, still on her knees beside Matt, forced herself to sit up, and, one hand resting on his arm, she turned her eyes seaward one last time. What she then saw caused her to close her eyes and to murmur a wordless prayer of exhausted and grateful thanksgiving. For she had seen, beside the red light, just narrowly to its left in the perceived distance, a point of green. The red light had not been a buoy, but the port running light of a vessel. Now it showed its starboard running light to her as well. The craft had moved forward and turned to its left in response to the flare, and was now approaching, bow on, toward Rebecca.

Afraid to ask her muscles to change her body's position and uncertain whether she could stand at all, she remained on her knees beside Matt, talking to him as the boat's outline gradually became apparent in now intermittent moonlight. The wind was dying, the sky was clearing, and she began to hear, at first faintly, the grumble of diesel engines, engines that drove a substantial fishing boat toward the narrow mouth of the inlet. She watched, fatigue now beginning to overwhelm her, as the craft, hugging the west side of the inlet, made its way gingerly past the ancient sea wall and into the watery enclosure.

And then she heard her name. She heard her name spoken—no, it had been shouted—not by supernatural energy this time, but by blood and lungs. And she knew the voice. It was a voice she had known all her life.

A searchlight from the boat began to probe the cliff wall. Ignoring her body's protests, she leaped to her feet and there, soaked with rain and blood and perspiration, layered with mud and sand and salt, Rebecca Manguson stood, erect, elegant, triumphant.

Her brother had come for her.

Chapter Nineteen

THE DIRECTOR OF THE INSTITUTE FOR SOCIAL RESEARCH found that he was trembling. He had been able to display his usual grave, indulgently condescending air with the police, showing his credential at the south porch of the cathedral. Now he stood alone along the south aisle and waited for the assistants to move to Holy Trinity Chapel with the sacred bread and wine. Jonathan Foster looked at his watch. It was not yet quarter past five.

How had it come to this, he thought to himself. He had never meant to have any but an honorable life, an educator's life of service. He had only wanted to hold positions that would allow him influence, surely a justifiable wish. After all, people wanted to be led. People wanted someone to make decisions on their behalf. And better he than someone else.

And now this. He was going to commit murder. He had avoided thinking that word to himself until now. But here in the cathedral somehow he needed to call things by their names. This was murder. Meredith Lancaster was forcing him to murder the bishop of St. David's. It was not as though he *wanted* to murder anyone. God would know that, he thought. But this was certainly murder. And it was certainly he who would do it. It was impossible. And yet here he was. Waiting for the assistants to place the vessels in the chapel. Just waiting to do his job. His murder.

And it would be the end. He knew that Lancaster would not be implicated. It would just be he, the director of the institute, who would be forever viewed as the murderer. Never mind that he had not brought the cyanide into the cathedral. Never mind that Lancaster had done

263

that himself, hours ago. Never mind that, if he had declined this role, he would have been killed before now. No one would understand. No one could possibly understand.

Foster looked up and toward the interior of the cathedral. It was happening again. He was being somehow compelled to look where he did not want to look. He moved in the direction toward which his eyes took him. He sat down at the end of a pew, his eyes now on the hymnal rack in front of him. In just moments he would be looking at a hymnal rack in Holy Trinity Chapel. But now he found himself reaching out and lifting from its niche not a hymnal but a prayer book. In the dim light he stared down at the small volume, then he opened it slowly. On the left-hand page his eyes fell upon words he could not interpret, and yet he could not seem to look elsewhere: "*Credaf yn un Duw, y Tad Hollalluog, gwneuthurwr nef a daear, a phob peth gweledig ac anweledig. Ac yn un Arglwydd Iesu Grist, unig-genedledig Fab Duw. . . .*"

His eyes moved themselves to the right-hand page, and there he read to himself: "I believe in one God, the Father Almighty, maker of heaven and earth, and of all things visible and invisible. And in one Lord Jesus Christ, the only-begotten Son of God. . . ."

Foster's hands were shaking. It became difficult to see the words. He could not hold the book steady. He placed it on his lap. Despite the chilly early morning air inside the building, he saw perspiration on the backs of his hands.

How had it come to this?

He heard a rustling noise and looked up. The assistants were moving the blessed elements into the chapel. He returned the prayer book to the rack and shut his eyes. Perhaps he could pray. After all, he was not unwilling to believe in God. He just could not seem to do it. And yet he certainly believed in Meredith Lancaster's Dark Masters. He could not disbelieve in them. He met them every day. It was they—the Others—who made him do things.

He sat for five minutes. Nothing happened in his mind. He was terrified, but he could not pray, because they would kill him. They would kill him even in the cathedral. They were everywhere. He was sure that they were everywhere.

It was time. Hardly aware of where he was, Foster moved haltingly, stumbling occasionally, along the south aisle toward the east end of the building. His breathing was labored. The cathedral was completely silent, nearly completely dark. He staggered on. Then it occurred to him that the reason he walked so unsteadily was the slope of the cathedral floor. Of course. The ancient earthquake. He was walking uphill. He would simply adjust for the slope.

Then he fell.

There are many ways to fall. This fall was the collapse of a man whose legs have ceased to work, stumbling in slow motion, toppling forward, arms and hands stretched out to arrest the fall long before the man has fallen far enough for hands and floor to meet. A parody of a fall.

But finally he lay on the hard, cold, stone floor of the south aisle. What was happening to him now, he thought to himself. Perhaps he should just turn and try to leave the building. Lancaster was probably going to have him killed anyway. Why should he not just leave without murdering someone himself? Of course. He would just retire from this miserable venture. It wouldn't really matter. In any case, he was tired. Very, very tired. Perhaps he could change. Perhaps he could even. . . .

Suddenly he heard voices in the far distance behind him. Others were beginning to arrive for the six o'clock service. He must hurry.

And so, in a hurry, a man ignores his final chance. In Jonathan Foster's case, it was to be the very last opportunity he would ever be given. The repeated hints, the mysterious urgings, the persistent tugs and pulls . . . all over now.

He who will not be saved will finally be given what he demands.

Foster picked himself up and moved doggedly toward Holy Trinity Chapel. His legs were not working properly, but he forced himself forward. He reached the archway and turned in, stooping slightly although the small entryway would actually have accommodated his full height. Moving now more quickly still, he slid between the two rows to a particular spot and clumsily and hastily lowered himself onto the cushioned kneeler. Glancing first at one archway and then at the other, and hearing nothing yet from the newly arrived worshipers, he removed the hymnal and opened it, his hands trembling now more than ever.

He stared incredulously into the empty compartment formed by the cutout pages of the book. He forced his mind to concentrate. Had Lancaster tricked him again? Was this some sort of test? If so, what was expected of him? And suddenly he was overwhelmed. It was too much. He had never meant anything terrible to happen. Why was he here at all? He looked up at the altar. The wine awaited him. He had but to produce the vial, empty the contents, and depart. The police would eventually come for him, but at least he would be facing ordinary human beings, not Meredith Lancaster and those Others.

But where was the vial? What had gone wrong? He closed the hymnal and replaced it, then, thinking better of that, he removed the book again and rose to his feet, the hymnal in his hand. He would await Lancaster's arrival and show him the empty book. He would explain that it wasn't his fault, that somehow the vial was not there. He couldn't be held responsible for the mistake. He had done as he had been directed. He looked again at his watch. It was nearly quarter 'til the hour. The other dignitaries and Lancaster himself would be arriving any minute. Desperately he walked back to the archway and stepped into the south aisle, searching his mind for some wisp of hope, some novel realization, some clever escape from this unexpected trap into which he became increasingly certain that he had fallen.

Looking back to his right down the south aisle, he saw several people coming his way in the medium distance. Three of them moved with the slow sense of self that told him they were among the special guests invited to this early service. Another was one of the policemen from the south porch guard unit. With him was a man whose face he recognized after a moment. It was Meredith Lancaster's driver. The two approached him, well ahead of the dignitaries. The policeman addressed Foster.

"I don't like to bother you, sir," said the man in a stage whisper, "but there's someone here says he's got to talk to you. Says he's Dr. Lancaster's chauffeur, sir."

Foster nodded and, with a gesture, dismissed the policeman, who turned and walked back along the aisle. Foster motioned for the driver to follow him in the other direction, out of earshot of those who were arriving. "Now," he said, looking closely at the ashen face of the man, "what is it?"

"Mr. Foster," he said in a gravelly, rushed, whisper, "I don't know what to do, sir. I don't know who to tell. It was awful, sir. It was the most terrible thing ever I've seen."

Foster raised his hand in another practiced gesture, nodding his head in concert with the movement to signal that things would be fine, if only one would remain calm and understand that he was speaking to one who could make things better . . . who could form a plan . . . who could make contacts and arrangements. "Just tell me what you saw, my good man. Just take your time."

The man's eyes darted right and left. "He was killed, sir. And Jake and Fred, too. They was all killed. It was the most terrible thing ever I've seen in my life, sir. They're all three dead. There's not even anything left of 'em, sir. They're dead *and* they're gone."

Patiently, calmly, ever so soothingly, Foster drew the story from the driver. And so he came in just minutes to understand that a young couple had somehow gotten into the cathedral an hour after midnight and had been surprised, as they were leaving, by Lancaster and his men. Then they had run, dashing through the town past all the guard units and onto the roadway to the cliffs. The driver described how he had overtaken them in the Mercedes, and had remained in the vehicle while Lancaster and his two guards had shot at the fleeing couple, killing at least one of them. And then the end had come, so swiftly and terribly that he could hardly understand what he saw and heard. But he was sure that, whatever it was, it came down like lightning but it was not lightning. And it killed. And after it killed, it made the three dead men stand there, dead, for many seconds. And then it blew them away. Impossible, it was. And the man had been so frightened that he had curled up in the automobile and had remained motionless for a very long time, more than three hours, before he could bring himself to his senses. But then he knew he had to tell someone, and he couldn't think of anyone to tell but Mr. Foster. He hoped he had done the right thing.

Jonathan Foster patted the terrified man on the shoulder. "There, there," he said comfortingly. "Everything is going to be just fine, good sir. Just fine indeed. And there'll be no need for you to tell the story to anyone else, you understand. Not ever."

The driver hurried back toward the cathedral entrance. And Foster, seeing him go, gave a deep, audible sigh of gratification and hope. He closed his eyes and said under his breath, "Finally. Finally." Then, looking up, he saw the bishop of St. David's himself approaching Holy Trinity Chapel. Quickly, the director of the Institute for Social Research, a spring in his step, entered the chapel and knelt with the others present.

As the small service began, a nondescript figure rose to its feet in the shadows of the still darkened south aisle from one of the countless crannies within which one might crouch unseen at that time of the morning. Sid Belton had observed Jonathan Foster's every move, unsurprised that it was Foster who had been assigned the task of lacing the wine with cyanide. But Foster's exchange with the chauffeur had affected the detective profoundly. Yes, Lancaster was dead. But Rebecca or Matt, and perhaps both, were dead as well. He swallowed hard. Walking softly back toward the extreme east end of the cathedral, he gritted his teeth against the emotion that surged within him. "I shoulda gone with 'em," he said to himself, knowing as he said it that he could not possibly have done so. "I shoulda gone with 'em."

Reaching the midpoint of the east transverse aisle, he sat down on the floor, now well away from the sounds of the chapel service, and put his face in his hands, just as he had hours earlier when his back had rested against the perimeter wall. He wiped his nose clumsily with his sleeve. Then his eyes. Then he repeated the process using his other sleeve. Then he moved his palms across his eyes in a futile effort to clear them of the salt moisture. Then he gave it up and simply cried. And his cries became sobs. He cried as he had not cried in his adult memory. And finally he began to relax. The sobs diminished.

After trying again to dry his cheeks and his eyes with his clothing and his hands, he looked up. He took a long, deep breath, and let his head fall slowly back until it rested against the cathedral wall. And he thought, and thrilled to the thought, of the endless file of Christians who had preceded him through these same aisles, within these same walls. The people. Their souls. And Rebecca and Matt among them.

And in that attitude he prayed.

Finally, a holy clarity having been restored to his mind, the detective began to compose a summary for himself. Lancaster was dead. The bishop was safe. The true documents were in the lock box, ready for the bishop's reading at the 9:30 service.

And sometime before then the two researchers would arrive.

Belton had no doubts in regard to Jonathan Foster's intentions. In the two hours following the early service and before preparations for the mid-morning service, Foster would seek to become Meredith Lancaster. He would reason that "the young couple" comprised the explanation for the missing vial. Somehow they had known about the murder plot, and had entered the cathedral and had taken the cyanide away. Very well. They had been taken care of already. And, with Lancaster dead, Foster would simply make all the arrangements in his stead. The bishop of St. David's would be grateful, very grateful indeed. Foster would arrange for a new key for the lock box. And at the appropriate time during the main service, Foster would walk before the television cameras with studied dignity to the box on which all eyes would focus. Exuding solemnity and humility, he would remove from it the leather folder, would ceremoniously present the folder to the bishop, and would stand beside him for the cameras, his eyes cast down with just the right touch of reverence. Foster would carry out the fraud with pious aplomb and his characteristic touch of muted panache. He would convince himself, as he had once before, that it was all Providential. The creed would become Jonathan Foster's creed, or so Foster would be thinking, up until the point at which the bishop began to read. At that point, if Foster were actually listening, he would find himself face to face with a most unexpected crisis.

And now, Foster would want those researchers for himself. The detective nodded in satisfaction in the darkness. Foster *was* Lancaster. He was simply a curiously benign, vaguely insipid, studiously officious version of the man. The detective's smile was grim. Evil could just as easily take the form of a Foster as of a Lancaster.

Belton clambered stiffly to his feet, straightened his shoulders, and turned toward the north aisle. He had work to do.

Members of the *Legati* still at the mansion had awakened in the Sunday morning darkness, and had assembled nervously in the underground meeting room by four o'clock, the earliest time at which, they had calculated, they might hear from Rebecca by telephone. They knew she might not take the time to stop and call from a public phone until she had driven further east from Solva than just one or two towns. She might not call, in fact, until she had driven all the way to Cardiff. Even so, the members felt it realistic to expect to hear from her by seven at the latest. And so, sleepily, they waited, several with their Bibles or prayer books in their hands.

But as the time dragged, Martha and Paul Clark found they could no longer maintain the pretense of calm expectation. Sometime after six o'clock they requested permission to go next door to the underground chapel. There they prayed and talked while the minutes ticked past. "Paul," said Martha finally, "are they all right? Tell me something, even if you're just making it up."

Paul took his wife's hand. He could not bring himself to smile or to say comforting words that he did not feel. "I don't know, dear," he whispered. "I just don't know.

"I've realized in the last two days how much comfort I took in Luke's presence on the Cambridge raid, not just his being in command, but his very presence with Rebecca and Matt. Without his being at St. David's every step of the way, I just can't recapture the sense of confidence I seemed to have then."

"I know, Paul," said Martha. "We've always thought of Luke as somehow invincible physically, and *always* able to make everything safe . . . not just for his sister, but for everybody around him. It's such a shock to think of his being wounded, of his being unable to be there with them every second."

At that moment, in the silence of the subterranean chapel, they heard the faint sound of a telephone's ring. Together they flew back into the hallway and, in seconds, stopped at the doorway of the meeting room. Jason Manguson and Lawrence Ashford stood facing Elisabeth. She held the telephone receiver against her ear and listened intently, her face a tense mask.

Suddenly, in a movement that sent a knife through Martha Clark's heart, Elisabeth turned her head abruptly and locked her eyes onto Martha's. Martha fell to her knees. A moan escaped her lips. Paul dropped to the floor beside her, his arms around her shoulders. Elisabeth looked away and jotted something on the notepad beside the telephone. Then she murmured her thanks into the phone, and returned the receiver to its cradle.

She raised her eyes to Martha's. "That was Luke. Matt was badly injured, dear. He and Rebecca were picked up by Luke and Tom at Porth Clais. Tom gave Matt emergency treatment throughout the boat trip back to Fishguard. Matt's just gone into surgery with Tom and a specialist that Tom had contacted in advance, and who was on standby. I've got the location and the phone numbers here, Martha. I'm so sorry, dear. I'm so sorry."

Martha sprang to her feet, raced to Elisabeth, took the slip of paper, and ran from the room, Paul and Jason at her heels. In no more than five minutes from their flying exit from the underground quarters, Jason was opening the main gate while the Alfa Romeo, with a squeal of rubber against the driveway surface, made its catlike way along the curving drive and through the gate.

With Martha at the wheel, they could reach Fishguard in just over three hours. If the thing could be done, she would do it.

At half past noon, the three members of the *Legati* remaining at the mansion—Elisabeth, Jason, and Lawrence Ashford—were just finishing sandwiches, their first meal on this interminable Sunday. And Elisabeth had just hung up the telephone, having held her fourth extended conversation with her children in the hours since Luke's first call had come in to his mother at about half past six.

"Matt has just come out of surgery," she reported to the two men. Although Lawrence Ashford had dozed from time to time, Jason had studied his wife's face and her verbal responses carefully throughout each conversation, trying to frame the words from Rebecca or Luke without actually hearing them. "Martha and Paul are with him," Elisabeth continued. "It looks as though there will need to be a series of operations to repair and rebuild the shoulder and upper arm, and they're not sure how much use he'll have of the limb after all is said and done. But the main worry, of course, is the skull fracture. They've relieved pressure from internal hemorrhage, but there will need to be more cranial surgery this afternoon and evening. Assuming he pulls through, they don't expect Matt to regain consciousness for quite some time, perhaps days."

There was a lengthy silence as each one, including Elisabeth herself, digested this news.

Then Lawrence Ashford sighed deeply, and inquired rather carefully, "And how are *your* children now, Elisabeth?"

"I can't get them to say a word about themselves, Lawrence. Rebecca says *she's* fine. Luke says *he's* fine. Each says the *other* is fine. It's like talking to the wall. Other than giving me whatever news they have about Matt, they just want to hear what *we* can tell *them* about things back at St. David's.

"And I suppose you heard what I've been saying to them about that? Not everything, Lawrence? Well, I simply explained to them that we've had one call from Detective Belton, but that a great deal of what we know has come from the BBC, which has saturated us with the story of the Great Lancaster Hoax.

"I said to Rebecca that the detective was marvelously successful at inducing the researchers to 'go public,' as he likes to say. The fact that Meredith Lancaster had been—to use Rebecca's term—'executed,' coupled with the fact that the bishop himself had been led to see the full story, made the researchers more than eager to explain the whole thing, first to Detective Belton and his Scotland Yard friends, then to the whole world in television interviews.

"And I told Rebecca that, once Martha can allow herself to think about the creed again, she will be gratified to know that the bishop quite gladly carried through with his reading. He liked what she had prepared very much, once he read through it. She'll be delighted, I think.

"So, Dr. Ashford, despite all the scandal, we've had, it seems, a marvelous reaffirmation this morning of portions of the history of the church and of the faith, and, especially, of the role St. David played in the Christian story on our island. And that's something lots of people didn't know much about until now.

"But, as you can imagine, I also had to give Rebecca the unhappy news about poor Jonathan Foster. I'm afraid that his suicide, apparently done while the main service—the 9:30 service—was underway, has been relegated to a footnote in most of the news stories.

"Of course, it is possible that it was not suicide. But going over those cliffs in broad daylight. . . .

"Such a sad, sad man. He will need our best prayers."

Wednesday morning had finally arrived. Rebecca rose from her knees in her bedroom and placed her prayer book on the dressing table, next to her Bible. She was excited. She had been away from her pupils for two long week-ends and seven full school days. That was much too long. Her mind played busily over the faces of the girls who would come tumbling into her classroom in just two hours. So few days remained in the school year. There was so much to be done in that time for each child.

Having completed her devotions, she strode briskly down the hallway of the flat and knocked on her brother's bedroom door. "Luke . . . Luke . . . it's time."

She moved into the kitchen and began to prepare a cold breakfast for them both. She knew that Luke would not let her help him move about on his wounded leg, but he would at least tolerate this. The drive from the Welsh coast to Birmingham, and then back home to London, had been hard on him. The small Alfa Romeo gave him no room to elevate his leg. And he had refused the pain medication, as usual.

She had wanted Luke to remain in Fishguard to recuperate alongside Matt. But, once Matt had regained consciousness on Monday morning, and had been pronounced out of danger by that afternoon, Luke had been determined that he would miss no more days of school than the single day of travel they would need to get home. And, to be truthful, Rebecca had felt the same. Here, with the children, was vocation; here was where they were needed.

And so, with the Clarks prepared to stay with Matt in Fishguard for as long as necessary, and with Tom Sutton remaining with them to minister to Matt and to drive all three of the Clarks back to Birmingham as soon as Matt could travel, Rebecca and Luke had bid them good-bye on Tuesday morning. The others had discreetly left Rebecca and Matt alone for a private parting.

But the farewell with Matt had not been satisfactory to Rebecca. There had been an awkwardness that she had not expected. In retrospect, she knew she should have. After all, when they had last been consciously together, they had been enmeshed in a web of danger from which escape had seemed extremely unlikely. Death had appeared imminent. And it had been under those extraordinary circumstances that they had kissed—almost desperately—outside the cathedral, and then had prayed together inside it, on their knees, in the moments before their climbing, sprinting, violence-filled escape.

Now it was different. Now they were safe. Family members were around them. And Matt was still weak from his wounds and his prolonged submission to anesthesia. He could not as yet remember enough of their flight from the cathedral to the cliffs to ask coherent questions, nor to hear and understand the answers if she had offered them.

All of that could wait.

Now, with glad impatience, Rebecca returned to Luke's door and raised her hand to knock again. But the door suddenly opened and Luke stood before her, fully dressed and clean shaven, leaning on his makeshift crutches. They laughed. "I'd been up for an hour before you knocked the first time," he said to her. "I could hardly sleep at all. I can't wait to see what my little characters have been up to for a week and a half."

Luke then made his other concession to his wound and his crutches. He allowed Rebecca to carry his briefcase for him on the short walk to his school. She opened the schoolhouse door for him, and walked beside him to his classroom. The building was empty except for the custodian's busy presence. She placed his briefcase on his desk and hugged him tightly. "I'll be back here at half past four, Luke. Do *not* try to walk home with this briefcase."

"Wouldn't think of it, dear," he replied, smiling broadly at her. "Wouldn't even think of it."

She laughed and left him happily unpacking his books and notes.

Mid-morning, Rebecca was just beginning to rearrange the girls' desks to begin grouped reading when she heard a knock at the classroom door. "Yes?" she called, and then watched as the receptionist and a custodian rolled into her room on a projector cart the largest and most elaborate arrangement of roses she could recall seeing in her life.

Every girl in the class stopped and stared, first at the flowers, then at their beloved teacher. Some of them stood and began to move, at first tentatively, then more confidently, toward Rebecca's desk.

"Miss Manguson!" one of them cried. "Here's a card."

Rebecca plucked the card from the midst of the roses' extravagant redness. A shy smile appeared on her face, followed by a spreading change of color on her cheeks, a delicate shade at once lighter and, in its subtlety, even more beautiful than that of the flowers.

"Ooooh, Miss Manguson!" came the chorus. "Who're they from?"

Rebecca looked up from the card. "They're from Matthew, girls." She looked down at the card again, her eyes welling. And then she repeated the words, almost to herself. "They're from Matthew."

About the Author

WALKER BUCKALEW RECEIVED A BACHELOR'S DEGREE IN English and religion from Duke University before serving as an officer on the aircraft carrier USS *Constellation*. Following his Navy service, Buckalew worked as a public school teacher and coach while earning his M.Ed. and Ph.D. degrees from the University of Wyoming.

Buckalew then embarked on a career in higher education, teaching at St. Lawrence University in Canton, New York, and the University of North Carolina at Asheville. He was later appointed president and chief academic officer at Cumberland University in Lebanon, Tennessee. Since 1989 he has served as a consultant to private schools throughout North America. He lives with his wife, Dr. Linda Mason Hall, in Wilmington, Delaware.